"Amelia Peabody Emerson, archeologist extraordinaire, and arguably the most potent female force to hit Egypt since Cleopatra, is digging in again!"
—*Philadelphia Inquirer*

"Plenty of interesting Egyptian and archeological lore, lots of danger."
—*New York Times Book Review*

"Amelia is rather like Indiana Jones, Sherlock Holmes, and Miss Marple all rolled into one."
—*Washington Post Book World*

"Elizabeth Peters is wickedly clever…[Her] women are smart, strong, bold, cunning, and highly educated, just like herself."
—*San Diego Reader*

"What's more fun than an Elizabeth Peters book? Not much that's legal!"
—*Salisbury Post* (NC)

"It's always fun to go on safari with this crew."
—*Anniston Star* (AL)

BOOKS BY ELIZABETH PETERS

Crocodile on the Sandbank

The Curse of the Pharaohs

The Hippopotamus Pool

The Last Camel Died at Noon

The Mummy Case

The Murders of Richard III

Naked Once More

Night Train to Memphis

Seeing a Large Cat

The Seventh Sinner

Silhouette in Scarlet

The Snake, the Crocodile and the Dog

THE CURSE OF THE PHARAOHS

ELIZABETH PETERS

GRAND CENTRAL
PUBLISHING

NEW YORK   BOSTON

Copyright © 1981 by Elizabeth Peters

This edition is published in arrangement with Dodd, Mead & Company.

Grand Central Publishing
Hachette Book Group
1290 Avenue of the Americas
New York, NY 10104
www.HachetteBookGroup.com

Grand Central Publishing is a division of Hachette Book Group, Inc.
The Grand Central Publishing name and logo is a trademark of Hachette Book Group, Inc.

The Hachette Speakers Bureau provides a wide range of authors for speaking events. To find out more, go to www.hachettespeakersbureau .com or call (866) 376-6591.

The publisher is not responsible for websites (or their content) that are not owned by the publisher.

Printed in the United States of America

Originally published in trade paperback by Hachette Book Group
First mass market edition: February 1988
Reissued: October 1992, April 2002
First oversize mass market edition: May 2013

10 9 8 7 6 5 4
OPM

To Phyllis Whitney

CHAPTER
ONE

The events I am about to relate began on a December afternoon, when I had invited Lady Harold Carrington and certain of her friends to tea.

Do not, gentle reader, be misled by this introductory statement. It is accurate (as my statements always are); but if you expect the tale that follows to be one of pastoral domesticity, enlivened only by gossip about the county gentry, you will be sadly mistaken. Bucolic peace is not my ambience, and the giving of tea parties is by no means my favorite amusement. In fact, I would prefer to be pursued across the desert by a band of savage Dervishes brandishing spears and howling for my blood. I would rather be chased up a tree by a mad dog, or face a mummy risen from its grave. I would rather be threatened by knives, pistols, poisonous snakes, and the curse of a long-dead king.

Lest I be accused of exaggeration, let me point out that I have had all those experiences, save one. However, Emerson once remarked that if I *should* encounter a band of Dervishes, five minutes of my nagging would unquestionably inspire even the mildest of them to massacre me.

Emerson considers this sort of remark humorous. Five years of marriage have taught me that even if one is unamused by the (presumed) wit of one's spouse, one does not say so. Some concessions to temperament are necessary if the marital state is to flourish. And I must confess that in most respects the state agrees with me. Emerson is a remarkable person, considering that he is a man. Which is not saying a great deal.

The state of wedlock has its disadvantages, however, and an accumulation of these, together with certain other factors, added to my restlessness on the afternoon of the tea party. The weather was dreadful—dreary and drizzling, with occasional intervals of sleety snow. I had not been able to go out for my customary five-mile walk; the dogs *had* been out, and had returned coated with mud, which they promptly transferred to the drawing-room rug; and Ramses...

But I will come to the subject of Ramses at the proper time.

Though we had lived in Kent for five years, I had never entertained my neighbors to tea. None of them has the faintest idea of decent conversation. They cannot tell a Kamares pot from a piece of prehistoric painted ware, and they have no idea who Seti the First was. On this occasion, however, I was forced into an exercise of civility which I would ordinarily abhor. Emerson had designs on a barrow on the property of Sir Harold, and—as he elegantly expressed it—it was necessary for us to "butter up" Sir Harold before asking permission to excavate.

It was Emerson's own fault that Sir Harold required buttering. I share my husband's views on the idiocy of fox hunting, and I do not blame him for personally escorting the fox off the field when it was about to be trapped, or run to earth, or whatever the phrase may be. I blame Emerson for pulling Sir Harold out of his saddle and thrashing him with his own riding crop. A brief, forceful lecture, together with the removal of the fox, would have gotten the point across. The thrashing was superfluous.

Initially Sir Harold had threatened to take Emerson to law. He was prevented by some notion that this would be unsportsmanlike. (Seemingly no such stigma applied to the pursuit of a single fox by a troop of men on horseback and a pack of dogs.) He was restrained from physically attacking Emerson by Emerson's size and reputation (not undeserved) for bellicosity. Therefore he had contented himself with cutting Emerson dead whenever they chanced to meet. Emerson never noticed when he was being cut dead, so matters had progressed peacefully enough until my husband got the notion of excavating Sir Harold's barrow.

It was quite a nice barrow, as barrows go—a hundred feet long and some thirty wide. These monuments are the tombs of antique Viking warriors, and Emerson hoped to discover the burial regalia of a chieftain, with perhaps evidences of barbaric sacrifice. Since I am above all things a fair-minded person, I will candidly confess that it was, in part, my own eagerness to rip into the barrow that prompted me to be civil to Lady Harold. But I was also moved by concern for Emerson.

He was bored. Oh, he tried to hide it! As I have said,

and will continue to say, Emerson has his faults, but unfair recrimination is not one of them. He did not blame *me* for the tragedy that had ruined his life.

When I first met him, he was carrying on archaeological excavations in Egypt. Some unimaginative people might not consider this occupation pleasurable. Disease, extreme heat, inadequate or nonexistent sanitary conditions, and a quite excessive amount of sand do mar to some extent the joys of discovering the treasures of a vanished civilization. However, Emerson adored the life, and so did I, after we joined forces, maritally, professionally, and financially. Even after our son was born we managed to get in one long season at Sakkara. We returned to England that spring with every intention of going out again the following autumn. Then our doom came upon us, as the Lady of Shalott might have said (indeed, I believe she actually did say so) in the form of our son, "Ramses" Walter Peabody Emerson.

I promised that I would return to the subject of Ramses. He cannot be dismissed in a few lines.

The child had been barely three months old when we left him for the winter with my dear friend Evelyn, who had married Emerson's younger brother Walter. From her grandfather, the irascible old Duke of Chalfont, Evelyn had inherited Chalfont Castle, and a great deal of money. Her husband—one of the few men whose company I can tolerate for more than an hour at a time—was a distinguished Egyptologist in his own right. Unlike Emerson, who prefers excavation, Walter is a philologist, specializing in the decipherment of the varied forms of the ancient Egyptian language.

He had happily settled down with his beautiful wife at her family home, spending his days reading crabbed, crumbling texts and his evenings playing with his ever-increasing family.

Evelyn, who is the dearest girl, was delighted to take Ramses for the winter. Nature had just interfered with her hopes of becoming a mother for the fourth time, so a new baby was quite to her taste. At three months Ramses was personable enough, with a mop of dark hair, wide blue eyes, and a nose which even then showed signs of developing from an infantile button into a feature of character. He slept a great deal. (As Emerson said later, he was probably saving his strength.)

I left the child more reluctantly than I had expected would be the case, but after all he had not been around long enough to make much of an impression, and I was particularly looking forward to the dig at Sakkara. It was a most productive season, and I will candidly admit that the thought of my abandoned child seldom passed through my mind. Yet as we prepared to return to England the following spring, I found myself rather looking forward to seeing him again, and I fancied Emerson felt the same; we went straight to Chalfont Castle from Dover, without stopping over in London.

How well I remember that day! April in England, the most delightful of seasons! For once it was not raining. The hoary old castle, splashed with the fresh new green of Virginia creeper and ivy, sat in its beautifully tended grounds like a gracious dowager basking in the sunlight. As our carriage came to a stop the doors opened and Evelyn ran out, her arms extended. Walter was close behind; he wrung his brother's hand

and then crushed me in a fraternal embrace. After the first greetings had been exchanged, Evelyn said, "But of course, you will want to see young Walter."

"If it is not inconvenient," I said.

Evelyn laughed and squeezed my hand. "Amelia, don't pretend with me. I know you too well. You are dying to see your baby."

Chalfont Castle is a large establishment. Though extensively modernized, its walls are ancient and fully six feet thick. Sound does not readily travel through such a medium, but as we proceeded along the upper corridor of the south wing, I began to hear a strange noise, a kind of roaring. Muted as it was, it conveyed a quality of ferocity that made me ask, "Evelyn, have you taken to keeping a menagerie?"

"One might call it that," Evelyn said, her voice choked with laughter.

The sound increased in volume as we went on. We stopped before a closed door. Evelyn opened it; the sound burst forth in all its fury. I actually fell back a pace, stepping heavily on the instep of my husband, who was immediately behind me.

The room was a day nursery, fitted up with all the comfort wealth and tender love can provide. Long windows flooded the chamber with light; a bright fire, guarded by a fender and screen, mitigated the cold of the old stone walls. These had been covered by paneling hung with pretty pictures and draped with bright fabric. On the floor was a thick carpet strewn with toys of all kinds. Before the fire, rocking placidly, sat the very picture of a sweet old nanny, her cap and apron snowy white, her rosy face calm, her hands busy with her knitting. Around the walls, in various postures of defense, were three children. Though they had grown considerably, I recognized these as the offspring of Evelyn and Walter. Sitting bolt upright in the center of the floor was a baby.

It was impossible to make out his features. All one could see was a great wide cavern of a mouth, framed in black hair. However, I had no doubt as to his identity.

"There he is," Evelyn shouted, over the bellowing of this infantile volcano. "Only see how he has grown!"

Emerson gasped. "What the devil is the matter with him?"

Hearing—how, I cannot imagine—a new voice, the infant stopped shrieking. The cessation of sound was so abrupt it left the ears ringing.

"Nothing," Evelyn said calmly. "He is cutting teeth, and is sometimes a little cross."

"Cross?" Emerson repeated incredulously.

I stepped into the room, followed by the others. The child stared at us. It sat foursquare on its bottom, its legs extended before it, and I was struck at once by its shape, which was virtually rectangular. Most babies, I had observed, tend to be spherical. This one had wide shoulders and a straight spine, no visible neck, and a face whose angularity not even baby fat could disguise. The eyes were not the pale ambiguous blue of a normal infant's, but a dark, intense sapphire; they met mine with an almost adult calculation.

Emerson had begun circling cautiously to the left, rather as one approaches a growling dog. The child's eyes swiveled suddenly in his direction. Emerson stopped. His face took on an imbecilic simper. He squatted. "Baby," he crooned. "Wawa. Papa's widdle Wawa. Come to nice papa."

"For God's sake, Emerson!" I exclaimed.

The baby's intense blue eyes turned to me. "I am your mother, Walter," I said, speaking slowly and distinctly. "Your mama. I don't suppose you can say Mama."

Without warning the child toppled forward. Emerson let out a cry of alarm, but his concern was unnecessary; the infant deftly got its four limbs under it and began crawling at an incredible speed, straight to me. It came to a stop at my feet, rocked back onto its haunches, and lifted its arms.

"Mama," it said. Its ample mouth split into a smile that produced dimples in both cheeks and displayed three small white teeth. "Mama. Up. Up, up, up, UP!"

Its voice rose in volume; the final UP made the windows rattle. I stooped hastily and seized the creature. It was surprisingly heavy. It flung its arms around my neck and buried its face against my shoulder. "Mama," it said, in a muffled voice.

For some reason, probably because the child's grip was so tight, I was unable to speak for a few moments.

"He is very precocious," Evelyn said, as proudly as if the child had been her own. "Most children don't speak properly until they are a year old, but this young man already has quite a vocabulary. I have shown him your photographs every day and told him whom they represented."

Emerson stood by me staring, with a singularly hangdog look. The infant released its stranglehold, glanced at its father, and—with what I can only regard, in the light of later experience, as cold-blooded calculation—

tore itself from my arms and launched itself through the air toward my husband.

"Papa," it said.

Emerson caught it. For a moment they regarded one another with virtually identical foolish grins. Then he flung it into the air. It shrieked with delight, so he tossed it up again. Evelyn remonstrated as, in the exuberance of its father's greeting, the child's head grazed the ceiling. I said nothing. I knew, with a strange sense of foreboding, that a war had begun—a lifelong battle, in which I was doomed to be the loser.

It was Emerson who gave the baby its nickname. He said that in its belligerent appearance and imperious disposition it strongly resembled the Egyptian pharaoh, the second of that name, who had scattered enormous statues of himself all along the Nile. I had to admit the resemblance. Certainly the child was not at all like its namesake, Emerson's brother, who is a gentle, soft-spoken man.

Though Evelyn and Walter both pressed us to stay with them, we decided to take a house of our own for the summer. It was apparent that the younger Emersons' children went in terror of their cousin. They were no match for the tempestuous temper and violent demonstrations of affection to which Ramses was prone. As we discovered, he was extremely intelligent. His physical abilities matched his mental powers. He could crawl at an astonishing speed at eight months. When, at ten months, he decided to learn to walk, he was unsteady on his feet for a few days; and at one time he had bruises on the end of his nose, his forehead, and his chin, for Ramses did nothing by halves—he fell and rose to fall again. He soon mastered the skill, however, and after that he was never still except when someone was holding him. By this time he was talking quite fluently, except for an annoying tendency to lisp, which I attributed to the unusual size of his front teeth, an inheritance from his father. He inherited from the same source a quality which I hesitate to characterize, there being no word in the English language strong enough to do it justice. "Bullheaded" is short of the mark by quite a distance.

Emerson was, from the first, quite besotted with the creature. He took it for long walks and read to it by the hour, not only from *Peter Rabbit* and other childhood tales, but from excavation reports and his own *History of Ancient Egypt,* which he was composing. To see Ramses, at fourteen months, wrinkling his brows over a sentence like "The theology of the Egyptians was a compound of fetishism, totemism and syncretism" was a sight as terrifying as it was comical. Even more terrifying was the occasional thoughtful nod the child would give.

After a time I stopped thinking of Ramses as "it." His masculinity was only too apparent. As the summer drew to a close I went, one day, to the estate agents and told them we would keep the house for another year. Shortly thereafter Emerson informed me that he had accepted a position as lecturer at the University of London.

There was never any need to discuss the subject. It was evident that we could not take a young child into the unhealthy climate of an archaeological camp; and it was equally obvious that Emerson could not bear to be parted from the boy. My own feelings? They are quite irrelevant. The decision was the only sensible solution, and I am always sensible.

So, four years later, we were still vegetating in Kent. We had decided to buy the house. It was a pleasant old place, Georgian in style, with ample grounds nicely planted—except for the areas where the dogs and Ramses excavated. I had no trouble keeping ahead of the dogs, but it was a running battle to plant things faster than Ramses dug them up. I believe many children enjoy digging in the mud, but Ramses' preoccupation with holes in the ground became absolutely ridiculous. It was all Emerson's fault. Mistaking a love of dirt for a budding talent for excavation, he encouraged the child.

Emerson never admitted that he missed the old life. He had made a successful career lecturing and writing; but now and then I would detect a wistful note in his voice as he read from the *Times* or the *Illustrated London News* about new discoveries in the Middle East. To such had we fallen—reading the ILN over tea, and bickering about trivia with county neighbors—we, who had camped in a cave in the Egyptian hills and restored the capital city of a pharaoh!

On that fateful afternoon—whose significance I was not to appreciate until much later—I prepared myself for the sacrifice. I wore my best gray silk. It was a gown Emerson detested because he said it made me look like a respectable English matron—one of the worst insults in his vocabulary. I decided that if Emerson disapproved, Lady Harold would probably consider the gown suitable. I even allowed Smythe, my maid, to arrange my hair. The ridiculous woman was always trying to fuss over my personal appearance. I seldom allowed her to do more than was absolutely necessary, having neither the time nor the patience for prolonged primping. On this occasion Smythe took full advantage. If I had not had a newspaper to read while she pulled and tugged at my hair and ran pins into my head, I would have screamed with boredom.

Finally she said sharply, "With all respect, madam, I cannot do this properly while you are waving that paper about. Will it please you to put it down?"

It did not please me. But time was getting on, and the newspaper story I had been reading—of which more in due course—only made me more discontented with the prospect before me. I therefore abandoned the *Times* and meekly submitted to Smythe's torture.

When she had finished the two of us stared at my reflection in the mirror with countenances that displayed our feelings—Smythe's beaming with triumph, mine the gloomy mask of one who had learned to accept the inevitable gracefully.

My stays were too tight and my new shoes pinched. I creaked downstairs to inspect the drawing room.

The room was so neat and tidy it made me feel quite depressed. The newspapers and books and periodicals that normally covered most of the flat surfaces had been cleared away. Emerson's prehistoric pots had been removed from the mantel and the what-not. A gleaming silver tea service had replaced Ramses' toys on the tea cart. A bright fire on the hearth helped to dispel the gloom of the gray skies without, but it did very little for the inner gloom that filled me. I do not allow myself to repine about what cannot be helped; but I remembered earlier Decembers, under the cloudless blue skies and brilliant sun of Egypt.

As I stood morosely contemplating the destruction of our cheerful domestic clutter, and recalling better days, I heard the sound of wheels on the gravel of the drive. The first guest had arrived. Gathering the robes of my martyrdom about me, I made ready to receive her.

There is no point in describing the tea party. It is not a memory I enjoy recalling and, thank heaven, subsequent events made Lady Harold's attitude quite unimportant. She is not the most stupid person I have ever met; that distinction must go to her husband; but she combines malice and stupidity to a degree I had not encountered until that time.

Remarks such as, "My dear, what a charming frock! I remember admiring that style when it first came out, two years ago," were wasted on me, for I am unmoved by insult. What did move me, to considerable vexation, was Lady Harold's assumption that my invitation to tea signified apology and capitulation. This assumption was apparent in every condescending word she said and in every expression that passed across her fat, coarse, common face.

But I perceive, with surprise, that I am becoming angry all over again. How foolish, and what a waste of time! Let me say no more—except to admit that I derived an unworthy satisfaction in beholding Lady Harold's ill-concealed envy of the neatness of the room, the excellence of the food, and the smart efficiency with which butler, footman, and parlormaid served us. Rose, my parlormaid, is always efficient, but on this occasion she outdid herself. Her apron was so starched it could have stood by itself, her cap ribbons fairly snapped as she moved. I recalled having heard that Lady Harold had a hard time keeping servants because of her parsimony and vicious tongue. Rose's younger sister had been employed by her...briefly.

Except for that minor triumph, for which I can claim no credit, the meeting was an unmitigated bore. The other ladies whom I had invited, in order to conceal my true motives, were all followers of Lady Harold; they did nothing but titter and nod at her idiotic remarks. An hour passed with stupefying slowness. It was clear that my mission was doomed to failure; Lady Harold would do nothing to accommodate me. I was beginning to wonder what would happen if I simply rose and left the room, when an interruption occurred to save me from that expedient.

I had—I fondly believed—convinced Ramses to remain quietly in the nursery that afternoon. I had accomplished this by bribery and corruption, promising him a visit to the sweetshop in the village on the following day. Ramses could consume enormous quantities of sweets without the slightest inconvenience to his appetite or digestive apparatus. Unfortunately his desire for sweets was not as strong as his lust for learning—or mud, as the case may be. As I watched Lady Harold devour the last of the frosted cakes I heard stifled outcries from the hall. They were followed by a crash—my favorite Ming vase, as I later learned. Then the drawing-room doors burst open and a dripping, muddy, miniature scarecrow rushed in.

It cannot be said that the child's feet left muddy prints. No; an unbroken stream of liquid filth marked his path, pouring from his person, his garments, and the unspeakable object he was flourishing. He slid to a stop before me and deposited this object in my lap. The stench that arose from it made its origin only too clear. Ramses had been rooting in the compost heap again.

I am actually rather fond of my son. Without displaying the fatuous adoration characteristic of his father, I may say that I have a certain affection for the boy. At that moment I wanted to take the little monster by the collar and shake him until his face turned blue.

Constrained, by the presence of the ladies, from this natural maternal impulse, I said quietly, "Ramses, take the bone from Mama's good frock and return it to the compost heap."

Ramses put his head on one side and studied his bone with a thoughtful frown. "I fink," he said, "it is a femuw. A femuw of a winocowus."

"There are no rhinoceroses in England," I pointed out.

"A a-stinct winocowus," said Ramses.

A peculiar wheezing sound from the direction of the doorway made me look in that direction in time to see Wilkins clap his hands to his mouth and turn suddenly away. Wilkins is a most dignified man, a butler among butlers, but I had once or twice observed that there were traces of a sense of humor beneath his stately exterior. On this occasion I was forced to share his amusement.

"The word is not ill chosen," I said, pinching my nostrils together with my fingers, and wondering how I could remove the boy without further damage to my drawing room. Summoning a footman to take him away was out of the question; he was an agile child, and his coating of mud made him as slippery as a frog. In his efforts to elude pursuit he would leave tracks across the carpet, the furniture, the walls, the ladies' frocks....

"A splendid bone," I said, without even trying to resist the temptation. "You must wash it before you show it to Papa. But first, perhaps Lady Harold would like to see it."

With a sweeping gesture, I indicated the lady.

If she had not been so stupid, she might have thought of a way of diverting Ramses. If she had not been so fat, she might have moved out of the way. As it was, all she could do was billow and shriek and sputter. Her efforts to dislodge the nasty thing (it *was* very nasty, I must admit) were in vain; it lodged in a fold of her voluminous skirt and stayed there.

Ramses was highly affronted at this unappreciative reception of his treasure.

"You will dwop it and bweak it," he exclaimed. "Give it back to me."

In his efforts to retrieve the bone he dragged it across several more square yards of Lady Harold's enormous lap. Clutching it to his small bosom, he gave her a look of hurt reproach before trotting out of the room.

I will draw a veil over the events that followed. I derive an unworthy satisfaction from the memory, even now; it is not proper to encourage such thoughts.

I stood by the window watching the carriages splash away and humming quietly to myself while Rose dealt with the tea-things and the trail of mud left by Ramses.

"You had better bring fresh tea, Rose," I said. "Professor Emerson will be here shortly."

"Yes, madam. I hope, madam, that all was satisfactory."

"Oh, yes indeed. It could not have been more satisfactory."

"I am glad to hear it, madam."

"I am sure you are. Now, Rose, you are not to give Master Ramses any extra treats."

"Certainly not, madam." Rose looked shocked.

I meant to change my frock before Emerson got home, but he was early that evening. As usual, he carried an armful of books and papers, which he flung helter-skelter onto the sofa. Turning to the fire, he rubbed his hands briskly together.

"Frightful climate," he grumbled. "Wretched day. Why are you wearing that hideous dress?"

Emerson has never learned to wipe his feet at the door. I looked at the prints his boots had left on the freshly cleaned floor. Then I looked at him, and the reproaches I had meant to utter died on my lips.

He had not changed physically in the years since we were wed. His hair was as thick and black and unruly as ever, his shoulders as broad, his body as straight. When I had first met him, he had worn a beard. He was now clean-shaven, at my request, and this was a considerable concession on his part, for Emerson particularly dislikes the deep cleft, or dimple, in his prominent chin. I myself approve of this little flaw; it is the only whimsical touch in an otherwise forbiddingly rugged physiognomy.

On that day his looks, manners, and speech were as usual. Yet there was something in his eyes.... I had seen the look before; it was more noticeable now. So I said nothing about his muddy feet.

"I entertained Lady Harold this afternoon," I said

in answer to his question. "Hence the dress. Have you had a pleasant day?"

"No."

"Neither have I."

"Serves you right," said my husband. "I told you not to do it. Where the devil is Rose? I want my tea."

Rose duly appeared, with the tea tray. I meditated, sadly, on the tragedy of Emerson, querulously demanding tea and complaining about the weather, like any ordinary Englishman. As soon as the door had closed behind the parlormaid, Emerson came to me and took me in his arms.

After an interval he held me out at arm's length and looked at me questioningly. His nose wrinkled.

I was about to explain the smell when he said, in a low, hoarse voice, "You are particularly attractive tonight, Peabody, in spite of that frightful frock. Don't you want to change? I will go up with you, and—"

"What is the matter with you?" I demanded, as he...Never mind what he did, it prevented him from speaking and made it rather difficult for me to speak evenly. "I certainly don't feel attractive, and I smell like moldy bone. Ramses has been excavating in the compost heap again."

"Mmmm," said Emerson. "My darling Peabody..."

Peabody is my maiden name. When Emerson and I first met, we did not hit it off. He took to calling me Peabody, as he would have addressed another man, as a sign of annoyance. It had now become a sign of something else, recalling those first wonderful days of our acquaintance when we had bickered and sneered at one another.

Yielding with pleasure to his embraces, I nevertheless felt sad, for I knew why he was so demonstrative.
The smell of Ramses' bone had taken him back to
our romantic courtship, in the unsanitary tombs of El
Amarna.

I left off feeling sad before long and was about to
accede to his request that we adjourn to our room; but
we had delayed too long. The evening routine was set
and established; we were always given a decent interval
alone after Emerson arrived, then Ramses was permitted to come in to greet his papa and take tea with us.
On that evening the child was anxious to show off his
bone, so perhaps he came early. It certainly seemed too
early to me, and even Emerson, his arm still around
my waist, greeted the boy with less than his usual
enthusiasm.

A pretty domestic scene ensued. Emerson took his
son, and the bone, onto his knee, and I seated myself
behind the teapot. After dispensing a cup of the genial
beverage to my husband and a handful of cakes to
my son, I reached for the newspapers, while Emerson
and Ramses argued about the bone. It *was* a femur—
Ramses was uncannily accurate about such things—
but Emerson claimed that the bone had once belonged
to a horse. Ramses differed. Rhinoceroses having been
eliminated, he suggested a dragon or a giraffe.

The newspaper story for which I searched was no
longer on the front page, though it had occupied this
position for some time. I think I can do no better than
relate what I then knew of the case, as if I were beginning a work of fiction; for indeed, if the story had not
appeared in the respectable pages of the *Times,* I would

have thought it one of the ingenious inventions of Herr Ebers or Mr. Rider Haggard—to whose romances, I must confess, I was addicted. Therefore, be patient, dear reader, if we begin with a sober narrative of facts. They are necessary to your understanding of later developments; and I promise you we will have sensations enough in due course.

Sir Henry Baskerville (of the Norfolk Baskervilles, not the Devonshire branch of the family), having suffered a severe illness, had been advised by his physician to spend a winter in the salubrious climate of Egypt. Neither the excellent man of medicine nor his wealthy patient could have anticipated the far-reaching consequences of this advice; for Sir Henry's first glimpse of the majestic features of the Sphinx inspired in his bosom a passionate interest in Egyptian antiquities, which was to rule him for the remainder of his life.

After excavating at Abydos and Denderah, Sir Henry finally obtained a firman to excavate in what is perhaps the most romantic of all Egyptian archaeological sites—the Valley of the Kings at Thebes. Here the god-kings of imperial Egypt were laid to rest with the pomp and majesty befitting their high estate. Their mummies enclosed in golden coffins and adorned with jewel-encrusted amulets, they hoped in the secrecy of their rock-cut tombs, deep in the bowels of the Theban hills, to escape the dreadful fate that had befallen their ancestors. For by the time of the Empire the pyramids of earlier rulers already gaped open and desolate, the royal bodies destroyed and their treasures dispersed. Alas for human vanity! The mighty pharaohs of the later period were no more immune to the depredations of tomb robbers than their ancestors had been. Every royal tomb found in the Valley had been despoiled. Treasures, jewels, and kingly mummies had vanished. It was assumed that the ancient tomb robbers had destroyed what they could not steal, until that astonishing day in July of 1881, when a group of modern thieves led Emil Brugsch, of the Cairo Museum, to a remote valley in the Theban mountains. The thieves, men from the village of Gurneh, had discovered what archaeologists had missed—the last resting place of Egypt's mightiest kings, queens, and royal children, hidden away in the days of the nation's decline by a group of loyal priests.

Not all the kings of the Empire were found in the thieves' cache, nor had all their tombs been identified. Lord Baskerville believed that the barren cliffs of the Valley still hid kingly tombs—even, perhaps, a tomb that had never been robbed. One frustration followed another, but he never abandoned his quest. Determined to dedicate his life to it, he built a house on the West Bank, half winter home, half working quarters for his archaeological staff. To this lovely spot he brought his bride, a beautiful young woman who had nursed him through a bout of pneumonia brought on by his return to England's damp spring climate.

The story of this romantic courtship and marriage, with its Cinderella aspect—for the new Lady Baskerville was a young lady of no fortune and insignificant family—had been prominently featured in the newspapers at the time. This event occurred before my own interest in Egypt developed, but naturally I had heard of Sir Henry; his name was known to every Egyptologist. Emerson had nothing good to say about him, but then Emerson did not approve of any other archaeologists, amateur or professional. In accusing Sir Henry of being an amateur he did the gentleman less than justice, for his lordship never attempted to direct the excavations; he always employed a professional scholar for that work.

In September of this year Sir Henry had gone to Luxor as usual, accompanied by Lady Baskerville and Mr. Alan Armadale, the archaeologist in charge. Their purpose during this season was to begin work on an area in the center of the Valley, near the tombs of Ramses II and Merenptah, which had been cleared by Lepsius in 1844. Sir Henry thought that the rubbish dumps thrown up by that expedition had perhaps covered the hidden entrances to other tombs. It was his intention to clear the ground down to bedrock to make sure nothing had been overlooked. And indeed, scarcely had the men been at work for three days when their spades uncovered the first of a series of steps cut into the rock.

(Are you yawning, gentle reader? If you are, it is because you know nothing of archaeology. Rock-cut steps in the Valley of the Kings could signify only one thing—the entrance to a tomb.)

The stairway went down into the rock at a steep angle. It had been completely filled with rock and rubble. By the following afternoon the men had cleared this away, exposing the upper portion of a doorway blocked with heavy stone slabs. Stamped into the mortar were the unbroken seals of the royal necropolis. Note that word, oh, reader—that word so simple and yet so fraught with meaning. Unbroken seals implied that the tomb had not been opened since the day when it was solemnly closed by the priests of the funerary cult.

Sir Henry, as his intimates were to testify, was a man of singularly phlegmatic temperament, even for a British nobleman. The only sign of excitement he displayed was a muttered, "By Jove," as he stroked his wispy beard. Others were not so blasé. The news reached the press and was duly published.

In accordance with the terms of his firman, Sir Henry notified the Department of Antiquities of his find; when he descended the dusty steps a second time he was accompanied by a distinguished group of archaeologists and officials. A fence had been hastily erected to hold back the crowd of sightseers, journalists, and natives, the latter picturesque in their long flapping robes and white turbans. Among the latter group one face stood out—that of Mohammed Abd er Rasul, one of the discoverers of the cache of royal mummies, who had betrayed the find (and his brothers) to the authorities and had been rewarded by a position in the Antiquities Department. Onlookers remarked on the profound chagrin of his expression and the gloomy looks of other members of the family. For once, the foreigners had stolen a march on them and deprived them of a potential source of income.

Though he had recovered from the illness that had brought him to Egypt and was (as his physician was later to report) in perfect health, Sir Henry's physique was not impressive. A photograph taken of him on that eventful day portrays a tall, stoop-shouldered man whose hair appears to have slid down off his head and adhered somewhat erratically to his cheeks and chin. Of manual dexterity he had none; and those who knew him well moved unobtrusively to the rear as he placed a chisel in position against the stone barricade and raised his hammer. The British consul did not know him well. The first chip of rock hit this unlucky gentleman full on the nose. Apologies and first aid followed. Now surrounded by a wide empty space, Sir Henry prepared to strike again. Scarcely had he raised the hammer when, from among the crowd of watching Egyptians, came a long ululating howl.

The import of the cry was understood by all who heard it. In such fashion do the followers of Mohammed mourn their dead.

There was a moment's pause. Then the voice rose again. It cried (I translate, of course): "Desecration! Desecration! May the curse of the gods fall on him who disturbs the king's eternal rest!"

Startled by this remark, Sir Henry missed the chisel and hit himself on the thumb. Such misadventures do not improve the temper. Sir Henry may be excused for losing his. In a savage voice he instructed Armadale, standing behind him, to capture the prophet of doom and give him a good thrashing. Armadale was willing; but as he approached the milling crowd the orator wisely ceased his cries and thereby became anonymous, for his friends all denied any knowledge of his identity.

It was a trivial incident, soon forgotten by everyone except Sir Henry, whose thumb was badly bruised.

At least the injury gave him an excuse to surrender his tools to someone who was able to use them more effectively. Mr. Alan Armadale, a young, vigorous man, seized the implements. A few skillful blows opened an aperture wide enough to admit a light. Armadale then respectfully stepped back, allowing his patron the honor of the first look.

It was a day of misadventures for poor Sir Henry. Seizing a candle, he eagerly thrust his arm through the gaping hole. His fist encountered a hard surface with such force that he dropped the candle and withdrew a hand from which a considerable amount of skin had been scraped.

Investigation showed that the space beyond the door was completely filled with rubble. This was not surprising, since the Egyptians commonly used such devices to discourage tomb robbers; but the effect was distinctly anticlimactic, and the audience dispersed with disappointed murmurs, leaving Sir Henry to nurse his barked knuckles and contemplate a long, tedious job. If this tomb followed the plans of those already known, a passageway of unknown length would have to be cleared before the burial chamber was reached. Some tombs had entrance passages over a hundred feet long.

Yet the fact that the corridor was blocked made the discovery appear even more promising than before. The *Times* gave the story a full column, on page three. The next dispatch to come from Luxor, however, rated front-page headlines.

Sir Henry Baskerville was dead. He had retired in perfect health (except for his thumb and his knuckles). He was found next morning stiff and stark in his bed.

On his face was a look of ghastly horror. On his high brow, inscribed in what appeared to be dried blood, was a crudely drawn uraeus serpent, the symbol of the divine pharaoh.

The "blood" turned out to be red paint. Even so, the news was sensational, and it became even more sensational after a medical examination failed to discover the cause of Sir Henry's death.

Cases of seemingly healthy persons who succumb to the sudden failure of a vital organ are certainly not unknown, nor, contrary to writers of thrillers, are they always due to the administration of mysterious poisons. If Sir Henry had died in his bed at Baskerville Hall, the physicians would have stroked their beards and concealed their ignorance in meaningless medical mumbo-jumbo. Even under these circumstances the story would have died a natural death (as Sir Henry was presumed to have done) had not an enterprising reporter from one of our less reputable newspapers remembered the unknown prophet's curse. The story in the *Times* was what one might expect of that dignified journal, but the other newspapers were less restrained. Their columns bristled with references to avenging spirits, cryptic antique curses, and unholy rites. But this sensation paled into insignificance two days later, when it was discovered that Mr. Alan Armadale, Sir Henry's assistant, had disappeared—vanished, as the *Daily Yell* put it, off the face of the earth!

By this time I was snatching the newspapers from Emerson each evening when he came home. Naturally I did not believe for an instant in the absurd tales of curses or supernatural doom, and when the news of young Armadale's disappearance became known I felt sure I had the answer to the mystery.

"Armadale is the murderer," I exclaimed to Emerson, who was on his hands and knees playing horsie with Ramses.

Emerson let out a grunt as his son's heels dug into his ribs. When he got his breath back he said irritably, "What do you mean, talking about 'the murderer' in that self-assured way? No murder was committed. Baskerville died of a heart condition or some such thing; he was always a feeble sort of fellow. Armadale is probably forgetting his troubles in a tavern. He has lost his position and will not easily find another patron so late in the season."

I made no reply to this ridiculous suggestion. Time, I knew, would prove me right, and until it did I saw no sense in wasting my breath arguing with Emerson, who is the stubbornest of men.

During the following week one of the gentlemen who had been present at the official opening of the tomb came down with a bad attack of fever, and a workman fell off a pylon at Karnak, breaking his neck. "The Curse is still operating," exclaimed the *Daily Yell*. "Who will be next?"

After the demise of the man who tumbled off the pylon (where he had been chiseling out a section of carving to sell to the illicit antiquities dealers), his fellows refused to go near the tomb. Work had come to a standstill after Sir Henry's death; now there seemed no prospect of renewing it. So matters stood on that cold, rainy evening after my disastrous tea party. For the past few days the Baskerville story had more or less subsided, despite the efforts of the *Daily Yell* to keep it alive by attributing every hangnail and stubbed toe in Luxor to the operation of the curse. No trace of the unfortunate (or guilty) Armadale had been found; Sir Henry Baskerville had been laid to rest among his forebears; and the tomb remained locked and barred.

I confess the tomb was my chief concern. Locks and bars were all very well, but neither would avail for long against the master thieves of Gurneh. The discovery of the sepulcher had been a blow to the professional pride of these gentlemen, who fancied themselves far more adept at locating the treasures of their ancestors than the foreign excavators; and indeed, over the centuries they had proved to be exceedingly skillful at their dubious trade, whether by practice or by heredity I would hesitate to say. Now that the tomb had been located they would soon be at work.

So, while Emerson argued zoology with Ramses, and the sleety rain hissed against the windows, I opened the newspaper. Since the beginning of *l'affaire Baskerville*, Emerson had been buying the *Yell* as well as the *Times*, remarking that the contrast in journalistic styles was a fascinating study in human nature. This was only an excuse; the *Yell* was much more entertaining to read. I therefore turned at once to this newspaper, noting that, to judge by certain creases and folds, I was not the first to peruse that particular article. It bore the title "Lady Baskerville vows the work must go on."

The journalist—"Our Correspondent in Luxor"—wrote with considerable feeling and many adjectives about the lady's "delicate lips, curved like a Cupid's bow, which quivered with emotion as she spoke" and "her tinted face which bore stamped upon it a deep acquaintance with grief."

"Bah," I said, after several paragraphs of this. "What drivel. I must say, Emerson, Lady Baskerville sounds like a perfect idiot. Listen to this. 'I can think of no more fitting monument to my lost darling than the pursuit of that great cause for which he gave his life.' Lost darling, indeed!"

Emerson did not reply. Squatting on the floor, with Ramses between his knees, he was turning the pages of a large illustrated volume on zoology, trying to convince the boy that his bone did not match that of a zebra—for Ramses had retreated from giraffes to that slightly less exotic beast. Unfortunately a zebra is rather like a horse, and the example Emerson found bore a striking resemblance to the bone Ramses was flourishing. The child let out a malevolent chuckle and remarked, "I was wight, you see. It is a zebwa."

"Have another cake," said his father.

"Armadale is still missing," I continued. "I told you he was the murderer."

"Bah," said Emerson. "He will turn up eventually. There has been no murder."

"You can hardly believe he has been drunk for a fortnight," I said.

"I have known men to remain drunk for considerably longer periods," said Emerson.

"If Armadale had met with an accident he, or his remains, would have been found by now. The Theban area has been combed—"

"It is impossible to search the western mountains thoroughly," Emerson snapped. "You know what they are like—jagged cliffs cut by hundreds of gullies and ravines."

"Then you believe he is out there somewhere?"

"I do. It would be a tragic coincidence, certainly, if he met with a fatal accident so soon after Sir Henry's death; the newspapers would certainly set up a renewed howl about curses. But such coincidences do happen, especially if a man is distracted by—"

"He is probably in Algeria by now," I said.

"Algeria! Why there, for heaven's sake?"

"The Foreign Legion. They say it is full of murderers and criminals attempting to escape justice."

Emerson got to his feet. I was pleased to observe that his eyes had lost their melancholy look and were blazing with temper. I noted, as well, that four years of relative inactivity had not robbed his form of its strength and vigor. He had removed his coat and starched collar preparatory to playing with the boy, and his disheveled appearance irresistibly recalled the unkempt individual who had first captured my heart. I decided that if we went straight upstairs there might be time, before we changed for dinner—

"It is time for bed, Ramses; Nurse will be waiting," I said. "You may take the last cake with you."

Ramses gave me a long, considering look. He then turned to his father, who said cravenly, "Run along, my boy. Papa will read you an extra chapter from his *History of Egypt* when you are tucked in your cot."

"Vewy well," said Ramses. He nodded at me in a manner reminiscent of the regal condescension of his namesake. "You will come and say good night, Mama?"

"I always do," I said.

When he had left the room, taking not only the last cake but the book on zoology, Emerson began pacing up and down.

"I suppose you want another cup of tea," I said.

What I really supposed was that since I had suggested the tea, he would say he did not want it. Like all men, Emerson is very susceptible to the cruder forms of manipulation. Instead he said gruffly, "I want a whiskey and soda."

Emerson seldom imbibes. Trying to conceal my concern, I inquired, "Is something wrong?"

"Not something. Everything. You know, Amelia."

"Were your students unusually dense today?"

"Not at all. It would be impossible for them to be duller than they normally are. I suppose it is all this talk in the newspapers about Luxor that makes me restless."

"I understand."

"Of course you do. You suffer from the same malaise— suffer even more than I, who am at least allowed to hover on the fringes of the profession we both love. I am like a child pressing its nose against the window of the toy shop, but you are not even permitted to walk by the place."

This flight of fancy was so pathetic, and so unlike Emerson's usual style of speaking, that it was with difficulty that I prevented myself from flinging my arms about him. However, he did not want sympathy. He wanted an alleviation of his boredom, and that I could not provide. In some bitterness of spirit I said, "And I have failed to obtain even a poor substitute for your beloved excavations. After today, Lady Harold will take the greatest pleasure in thwarting any request we might make. It is my fault; I lost my temper."

"Don't be a fool, Peabody," Emerson growled. "No one could make an impression on the solid stupidity of that woman and her husband. I told you not to attempt it."

This touching and magnanimous speech brought tears to my eyes. Seeing my emotion, Emerson added, "You had better join me in a little spirituous consolation. As a general rule I do not approve of drowning one's sorrows, but today has been a trial for both of us."

As I took the glass he handed me I thought how shocked Lady Harold would have been at this further evidence of unwomanly habits. The fact is, I abominate sherry, and I like whiskey and soda.

Emerson raised his glass. The corners of his mouth lifted in a valiant and sardonic smile. "Cheers, Peabody. We'll weather this, as we have weathered other troubles."

"Certainly. Cheers, my dear Emerson."

Solemnly, almost ritually, we drank.

"Another year or two," I said, "and we might consider taking Ramses out with us. He is appallingly healthy; sometimes I feel that to match our son against the fleas and mosquitoes and fevers of Egypt is to place the country under an unfair disadvantage."

This attempt at humor did not win a smile from my husband. He shook his head. "We cannot risk it."

"Well, but the boy must go away to school eventually," I argued.

"I don't see why. He is getting a better education from us than he could hope to obtain in one of those pestilential purgatories called preparatory schools. You know how I feel about them."

"There must be a few decent schools in the country."

"Bah." Emerson swallowed the remainder of his whiskey. "Enough of this depressing subject. What do you say we go upstairs and—"

He stretched out his hand to me. I was about to take it when the door opened and Wilkins made his appearance. Emerson reacts very poorly to being interrupted when he is in a romantic mood. He turned to the butler and shouted, "Curse it, Wilkins, how dare you barge in here? What is it you want?"

None of our servants is at all intimidated by Emerson. Those who survive the first few weeks of his bellowing and temper tantrums learn that he is the kindest of men. Wilkins said calmly, "I beg your pardon, sir. A lady is here to see you and Mrs. Emerson."

"A lady?" As is his habit when perplexed, Emerson fingered the dent in his chin. "Who the devil can that be?"

A wild thought flashed through my mind. Had Lady Harold returned, on vengeance bent? Was she even now in the hall carrying a basket of rotten eggs or a bowl of mud? But that was absurd, she would not have the imagination to think of such a thing.

"Where is the lady?" I inquired.

"Waiting in the hall, madam. I attempted to show her into the small parlor, but—"

Wilkins' slight shrug and raised eyebrow finished the story. The lady had refused to be shown into the parlor. This suggested that she was in some urgency, and it also removed my hope of slipping upstairs to change.

"Show her in, then, Wilkins, if you please," I said.

The lady's urgency was even greater than I had supposed. Wilkins had barely time to step back out of the way before she entered; she was advancing toward us when he made the belated announcement: "Lady Baskerville."

CHAPTER
TWO

The words fell on my ears with almost supernatural force. To see this unexpected visitor, when I had just been thinking and talking about her (and in no kindly terms) made me feel as if the figure now before us was no real woman, but the vision of a distracted mind.

And I must confess that most people would have considered her a vision indeed, a vision of Beauty posing for a portrait of Grief. From the crown of her head to her tiny slippers she was garbed in unrelieved black. How she had passed through the filthy weather without so much as a mud stain I could not imagine, but her shimmering satin skirts and filmy veils were spotless. A profusion of jet beads, sullenly gleaming, covered her bodice and trailed down the folds of her full skirt. The veils fell almost to her feet. The one designed to cover her face had been thrown back so that her pale, oval countenance was framed by the filmy puffs and folds. Her eyes were black; the brows lifted in a high curve that gave her a look of perpetual and innocent surprise. There was no color in her cheeks, but her mouth was a full rich scarlet. The effect of this was startling in the extreme; one could not help thinking of the damnably lovely lamias and vampires of legend.

Also, one could not help thinking of one's mud-stained, unbecoming gown, and wonder whether the aroma of whiskey covered the smell of moldy bone, or the reverse. Even I, who am not easily daunted, felt a pang of self-consciousness. I realized that I was trying to hide my glass, which was still half full, under a sofa cushion.

Though the pause of surprise—for Emerson, like myself, was gaping—seemed to last forever, I believe it was only a second or two before I regained my self-possession. Rising to my feet, I greeted our visitor, dismissed Wilkins, offered a chair and a cup of tea. The lady accepted the chair and refused the tea. I then expressed my condolences on her recent bereavement, adding that Sir Henry's death was a great loss to our profession.

This statement jarred Emerson out of his stupor, as I had thought it might, but for once he showed a modicum of tact, instead of making a rude remark about Sir Henry's inadequacies as an Egyptologist. Emerson saw no reason why anything, up to and including death, should excuse a man from poor scholarship.

However, he was not so tactful as to agree with my compliment or add one of his own. "Er—humph," he said. "Most unfortunate. Sorry to hear of it. What the deuce do you suppose has become of Armadale?"

"Emerson," I exclaimed. "This is not the time—"

"Pray don't apologize." The lady lifted a delicate white hand, adorned with a huge mourning ring made of braided hair—that of the late Sir Henry, I presumed.

She turned a charming smile on my husband. "I know Radcliffe's good heart too well to be deceived by his gruff manner."

Radcliffe indeed! I particularly dislike my husband's first name. I was under the impression that he did also. Instead of expressing disapproval he simpered like a schoolboy.

"I was unaware that you two were previously acquainted," I said, finally managing to dispose of my glass of whiskey behind a bowl of potpourri.

"Oh, yes," said Lady Baskerville, while Emerson continued to grin foolishly at her. "We have not met for several years; but in the early days, when we were all young and ardent—ardent about Egypt, I mean—we were well acquainted. I was hardly more than a bride— too young, I fear, but my dear Henry quite swept me off my feet."

She dabbed at her eyes with a black-bordered kerchief.

"There, there," said Emerson, in the voice he sometimes uses with Ramses. "You must not give way. Time will heal your grief."

This from a man who curled up like a hedgehog when forced into what he called society, and who never in his life had been known to utter a polite cliché! He began sidling toward her. In another moment he would pat her on the shoulder.

"How true," I said. "Lady Baskerville, the weather is inclement, and you seem very tired. I hope you will join us for dinner, which will be served shortly."

"You are very kind." Lady Baskerville removed her handkerchief from her eyes, which appeared to be perfectly dry, and bared her teeth at me. "I would not dream of such an intrusion. I am staying with friends in the neighborhood, who are expecting me back this evening. Indeed, I would not have come so unceremoniously, unexpected and uninvited, if I had not had an urgent matter to put before you. I am here on business."

"Indeed," I said.

"Indeed?" Emerson's echo held a questioning note; but in fact I had already deduced the nature of the lady's business. Emerson calls this jumping to conclusions. I call it simple logic.

"Yes," said Lady Baskerville. "And I will come to the point at once, rather than keep you any longer from your domestic comforts. I gather, from your question about poor Alan, that you are au courant about the situation in Luxor?"

"We have followed it with interest," Emerson said.

"We?" The lady's glowing black eyes turned to me with an expression of curiosity. "Ah, yes, I believe I did hear that Mrs. Emerson takes an interest in archaeology. So much the better; I will not bore her if I introduce the subject."

I retrieved my glass of whiskey from behind the potpourri. "No, you will not bore me," I said.

"You are too good. To answer your question, then, Radcliffe: no trace has been found of poor Alan. The situation is swathed in darkness and in mystery. When I think of it I am overcome."

Again the dainty handkerchief came into play. Emerson made clucking noises. I said nothing, but drank my whiskey in ladylike silence.

At last Lady Baskerville resumed. "I can do nothing

about the mystery surrounding Alan's disappearance; but I am in hopes of accomplishing something else, which may seem unimportant compared with the loss of human life, but which was vital to the interests of my poor lost husband. The tomb, Radcliffe—the tomb!"

Leaning forward, with clasped hands and parted lips, her bosom heaving, she fixed him with her great black eyes; and Emerson stared back, apparently mesmerized.

"Yes, indeed," I said. "The tomb. We gather, Lady Baskerville, that work has come to a standstill. You know, of course, that sooner or later it will be robbed, and all your husband's efforts wasted."

"Precisely!" The lady turned the clasped hands, the lips, the bosom, et cetera, et cetera, on me. "How I do admire your logical, almost masculine, mind, Mrs. Emerson. That is just what I was trying to express, in my poor silly way."

"I thought you were," I said. "What is it you want my husband to do?"

Thus directed, Lady Baskerville had to get to the point. How long she would have taken if she had been allowed to ramble on, heaven only knows.

"Why, to take over the direction of the excavation," she said. "It must be carried on, and without delay. I honestly believe my darling Henry will not rest quietly in the tomb while this work, possibly the culmination of his splendid career, is in peril. It will be a fitting memorial to one of the finest—"

"Yes, you said that in your interview in the *Yell*," I interrupted. "But why come to us? Is there no scholar in Egypt who could take on the task?"

"But I came first to you," she exclaimed. "I know Radcliffe would have been Henry's first choice, as he is mine."

She had not fallen into my trap. Nothing would have enraged Emerson so much as the admission that she had approached him only as a last resort. And, of course, she was quite correct; Emerson *is* the best.

"Well, Emerson?" I said. I confess, my heart was beating fast as I awaited his answer. A variety of emotions struggled for mastery within my breast. My feelings about Lady Baskerville have, I trust, been made plain; the notion of my husband spending the remainder of the winter with the lady was not pleasing to me. Yet, having beheld his anguish that very evening, I could not stand in his way if he decided to go.

Emerson stood staring at Lady Baskerville, his own feelings writ plainly across his face. His expression was that of a prisoner who had suddenly been offered a pardon after years of confinement. Then his shoulders sagged.

"It is impossible," he said.

"But why?" Lady Baskerville asked. "My dear husband's will specifically provides for the completion of any project that might have been in progress at the time of his demise. The staff—with the exception of Alan—is in Luxor, ready to continue. I confess that the workers have shown a singular reluctance to return to the tomb; they are poor, superstitious things, as you know—"

"That would present no problem," Emerson said, with a sweeping gesture. "No, Lady Baskerville; the difficulty is not in Egypt. It is here. We have a young child. We could not risk taking him to Luxor."

There was a pause. Lady Baskerville's arched brows rose still higher; she turned to me with a look that expressed the question she was too well bred to voice aloud. For really, the objection was, on the face of it, utterly trivial. Most men, given an opportunity such as the one she had offered, would coolly have disposed of half a dozen children, and the same number of wives, in order to accept. It was because this idea had, obviously, not even passed through Emerson's mind that I was nerved to make the noblest gesture of my life.

"Do not consider that, Emerson," I said. I had to pause, to clear my throat; but I went on with a firmness that, if I may say so, did me infinite credit. "Ramses and I will do very well here. We will write every day—"

"Write!" Emerson spun around to face me, his blue eyes blazing, his brow deeply furrowed. An unwitting observer might have thought he was enraged. "What are you talking about? You know I won't go without you."

"But—" I began, my heart overflowing.

"Don't talk nonsense, Peabody. It is out of the question."

If I had not had other sources of deep satisfaction at that moment, the look on Lady Baskerville's face would have been sufficient cause for rejoicing. Emerson's response had taken her completely by surprise; and the astonishment with which she regarded me, as she tried to find some trace of the charms that made a man unwilling to be parted from me, was indeed delightful to behold.

Recovering, she said hesitantly, "If there is any question of a proper establishment for the child—"

"No, no," said Emerson. "That is not the question. I am sorry, Lady Baskerville. What about Petrie?"

"That dreadful man?" Lady Baskerville shuddered. "Henry could not abide him—so rude, so opinionated, so vulgar."

"Naville, then."

"Henry had such a poor opinion of his abilities. Besides, I believe he is under obligation to the Egypt Exploration Fund."

Emerson proposed a few more names. Each was unacceptable. Yet the lady continued to sit, and I wondered what new approach she was contemplating. I wished she would get on with it, or take her leave; I was very hungry, having had no appetite for tea.

Once again my aggravating but useful child rescued me from an unwelcome guest. Our good-night visits to Ramses were an invariable custom. Emerson read to him, and I had my part as well. We were late in coming, and patience is not a conspicuous virtue of Ramses. Having waited, as he thought, long enough, he came in search of us. How he eluded his nurse and the other servants on that particular occasion I do not know, but he had raised evasion to a fine art. The drawing-room doors burst open with such emphasis that one looked for a Herculean form in the doorway. Yet the sight of Ramses in his little white nightgown, his hair curling damply around his beaming face, was not anticlimactic; he looked positively angelic, requiring only wings to resemble one of Raphael's swarthier cherubs.

He was carrying a large folder, clasping it to his infantile bosom with both arms. It was the manuscript of *The History of Egypt*. With his usual single-minded determination he gave the visitor only a glance before trotting over to his father.

"You pwomised to wead to me," he said.

"So I did, so I did." Emerson took the folder. "I will come soon, Ramses. Go back to Nurse."

"No," said Ramses calmly.

"What a little angel," exclaimed Lady Baskerville.

I was about to counter this description with another, more accurate, when Ramses said sweetly, "And you are a pitty lady."

Little did the lady know, as she smiled and blushed, that the apparent compliment was no more than a simple statement of fact, implying nothing of Ramses' feelings of approval or disapproval. In fact, the slight curl of his juvenile lip as he looked at her, and the choice of the word "pretty" rather than "beautiful" (a distinction which Ramses understood perfectly well) made me suspect that, with that fine perception so surprising in a child of his age, which he has inherited from me, he held certain reservations about Lady Baskerville and would, if properly prompted, express them with his customary candor.

Unfortunately, before I could frame an appropriate cue, his father spoke, ordering him again to his nurse, and Ramses, with that chilling calculation that is such an integral part of his character, decided to make use of the visitor for his own purposes. Trotting quickly to her side, he put his finger in his mouth (a habit I broke him of early in his life) and stared at her.

"Vewy pitty lady. Wamses stay wif you."

"Dreadful hypocrite," I said. "Begone."

"He is adorable," murmured Lady Baskerville. "Dear

little one, the pretty lady must go away. She would stay if she could. Give me a kiss before I go."

She made no attempt to lift him onto her lap, but bent over and offered a smooth white cheek. Ramses, visibly annoyed at his failure to win a reprieve from bed, planted a loud smacking kiss upon it, leaving a damp patch where once pearl powder had smoothly rested.

"I will go now," Ramses announced, radiating offended dignity. "You come soon, Papa. You too, Mama. Give me my book."

Meekly Emerson surrendered his manuscript and Ramses departed. Lady Baskerville rose.

"I too must go to my proper place," she said, with a smile. "My heartfelt apologies for disturbing you."

"Not at all, not at all," said Emerson. "I am only sorry I was unable to be of help."

"I too. But I understand now. Having seen your darling child and met your charming wife—" Here she grinned at me, and I grinned back—"I comprehend why a man with such affable domestic ties would not wish to leave them for the danger and discomfort of Egypt. My dear Radcliffe, how thoroughly domesticated you have become! It is delightful! You are quite the family man! I am happy to see you settled down at last after those adventurous bachelor years. I don't blame you in the least for refusing. Of course none of us believes in curses, or anything so foolish, but there is certainly something strange going on in Luxor, and only a reckless, bold, free spirit would face such dangers. Good-bye, Radcliffe—Mrs. Emerson—such a pleasure to have met you—no, don't see me out, I beg. I have troubled you enough."

The change in her manner during this speech was remarkable. The soft murmuring voice became brisk and emphatic. She did not pause for breath, but shot out the sharp sentences like bullets. Emerson's face reddened; he tried to speak, but was not given the opportunity. The lady glided from the room, her black veils billowing out like storm clouds.

"Damn!" said Emerson. He stamped his foot.

"She was very impertinent," I agreed.

"Impertinent? On the contrary, she tried to state the unpalatable facts as nicely as possible. 'Quite the family man! Settled down at last!' Good Gad!"

"Now you are talking just like a man," I began angrily.

"How surprising! I am not a man, I am a domesticated old fogy, without the courage or the daring—"

"You are responding precisely as she hoped you would," I exclaimed. "Can't you see that she chose every word with malicious deliberation? The only one she did not employ was—"

"Henpecked. True, very true. She was too courteous to say it."

"Oh, so you think you are henpecked, do you?"

"Certainly not," said Emerson, with the complete lack of consistency the male sex usually exhibits during an argument. "Not that you don't try—"

"And you try to bully me. If I were not such a strong character—"

The drawing-room doors opened. "Dinner is served," said Wilkins.

"Tell Cook to put it back a quarter of an hour," I said. "We had better tuck Ramses in first, Emerson."

"Yes, yes. I will read to him while you change that abominable frock. I refuse to dine with a woman who looks like an English matron and smells like a compost heap. How dare you say that I bully you?"

"I said you tried. Neither you nor any other man will ever succeed."

Wilkins stepped back as we approached the door.

"Thank you, Wilkins," I said.

"Certainly, madam."

"As for the charge of henpecking—"

"I beg your pardon, madam?"

"I was speaking to Professor Emerson."

"Yes, madam."

"Henpecking was the word I used," snarled Emerson, allowing me to precede him up the stairs. "And henpecking was the word I meant."

"Then why don't you accept the lady's offer? I could see you were panting to do so. What a charming time you two could have, night after night, under the soft Egyptian moon—"

"Oh, don't talk like a fool, Amelia. The poor woman won't go back to Luxor; her memories would be too much to bear."

"Ha!" I laughed sharply. "The naivety of men constantly astonishes me. Of course she will be back. Especially if you are there."

"I have no intention of going."

"No one is preventing you."

We reached the top of the stairs. Emerson turned to the right, to continue up to the nursery. I wheeled left, toward our rooms.

"You will be up shortly, then?" he inquired.

"Ten minutes."

"Very well, my dear."

It required even less than ten minutes to rip the gray gown off and replace it with another. When I reached the night nursery the room was dark except for one lamp, by whose light Emerson sat reading. Ramses, in his crib, contemplated the ceiling with rapt attention. It made a pretty little family scene, until one heard what was being said.

"...the anatomical details of the wounds, which included a large gash in the frontal bone, a broken malar bone and orbit, and a spear thrust which smashed off the mastoid process and struck the atlas vertebra, allow us to reconstruct the death scene of the king."

"Ah, the mummy of Seqenenre," I said. "Have you got as far as that?"

From the small figure on the cot came a reflective voice. "It appeaws to me that he was muwduwed."

"What?" said Emerson, baffled by the last word.

"Murdered," I interpreted. "I would have to agree, Ramses; a man whose skull has been smashed by repeated blows did not die a natural death."

Sarcasm is wasted on Ramses. "I mean," he insisted, "that it was a domestic cwime."

"Out of the question," Emerson exclaimed. "Petrie has also put forth that absurd idea; it is impossible because—"

"Enough," I said. "It is late and Ramses should be asleep. Cook will be furious if we do not go down at once."

"Oh, very well." Emerson bent over the cot. "Good night, my boy."

"Good night, Papa. One of the ladies of the hawem did it, I think."

I seized Emerson by the arm and pushed him toward the door, before he could pursue this interesting suggestion. After carrying out my part of the nightly ritual (a description of which would serve no useful purpose in the present narrative), I followed Emerson out.

"Really," I said, as we went arm in arm along the corridor, "I wonder if Ramses is not too precocious. Does he know what a harem is, I wonder? And some people might feel that reading such a catalog of horrors to a child at bedtime will not be good for his nerves."

"Ramses has nerves of steel. Rest assured he will sleep the sleep of the just and by breakfast time he will have his theory fully developed."

"Evelyn would be delighted to take him for the winter."

"Oh, so we are back to that, are we? What sort of unnatural mother are you, that you can contemplate abandoning your child?"

"I must choose, it appears, between abandoning my child or my husband."

"False, utterly false. No one is going to abandon anyone."

We took our places at the table. The footman, watched critically by Wilkins, brought on the first course.

"Excellent soup," Emerson said, in a pleased voice. "Tell Cook, will you please, Wilkins?"

Wilkins inclined his head.

"We are going to settle this once and for all," Emerson went on. "I refuse to have you nagging me for days to come."

"I never nag."

"No, because I don't permit it. Get this straight, Amelia: I am not going to Egypt. I have refused Lady Baskerville's offer, and do not mean to reconsider. Is that plain enough?"

"You are making a grave mistake," I said. "I think you should go."

"I am well aware of your opinion. You express it often enough. Why can't you allow me to make up my own mind?"

"Because you are wrong."

There is no need to repeat the remainder of the discussion. It continued throughout the meal, with Emerson appealing from time to time to Wilkins, or to John, the footman, to support a point he was trying to make. This made John, who had been with us only a few weeks, very nervous at first. Gradually, however, he became interested in the discussion and added comments of his own, ignoring the winks and frowns of Wilkins, who had long since learned how to deal with Emerson's unconventional manners. To spare the butler's feelings I said we would have coffee in the drawing room, and John was dismissed, though not before he had said earnestly, "You had better stay here, sir; them natives is strange people, and I'm sure, sir, we would all miss you if you was to go."

Dismissing John did not dismiss the subject, for I stuck to it with my usual determination, despite Emerson's efforts to introduce other topics of conversation. He finally flung his coffee cup into the fireplace with a shout of rage and stormed out of the drawing room. I followed.

When I reached our bedchamber, Emerson was undressing. Coat, tie, and collar were draped inappropriately over various articles of furniture, and buttons flew around the room like projectiles as he removed his shirt.

"You had better purchase another dozen shirts the next time you are in Regent Street," I said, ducking as a button whizzed past my face. "You will need them if you are going abroad."

Emerson whirled. For so burly and broad-chested a man he is surprisingly quick in his movements. In one stride he bridged the space between us. Taking me by the shoulders, he...

But here I must pause for a brief comment. Not an apologia—no, indeed! I have always felt that the present-day sanctimonious primness concerning the affection between the sexes, even between husband and wife—an affection sanctified by the Church and legalized by the Nation—is totally absurd. Why should a respectable, interesting activity be passed over by novelists who pretend to portray "real life"? Even more despicable, to my mind, are the circumlocutions practiced by writers on this subject. Not for me the slippery suavity of French or the multi-syllabled pretentiousness of Latin. The good old Anglo-Saxon tongue, the speech of our ancestors, is good enough for me. Let the hypocrites among you, readers, skip the following paragraphs. Despite my reticence on the subject the more discerning will have realized that my feelings for my husband, and his for me, are of the warmest nature. I see no reason to be ashamed of this.

To return to the main stream of the argument, then:

Taking me by the shoulders, Emerson gave me a hearty shake.

"By Gad," he shouted. "I will be master in my own house! Must I teach you again who makes decisions here?"

"I thought we made them together, after discussing problems calmly and courteously."

Emerson's shaking had loosened my hair, which is thick and coarse and does not yield easily to restraint. Still holding me by one shoulder, he passed the fingers of his other hand into the heavy knot at the back of my neck. Combs and hairpins went flying. The hair tumbled down over my shoulders.

I do not recall precisely what he said next. The comment was brief. He kissed me. I was determined not to kiss him back; but Emerson kisses very well. It was some time before I was able to speak. My suggestion that I call my maid to help me out of my frock was not well received. Emerson offered his services. I pointed out that his method of removing a garment often rendered that garment unserviceable thereafter. This comment was greeted with a wordless snort of derision and a vigorous attack upon the hooks and eyes.

After all, much as I commend frankness in such matters, there are areas in which an individual is entitled to privacy. I find myself forced to resort to a typographical euphemism.

*   *   *

By midnight the sleet had stopped falling, and a brisk east wind shook the icy branches of the trees outside our window. They creaked and cracked like spirits of darkness, protesting attack. My cheek rested against my husband's breast; I could hear the steady rhythmic beat of his heart.

"When do we leave?" I inquired softly.

Emerson yawned. "There is a boat on Saturday."

"Good night, Emerson."

"Good night, my darling Peabody."

CHAPTER
THREE

Reader, do you believe in magic—in the flying carpets of the old Eastern romances? Of course you don't; but suspend your disbelief for a moment and allow the magic of the printed word to transport you across thousands of miles of space and many hours of time to a scene so different from wet, cold, dismal England that it might be on another planet. Picture yourself sitting with me on the terrace of Shepheard's Hotel in Cairo. The sky is a brilliant porcelain blue. The sun casts its benevolent rays impartially on rich merchants and ragged beggars, on turbaned imams and tailored European tourists—on all the infinitely varied persons who compose the bustling crowds that traverse the broad thoroughfare before us. A bridal procession passes, preceded by musicians raising cacophonous celebration with flutes and drums. The bride is hidden from curious eyes by a rose silk canopy carried by four of her male relations. Poor girl, she goes from one owner to another, like a bale of merchandise; but at that moment even my indignant contemplation of that most iniquitous of Turkish customs is mellowed by my joy in being where I am. I am filled with the deepest satisfaction. In a few moments Emerson will join me and we will set out for the Museum.

Only one ripple mars the smooth surface of my content. Is it concern for my little son, so far from his mother's tender care? No, dear reader, it is not. The thought that several thousands of miles separate me from Ramses inspires a sense of profound peace such as I have not known for years. I wonder that it never before occurred to me to take a holiday from Ramses.

I knew he would receive from his doting aunt care as tender and devoted as he could expect at home. Walter, who had followed Ramses' developing interest in archeology with profound amusement, had promised to give him lessons in hieroglyphs. I did feel a trifle guilty about Evelyn's children, who were, as Emerson put it, "in for a long, hard winter." But after all, the experience would probably be good for their characters.

It had, of course, proved impossible to leave as soon as Emerson optimistically expected. For one thing, the holidays were almost upon us, and it would have been impossible to leave Ramses only a few days before Christmas. So we spent the festal season with Walter and Evelyn, and by the time we took our departure, on Boxing Day, even Emerson's grief at parting from his son was mitigated by the effects of a week of juvenile excitement and overindulgence. All the children except Ramses had been sick at least once, and Ramses had set the Christmas tree on fire, frightened the nursery maid into fits by displaying his collection of engravings of mummies (some in an advanced state of decrepitude), and . . . But it would require an entire volume to describe all Ramses' activities. On the morning of our departure his infantile features presented a horrific appearance, for he had been badly scratched by little Amelia's kitten while trying to show the animal how to stir the plum pudding with its paw. As the kitchen echoed to the outraged shrieks of the cook and the growls of the cat, he had explained that, since every other member of the household was entitled to stir the pudding for luck in the coming year, he had felt it only fair that the pets should share in the ceremony.

With such memories, is it any wonder that I contemplated a few months away from Ramses with placid satisfaction?

We took the fastest possible route: train to Marseilles, steamer to Alexandria, and train to Cairo. By the time we reached our destination my husband had shed ten years, and as we made our way through the chaos of the Cairo train station he was the old Emerson, shouting orders and expletives in fluent Arabic. His bull-like voice made heads turn and eyes open wide, and we were soon surrounded by old acquaintances, grinning and calling out greetings. White and green turbans bobbed up and down like animated cabbages, and brown hands reached out to grasp our hands. The most touching welcome came from a wizened old beggar, who flung himself on the ground and wrapped his arms around Emerson's dirty boot, crying, "Oh, Father of Curses, you have returned! Now I can die in peace!"

"Bah," said Emerson, trying not to smile. Gently disengaging his foot, he dropped a handful of coins onto the old man's turban.

I had cabled Shepheard's to book rooms as soon as

we decided to accept Lady Baskerville's offer, for the hotel is always crowded during the winter season. A magnificent new structure had replaced the rambling old building we had stayed in so often. Italianite in style, it was an imposing edifice with its own generating plant—the first hotel in the East to have electric lights. Emerson grumbled at all the unnecessary luxury. I myself have no objection to comfort so long as it does not interfere with more important activities.

We found messages awaiting us from friends who had heard of Emerson's appointment. There was also a note from Lady Baskerville, who had preceded us by a few days, welcoming us back to Egypt and urging us to proceed as soon as possible to Luxor. Conspicuous by its absence was any word from the Director of Antiquities. I was not surprised. Monsieur Grebaut and Emerson had never admired one another. It would be necessary for us to see him, and Grebaut was making certain we would have to sue humbly for an audience, like any ordinary tourists.

Emerson's comments were profane. When he had calmed down a little, I remarked, "All the same, we had better call on him at once. He can, if he wishes, make difficulties for us."

This sensible suggestion brought on another spell of ranting, in the course of which Emerson predicted Grebaut's future residence in a warm and uncomfortable corner of the universe, and declared that he himself would rather join the rascal in that place than make the slightest concession to rude officiousness. I therefore abandoned the subject for the time being and agreed to Emerson's proposal that we go first to Aziyeh, a village near Cairo from which he had in the past recruited his workmen. If we could take with us to Luxor a skeleton crew of men who were not infected with the local superstitions, we could begin work at once and hope to recruit other workers after success had proved their fears to be vain.

This concession put Emerson in a better mood, so that I was able to persuade him to dine downstairs instead of going to a native eating place in the bazaar. Emerson prefers such places, and so do I; but as I pointed out, we had been a long time away and our resistance to the local diseases had probably decreased. We dared not risk illness, for the slightest malaise would be interpreted as further evidence of the pharaoh's curse.

Emerson was forced to agree with my reasoning. Grumbling and swearing, he got into his boiled shirt and black evening suit. I tied his tie for him and stood back to observe him with pardonable pride. I knew better than to tell him he looked handsome, but indeed he did; his sturdy, upright frame and square shoulders, his thick black hair and his blue eyes blazing with temper formed a splendid picture of an English gentleman.

I had another reason for wishing to dine at the hotel. Shepheard's is the social center for the European colony, and I hoped to meet acquaintances who could bring us up to date on the news of the Luxor expedition.

Nor was I disappointed. When we entered the gilded dining hall the first person I saw was Mr. Wilbour, whom the Arabs call Abd er Dign because of his magnificent beard. White as the finest cotton, it sweeps down to the center of his waistcoat and frames a face both benevolent and highly intelligent. Wilbour had wintered in Egypt for many years. Rude gossip whispered of a political peccadillo in his native New York City, which made it expedient for him to avoid his homeland; but we knew him as an enthusiastic student of Egyptology and a patron of young archeologists. Seeing us, he came at once to greet us and ask us to join his party, which included several other old friends.

I took care to seat myself between Emerson and the Reverend Mr. Sayce; there had been an acrimonious exchange of letters the previous winter on the subject of certain cuneiform tablets. The precaution proved useless. Leaning across me, his elbow planted firmly on the table, Emerson called loudly, "You know, Sayce, that the people at Berlin have confirmed my date for the tablets from Amarna? I told you you were off by eight hundred years."

The Reverend's gentle countenance hardened; and Wilbour quickly intervened. "There was a rather amusing story about that, Emerson; did you hear how Budge managed to trick Grebaut out of those tablets?"

Emerson disliked Mr. Budge of the British Museum almost as much as he did Grebaut, but that evening, with the Director's discourtesy fresh in his mind, he was pleased to hear of anything to Grebaut's discredit. Distracted from his attack on the Reverend, he replied that we had heard rumors of the event but would be glad of a first-hand account.

"It was really a most reprehensible affair in every way," Wilbour said, shaking his head. "Grebaut had already warned Budge that he would be arrested if he continued to purchase and export antiquities illegally.

Quite unperturbed, Budge went straight to Luxor and bought not only eighty of the famous tablets but a number of other fine objects. The police promptly moved in, but Grebaut had neglected to provide them with a warrant, so they could only surround the house and wait for our popular Director of Antiquities to arrive with the requisite authority. In the meantime they saw no harm in accepting a fine meal of rice and lamb from the manager of the Luxor Hotel—next to which establishment Budge's house happened to be located. While the honest gendarmes gorged themselves, the hotel gardeners dug a tunnel into the basement of Budge's house and removed the antiquities. By a strange coincidence Grebaut's boat had run aground twenty miles north of Luxor, and he was still there when Budge set out for Cairo with his purchases, leaving the police to guard his empty house."

"Shocking," I said.

"Budge is a scoundrel," Emerson said. "And Grebaut is an idiot."

"Have you seen our dear Director yet?" Sayce inquired.

Emerson made rumbling noises. Sayce smiled. "I quite agree with you. All the same, you will have to see him. The situation is bad enough without incurring Grebaut's enmity. Are you not afraid of the curse of the pharaohs?"

"Bah," said Emerson.

"Quite! All the same, my dear chap, you won't find it easy to hire workers."

"We have our methods," I said, kicking Emerson in the shin to prevent him from explaining those methods.

Not that there was anything underhanded in what we planned; no, indeed. I would never be a party to stealing skilled workmen from other archaeologists. If our men from Aziyeh preferred to come with us, that was their choice. I simply saw no point in discussing the possibility before we had made our arrangements. I think Mr. Wilbour suspected something, however; there was an amused gleam in his eyes as he looked at me, but he said nothing, only stroked his beard in a contemplative fashion.

"So what is happening in Luxor?" I asked. "I take it the curse is still alive and well?"

"Good heavens, yes," Mr. Insinger, the Dutch archaeologist, answered. "Marvels and portents abound. Hassan ibn Daoud's pet goat gave birth to a two-headed kid, and ancient Egyptian ghosts haunt the Gurneh hills."

He laughed as he spoke, but Mr. Sayce shook his head sadly.

"Such are the superstitions of paganism. Poor ignorant people!"

Emerson could not let such a statement pass. "I can show you equal ignorance in any modern English village," he snapped. "And you can hardly call the creed of Mohammed paganism, Sayce; it worships the same God and the same prophets you do."

Before the Reverend, flushing angrily, could reply, I said quickly, "It is a pity Mr. Armadale is still missing. His disappearance only adds fuel to the fire."

"It would scarcely improve matters if he were found, I fear," Mr. Wilbour said. "Another death, following that of Lord Baskerville—"

"You believe he is dead, then?" Emerson asked, giving me a sly look.

"He must have perished or he would have turned up by now," Wilbour replied. "No doubt he met with a fatal accident while wandering the hills in a state of distraction. It is a pity; he was a fine archaeologist."

"At any rate, their fears may keep the Gurnawis from trying to break into the tomb," I said.

"You know better than that, my dear Mrs. Emerson," said Insinger. "At any rate, with you and Mr. Emerson on the job, we need not worry about the tomb."

Nothing of further consequence was said that evening, only speculations as to what marvels the tomb might contain. We therefore bid our friends good night as soon as the meal was concluded.

The hour was still early, and the lobby was crowded with people. As we approached the staircase someone darted out from among the throng and caught my arm.

"Mr. and Mrs. Emerson, I presume? Sure, and I've been looking forward to a chat with you. Perhaps you will do me the honor of joining me for coffee or a glass of brandy."

So confident was the tone, so assured the manner, that I had to look twice before I realized that the man was a total stranger. His boyish figure and candid smile made him appear, at first, far too young to be smoking the cigar that protruded at a jaunty angle from his lips. Bright-red hair and a liberal sprinkling of freckles across a decidedly snub nose completed the picture of brash young Ireland, for his accent had been unmistakably of that nation. Seeing me stare at his cigar, he immediately flung it into a nearby container.

"Your pardon, ma'am. In the pleasure of seeing you I forgot my manners."

"Who the devil are you?" Emerson demanded.

The young man's smile broadened. "Kevin O'Connell, of the *Daily Yell*, at your service. Mrs. Emerson, how do you feel about seeing your husband brave the pharaoh's curse? Did you attempt to dissuade him, or do you—"

I caught my husband's arm with both hands and managed to deflect the blow he had aimed at Mr. O'Connell's prominent chin.

"For pity's sake, Emerson—he is half your size!"

This admonition, as I expected, had the effect that an appeal to reason, social decorum, or Christian meekness would not have had. Emerson's arm relaxed and his cheeks turned red—though, I fear, with rising anger rather than shame. Seizing my hand, he proceeded at a brisk pace up the stairs. Mr. O'Connell trotted after us, spouting questions.

"Would you care to venture an opinion as to what has become of Mr. Armadale? Mrs. Emerson, will you take an active part in the excavation? Mr. Emerson, were you previously acquainted with Lady Baskerville? Was it, perhaps, old friendship that prompted you to accept such a perilous position?"

It is impossible to describe the tone of voice in which he uttered the word "friendship," or the indelicate overtone with which he invested that harmless word. I felt my own face grow warm with annoyance. Emerson let out a muted roar. His foot lashed out, and with a startled yelp Mr. O'Connell fell backward and rolled down the stairs.

As we reached the turn of the stair I glanced back

and saw, to my relief, that Mr. O'Connell had taken no serious injury. He had already regained his feet and, surrounded by a staring crowd, was engaged in brushing off the seat of his trousers. Meeting my eye, he had the effrontery to wink at me.

Emerson had his coat, tie, and half the buttons of his shirt off before I closed the door of our room.

"Hang it up," I said, as he was about to toss his coat onto a chair. "I declare, Emerson, that is the third shirt you have ruined since we left. Can you never learn—"

But I never finished the admonition. Obeying my order, Emerson had flung open the doors of the wardrobe. There was a flash of light and a thud; Emerson leaped back, one arm held at an unnatural angle. A bright line of red leaped up across his shirt sleeve. Crimson drops rained onto the floor, spattering the handle of the dagger that stood upright between Emerson's feet. Its haft still quivered with the force of its fall.

II

Emerson's hand clamped down on his forearm. The rush of blood slowed and stopped. A pain in the region of my chest reminded me that I was holding my breath. I let it out.

"That shirt was ruined in any case," I said. "Do, pray, hold your arm out so that you do not drip onto your good trousers."

I make it a rule always to remain calm. Nevertheless, it was with considerable speed that I crossed the room, snatching a towel from the washstand as I passed it. I had brought medical supplies with me, as is my custom; in a few moments I had cleaned and bandaged the wound which, fortunately, was not deep. I did not even mention a physician. I was confident that Emerson shared my own feelings on that matter. The news of an accident to the newly appointed director of the Luxor expedition could have disastrous consequences.

When I had finished I leaned back against the divan; and I confess I was unable to repress a sigh. Emerson looked at me seriously. Then a slight smile curved the corners of his mouth.

"You are a trifle pale, Peabody. I trust we are not going to have a display of female vapors?"

"I fail to see any humor in the situation."

"I am surprised at you. For my part, I am struck by the ludicrous ineptitude of the whole business. As nearly as I can make out, the knife was simply placed on the top shelf of the wardrobe, which rests somewhat insecurely on wooden pegs. The vigor of my movement in opening the door caused the weapon to topple out; it was pure accident that it struck me instead of falling harmlessly to the floor. Nor could the unknown have been sure that I would be the one to . . . ." As realization dawned, anger replaced the amusement on his face, and he cried out, "Good Gad, Peabody, you might have been seriously injured if you had been the one to open that wardrobe!"

"I thought you had concluded that no serious injury was contemplated," I reminded him. "No masculine vapors, Emerson, if you please. It was meant as a warning, nothing more."

"Or as an additional demonstration of the effectiveness of the pharaoh's curse. That seems more likely. No one who knows us would expect that we would be deterred from our plans by such a childish trick. Yet unless the incident becomes public knowledge it will be wasted effort."

Our eyes met. I nodded. "You are thinking of Mr. O'Connell. Would he really go to such lengths in order to get a story?"

"These fellows will stop at nothing," Emerson said with gloomy conviction.

He was certainly in a position to know, for during his active career he had featured prominently in sensational newspaper stories. As one reporter had explained to me, "He makes such splendid copy, Mrs. Emerson—always shouting and striking people."

There was some truth in this statement, and Emerson's performance that evening would undoubtedly make equally splendid copy. I could almost see the headlines: "Attack on our reporter by famous archaeologist! Frenzied Emerson reacts violently to question about his intimacy with dead man's widow!"

No wonder Mr. O'Connell had looked so pleased after being kicked down the stairs. He would consider a few bruises a small price to pay for a good story. I remembered his name now. He had been the first to break the story about the curse—or rather, to invent it.

There was no question about Mr. O'Connell's scruples, or lack thereof. Certainly he would have had no difficulty in gaining access to our room. The locks were flimsy, and the servants were amenable to bribery. But was he capable of planning a trick that might have ended in injury, however slight? I found that hard to believe. Brash, rude, and unscrupulous he might be, but I am an excellent judge of character, and I had seen no trace of viciousness in his freckled countenance.

We examined the knife but learned nothing from it; it was a common type, of the sort that can be bought in any bazaar. There was no point in questioning the servants. As Emerson said, the less publicity, the better. So we retired to our bed, with its canopy of fine white mosquito netting. In the ensuing hour I was reassured as to the negligibility of Emerson's wound. It did not seem to inconvenience him in the slightest.

III

We set out for Aziyeh early next morning. Though we had sent no message ahead, the news of our coming had spread, by that mysterious unseen means of communication common to primitive people, so that when our hired carriage stopped in the dusty village square, most of the population was assembled to greet us. Towering over the other heads was a snowy turban surmounting a familiar bearded face. Abdullah had been our reis, or foreman, in the past. His beard was now almost as white as his turban, but his giant frame looked as strong as ever, and a smile of welcome struggled with his instinctive patriarchal dignity as he pushed forward to shake our hands.

We retired to the house of the sheikh, where half the male population crowded into the small parlor. There we sat drinking sweet black tea and exchanging compliments, while the temperature steadily rose. Long periods of courteous silence were broken by repeated comments of "May God preserve you" and "You have honored us." This ceremony can take several hours, but Emerson's audience knew him well, and they exchanged amused glances when, after a mere twenty minutes, he broached the reason for our visit.

"I go to Luxor to carry on the work of the lord who died. Who will come with me?"

The question was followed by soft exclamations and well-feigned looks of surprise. That the surprise was false I had no doubt. Abdullah's was not the only familiar face in the room; many of our other men were there as well. The workers Emerson had trained were always in demand, and I did not doubt that these people had left other positions in order to come to us. Obviously they had anticipated the request and had, in all probability, already decided what they would do.

However, it is not the nature of Egyptians to agree to anything without a good deal of debate and discussion. After an interval Abdullah rose to his feet, his turban brushing the low ceiling.

"Emerson's friendship for us is known," he said. "But why does he not employ the men of Luxor who worked for the dead lord?"

"I prefer to work with my friends," Emerson replied. "Men I can trust in danger and difficulty."

"Ah, yes." Abdullah stroked his beard. "Emerson speaks of danger. It is known that he never lies. Will he tell us what danger he means?"

"Scorpions, snakes, landslides," Emerson shot back. "The same dangers we men have always faced together."

"And the dead who will not die, but walk abroad under the moon?"

This was a much more direct question than I had anticipated. Emerson, too, was caught off guard. He did not answer immediately. Every man in the room sat with his eyes fixed unwinkingly on my husband.

At last he said quietly, "You of all men, Abdullah, know that there is no such thing. Have you forgotten the mummy that was no mummy, but only an evil man?"

"I remember well, Emerson, but who is to say that such things cannot exist? They say that the lord who is dead disturbed the sleep of the pharaoh. They say—"

"They are fools who say so," Emerson interrupted. "Has not God promised the faithful protection against evil spirits? I go to carry on the work. I look for *men* to come with me, not fools and cowards."

The issue had never really been in doubt. When we left the village we had our crew, but thanks to Abdullah's piously expressed doubts we had to agree to a wage considerably higher than was customary. Superstition has its practical uses.

IV

On the following morning I sat, as I have described, on the terrace of Shepheard's and reviewed the events of the past two days. You will now comprehend, reader, why a single small cloud cast a faint shadow on the brightness of my pleasure. The cut on Emerson's arm was healing nicely, but the doubts that incident had raised were not so easily cured. I had taken it for granted that the death of Lord Baskerville and the disappearance of his assistant were parts of a single, isolated tragedy, and that the so-called curse was no more than the invention of an enterprising journalist. The strange case of the knife in the wardrobe raised another and more alarming possibility.

It is foolish to brood about matters one cannot control, so I dismissed the problem for the moment and enjoyed the constantly changing panorama unrolling before me until Emerson finally joined me. I had sent a messenger to Monsieur Grebaut earlier, informing him that we planned to call on him that morning. We were going to be late, thanks to Emerson's procrastination, but when I saw his scowl and his tight-set lips I realized I was fortunate to persuade him to go at all.

Since we were last in Egypt the Museum had been moved from its overcrowded quarters at Boulaq to the Palace of Gizeh. The result was an improvement in the amount of space only; the crumbling, overly ornate decorations of the palace were poorly suited for purposes of display, and the antiquities were in wretched condition. This increased Emerson's bad temper; he was red with annoyance by the time we reached the office, and when a supercilious secretary informed us that we must come back another day, since the Director was too busy to see us, he pushed the young man rudely aside and hurled himself at the door of the inner office.

I was not surprised when it failed to yield, for I had heard a sound like that of a key being turned in a lock. Locks do not hinder Emerson when he wishes to proceed; a second, more vigorous assault burst the door open. With a consoling smile at the cowering secretary I followed my impetuous husband into Grebaut's sanctum.

The room was crowded to the bursting point with open boxes containing antiquities, all awaiting examination and classification. Pots of baked clay, scraps of wood from furniture and coffins, alabaster jars, ushabtis, and dozens of other items overflowed the packing cases onto tables and desk.

Emerson let out a cry of outrage. "It is worse than it was in Maspero's day! Curse the rascal, where is he? I want to give him a piece of my mind!"

When antiquities are visible, Emerson is blind to all else. He did not observe the toes of a pair of rather large boots protruding from under a drapery that covered one side of the room.

"He appears to have stepped out," I replied, watching the boots. "I wonder if there is a door behind those draperies."

The polished toes shrank until only a bare inch remained visible. I assumed Grebaut was pressed up against a wall or a closed window and could retreat no further. He is a rather stout man.

"I have no intention of searching for the wretch," Emerson announced loudly. "I will leave him a note." He began to scrabble in the litter atop the Director's desk. Grebaut's papers and correspondence went flying.

"Calm yourself, Emerson," I said. "Monsieur Grebaut won't thank you for making a mess of his desk."

"I could not make it worse than it is." Emerson tossed away papers with both hands. "Just let me come face to face with that imbecile! He is totally incompetent. I intend to demand his resignation."

"I am thankful he is not here," I said, glancing casually at the drapery. "You have such a temper, Emerson;

you are really not accountable for your actions at times like this, and I would hate for you to injure the poor man."

"I would like to injure him. I would like to break both his arms. A man who would allow such neglect—"

"Why don't you leave a message with the secretary?" I suggested. "He must have pen and paper on his desk. You will never find it there."

With a final gesture that sent the remaining papers sailing around the room, Emerson stamped out. The secretary had fled. Emerson seized his pen and began scribbling furiously on a sheet of paper. I stood in the open doorway, one eye on Emerson, one eye on the boots; and I said loudly, "You might suggest, Emerson, that Monsieur Grebaut send the firman giving you charge of the expedition to our hotel. That will save you another trip."

"Good idea," Emerson grunted. "If I have to come again I *will* murder that moron."

Gently I closed the door of Grebaut's office.

We took our departure. Three hours later a messenger delivered the firman to our room.

CHAPTER FOUR

On my first trip to Egypt I had traveled by dahabeeyah. The elegance and charm of that mode of travel can only be dimly imagined by those who have not experienced it. My boat had been equipped with every comfort, including a grand piano in the salon and an outdoor sitting room on the upper deck. How many blissful hours did I spend there, under the billowing sails, drinking tea and listening to the songs of the sailors while the magnificent panorama of Egyptian life glided by on either side—villages and temples, palm trees, camels, and holy hermits perched precariously on pillars. How fond were my memories of that journey, which had culminated in my betrothal to my spouse! How gladly would I have repeated that glorious experience!

Alas, on this occasion we could not spare the time. The railroad had been extended as far south as Assiût, and since it was by far the fastest means of travel, we endured eleven hours of heat, jolting, and dust. From Assiût we took a steamer for the remaining distance. Though less uncomfortable than the train, it was a far cry from my dear dahabeeyah.

On the day we were to dock at Luxor I was on deck at dawn, hanging over the rail and gaping like any ignorant Cook's tourist. The Luxor temple had been cleared of the shacks and huts that had so long marred its beauty; its columns and pylons glowed rosy pink in the morning light as the steamer glided in to the dock.

Here the peaceful visions of the past were replaced by noisy modern bustle, as porters and guides converged on the disembarking passengers. The dragomen of the Luxor hotels shouted out the advantages of their various hostelries and attempted to drag bewildered tourists into the waiting carriages. No one bothered us.

Emerson went off to collect our luggage and locate our workmen, who had traveled in the same boat. Leaning on my parasol, I gazed complacently at the scene and took deep breaths of the soft air. Then a hand touched my arm, and I turned to meet the intense gaze of a stout young man wearing gold-rimmed spectacles and the most enormous pair of mustaches I had ever seen. The ends of them curled up and around like the horns of a mountain goat.

Heels together, body stiff, he bent himself at the waist and said, "Frau Professor Emerson? Karl von Bork, the epigrapher of the ill-fated Baskerville expedition. To Luxor I give you greeting. By Lady Baskerville was I sent. Where is the Professor? Long have I to the honor of meeting him looked forward. The brother of the so distinguished Walter Emerson—"

This rapid spate of conversation was all the more remarkable because the young man's face remained utterly expressionless throughout. Only his lips and the gigantic mustache above them moved. As I was to

learn, Karl von Bork spoke seldom, but once he began
to talk, it was virtually impossible to stop him except by
the means I adopted on that occasion.

"How do you do," I said loudly, drowning out his
last words. "I am pleased to meet you. My husband is
just...Where is he? Ah, Emerson; allow me to present
Herr von Bork."

Emerson grasped the young man's hand. "The epigrapher? Good. I trust you have a boat ready—one of
sufficient size. I have brought twenty men with me
from Cairo."

Von Bork bowed again. "An excellent idea, Herr
Professor. A stroke of genius! But I had expected nothing less from the brother of the distinguished—"

I interrupted this speech, as I had interrupted the
first; and we found that when Herr von Bork was not
talking he was efficient enough to please even my
demanding husband. The felucca he had hired was
commodious enough to hold us all. Our men gathered
in the bow, looking loftily at the boatmen and making
comments about the stupidity of Luxor men. The great
sails swelled, the prow dipped and swung about; we
turned our backs on the ancient temples and modern
houses of Luxor and moved out onto the broad bosom
of the Nile.

I could not help but be keenly sensitive to the impli-
cations of this westward journey, the same one made
by generations of Thebans when, the troubles of life
behind them, they set sail on the road to heaven. The
rugged western cliffs, gilded by the morning sun, had
for thousands of years been honeycombed by tombs
of noble, pharaoh, and humble peasant. The ruined

remains of once-great mortuary temples began to take shape as we drew near the shore: the curving white colonnades of Deir el Bahri, the frowning walls of the Ramesseum, and, towering above the plain, those colossal statues that alone remained of Amenhotep the Third's magnificent temple. Even more evocative were the wonders we could not see—the hidden, rock-cut sepulchers of the dead. As I looked, my heart swelled within me, and the last four years in England seemed but a horrid dream.

The sound of von Bork's voice roused me from my blissful contemplation of that gigantic cemetery. I hoped the young man would not continue to refer to Emerson as the brother of the distinguished Walter. Emerson has the highest regard for Walter's abilities, but one could hardly blame him for taking umbrage at being regarded only as an appendage to his brother. Von Bork's specialty was the study of the ancient language, so it was not surprising that he should venerate Walter's contributions to that field.

However, von Bork was merely telling Emerson the latest news.

"I have, at Lady Baskerville's orders, a heavy steel door at the entrance to the tomb erected. In the Valley reside two guards under the authority of a sub-inspector of the Antiquities Department—"

"Useless!" Emerson exclaimed. "Many of the guards are related to the tomb robbers of Gurneh, or are so woefully superstitious that they will not leave their huts after dark. You ought to have guarded the tomb yourself, von Bork."

"*Sie haben recht*, Herr Professor," the young German

murmured submissively. "But difficult it was; only Milverton and myself remain, and he of a fever has been ill. He—"

"Mr. Milverton is the photographer?" I asked.

"Quite correct, Frau Professor. The expedition staff of the finest was; now that you and the Professor have come, only an artist is lacking. Mr. Armadale that task performed, and I do not—"

"But that is a serious lack," Emerson remarked. "Where are we to find an artist? If only Evelyn had not abandoned a promising career. She had a nice touch. She might have amounted to something."

Considering that Evelyn was one of the wealthiest women in England, the devoted mother of three lovely children and the adoring wife of a man who doted on her every movement, I could not see that she had lost a great deal. However, I knew there was no sense in pointing this out to Emerson. I therefore contented myself with remarking, "She has promised to come out with us again after the children are in school."

"Yes, but when will that be? She keeps on producing the creatures in endless succession and shows no sign of stopping. I am fond of my brother and his wife, but a continual progression of miniature Evelyns and Walters is a bit too much. The human race—"

When the human race entered the discussion I stopped listening. Emerson is capable of ranting on that subject for hours.

"If I may suggest," von Bork said hesitantly.

I looked at him in surprise. The tentative tone was quite unlike his usual confident voice, and although his countenance remained impassive, his sunburned cheeks had turned a trifle pink.

"Yes, certainly," said Emerson, as surprised as I.

Von Bork cleared his throat self-consciously. "There is a young lady—an English lady—in Luxor village who is an accomplished painter. In an emergency she might be persuaded..."

Emerson's face fell. I sympathized; I shared his opinion of young lady artists of the amateur persuasion.

"It is early days yet," I said tactfully. "When we have uncovered something worth copying, we can worry about a painter. But I thank you for the suggestion, Herr von Bork. I believe I will call you Karl. It is easier and more friendly. You do not object, I hope?"

By the time he had finished assuring me that he did not, we were docking on the west bank.

Thanks to Karl's efficiency and Emerson's curses, we soon found ourselves mounted on donkeyback and ready to proceed. Leaving Abdullah to arrange for the transport of the men and the baggage, we set out across the fields, now green with crops. The pace of a donkey is leisurely in the extreme, so we were able to converse as we rode along; and as we came near to the place where the fertile black soil left by the annual inundation gives way to the red desert sands, Emerson said abruptly, "We will go by way of Gurneh."

Karl was more relaxed now that he had performed his task of greeting and transporting us without mishap; I observed that when he was calm he was able to keep his verbs straight instead of relapsing into tortuous German sentence structure.

"It is not the direct path," he objected. "I had thought you and Mrs. Emerson would wish to rest and refresh yourselves after—"

"I have my reasons for suggesting it," Emerson replied.

"Aber natürlich! Whatever the Professor wishes."

Our donkeys crossed into the desert, a line so distinct that their front feet pressed the hot sands while their back feet were still on the cultivated land. The village of Gurneh is several hundred yards beyond the cultivation, in the rocky foothills of the mountains. The huts of sun-dried brick blend into the pale-brown rock of the hillside. One might wonder why the residents, who have lived in this place for hundreds of years, do not seek a more comfortable locale. They have solid economic reasons for remaining, for they make their livelihood on that spot. Between the huts and under their very floors lie the ancient tombs whose treasures form the inhabitants' source of income. In the hills behind the village, a convenient half-hour's walk away, are the narrow valleys where the kings and queens of the Empire were buried.

We heard the sounds of the village before we could make out its dwellings—the voices of children, the barking of dogs, and the bleating of goats. The cupola of the old village mosque could be seen on the desert slope, and a few palms and sycamores half concealed a row of antique columns. Emerson headed toward these, and before long I realized why he had chosen that route. A precious spring of water was there, with a broken sarcophagus serving as a cattle trough. The village well is always a scene of much activity, with women filling their jars and men watering their beasts. Silence descended upon the group as we approached, and all movement was suspended. The jars remained poised in the arms of the women; the men stopped smoking and gossiping as they stared at our little caravan.

Emerson called out a greeting in sonorous Arabic. He did not pause or wait for a reply. At as stately a pace as a small donkey could command he rode past, with Karl and me following. Not until we had left the well far behind did I hear the sounds of renewed activity.

As our patient beasts plodded across the sand, I allowed Emerson to remain a few feet ahead, a position he much enjoys and seldom obtains. I could see by the arrogant set of his shoulders that he fancied himself in the role of gallant commander, leading his troops; and I saw no reason to point out that no man can possibly look impressive on donkeyback, particularly when his legs are so long he must hold them out at a forty-five-degree angle to keep his feet from dragging on the ground. (Emerson is not unusually tall; the donkeys are unusually small.)

"For what was this?" Karl asked in a low voice, as we rode side by side. "I understand it not. To ask the Professor I do not dare; but you, his companion and—"

"I have not the least objection to explaining," I replied. "Emerson has flung down the gauntlet to that pack of thieves. In effect he has said: 'I am here. I do not fear you. You know who I am; interfere with me at your peril.' It was well done, Karl; one of Emerson's better performances, if I may say so."

Unlike Karl, I had not troubled to moderate my voice. Emerson's shoulders twitched irritably, but he did not turn around. After an interval we rounded a rocky spur and saw before us the curving bay that shelters the ruined temples of Deir el Bahri, near which the house was situated.

Most readers, I imagine, are familiar with the appearance of the now-famous Baskerville Expedition House, since photographs and engravings of it have been featured in numerous periodicals. I had never happened to see the place myself, since it was still under construction on the occasion of our last visit to Luxor, and though I had seen reproductions and plans, my first sight of the place impressed me considerably. Like most Eastern houses it was built around a courtyard, with rooms on all four sides. A wide gate in the center of one side admitted visitors to the courtyard, onto which the chambers opened. The material was the usual mud brick, neatly plastered and whitewashed, but the size was enormous, and it had suited Lord Baskerville's fancy to decorate it in ancient Egyptian style. The gate and the windows were capped by wooden lintels painted with Egyptian motifs in bright colors. Along one side a row of columns with gilded lotus capitals supported a pleasant shady loggia, where orange and lemon trees grew in earthenware pots and green vines twined around the columns. A nearby spring provided water for palm and fig trees; and in the brilliant sunlight the white walls and archaic decoration reminded us of what the ancient palaces must have looked like before time reduced them to heaps of mud.

My husband has no appreciation of architecture unless it is three thousand years old. "The devil!" he exclaimed. "What a frightful waste of money!"

We had slowed our animals to a walk, the better to appreciate our first view of our new home. My donkey misinterpreted this gesture. It came to a complete standstill. I refused Karl's offer of a stick—I do not believe in beating animals—and spoke sternly to the donkey. It gave me a startled look and then proceeded. I promised myself that as soon as I had time I would examine the animal and any others hired by Lord Baskerville. These poor beasts were wretchedly treated and often suffered from saddle sores and infections caused by inadequate cleanliness. I never permitted that sort of thing in my other expeditions and did not intend to allow it here.

The wooden gates swung open as we approached, and we rode directly into the courtyard. Pillars supported a cloister-like walkway, roofed with red tiles, which ran along three sides. All the rooms opened onto this open-sided corridor, and at my request Karl took us on a brief tour of inspection. I could not help but be impressed at the forethought that had gone into the arrangement of the house; if I had not known better, I would have thought a woman had planned it. A number of bedchambers, small but comfortable, had been designed for the use of the staff and for visitors. Larger chambers, as well as a small room which served as a bath, had been reserved for Lord and Lady Baskerville. Karl informed us that his lordship's room was now ours and I found the arrangements all I could wish. One section of the room had been fitted out as a study, with a long table and a row of bookshelves containing an Egyptological library.

Today such accommodations are not unique, and

archaeological staffs are often large; but at that time, when an expedition sometimes consisted of one harassed scholar directing the diggers, keeping his own records and accounts, cooking his own meals and washing his own stockings—if he bothered to wear them—Baskerville House was a phenomenon. One entire wing contained a large dining room and a sizable parlor or common room, which opened onto the columned loggia. The furnishings of this latter chamber were a curious blend of the ancient and modern. Woven mattings covered the floor, and filmy white curtains at the long French doors helped to keep out insects. Chairs and couches were of royal-blue plush; the picture frames and mirrors were heavily carved and gilded. There was even a Gramophone with a large collection of operatic recordings, the late Sir Henry having been a devotee of that form of music.

As we entered, a man rose from the sofa on which he had been reclining. His pallor, and the unsteadiness of his gait as he advanced to meet us, rendered Karl's introduction unnecessary; this was the ailing Mr. Milverton. I immediately led him back to the sofa and placed my hand on his brow.

"Your fever is gone," I said. "But you are still suffering from the debility produced by the illness and should not have left your bed."

"For heaven's sake, Amelia, restrain yourself," Emerson grumbled. "I had hoped that on this expedition you would not succumb to your delusion that you are a qualified physician."

I knew the cause of his ill temper. Mr. Milverton was an extremely handsome young fellow. The slow smile that spread across his face as he glanced from me to my husband showed even white teeth and well-cut lips. His golden locks fell in becoming disarray over a high white brow. Yet his good looks were entirely masculine and his constitution had not been seriously impaired by his illnesss; the breadth of his chest and shoulders were those of a young athlete.

"You are more than kind, Mrs. Emerson," he said. "I assure you, I am quite recovered and have been looking forward to meeting you and your famous husband."

"Humph," said Emerson, in a slightly more genial tone. "Very well; we will begin tomorrow morning—"

"Mr. Milverton should not risk the noonday sun for several days," I said.

"Again I remind you," said Emerson, "that you are not a physician."

"And I remind you of what happened to you on one occasion when you disregarded my medical advice."

A singularly evil look spread over Emerson's features. Deliberately he turned from me to Karl. "And where is Lady Baskerville?" he inquired. "A delightful woman!"

"She is," said Karl. "And I have for you, Professor, a particular message from that most distinguished lady. She stays at the Luxor Hotel; it would not be proper, you understand, for her to inhabit this place without another lady to companion her, now that her esteemed husband—"

"Yes, yes," Emerson said impatiently. "What is the message?"

"She wishes you—and Mrs. Emerson, of course—to dine with her this evening at the hotel."

"Splendid, splendid," Emerson exclaimed vivaciously. "How I look forward to the meeting!"

Needless to say, I was quite amused at Emerson's transparent attempt to annoy me by professing admiration for Lady Baskerville. I said calmly, "If we are dining at the hotel you had better unpack, Emerson; your evening clothes will be sadly wrinkled. You, Mr. Milverton, must go back to bed at once. I will visit you shortly to make sure you have everything you need. First I will inspect the kitchen and speak to the cook. Karl, you had better introduce me to the domestic staff. Have you had difficulty in keeping servants?"

Taking Karl firmly by the arm, I left the room before Emerson could think of a reply.

The kitchen was in a separate building behind the main house, a most sensible arrangement in a hot climate. As we approached, a variety of delicious aromas told me that luncheon was being prepared. Karl explained that most of the house servants were still at their jobs. Apparently they felt there was no danger in serving the foreigners so long as they did not actively participate in the desecration of the tomb.

I was pleased to recognize an old acquaintance in Ahmed the chef, who had once been employed at Shepheard's. He seemed equally happy to see me. After we had exchanged compliments and inquiries concerning the health of our families I took my leave, happy to find that in this area at least I would not have to exercise constant supervision.

I found Emerson in our room going through his books and papers. The suitcases containing his clothes had not been opened. The young servant whose task it was to unpack them squatted on the floor, talking animatedly with Emerson.

"Mohammed has been telling me the news," Emerson said cheerfully. "He is the son of Ahmed the chef—you remember—"

"Yes, I have just spoken to Ahmed. Luncheon will be ready shortly." As I spoke I extracted the keys from Emerson's pocket; he continued to sort his papers. I handed the keys to Mohammed, a slender stripling with the luminous eyes and delicate beauty these lads often exhibit; with my assistance he soon completed his task and departed. I observed with pleasure that he had filled the water jar and laid out towels.

"Alone at last," I said humorously, unbuttoning my dress. "How refreshing that water looks! I am sadly in need of a wash and change, after last night."

I hung my dress in the wardrobe and was about to turn when Emerson's arms came round my waist and pressed me close.

"Last night was certainly unsatisfactory," he murmured (or at least he thought he was murmuring; Emerson's best attempt at this sound is a growling roar, exceedingly painful to the ear). "What with the hardness of the bunks and their extreme narrowness, and the motion of the ship—"

"Now, Emerson, there is no time for that now," I said, attempting to free myself. "We have a great deal to do. Have you made arrangements for our men?"

"Yes, yes, it is all taken care of. Peabody, have I ever told you how much I admire the shape of your—"

"You have." I removed his hand from the area in question, though I confess it required some willpower for me to do so. "There is no time for that now. I would like to walk across to the Valley this afternoon and have a look at the tomb."

It is no insult to me to admit that the prospect of archaeological investigation is the one thing that can distract Emerson from what he was doing at that moment.

"Hmmm, yes," he said thoughtfully. "It will be hot as the hinges of Hades, you know."

"All the better; the Cook's people will have gone and we will enjoy a little peace and quiet. We must leave immediately after luncheon if we are to dine with Lady Baskerville this evening."

So it was agreed, and for the first time in many years we assumed our working attire. A thrill permeated my being to its very depths when I beheld my dear Emerson in the garments in which he had first won my heart. (I speak figuratively, of course; those original garments had long since been turned into rags.) His rolled-up sleeves bared his brawny arms, his open collar displayed his strong brown throat. With an effort I conquered my emotion and led the way to the dining room.

Karl was waiting for us. I was not surprised to find him prompt at his meals; his contours indicated that a poor appetite was not one of his difficulties. A look of faint surprise crossed his features when he saw me.

In my early days in Egypt I had been vexed by the convention that restricted women to long, inconveniently trailing skirts. These garments are wholly unsuited to climbing, running, and the active aspects of archaeological excavation. I had progressed from skirts to Rationals, from Rationals to a form of bloomer; in my last season I had taken the bull by the horns and ordered a costume that seemed to me to combine utility with womanly modesty. In a land where snakes and scorpions abound, stout boots are a necessity. Mine reached to the knees and there met my breeches, cut with considerable fullness, and tucked into the boot tops in order to avoid any possibility of accidental disarrangement. Over the breeches I wore a knee-length tunic, open at the sides to allow for the stretching of the lower limbs to their widest extent, in case rapid locomotion, of pursuit or of flight, became desirable. The costume was completed by a broad-brimmed hat and a stout belt equipped with hooks for knife, pistol, and other implements.

A similar costume became popular for hunting a year or two later, and although I never received any credit for my innovation, I do not doubt that it was my example that broke the ice.

When he heard of our plans for that afternoon, Karl offered to accompany us, but we declined, wishing to be alone on this first occasion. There is a carriage road, of sorts, leading through a cleft in the cliffs to the Valley where the royal dead of Egypt were entombed; but we took the more direct path, over the high plateau behind Deir el Bahri. Once we left the shady grove and the gardens the sun beat down upon us; but I could not repine, as I remembered the dreary winter weather and tedious routine we had left behind.

A brisk scramble up a rocky, steep incline brought us to the top of the plateau. There we paused for a moment to catch our breath and enjoy the view. Ahead lay a rough waste of barren stone; behind and below, the width of the Nile Valley lay spread out like a master painting. The temple of Queen Hatasu, cleared by

Maspero, looked like a child's model. Beyond the desert the fields bordered the river like an emerald-green ribbon. The air was so clear that we could make out the miniature shapes of the pylons and columns of the eastern temples. To the south rose the great pyramid-shaped peak known as the Goddess of the West, she who guards the ancient sepulchers.

Emerson began to hum. He has a perfectly appalling singing voice and no idea whatever of pitch, but I made no objection, even when words emerged from his drone.

> ...from Coffee and from
> supper rooms, from Poplar to Pall Mall,
> The girls on seeing me exclaim, "O what a
> champagne swell!"

I joined in.

> Champagne Charlie is my name, good for any game
> at night, boys, who'll come and join me in a spree?

Emerson's hand reached for mine. In perfect harmony of soul (if not voice) we proceeded; and I did not feel that our melodies profaned that solemn spot since they arose from joyful anticipation of a noble work.

At the end of our stroll we found ourselves on the edge of a cliff looking down into a canyon. Rocky walls and barren floor were of the same unrelieved drab brown, bleached by the sunlight to the color of a pale and unpalatable pudding. A few small patches of shadow, abbreviated by the height of the sun, were the only breaks in the monotony—except for the rectangular black openings that had given the Valley of the Kings its name. They were the doorways of royal tombs.

I was gratified to observe that my hope of relative privacy had been correct. The tourists had departed to their hotels, and the only living objects to be seen were shapeless bundles of rags that covered the sleeping forms of the Egyptian guides and guards whose work lay in the Valley. But no!—with chagrin I revised my first impression when I beheld a moving figure. It was too far away for me to see more than its general outline, which was that of a tall male person in European clothing. It appeared to be engaged in rapt contemplation of the surrounding cliffs.

Though we had never visited the tomb which was the object of our present quest, I have no doubt that Emerson could have drawn an accurate map of its precise location. I know I could have. Our eyes were drawn to it as if by a magnet.

It lay below, on the opposite side of the Valley from where we stood. The steep, almost vertical configuration of the cliffs framed it like a theatrical backdrop. At the foot of the cliff was a long slope of rock and gravel, broken by heaps of rubble from earlier excavations, and by a few modern huts and storage buildings. A triangular cut into the gravel framed the doorway of the tomb of Ramses VI. Below this, and to the left, I saw the stout iron gate to which Karl had referred. Two dusty bundles—the alert guards Grebaut had appointed to guard the tomb—lay near the gate.

Emerson's hand tightened on mine. "Only think," he said softly, "what wonders that bare rock still hides!

The tombs of Thutmose the Great, of Amenhotep the Second and Queen Hatasu....Even another cache of royal mummies like the one found in 1881. Which of them awaits our labor?"

I shared his sentiments, but his fingers were crushing my hand. I pointed this out. With a deep sigh Emerson returned to practicality. Together we scrambled down the path to the floor of the Valley.

The sleeping guards did not stir even when we stood over them. Emerson prodded one bundle with his toe. It quivered; a malevolent black eye appeared among the rags, and from a concealed mouth a spate of vulgar Arabic curses assailed us. Emerson replied in kind. The bundle sprang to its feet and the rags parted to reveal one of the evilest faces I have ever beheld, seamed by lines and scars. One eye was a milkywhite, sightless blank. The other eye glared widely at Emerson.

"Ah," said my husband, in Arabic, "it is thou, Habib. I thought the police had locked thee up forever. What madman gave to thee a task proper to an honest man?"

They say the eyes are the mirror of the soul. In this case Habib's one serviceable orb displayed, for a moment, the intensity of his real feelings. Only for a moment; then he groveled in a deep obeisance, mumbling greetings, apologies, explanations—and assurances that he had given over his evil ways and merited the trust of the Antiquities Department.

"Humph," said Emerson, unimpressed. "Allah knows thy true heart, Habib; I have not his all-seeing eye, but I have my doubts. I am going into the tomb. Get out of the way."

The other guard had roused himself by this time

and was also bowing and babbling. His countenance was not quite as villainous as Habib's, probably because he was somewhat younger.

"Alas, great lord, I have no key," said Habib.

"But I have," said Emerson, producing it.

The gate had been cemented into place across the doorway. The bars were stout, the padlock massive; yet I knew they would prove no lasting impediment to men who have been known to tunnel through solid rock in order to rob the dead. When the grille swung open we were confronted with the sealed doorway that had frustrated Lord Baskerville on the last day of his life. Nothing had been touched since that hour. The small hole opened by Armadale still gaped, the only break in the wall of stones.

Lighting a candle, Emerson held it to the opening and we both looked in, bumping heads in our eagerness. I had known what to expect, and yet it was dampening to the spirits to behold a heap of rocky rubble that completely concealed whatever lay beyond.

"So far, so good," Emerson remarked. "No one has attempted to enter since Baskerville's death. Frankly, I expected that our friends from Gurneh would have tried to break in long before this."

"The fact that they have not makes me suspect that we have a long job ahead of us," I said. "Perhaps they are waiting for us to clear the passageway so they can get at the burial chamber without having to engage in boring manual labor."

"You may be right. Though I hope you are wrong about the extent of clearance necessary; as a rule the rubble fill does not extend beyond the stairwell."

"Belzoni mentions climbing over heaps of rubble when he entered Seti's tomb, in 1844," I reminded him.

"The cases are hardly parallel. That tomb had been robbed and re-used for later burials. The debris Belzoni described..."

We were engaged in a delightfully animated archaeological discussion when there was an interruption. "Hello, down there," called a loud, cheery voice. "May I join you, or will you come up?"

Turning, I beheld a form silhouetted against the bright rectangle of the opening at the head of the stairs. It was that of the tall personage I had noticed earlier, but I could not see it clearly until we had ascended the stairs—for Emerson promptly replied that we would come up. He was not anxious to have any stranger approach his new toy.

The form revealed itself to be that of a very tall, very thin gentleman with a lean, humorous face and hair of that indeterminate shade which may be either fair or gray. His accent had already betrayed his nationality, and as soon as we emerged from the stairway he continued in the exuberant strain typical of the natives of our erstwhile colony. (I flatter myself that I reproduce the peculiarities of the American dialect quite accurately.)

"Well, now, I declare, this is a real sure-enough pleasure. I don't need to ask who you are, do I? Let me introduce myself—Cyrus Vandergelt, New York, U.S.A.—at your service, ma'am, and yours, Professor Emerson."

I recognized the name, as anyone familiar with Egyptology must have done. Mr. Vandergelt was the American equivalent of Lord Baskerville—enthusiastic amateur, wealthy patron of archaeology.

"I knew you were in Luxor," Emerson remarked unenthusiastically, taking the hand Mr. Vandergelt had thrust at him. "But I did not expect to meet you so soon."

"You probably wonder what I am doing here at this goldurned hour," Vandergelt replied with a chuckle. "Well, folks, I am just like you—we are birds of a feather. It would take more than a little heat to keep me from what I mean to do."

"And what is that?" I inquired.

"Why, to meet you, sure enough. I figured you would get out here just the minute you arrived. And, ma'am, if you will permit me to say so, the sight of you would make any effort worthwhile. I am—I make no bones about it, ma'am, indeed I say it with pride—I am a most assiduous admirer of the ladies and a connoisseur, in the most respectable sense, of female loveliness."

It was impossible to take offense at his words, they displayed such irrepressible trans-Atlantic good humor and such excellent taste. I allowed my lips to relax into a smile.

"Bah," said Emerson. "I know you by reputation, Vandergelt, and I know why you are here. You want to steal my tomb."

Mr. Vandergelt grinned broadly. "I sure would if I could. Not just the tomb, but you and Mrs. Emerson to dig it out for me. But"—and here he became quite serious—"Lady Baskerville has set her heart on doing this as a memorial to the dear departed, and I am not the man to stand in a lady's way, particularly when her aim is so fraught with touching sentiment. No, sir;

Cyrus Vandergelt is not the man to try low tricks. I only want to help. Call on me for any assistance you may require."

As he spoke, he straightened to his full height—which was well over six feet—and raised his hand as if taking an oath. It was an impressive sight; one almost expected to see the Stars and Bars waving in the breeze and hearing the stirring strains of "Oh Beautiful America."

"You mean," Emerson retorted, "that you want to get in on the fun."

"Ha, ha," said Vandergelt cheerfully. He gave Emerson a slap on the back. "I said we were alike, didn't I? There's no fooling a sharp lad like you. Sure I do. If you don't let me play, I'll drive you crazy thinking of excuses to drop in. No, but seriously, folks, you're going to need all the help you can get. Those Gurneh crooks are going to be on you like a hornets' nest, and the local imam is stirring up the congregation in a fancy way. If I can't do anything else, I can at least help guard the tomb, and the ladies. But look, why are we standing here jawing in the hot sun? I've got my carriage down at the other end of the Valley; let me give you a lift home and we can talk some more."

We declined this offer, and Mr. Vandergelt took his leave, remarking, "You haven't seen the last of me, folks. You're dining with Lady Baskerville tonight? Me, too. I'll see you then."

I fully expected a diatribe from Emerson on Mr. Vandergelt's manners and motives, but he was uncharacteristically silent on the subject. After a further examination of what little could be seen we prepared to go; and then I realized Habib was no longer with us. The other guard burst into a garbled explanation, which Emerson cut short.

"I was about to dismiss him anyway," he remarked, addressing me but speaking in Arabic for the benefit of anyone who might be listening. "Good riddance."

The shadows were lengthening when we started the climb up the cliff, and I urged Emerson, who was preceding me, to greater haste. I wanted ample time to prepare for the evening's encounter. We had almost reached the top when a sound made me glance up. I then seized Emerson by the ankles and pulled him down. The boulder which I had seen teetering on the brink missed him by less than a foot, sending splinters of rock flying in every direction when it struck.

Slowly Emerson rose to his feet. "I do wish, Peabody, that you could be a little less abrupt in your methods," he remarked, using his sleeve to wipe away the blood that was dripping from his nose. "A calm 'Watch out, there,' or a tug at my shirttail would have proved just as effective, and less painful."

This was a ridiculous statement, of course; but I was given no time to reply to it, for as soon as Emerson had ascertained, with one quick glance, that I was unharmed, he turned and began to climb with considerable speed, vanishing at last over the rim of the cliff. I followed. When I reached the top he was nowhere in sight, so I sat down on a rock to wait for him, and—to be candid—to compose my nerves, which were somewhat shaken.

The tentative theory I had briefly considered in Cairo was now strengthened. Someone was determined to prevent Emerson from continuing the work Lord

Baskerville had begun. Whether the latter's death had formed part of this plan, or whether the unknown miscreant had made use of a tragic accident in order to further his scheme I could not then make out, but I felt sure we had not seen the last of attempts aimed at my husband. How glad I was that I had yielded to what had seemed a selfish impulse and come with him. The apparent conflict between my duty to my husband and my duty to my child had been no conflict. Ramses was safe and happy; Emerson was in deadly danger, and my place was at his side, guarding him from peril.

As I mused I saw Emerson reappear from behind a heap of boulders some distance from the path. His face was smeared with blood, and his eyes bulged with rage, so that he presented quite a formidable sight.

"He got away, did he?" I said.

"Not a trace. I would not have left you," he added apologetically, "but that I felt sure the rascal had taken to his heels the moment the rock fell."

"Nonsense. The attempt was aimed at you, not at me—although the perpetrator does not seem to care whom he endangers. The knife—"

"I don't believe the two incidents can be related, Amelia. The hands that pushed this rock were surely the filthy hands of Habib."

This suggestion made a certain amount of sense. "But why does he hate you so much?" I asked. "I could see you were on bad terms, but attempted murder...."

"I was responsible for his being apprehended on the criminal charge I spoke of." Emerson accepted the handkerchief I gave him and attempted to clean his face while we walked on.

"What was his crime? Stealing antiquities?"

"That, of course. Most of the Gurneh men are involved in the antiquities game. But the case that brought him to justice, through me, was of a different and very distressing nature. Habib once had a daughter. Her name was Aziza. When she was a small child she worked for me as a basket girl. As she matured she turned into an unusually pretty young woman, slight and graceful as a gazelle, with big dark eyes that would melt any man's heart."

The tale Emerson proceeded to unfold would indeed have melted the hardest heart—even that of a man. The girl's beauty made her a valuable property, and her father hoped to sell her to a wealthy landowner. Alas, her beauty attracted other admirers, and her innocence rendered her vulnerable to their wiles. When her shame became known the rich and repulsive buyer rejected her, and her father, enraged at losing his money, determined to destroy a now-valueless object. Such things are done more often than the British authorities like to admit; in the name of "family honor" many a poor woman has met a ghastly fate at the hands of those who should have been her protectors. But in this case the girl managed to escape before the murderer had completed his vile act. Beaten and bleeding, she staggered to the tent of Emerson, who had been kind to her.

"Both her arms were broken," said Emerson, in a soft, cold voice quite unlike his usual tones. "She had tried to shield her head from the blows of her father's club. How she eluded him, or walked so far in her condition, I cannot imagine. She collapsed at my feet. I made her as comfortable as I could and ran to get help.

In the few moments I was gone, Habib, who must have been close behind her, entered my tent and crushed her skull with a single blow.

"I returned in time to see him running away. One glance told me I could do no more for poor Aziza, so I went in pursuit. I gave him a good beating before I turned him over to the police. He got off much more lightly than he deserved, for of course the native courts found his motive entirely reasonable. If I had not threatened the sheikh with various unpleasant things he would probably have set Habib free."

I pressed his arm sympathetically. I understood why he had not mentioned the story; even now the memory affected him deeply. The softer side of Emerson's character is not known to many people, but those who are in trouble instinctively sense his real nature and seek him out, as the unhappy girl had done.

After a moment of thoughtful silence he shook himself and said, in his usual careless tone, "So take care with Mr. Vandergelt, Amelia. He was not exaggerating when he called himself an admirer of the fair sex, and if I learn that you have yielded to his advances I will beat you."

"I will take care that you don't catch me, never fear. But, Emerson, we are going to have a hard time solving this case if we hope to do it by using you as bait. There are too many people in Egypt who would like to kill you."

CHAPTER
FIVE

A magnificent sunset turned the reflecting water to a shimmering scarf of crimson and gold as we set sail for the east bank and our appointment with Lady Baskerville. Emerson was sulking because I had insisted we take a carriage from the house to the quay. No man but Emerson would have considered walking across the fields in full evening kit, much less expect me to trail my red satin skirts and lace ruffles through the dirt; but Emerson is unique. When he behaves irrationally it is necessary to be firm with him.

He cheered up, however, when we embarked, and indeed few people could fail to be moved to enjoyment at such sensations. The cool evening breeze bathed our faces, the felucca slid smoothly across the water, and before us unrolled the glorious panorama of Luxor— the vivid green of palms and gardens, the statues and pillars and pylons of the Theban temples. A carriage was waiting for us and it bore us swiftly through the streets to the Luxor Hotel, where Lady Baskerville was staying.

As we entered the lobby the lady came gliding to

meet us, her hands outstretched. Although she wore black I did not consider the gown suitable for a recently bereaved widow. The abominable bustle, which had so vexed me in the past, was on its way out. Lady Baskerville's gown was of the latest style, with only a small drapery behind. The layers of black net forming the skirts were so full and the puffs of fabric at her shoulders so exaggerated that her waist looked ridiculously small. She was tightly corseted, and the extent of shoulder and throat exposed was, in my opinion, almost indecent. The waxy white flowers crowning her upswept hair were also inappropriate.

(I do not apologize for this digression into fashion. Not only is it intrinsically interesting, but it shows something of the woman's character.)

Lady Baskerville gave me her fingertips and clasped Emerson's hand warmly. She then turned to introduce us to her companion.

"We met earlier," said Cyrus Vandergelt, beaming down at us. "It sure is nice to see you folks again. Mrs. Emerson, may I say your dress is right pretty. That red color suits you."

"Let us go in to dinner," Lady Baskerville said, with a slight frown.

"I thought Miss Mary and her friend were joining us," Vandergelt said.

"Mary said she would come if she were able. But you know her mother."

"I sure enough do!" Vandergelt rolled his eyes heavenward. "Have you met Madame Berengeria, Mrs. Emerson?"

I indicated that I had not had the pleasure. Vandergelt went on, "She claims she came here to study ancient Egyptian religion, but I opine it's because living is cheap. I don't like to speak ill of any member of the fair sex, but Madame Berengeria is an awful woman."

"Now, Cyrus, you must not be unkind," said Lady Baskerville, who had listened with a faint pleased smile. She enjoyed hearing other women criticized as much as she disliked hearing them complimented. "The poor thing cannot help it," she went on, turning to Emerson. "I believe her mind is deficient. We are all very fond of Mary, so we tolerate her mother; but the poor child is kept dancing attendance on the old...on the unfortunate creature, and can seldom get away."

Emerson shifted restlessly from one foot to the other and inserted a finger under his collar, as he does when he is uncomfortable or bored. Reading these signs correctly—as any married woman would—Lady Baskerville was turning toward the dining salon when Mr. Vandergelt let out a muffled exclamation.

"Holy shucks!" (At least I believe that was the phrase.) "How the dickens—look who's here. You didn't invite her, did you?"

"Certainly not." Lady Baskerville's voice had a distinct rasp as her eyes lit on the person who had prompted Vandergelt's remark. "That would not prevent her from coming, though. The woman has the manners of a peasant."

Coming toward us was a singular pair. One was a young lady dressed modestly in a somewhat out-of-date evening frock of pale-yellow voile. Ordinarily she would have captured anyone's attention, for she was the possessor of an unusually exotic style of beauty; her olive skin and dark, long-lashed eyes, her delicate features and slender frame were so like those of the aristocratic Egyptian ladies depicted in the tomb paintings that her modern dress looked out of place, like a riding habit on an antique statue of Diana. One expected to see diaphanous linen robes, collars of turquoise and carnelian, anklets and bracelets of gold adorning her limbs.

All these, and more, bedecked the woman who was with her, and whose extraordinary appearance drew the eye from the girl's pretty face. She was an extremely large woman, standing several inches taller than her daughter and being correspondingly broad. The linen robe she wore was no longer pure white, but a dingy gray. The beaded collar that attempted in vain to cover her ample bosom was a cheap imitation of the jewels worn by pharaohs and their ladies. On her very large feet were skimpy sandals; around the imprecise region of her waist a brightly embroidered sash had been knotted. Her hair was a huge black beehive surmounted by a bizarre headdress consisting of feathers, flowers, and cheap copper ornaments.

I pinched Emerson. "If you say just one of the words that are in your mind..." I hissed, leaving the threat unspecified.

"I'll keep quiet if you will," Emerson replied. His shoulders were shaking and his voice quivered.

"And try not to laugh," I added.

A stifled whoop was the only answer.

Madame Berengeria swept toward us, towing her daughter along in her wake. A closer examination confirmed what I had suspected—that the unnaturally black hair was a wig, like those worn by the ancients. The contrast between this dreadful object, which appeared to be constructed of horsehair, and Miss Mary's soft, shining locks would have been amusing if it had not been so horrid.

"I came," Madame Berengeria announced dramatically. "The messages were favorable. I was given the strength to endure a meeting devoid of spiritual comfort."

"How nice," said Lady Baskerville, baring her long white teeth as if she thirsted to sink them in the other woman's throat. "Mary, my child, I am delighted to see you. Let me present you to Professor and Mrs. Emerson."

The girl acknowledged the introduction with a shy smile. She had very pretty, old-fashioned manners—which she had certainly not learned from her mother. Emerson, his amusement forgotten, studied the girl with a blend of pity and admiration, and I wondered if her lovely face, so Egyptian in character, had reminded him of the murdered Aziza.

Without waiting to be introduced, Madame thrust herself forward, catching Emerson's hand and holding it, with odious familiarity, in both of hers. Her fingers were stained with henna and quite dirty.

"We need no formal presentation, Professor," she boomed, in a voice so loud that the few heads that had not turned to mark her entrance now swiveled in our direction. "Or may I call you...Set-nakhte?"

"I don't see why the devil you should," Emerson replied in astonishment.

"You don't remember." They were almost of a height, and she had come so close to him that when she let out a gusty sigh Emerson's hair waved wildly. "It is not given to all of us to remember former lives," she went on. "But I had hoped...I was Ta-weseret, the Queen, and you were my lover."

"Good Gad," Emerson exclaimed. He tried to free his hand, but the lady hung on. Her grip must have been as strong as a man's, for Emerson's fingers turned white as hers tightened.

"Together we ruled in ancient Waset," Madame Berengeria continued raptly. "That was after we had murdered my wretched husband, Ramses."

Emerson was distracted by this inaccuracy. "But," he protested, "Ramses was not the husband of Ta-weseret, and it is not at all certain that Set-nakhte—"

"Murdered!" Madame Berengeria shouted, causing Emerson to flinch back. "Murdered! We suffered for that sin in other lives, but the grandeur of our passion...Ah, Set-nakhte, how could you forget?"

Emerson's expression, as he contemplated the self-proclaimed partner of his passion, was one I will long remember with enjoyment. However, the woman was beginning to wear on me, and when my husband cast a look of piteous appeal in my direction, I decided to intervene.

I always carry a parasol. I find it invaluable in many different ways. My working parasol is of stout black bombazine with a steel shaft. Naturally the one I carried that evening matched my frock and was eminently suitable for formal occasions. I brought it down smartly on Madame Berengeria's wrist. She yelped and let go of Emerson.

"Dear me, how careless of me," I said.

For the first time the lady looked directly at me.

Black kohl, lavishly smeared around her eyes, made her look as if she had suffered a severe beating. The orbs themselves were unusual. The irises were of an indeterminate shade between blue and gray, and so pale that they blended with the muddy white of the eye. The pupils were dilated to an unusual degree. Altogether it was a most unpleasant set of optics, and the concentrated and venomous intelligence with which they regarded me assured me of two things: one, that I had made an enemy; two, that Madame's eccentricities were not entirely without calculation.

Lady Baskerville seized Mr. Vandergelt's arm; I took possession of my poor gaping Emerson; and leaving Madame and her unfortunate daughter to bring up the rear, we proceeded to the dining salon. A table had been prepared for us, and it was there that the next difficulty arose, caused, as one might have expected, by Madame Berengeria.

"There are only six places," she exclaimed, settling herself at once into the nearest chair. "Did not Mary tell you, Lady Baskerville, that my young admirer will also be dining?"

The effrontery of this was so enormous as to leave the hearers with nothing to say. Shaking with fury, Lady Baskerville summoned the maitre d'hôtel and requested that an additional place be set. In defiance of custom I placed Emerson firmly between myself and our hostess, which left Mr. Vandergelt to partner Madame Berengeria. Her appearance had thrown the arrangements out in every conceivable way, for there was now an uneven number of ladies and gentlemen. The empty chair awaiting Madame Berengeria's "admirer" chanced to be between me and Miss Mary. So preoccupied was I with other matters that it did not occur to me to wonder who this person might be. I was taken completely by surprise when a familiar freckled face surmounted by an equally well-known shock of flaming red hair made its appearance.

"Heartfelt apologies for my tardiness, Lady Baskerville," said Mr. O'Connell, bowing. "'Twas unavoidable, I assure you. What a pleasure to see so many friends! Is this my place? Sure an' I couldn't want a better one."

As he spoke he inserted himself neatly into the vacant chair and bestowed an inclusive hearty smile upon the party.

Seeing, by the intensifying livid hue of his countenance, that Emerson was on the verge of an explosive comment, I trod heavily upon his foot.

"I did not expect to meet you here, Mr. O'Connell," I said. "I trust you have recovered from your unfortunate accident."

"Accident?" Mary exclaimed, her soft dark eyes widening. "Mr. O'Connell, you did not tell me—"

"It was nothing," O'Connell assured her. "I clumsily lost my footing and fell down a few stairs." He looked at me, his eyes narrowed with amusement. "'Tis kind you are, Mrs. Emerson, to be remembering such a trivial incident."

"I am relieved to hear that you considered it trivial," I said, maintaining my pressure on Emerson's foot, which twitched and writhed under the sole of my shoe.

Mr. O'Connell's eyes were as innocent as limpid

pools of water. "To be sure I did. I only hope my editors feel the same."

"I see," I said.

Waiters bustled up carrying bowls of clear soup, and the meal began. Conversation also began, each person turning to his dinner partner. Thanks to Madame, this comfortable social custom was confused by the presence of an extra person, and I found myself with no one to talk to. I did not object; sipping my soup, I was able to eavesdrop on the other conversations in turn, to my edification and entertainment.

The two young people seemed on friendly terms. Indeed, I suspected Mr. O'Connell's feelings were somewhat warmer; his eyes never left the girl's face and his voice took on the soft, caressing tones that are typical of the Irish. Though Mary evidently enjoyed his admiration, I was not sure that her affections were seriously engaged. I also observed that though Madame Berengeria was regaling Mr. Vandergelt with a description of her romance with Set-nakhte, she kept a close eye on the young people. Before long she turned abruptly and interrupted O'Connell in the middle of a compliment. This freed Vandergelt; catching my eye, he pantomimed a sigh of relief and joined in the discussion between Emerson and Lady Baskerville.

Thanks to Emerson, this had taken a strictly archaeological turn, despite Lady Baskerville's sighs and fluttering lashes and repeated thanks for his gallantry in coming to the rescue of a poor lonely widow. Happily impervious to these hints, Emerson continued to explain his plans for excavating the tomb.

Do not believe for an instant, reader, that I had lost sight of what had now become my main object. To discover the murderer of Lord Baskerville was no longer a matter of purely intellectual interest. Mr. O'Connell might have been responsible for the injury to Emerson in Cairo (though I doubted this); the villainous Habib might have been the motive power behind the boulder that had so narrowly missed him that very day. *Might*, I say; for I felt sure that two attempts in such a short space of time had a deeper and more sinister significance. The person who had murdered Baskerville now had designs on the life of my husband, and the sooner I discovered his identity, the sooner Emerson would be safe.

I use the masculine pronoun for reasons of grammatical simplicity, but I could not dismiss the possibility that a woman's hand had wielded the death weapon (whatever that might have been). Indeed, as I looked around the table I felt I had never beheld such a suspicious-looking group of persons.

That Lady Baskerville was capable of murder I did not doubt. Why she should want to kill her husband I did not know at that time, but I felt sure that a brief investigation would provide a motive and also explain how she had managed the two attacks on Emerson.

As for Mr. Vandergelt, amiable as he appeared to be, I had to consider him a suspect. We all know how ruthlessly these American millionaires crush their rivals as they climb to power. Vandergelt had lusted after Lord Baskerville's tomb. Some might consider that an inadequate motive for murder, but I knew the archaeological temperament too well to dismiss it.

As if she felt my speculative glance move to her,

Madame Berengeria looked up from the roast mutton she was stuffing into her mouth. Once again her pallid eyes glowed with hate. No need to ask myself if she was capable of committing murder! She was certainly mad, and the actions of a madwoman are unaccountable. She might have hailed Lord Baskerville as a long-lost lover and killed him when he rejected her, as any normal man must.

Madame Berengeria continued to wolf her food and I turned my attention to her daughter, who was listening in silence to Mr. O'Connell's low-voiced remarks. She was smiling, but it was a sad smile; the bright lights of the salon showed the shabbiness of her frock and the weary lines in her young face. I immediately removed her from my list of suspects. The fact that she had not yet exterminated her mother proved that she was incapable of violence.

Mr. O'Connell? Without a doubt he must be on my list. He was on good terms with all three of the ladies, which indicated a sly and hypocritical turn of character. To win Mary's regard would not be difficult; the child would respond to any show of kindness or affection. In order to facilitate his acquaintance with the girl, O'Connell had ingratiated himself with her mother, by sheer duplicity and falsehood (for no one could honestly admire, or even tolerate, the woman). The same slippery slyness probably accounted for his acceptance by Lady Baskerville. He had written about her in the most disgustingly sentimental terms, and she was vain enough to be deceived by empty flattery. In short, his was not a character to be trusted.

Of course those present did not exhaust all the possible suspects. The missing Armadale was high on my list, and Karl von Bork and Milverton might have motives as yet unknown to me. I did not doubt that as soon as I applied myself seriously to the problem, the answer would be easily discovered; and, to be truthful, the prospect of a little detective work was not at all displeasing.

In such entertaining speculations the meal passed, and we prepared to retire to the lounge. Madame Berengeria had eaten everything she could get her hands on, and her round face shone greasily. So must ancient Egyptian diners have looked, at the end of a formal party, when the cone of scented fat atop their wigs had melted and run down their faces. She had also drunk vast quantities of wine. When we rose from the table she caught her daughter's arm and leaned heavily against her. Mary's knees buckled under the weight. Mr. O'Connell promptly came to her rescue, or rather, he tried to, for when he took Madame's other arm she pulled away from him.

"Mary will help me," she muttered. "Dear daughter— help Mother—good daughter never leaves Mother...."

Mary turned pale. Supporting Madame, she said in a low voice, "Perhaps you would call a carriage, Mr. O'Connell. We had better not stay. Mother, you are unwell."

"Never felt better," Madame Berengeria declared. "Have a little coffee. Must talk to old lover—Amenhotep— I called him the Magnificent—he was, too—you remember your darling queenie, don't you, Amen?"

Releasing her daughter's arm, she lunged at Emerson.

But this time she had underestimated my husband. On the first occasion he had been caught off guard; now he acted, and Emerson is seldom, if ever, restrained from action by any remote notion of what is socially acceptable. Catching the lady in a paralyzing grip, he frogmarched her toward the door, calling out, "A carriage here! Madame Berengeria's carriage, if you please!"

The hotel porter leaped to assist him. Mary started after them. O'Connell caught her hand.

"Can you not stay? I haven't had a chance to talk to you—"

"You know I cannot. Good night, everyone. Lady Baskerville, my thanks—and apologies—"

Slim and graceful in her shabby frock, her head bowed, she followed the porters who were dragging her mother out the door.

Mr. O'Connell's countenance plainly displayed his chagrin and his affectionate concern. I began to warm to the young man; but then he gave himself a sort of shake and remarked, "Well, Mrs. Emerson, have you changed your mind about that interview? Your thoughts on arriving in Luxor would interest my readers enormously."

The transformation of his face was extraordinary. His eyes sparkled with malice, his mouth curved in a tight-lipped half-moon grin. This expression, which I thought of as his journalist's face, reminded me of the leprechauns and mischievous elves which are said to abound in the Emerald Isle.

Not wishing to dignify the suggestion with a reply, I ignored it. Fortunately Emerson had not heard the question. Leaning on the back of Lady Baskerville's chair, he was explaining his plans for the next day. "And," he added, glancing at me, "since we must be out at the first light, we had better be getting back, eh, Amelia?"

I promptly rose. To my surprise, so did Lady Baskerville.

"I am packed and ready. If you will summon the porter, Radcliffe?" Seeing my expression, she smiled sweetly at me. "Had I not explained that I mean to go with you, Mrs. Emerson? Now that you are here, I need not fear scandal if I resume my old place, hallowed by so many fond memories."

I need not say that my response was perfectly calm and courteous.

II

I had feared the presence of Lady Baskerville in the adjoining room might inhibit Emerson to some extent. It did, in the beginning. Casting an irritated glance at the closed portal, which I had promptly bolted, he muttered, "Curse it, Amelia, this is going to be a nuisance; I shan't be able to say a thing for fear of being overheard." However, as time went on he became so involved in what he was doing that all reserve fled and all external distractions were forgotten. My own contributions toward achieving this end were not inconsiderable.

Lying at peace in my husband's arms, I drifted off to sleep. But we were not destined for a quiet rest that night. Scarcely, it seemed, had my eyelids closed when I was reft of slumber by an outrageous howl, so penetrating that it seemed to come from within our very chamber.

I pride myself on being able to arise from meditation

or sleep fully alert and ready for whatever action seems required. Rising up, I prepared to bound out of bed. Unfortunately I had not completely readjusted to the sleeping arrangements necessary in that clime; and, as I had done on another memorable occasion, I plunged headlong into the mosquito netting draped around the bed. My efforts to free myself only wound the fabric more tightly around me. The howling continued. It had now been joined by cries of alarm from elsewhere in the house.

"Help me, Emerson," I cried irritably. "I am entangled in the netting. Why do you not arise?"

"Because," said a faint voice from the bed, "you stepped onto my stomach when you stood up. I have just now recovered my breath."

"Then employ it, if you please, in action rather than words. Unloose me."

Emerson obeyed. It is not necessary to reproduce the comments he made while doing so. Once he had freed me he ran to the door. As his form crossed the band of moonlight from the open window I let out a shriek.

"Emerson, your trousers—your dressing gown— something—"

With a violent oath Emerson snatched up the first garment that came to hand. It proved to be the one I had discarded upon retiring, a nightgown of thin white linen trimmed with wide bands of lace. Tossing this at me, with an even more violent oath, he began searching for his clothes. By the time we reached the courtyard the shrieks had stopped, but the excitement had not subsided. All the members of the expedition were gathered around a servant who sat on the ground with his arms over his head, rocking back and forth and moaning. I recognized Hassan, one of Lord Baskerville's men, who was employed as a night watchman.

"What has happened?" I demanded of the person nearest me. This happened to be Karl, who was standing with his arms folded and every hair in his mustache neatly in place. He was fully dressed. Bowing, in his formal German fashion, he replied calmly, "The foolish person claims he saw a ghost. You know how superstitious these people are; and at the present time—"

"How ridiculous," I said, in considerable disappointment. I had hoped the disturbance might have been caused by the murderer of Lord Baskerville, returning to the scene of the crime.

Emerson seized Hassan by the neck and hoisted him up off the ground. "Enough!" he shouted. "Art thou a man, or a dribbling infant? Speak; tell me what sight brought our valiant watchman to this pass."

Emerson's methods, though unconventional, are usually effective. Hassan's sobs died away. He began kicking his feet, and Emerson lowered him till his dusty bare soles rested on the beaten earth of the courtyard.

"Oh, Father of Curses," he gulped. "Wilt thou protect thy servant?"

"Certainly, certainly. Speak."

"It was an efreet, an evil spirit," Hassan whispered, rolling his eyes. "The spirit of the one with the face of a woman and the heart of a man."

"Armadale!" Mr. Milverton exclaimed.

He and Lady Baskerville were standing side by side. Her delicate white hands clutched his sleeve, but it would be hard to say which of them was supporting the other, for he was as pale as she.

Hassan nodded vigorously, or at least he tried to do so; Emerson was still holding him by the throat.

"The hand of the Father of Curses renders speech difficult," he complained.

"Oh, sorry," Emerson said, releasing him.

Hassan rubbed his bony neck. He had recovered from his initial fright, and there was a crafty gleam in his eyes that made me suspect he was beginning to enjoy being the center of attention.

"I saw it clearly in the moonlight, as I made my rounds," he said. "The very form and image of the one with the face—"

"Yes, yes," Emerson interrupted. "What was he doing?"

"Creeping through the shadows like a serpent or a scorpion or an evil djinn! He wore the long linen robe of a corpse, and his face was thin and drawn, with staring eyes and—"

"Stop that!" Emerson roared. Hassan subsided, with another roll of his eyes, as if he were judging the effect of the ghost story on his audience.

"The superstitious fellow was dreaming," Emerson said, addressing Lady Baskerville. "Return to bed. I will see to it that he—"

Like many of the men, Hassan understood English much better than he spoke it. "No!" he exclaimed. "It was no dream, I swear; I heard the jackals howling in the hills, I saw the grass blades bend under his feet. He went to one of the windows, oh, Father of Curses—one of the windows there."

He gestured toward the side of the house in which all our rooms were located.

Karl let out a grunt. Lady Baskerville's face turned muddy gray. But Milverton's reaction was the most dramatic. With a queer soft sigh he folded at the knees and fell to the ground in a dead faint.

III

"It means nothing," I said, some time later, as Emerson and I again prepared to retire. "I told you the young man was not fully recovered; the shock and excitement were too much for him."

Emerson was standing on a chair trying to get the mosquito netting back in place. He had irritably refused my suggestion that I call one of the servants to do the job.

"I am surprised at you, Amelia," he grunted. "I made sure you would take that faint as a sign of guilt."

"Don't be absurd. Armadale is the murderer; I have insisted on that all along. Now we know he is still alive, and in the area."

"We know nothing of the kind. Hassan is perfectly capable of imagining the spirits of Ramses One through Twelve, simultaneously. Forget it and come to bed."

He descended from the chair. To my astonishment I saw that he had the netting in place. Emerson is constantly displaying talents I never knew he had. So I did as he suggested.

CHAPTER SIX

Despite our disturbed night we were awake before daylight. It was a glorious morning. To breathe the air was like drinking chilled white wine. When the sun lifted in majesty over the horizon the western cliffs blushed rosy red in welcome. Larks rose singing to greet the dawn, and all objects shone with a luster that made them appear newly washed—a most deceptive appearance, I might add, since cleanliness is not a conspicuous characteristic of the inhabitants of Upper Egypt or their belongings.

By sunrise we were riding across the plain, through fields of waving barley and ripening vegetables. It was necessary to carry a certain amount of gear with us, so we took this route rather than the shorter, more difficult path over the cliffs. Following us in a ragged but cheerful procession were our loyal men from Aziyeh. I felt quite like a general of a small army; when my rising spirits demanded an outlet I turned in my saddle and raised my arm with a shout of "Huzzah!" to which our troop responded with a cheer and Emerson with a snarl of "Don't make an ass of yourself, Amelia."

Abdullah marched at the head of his men, his vigorous stride and keen brown face belying his years. We encountered the usual morning crowd—women in long brown gulabeeyahs carrying naked children, donkeys almost hidden under their loads of brushwood, haughty camels and their drivers, peasants with rakes and hoes setting out for the fields. Abdullah, who has a fine voice, struck up a song. The men joined in the chorus, and I heard a note of defiance in the way they sang. The watchers muttered and nudged one another. Though no one offered a hostile gesture, I was glad when we left the cultivated land and entered the narrow opening in the cliffs. The towering rocks that guard the entrance had been shaped by wind and water into weird suggestions of watchful statues, though the very idea of water in that now desolate place seems fantastic. The pale limestone walls and chalky ground are as lifeless as the icy wastes of the north.

As we entered the Valley proper we saw that a large crowd had assembled near our tomb. My eye was caught by one man, conspicuous by his unusual height and heavy farageeyeh, the outer robe worn chiefly by men of the learned professions. His arms folded, his wiry black beard jutting out, he stood alone; the others, jostling and shoving one another, had left a respectful space around him. His green turban proclaimed him a descendant of the Prophet; his stern face and fixed, deep-set eyes gave the impression of a forceful and commanding personality.

"That is the local holy man," Karl said. "I feel I must warn you, Professor, that he has been hostile to—"

"Unnecessary," Emerson replied. "Be silent and keep out of the way."

Dismounting, he turned to face the imam. For a moment the two confronted one another in silence. I confess I had seldom seen two more impressive men. They seemed to transcend individuality and become symbols of two ways of life: the past and the future, the old superstition and the new rationalism.

But I digress.

Solemnly the imam raised his hand. His bearded lips parted.

Before he could utter a word, Emerson said loudly, "*Sabâhkum bilkheir*, Holy One. Have you come to bless the work? *Marhaba*—welcome."

Emerson maintains, justly or unjustly, that all religious leaders are showmen at heart. This man reacted to being "upstaged" as any skilled actor would, conquering the anger that flared in his eyes and replying, with scarcely a pause, "I bring no blessing but a warning. Will you risk the curse of the Almighty? Will you profane the dead?"

"I come to save the dead, not profane their tombs," Emerson replied. "For centuries the men of Gurneh have strewn the sands with their pitiful bones. As for curses, I do not fear efreets and demons, for the God we both worship has promised us protection against evil. I invoke His blessing on our work of rescue! *Allâhu akbar; lâ ilâha illa'llâh!*" Sweeping off his hat, he turned toward Mecca and raised his hands to each side of his face in the gesture prescribed for the recitation of the *takbir*.

I could hardly repress a shout of "bravo!" A murmur

of surprise and approval rippled through the watchers. Emerson held his theatrical pose just long enough. Clapping his hat back on his head before his surprised adversary could think of a fitting reply, he said briskly, "Now then, Holy One, you will excuse me if I get to work."

Without further ado he started down the steps. The imam, recognizing defeat with the dignity his office demanded, turned on his heel and walked away, followed by part of the audience. The rest squatted down on their haunches and prepared to watch us work— hoping, no doubt, for a catastrophe of some kind.

I was about to follow Emerson when I realized that the dispersal of the crowd had revealed a form thus far concealed in their ranks. Mr. O'Connell's fiery-red hair was hidden by an inordinately large solar kepi. He was scribbling busily in a notebook. Feeling my eyes upon him, he looked up and raised his hat.

"Top of the morning to you, Mrs. Emerson. I hope you are not tired after your disturbed night?"

"How did you know about that?" I demanded. "And what the—that is, what are you doing here?"

"Why, this is a public place, to be sure. The opening of the tomb is important news. Your husband has already given me a first-rate lead. What an actor he is!"

He had not answered my first question. Obviously he had sources of information within our very household and was not inclined to betray them. As for the second point, he ws quite correct; we might prevent him from entering the tomb, but we could not keep him from watching. As I stared angrily at him he coolly produced a folding stool, opened it, and seated himself. Then he poised his pencil over his notebook and regarded me expectantly.

I felt a new sympathy for the imam. Like him, I had been left with nothing to say. So, following his example, I retreated with as much dignity as I could command.

Descending the stairs, I found that Emerson had unlocked the iron gate and was conversing with the guards—not the ill-favored Habib and his friend, but two of our own men. Being unaware that Emerson had taken this step, I remarked upon it.

"You must think me a fool if you believe I would neglect such an elementary precaution," Emerson replied. "I am not at all sure that such measures will suffice, however. Once we have the passage cleared, it may be necessary for one of us to spend the night here. When Milverton is healthy enough to satisfy you, there will be three of us—"

"Four," I corrected, taking a firm hold of my parasol.

There was a certain amount of grumbling from the men when they realized they would have to carry away the baskets of debris. This menial chore was usually delegated to children, but Emerson had determined not to ask for any help from the villagers. Once they saw that the work was proceeding without incident, they would come to us. At least we had counted on that; but events like our "ghost" of the night before would not help matters. If only we could catch the elusive Armadale!

When the men saw that Karl, Emerson, and I pitched in with the work they stopped complaining. Indeed, Abdullah was horrified when I raised the first basket of rock in my arms and prepared to carry it off.

"Obviously you have forgotten my habits, Abdullah," I said. "You have seen me do ruder labor than this."

The old man smiled. "I have not forgotten your temper, at least, Sitt Hakim. It would take a braver man than Abdullah to prevent you from acting as you choose."

"There is no such man," I retorted. I was pleased with this remark, for it conveyed a delicate compliment as well as being a simple statement of fact. I then asked my husband where he wished to form the refuse dump, since my basket would have the honor of being the first to be deposited there.

Emerson looked up over the rim of the staircase and stroked his chin thoughtfully. "There," he said, pointing to a spot to the southwest, near the entrance to Ramses the Sixth's tomb. "There can be nothing of interest in that area; the ruins are only the remains of ancient workmen's huts."

As I trudged back and forth with my basket I was, at first, a strifle self-conscious under Mr. O'Connell's steady regard and unfailing smile, for I knew he was drawing a verbal portrait of me for the benefit of his readers. Gradually, however, I forgot him in the pressure of work. The pile of debris mounted with what seemed painful slowness. Since I did not enter the tomb, but received my loaded basket from the man who had filled it, I had no way of measuring the progress being made, and I found it devilish discouraging, as Emerson might have said.

I also developed a considerable respect for the humble basket children. How they could run merrily back and forth, singing and making jokes, I did not know; I was dripping with perspiration and conscious of unfamiliar aches in various portions of my anatomy.

The tourists gathered as the morning went on, and in addition to the fence around the tomb itself, it became necessary to string ropes along the path between the entrance and the rubbish dump. The more impertinent tourists ignored these, and I was constantly having to shove gaping idiots aside. Half blinded by sun, dust, and perspiration, I paid no more attention to these forms than was necessary to propel them out of my way, so that when I encountered a very elaborate pale-gray walking gown trimmed with black lace, in the exact center of the path, I gave it a little nudge with my elbow in passing. A shriek, echoed by a masculine exclamation, made me pause. Wiping my sleeve across my brow to clear my vision, I recognized Lady Baskerville. No doubt it was her corsets that prevented her from bending at the waist; her entire body was tilted backward, as stiff as a tree trunk, her heels resting on the ground and her shoulders supported by Mr. Vandergelt. She glowered at me from under the flower-trimmed bonnet, which had fallen over her brow.

"Good morning, Mrs. Emerson," said Mr. Vandergelt. "I sure hope you'll excuse me for not removing my hat."

"Certainly. Good morning, Lady Baskerville; I did not see you. Excuse *me* while I empty this basket."

When I returned Lady Baskerville was standing upright, adjusting her hat and her temper. The sight of me, unkempt, dusty and damp, restored her equanimity. She gave me a pitying smile.

"My dear Mrs. Emerson, I never expected to see you engaged in menial labor."

"It is necessary," I replied briefly. "We could do with a few more workers." I inspected her from head to toe and saw her face go rigid with indignation before I added, "I hope Mr. Milverton is better?"

"You saw him yourself earlier, I am told," Lady Baskerville replied, following after me, for of course I did not pause in my work any longer than was absolutely necessary.

"Yes, I told him to stay indoors today."

I was about to continue when a shout from the tomb made me drop my basket and break into a trot. The watching crowd also realized the significance of that cry; they pressed so close around the entrance that I had to shove through them to reach the steps, and only Emerson's outraged gestures kept several of them from following me down.

The men were working close enough to the entrance to render artificial lighting unnecessary, but at first my eyes were dazzled by the abrupt transition from bright sunlight to gloom. Then I saw what had caused the excitement. On one wall, now cleared to a depth of several feet, was part of a painting. Greater than life size, it showed the upper portion of the body of a male figure, one hand lifted in benediction. The colors shone as brightly as they had on that far-off day when the artist had applied them: the red-brown of the skin, the corals and greens and lapis blues of the beaded collar, the gold of the tall plumes crowning the black head.

"Amon," I exclaimed, recognizing the insignia of that god. "Emerson, how splendid!"

"The workmanship is as fine as the tomb of Seti the First," Emerson said. "We will have to go slowly to avoid damaging the paint."

Vandergelt had followed us down the stairs. "You

are going to remove all the debris? Why not tunnel through it, to reach the burial chamber sooner?"

"Because I am not interested in providing a journalistic sensation, or making it easier for the Gurnawis to rob the tomb."

"You've got me there," Vandergelt said, with a smile. "Much as I'd like to stay, Professor, I reckon I had better get Lady Baskerville back home."

We kept at it until early in the evening. By the time we stopped, several yards of the tunnel lay open, and two splendid paintings had been brought to light, one on either wall. They formed part of a procession of gods. Not only Amon but Osiris and Mut and Isis had made their appearance. There were inscriptions, which Karl was eagerly copying, but to our disappointment the name of the tomb owner had not appeared.

After locking the iron grille and the door of the little shed that had been built to hold our equipment, we started back to Baskerville House. Darkness stretched long blue velvet arms toward us as we proceeding eastward; but behind us, toward the west, the last sullen streaks of sunset scarred the sky, like bleeding wounds.

II

Emerson may—and does—sneer at unnecessary luxuries; but I noticed that he did not scruple to avail himself of the comforts of the pleasant little bathroom next to our bedchamber. I heard the servants refilling the great earthenware jars as I completed my own ablutions;

and very enjoyable the cool water was, I must say, after a day in the sun and dust. Emerson followed me; and I smiled to myself as his voice rose in song. It had to do, I believe, with a young man on a trapeze.

A late tea was set out when we went to the elegant drawing room. The windows opened onto the vine-shaded loggia, and the scent of jasmine pervaded the chamber.

We were the first to come, but scarcely had I taken my seat behind the tea tray when Karl and Mr. Milverton made their appearance, and a moment later we were joined by Mr. Vandergelt, who strolled in through the French doors with the familiarity of an old friend.

"I was invited," he assured me, as he bowed over my hand. "But I'm bound to admit I'd have butted in anyhow, I am so anxious to hear what you found today. Where is Lady Baskerville?"

Even as he inquired the lady swept in, trailing ruffles and laces, and carrying a spray of sweet white jasmine. After a (I hardly need add) courteous discussion as to which of us should dispense the genial beverage, I filled the cups. Emerson then condescended to give a brief but pithy lecture on the day's discoveries.

He began, generous creature that he is, by mentioning my own not inconsiderable contributions. I had spent the last hours of the afternoon sifting through the debris removed from the passageway. Few excavators bother with this task when they are in quest of greater goals, but Emerson has always insisted on examining every square inch of the fill, and in this case our efforts had been rewarded. With some pride I displayed my finds, which had been set out on a tray: a heap of pottery shards (common buff ware), a handful of bones (rodent), and a copper knife.

Lady Baskerville let out a gasp of laughter.

"My poor dear Mrs. Emerson: All that effort for a handful of rubbish."

Mr. Vandergelt stroked his goatee. "I'm not so sure about that, ma'am. They may not look like much, but I'll be doggoned surprised if they don't mean something—something not too good. Eh, Professor?"

Emerson nodded grudgingly. He does not like to have his brilliant deductions anticipated. "You are sharp, Vandergelt. Those bits of broken pottery came from a jar that was used to hold scented oil. I very much fear, Lady Baskerville, that we are not the first to disturb the pharaoh's rest."

"I don't understand." Lady Baskerville turned to Emerson with a pretty little gesture of bewilderment.

"But it is only too clear," Karl exclaimed. "Such perfumed oil was buried with the dead man for his use in the next world, as were foodstuffs, clothing, furniture, and other necessities. We know this from the tomb reliefs and from the papyrus that—"

"Very well, very well," Emerson interrupted. "What Karl means, Lady Baskerville, is that such shards could be found in the outer corridor only if a thief had dropped one of the jars as he was carrying it out."

"Perhaps it was dropped on the way in," suggested Milverton cheerfully. "My servants are always breaking things."

"In that case the broken jar would have been swept up," said Emerson. "No; I am almost certain that the tomb was entered after the burial. A difference in the consistency of the filling material indicates that a tunnel had been dug through it."

"And re-filled," said Vandergelt. He shook his finger playfully at Emerson. "Now, Professor, you're trying to get us all het up. But I'm on to you. The thieves' tunnel wouldn't have been filled up, and the necropolis seals re-applied, if the tomb had been empty."

"Then you believe there are treasures yet to be found?" Lady Baskerville asked.

"If we found nothing more than painted reliefs of the quality we have uncovered thus far, the tomb would be a treasure," Emerson replied. "But, in fact, Vandergelt is right again." He gave the American a malignant look. "I do believe there is a chance the thieves never reached the burial chamber."

Lady Baskerville exclaimed with delight. I turned to Milverton, who was seated beside me, his expression one of poorly concealed amusement.

"Why do you smile, Mr. Milverton?"

"I confess, Mrs. Emerson, that I find all this fuss over a few bits of broken pottery somewhat bewildering."

"That is a strange thing for an archaeologist to say."

"But I am no archaeologist, only a photographer, and this is my first venture into Egyptology." His eyes shifted; they continued to avoid mine as he continued rapidly. "In fact, I had begun to have doubts about my usefulness even before Lord Baskerville's unfortunate death. Now that he is gone I don't believe...that is, I feel I can do better...."

"What?" Lady Baskerville had overheard, despite the fact that Milverton's voice had been scarcely louder than a murmur. "What are you saying, Mr. Milverton? You cannot be thinking of leaving us?"

The wretched young man turned all colors of the rainbow. "I was telling Mrs. Emerson that I don't believe I can be of use here. My state of health—"

"Nonsense!" Lady Baskerville exclaimed. "Dr. Dubois assured me you are making a splendid recovery, and that you are better off here than alone in a hotel. You mustn't run away."

"We need you," Emerson added. "We are desperately understaffed, Milverton, as you know."

"But I have no experience—"

"Not in archaeology, perhaps. But what we need are guards and supervisors. Besides, I assure you, your special skills will be required as soon as you are able to come out with us."

Under my husband's keen regard the young man squirmed like a schoolboy being quizzed by a stern master. The analogy was irresistible; Milverton was the very model of a young English gentleman of the finest type, and it was difficult to see in his fresh, candid face anything except normal embarrassment. I flatter myself, however, that I can see beyond the obvious. Milverton's behavior was highly suspicious.

He was saved from answering by Karl, who had been eagerly examining the pottery fragments in the hope of finding writing on them. Now the young German looked up and said, "Excuse me, Herr Professor, but have you considered my suggestion regarding an artist? Now that paintings have been found—"

"Quite, quite," Emerson said. "An artist would certainly be useful."

"Especially," Vandergelt added, "since there is so much antagonism toward your work. I wouldn't put it past the local hoodlums to destroy the paintings out of spite."

"They will have to get to them first," Emerson said grimly.

"I am sure your guards are trustworthy. All the same—"

"You need not belabor the point. I'll give the girl a try."

Milverton had relaxed as the attention of the others was directed away from him. Now he sat up with a start.

"Is it Miss Mary of whom you speak? You cannot be serious. Karl, how can you suggest—"

"But she is a fine artist," Karl said.

"Granted. But it is out of the question for her to risk herself."

Karl turned beet red. "Risk? *Was ist's? Was haben Sie gesagt? Niemals würde ich*…Excuse me, I forget myself; but that I would endanger—"

"Nonsense, nonsense," shouted Emerson, who had apparently decided never to let the young German complete a sentence. "What do you mean, Milverton?"

Milverton got to his feet. Despite the grave doubts his peculiar behavior had raised in my mind, I could not help but admire him at that moment: pale as linen, his handsome blue eyes burning, his manly figure erect, he halted the general outcry with a dramatic gesture.

"How can you all be so blind? Of course there is risk. Lord Baskerville's mysterious death, Armadale missing, the villagers threatening….Am I the only one among you who is willing to face the truth? Be it so! And be assured I will not shirk my duty as an Englishman and a gentleman! Never will I abandon Miss Mary—or you, Lady Baskerville—or Mrs. Emerson—"

Seeing that he was losing the superb emotional import of his speech, I rose and seized him by the arm.

"You are overexcited, Mr. Milverton. I suspect you are not fully recovered. What you need is a good dinner and a quiet night. Once you have regained your health, these fancies will no longer trouble you."

The young man gazed at me with troubled eyes, his sensitive lips quivering, and I felt constrained to add, "The natives call me 'Sitt Hakim,' the lady doctor, you know; I assure you that I know what is best for you. Your own mother would advise you as I have done."

"Now that makes good sense," Vandergelt exclaimed heartily. "You listen to the lady, young fellow; she's a sharp one."

Dominated by a stronger personality (I refer to my own, of course), Mr. Milverton nodded submissively and said no more.

However, the effects of his outburst could not be dismissed so easily. Karl was silent and sullen for the remainder of the evening; it was clear, from the angry looks he shot at the other young man, that he had not forgotten or forgiven Milverton for his accusation. Lady Baskerville also seemed upset. After dinner, when Mr. Vandergelt prepared to return to the hotel, he urged her to come with him. She refused with a laugh; but in my opinion the laughter was hollow.

Vandergelt took his departure, bearing with him a note that he had promised to deliver to Mary, and the rest of us retired to the drawing room. I allowed Lady Baskerville to dispense the coffee, thinking that domestic and soothing activity would calm her nerves, which it undoubtedly would have done if the others had cooperated with me in behaving normally. But Karl sulked, Emerson relapsed into the blank-faced silence that is indicative of his more contemplative moods, and Milverton was so nervous he could hardly sit still. It was with considerable relief that I heard Emerson declare we must all retire early, in view of the hard day's work ahead of us.

Lady Baskerville accompanied us as we crossed the courtyard. I noticed that she stayed close to us, and I wondered if she was afraid to be alone with one or another of the young men. Had there been a veiled threat in Milverton's speech? Had Karl's sudden display of anger suggested to her that he was not incapable of violence?

Milverton was not far behind us. I was relieved to see him leave the room, not only because he needed his rest, but because it seemed inadvisable for the two men to be left alone, in view of the antagonism between them. His hands in his pockets, his head bowed, he strolled slowly along, and he was still in the courtyard when we reached our doors. Lady Baskerville's was next to ours; we paused to bid her a courteous good night. Scarcely had she stepped into the room, however, when an appalling shriek burst from her lips and she staggered back, her arms outthrust as if to ward off an attacker.

I reached the lady first and supported her swaying frame while Emerson snatched a lantern and ran into the room to see what had caused such alarm. As usual, Lady Baskerville was rudely unappreciative of my attentions. She wrenched herself from me and flung herself into the arms of Milverton, who had rushed to her side.

"Help me, Charles, help me!" she cried. "Save me from—from—"

I itched to slap her, but could not do so because her face was buried against Milverton's shoulder. At that moment an incongruous sound reached my ears. It was the sound of my husband's hearty laugh.

"Come and see, Amelia," he called.

Pushing Lady Baskerville and Milverton out of the way, I entered the room.

Though smaller than the chamber formerly occupied by his lordship, it was of ample size and decorated with feminine delicacy. Soft matting covered the floor; the china vessels were of fine porcelain, painted with flowers. Under the window stood a dressing table equipped with crystal lamps and polished mirrors. Emerson stood by the table, holding the lantern high.

Firmly planted in the center of the tabletop, surrounded by the little pots and jars that contained Lady Baskerville's beauty aids, was a huge brindled cat. Its shape and its pose were startlingly similar to the statues of felines that have come down to us in great number from ancient Egypt, and the color of its fur was like that shown in the paintings—a ticked brownish and fawn pattern. The triple mirror behind the animal reflected its form, so that it seemed as if not one but an entire pride of ancient Egyptian cats confronted us. Unsympathetic as I am with female vapors in any form, I could not entirely blame Lady Baskerville for behaving as she had; the lantern light turned the creature's eyes to great luminous pools of gold, and they seemed to stare directly into mine with a cold intelligence.

Emerson is insensitive to subtler nuances. Putting out his hand, he tickled the descendant of Bastet, the cat goddess, under its lean chin.

"Nice kitty," he said, smiling. "Whose pet is it, I wonder? It is not wild; see how sleek and fat it is."

"Why, it is Armadale's cat," Milverton exclaimed. Supporting Lady Baskerville, he advanced into the room. The cat closed its eyes and turned its head so that Emerson's fingers could reach the spot under its ears. With its glowing orbs hidden and its purr resounding through the room, it lost its uncanny appearance. Now I could not imagine what Lady Baskerville had made such a fuss about, especially since the cat was known to her personally.

"I wonder where it has been all this time?" Milverton went on. "I haven't seen it since Armadale disappeared. We called it his, and he made himself responsible for its care, but in fact it was something of a house mascot, and we were all fond of it."

"I was not fond of it," Lady Baskerville exclaimed. "Horrid, slinking beast, always leaving dead mice and insects on my bed—"

"That is the nature of cats," I replied, studying the beast with more favor. I had never been particularly fond of cats. Dogs are more English, I believe. I now began to realize that felines may be excellent judges of character, and this belief was confirmed when the cat rolled over and embraced Emerson's hand with its paws.

"Precisely," Milverton said, helping Lady Baskerville

to a chair. "I remember hearing his lordship explain that. The ancient Egyptians domesticated cats because of their ability to control rodents—a useful talent in an agricultural society. When Bastet brought her mice to you, Lady Baskerville, she was paying you a delicate attention."

"Ugh," said Lady Baskerville, fanning herself with her handkerchief. "Get the dreadful creature out of here. And do make certain, Mr. Milverton, that it has not left me any other 'attentions.' Where is my maid? If she had been here, as was her duty—"

The door opened, and the apprehensive visage of a middle-aged Egyptian woman appeared.

"Oh, there you are, Atiyah," Lady Baskerville said angrily. "Why weren't you here? What do you mean, allowing this animal to get in?"

From the bewilderment on the woman's face I could see that she understood very little English. Her mistress's anger was only too apparent from her tone, however; Atiyah began to babble in Arabic, explaining that the cat had come in through the window and she had been unable to put it out. Lady Baskerville continued to berate her in English and Atiyah continued to wail in Arabic until Emerson put an end to the performance by scooping the cat up in his arms and marching to the door.

"Pull your curtains and go to bed, Lady Baskerville. Come along, Amelia. Go to your room, Mr. Milverton. Ridiculous business," he added, and strode out. The cat peered at us from over his shoulder.

When we reached our room Emerson put the animal on the floor. It immediately jumped onto the bed and began washing itself. I advanced toward it, somewhat tentatively—not through fear, but because I had never been intimately acquainted with cats. As I put out my hand it rolled over and began to purr.

"Interesting," said Emerson. "That is a position of submission, Amelia; by exposing its soft and vulnerable underbelly it demonstrates that it trusts you. It is unusually tame. I am surprised that it has managed to fend for itself so long."

This aspect of the matter had not occurred to me. Scratching the cat's stomach (a surprisingly pleasant sensation, I confess), I considered the point.

"Emerson," I cried. "It has been with Armadale! Do you suppose it could lead us to him?"

"You know nothing of the nature of cats," Emerson replied, unbuttoning his shirt.

As if to prove him correct, the cat wound all its limbs around my arm and sank its teeth into my hand. I gazed at it in shocked surprise.

"Release your grip at once," I said severely. "You may mean this as another delicate attention, but I assure you it is not appreciated by the recipient."

The cat at once obeyed and licked my fingers apologetically. It then stretched. Its body elongated to a perfectly astonishing degree, as if its muscles were made of India rubber. In a series of agile bounds it passed through the window and disappeared into the night.

I examined my hand. The cat's teeth had left dents in the skin, but had not drawn blood.

"A curious way of demonstrating affection," I remarked. "But it seems a most intelligent creature. Should we not go in search of it?"

"It is a nocturnal animal," Emerson replied. "Now don't get into one of your fits of enthusiasm, Amelia, the way you always do when some new subject captures your agile imagination. Leave the cat to do what cats do in the nighttime—an activity, let me add, that we might emulate."

However, we did not do so. Overcome by the fatigues of the day, we were swiftly overcome by slumber so profound that no sound from without disturbed our rest. Yet at some time in the dark hours before the dawn, not far from our open window, Hassan the watchman met the jackal god of cemeteries and set out on the road to the West.

III

Unfortunately we had no chance of hiding this latest evidence of "the curse of the pharaoh." Hassan's body was discovered by a fellow servant, whose woeful ululations roused us from sleep. Departing unceremoniously by way of our bedroom window, Emerson was the first on the scene. I need not say that I was close behind him. We were in time to see the shirttails of the discoverer vanish into the grove. Attributing this disappearance to the horror primitive people feel for a dead body, Emerson did not attempt to call him back, but knelt and turned the dusty bundle of cotton over onto its back.

The blank staring eyes and livid face confronted me almost with a look of accusation. I had not found Hassan a prepossessing character; but a wave of pity and indignation washed over me, and I vowed on the spot that his murderer would not go unpunished.

I said as much to Emerson. Intent on the limp form, which he was examining with some care, he remarked acrimoniously, "There you go again, Amelia, jumping to conclusions. What makes you think the man was murdered?"

"What makes you think he was not?"

"I don't know how the devil he died." Emerson rose to his feet, slapping absently at the cloud of small insects that swarmed around him. "There is a bump on the back of his head, but it was certainly not enough to kill him. Other than that, there is not a mark on him. But there are plenty of fleas.... Curse it, I am going to be late for work."

The pace of life in Egypt is slow, and death is commonplace. Ordinarily the authorities would have taken their time in responding to a summons such as ours. But our case was different. If I had required any demonstration of the passionate interest in our affairs that possessed all of Luxor, I would have found it in the speed with which the police appeared on the scene.

Emerson had already left for the Valley, at my suggestion. I had pointed out that it was unnecessary for both of us to waste working hours, for he could add nothing to what I knew of the matter; and since this accorded with his own inclinations, he did not object. I saw no reason to mention my chief reason for wanting him away. I anticipated that the press would soon descend on the house and felt that we were providing enough of a journalistic thrill without any additional contributions from my husband.

Eventually the body of poor Hassan was removed, though not without considerable discussion as to its disposition; for the constable wished to restore it to the family, whereas I insisted on a postmortem. I won my point, naturally, but it was obvious, from the way the men shook their heads and murmured, that they considered such investigation unnecessary. Hassan had been killed by an efreet, the ghost of the pharaoh; why look for further evidence?

CHAPTER
SEVEN

Eager as I was to depart at once, I felt obliged to inquire after Lady Baskerville. She was in bed, with her Egyptian maid in attendance. The dark circles under her eyes and the pallor of her cheeks assured me that her complaints of being quite overcome were not entirely fictitious.

"When will this horror end?" she demanded, wringing her hands.

"I am sure I have no idea," I replied. "Is there anything I can do for you, Lady Baskerville, before I go?"

"No. No, I believe I will try to sleep. I had the most dreadful dreams."

I took my departure, before she could tell me about her dreams. It was a pleasure to assume my working garb and set out in the fresh morning air.

Yet dark forebodings haunted me during my walk, for I well knew that once word of Hassan's death got out, even our dedicated workmen might throw down their tools and refuse to enter the accursed tomb. Emerson was not the man to stand meekly aside and let his orders be defied. He would resist—the men would turn on him—attack him.... My affectionate imagination presented me with a ghastly image. I could see my husband's life blood soaking into the white dust, and the men trampling his fallen body as they fled. By the time I reached the cliff overlooking the Valley, I was running.

One glance told me that the tragedy I had envisioned had not occurred, though it was clear that news of the latest disaster had spread. The crowd of the previous day had multiplied tenfold. Among the watchers I saw three of our men reinforcing the fence around the work area. They had not rebelled; they were loyal. I do not scruple to admit that a tear of relief dampened my eye. Brushing it resolutely aside, I descended.

Once again my trusty parasol proved its usefulness. By poking it at the backs of the crowd, I won a path through to the stairs. One of the basket men was just coming up. I greeted him effusively. He mumbled something and would not meet my eye. Again my apprehensions rose. Before they could flower into hysteria I heard the sound I yearned to hear—Emerson's voice raised in a blistering Arabic swear word.

It was echoed, bizarrely, by a girl's soft laugh. Squinting into the shadows below, I saw Miss Mary perched on a stool at the bottom of the stairs. Her position must have been uncomfortable, for she was pressed against the wall in order to leave a path for the basket men. But she appeared quite cheerful; greeting me with a shy smile, she said softly, "The Professor does not realize, I am sure, that my Arabic is quite fluent. Pray don't tell him; he needs some outlet for his feelings."

I did not doubt that she found her cramped, hot position a pleasant change from her usual morning's occupation, for any activity that did not include her mother must be pleasurable. However, I found her cheerfulness somewhat frivolous under the circumstances, and I was about to utter a kindly reproof when her pretty face grew sober and she went on, "I am so sorry you had such a distressing experience this morning. I did not learn of it until I arrived here; but I assure you, Mrs. Emerson, that I want to help in any way I can."

This speech convinced me that my initial appraisal of the girl's character had not been at fault. Her cheerfulness was simply an effort to keep her chin up, in the best British tradition. I replied warmly, "You must call me Amelia; we will be working together, I hope, for a long time."

She was about to reply when Emerson came storming out and told me to get to work. I drew him aside. "Emerson," I said in a soft voice, "it is time we took action to end this nonsense about the curse, instead of simply ignoring it. We can only lose that way; every incident will be interpreted as a new instance of supernatural hostility unless—"

"For the love of heaven, Amelia, don't make a speech," Emerson snapped. "I see the point you are attempting to make; proceed, if you are able, to a specific suggestion."

"I was about to do so when you so rudely interrupted me," I replied spiritedly. "The men seem perturbed by last night's accident. Give them a day or two away from the tomb; set them to work searching for Armadale. If we can find him and prove he was responsible for Lord Baskerville's death—"

"How the devil can we hope to find him when weeks of search produced nothing?"

"But we know he was here, on our very doorstep (so to speak) less than twelve hours ago! Hassan saw the man himself, not his ghost; Armadale must have returned last night and murdered Hassan in order to escape discovery. Or Hassan may have attempted to blackmail him—"

"Good Gad, Amelia, will you attempt to control your rampageous imagination? I admit that what you have suggested is possible. It had, of course, already occurred to me as one explanation among many—"

"You never thought of it until this moment," I said indignantly. "It is just like you to claim the credit for my—"

"Why should I wish to claim credit for such a wild, farfetched—"

"Kindly lower your voice."

"I never raise my voice," Emerson bellowed. A ghostly echo came rolling back from the depths of the tomb, as if the king's spirit were objecting to being awakened.

"Then you will not do as I suggest?"

Emerson's voice dropped to a thunderous growl. "I came here to excavate, Amelia, not to play Sherlock Holmes, a role, let me point out, for which you are no better equipped than I. If you wish to assist me, get to work. If you do not, return to the house and drink tea with Lady Baskerville."

Whereupon he charged back into the tomb. Turning, I met the wide, apprehensive gaze of Mary. I smiled at her.

"Pay no attention to the Professor, Mary. His bark is worse than his bite."

"Oh, I know that. I..." The girl raised a trembling

hand to brush a lock of hair from her brow. "I am not at all afraid of the Professor."

"You aren't afraid of me, I hope," I said, laughing.

"Oh, no," Mary replied quickly.

"I should hope not. My temper is always mild—though at times Emerson would try the patience of a saint. That is one of the small difficulties of the married state, my dear, as you will discover."

"It is most unlikely that I will," Mary replied bitterly. Before I could pursue this interesting comment, she went on, "I could not help overhearing, Mrs. Emerson. Do you really believe poor Alan is still alive?"

"What other explanation can there be?"

"I don't know. I cannot explain the mystery, but I am sure Alan would never have harmed Lord Baskerville. He was the gentlest of men."

"You knew him well?"

Mary blushed and lowered her eyes. "He...he had done me the honor to ask me to be his wife."

"My dear child." I placed a sympathetic hand on her shoulder. "I did not know you were engaged to Mr. Armadale, or I would not have spoken so critically of him."

"No, no, we were not engaged. I was obliged to tell him his hopes could never be realized."

"You did not love him?"

The girl gave me a strange look, in which surprise and amusement were blended with a fatalism unexpected in one of her tender years. "How often does love come in question, Mrs. Emerson?"

"It is—it should be—the only possible basis for marriage," I exclaimed.

Mary continued to study me curiously. "You really believe that! Oh, do forgive me; I did not intend—"

"Why, there is nothing to forgive, my dear. I am always pleased to pass on the benefit of my age and experience to the young, and at the risk of hubris I must say that I consider my marriage a sterling example of what that condition can and should be. My feelings for Emerson, and his for me, are too deep to be concealed. I am the most fortunate of women. And he considers himself the most fortunate of men. I am sure he would say so, if he ever discussed such matters."

Mary was overtaken with a sudden fit of coughing. Struggling heroically to control it, she covered her face with her hands. I administered a brisk slap on the back, remarking, "You had better come up out of the dust for a while."

"No, thank you; I am quite all right now. It was... something caught in my throat. Mrs. Emerson—"

"Amelia. I insist."

"You are too kind. I would like, if I may, to return to the subject of Alan Armadale."

"By all means. I am not so narrow-minded, I hope, to refuse to entertain other hypotheses."

"I certainly cannot blame you for suspecting poor Alan," Mary said ruefully. "You are not the first to do so. But if you had been acquainted with him, you would know he could not be guilty of such a vile act. Lord Baskerville was his patron, his benefactor. Alan was devoted to him."

"Then what do you think has become of Mr. Armadale?"

"I fear he has met with a fatal accident," Mary said. Her voice was grave but composed; it assured me that her feelings for the missing man, though affectionate, were not of that degree of tenderness that made it impossible for me to discuss his guilt or innocence freely. She went on, "He had been in a strange mood for several weeks preceding Lord Baskerville's death: wildly gay one moment, gloomy and silent the next. I wondered if my refusal of his offer of marriage was preying on his mind—"

"That hardly seems likely," I interrupted, attempting to reassure her.

"Believe me, I do not assess my charms so highly," Mary replied, with a faint smile. "He took it well at the time; it was not until a week or so later that he began to exhibit the characteristics I speak of, and he did not renew his offer. Something was certainly amiss with him—whether physical or spiritual, I cannot say. Naturally we were all shocked by Lord Baskerville's mysterious death, but Alan's reaction...He was like the man in the poem—perhaps you know the one I am thinking of—fearful to turn his head lest he see some foul fiend close behind. I am convinced that his mind gave way and that he wandered into the mountains, where he met with an untimely end."

"Humph," I muttered. "That is conceivable. Though I find it hard to believe that Lord Baskerville's death could affect him so strongly. His lordship was not, I believe, the sort of man who was capable of winning the devoted love of his subordinates."

"Really," Mary said hesitantly, "I would not like—"

"Your discretion does you credit. *Nil nisi bonum*, and all that; but remember, Mary, we are investigating the poor man's death, and this is no time—"

"This is no time for gossip," shouted a voice behind

me. Mary started and dropped her pencil. I turned to behold Emerson, his pose one of extreme belligerence, his face flushed with heat and anger. "You are not investigating anything," he went on. "Get that clear in your mind, Amelia, if you can. Stop interfering with my artist and return to your rubbish heap, or I will put you over my shoulder and carry you back to the house."

Without waiting for an answer he vanished into the interior of the tomb.

"Men are such cowards," I said indignantly. "He knew I had more to say. Well, I will deal with him later; it would make a bad impression on the men if I were to follow him and point out the weakness of his argument. I am glad we had this little talk, Mary."

With a reassuring pat on the shoulder, I left the girl to her work. Not that I was at all intimidated by Emerson's anger—no, indeed. I wanted to think over what the girl had told me. She had given me much food for thought. I was particularly struck by her description of Armadale's strange behavior preceding the death of Lord Baskerville. What she failed to see, being fond of the young man, was that this phenomenon only strengthened the theory that Armadale had murdered his patron. The absence of a motive had been one of the things in Armadale's favor; but a maniac needs no motive, as we know from our studies of criminal behavior.

II

Upon returning to the house that evening, tired and hot and out of sorts, it was no pleasure to be told that

Lady Baskerville wanted to see us immediately. Emerson replied with a single vehement word and went stamping off to our room. I delayed a moment in order to reassure the messenger, who had turned quite green with terror.

Atiyah, Lady Baskerville's attendant, was a Cairene and a Copt, and therefore was not popular with the Moslem servants. A shy, timid creature of indeterminate age—as are most Egyptian women, once they pass the brief bloom of youth—she spent most of her time in Lady Baskerville's chamber attending to her duties or in the small room in the servants' wing that had been assigned to her use. Lady Baskerville was constantly reprimanding her. Once, after overhearing such a lecture, I asked the lady why she did not employ an English maid, since Atiyah seemed so inadequate. The lady replied, with a curl of her handsome lip, that Lord Baskerville had preferred not to incur the expense. That accorded with what I had heard of his lordship's peculiar blend of professional extravagance and personal parsimony—he had, for instance, never employed a manservant while in Egypt—but I suspected the true reason was that Lady Baskerville could not have bullied and berated a free-born Englishwoman as she did the humble native.

I therefore made it a point to speak gently to the woman, whose hands were fumbling with a string of carved wooden beads, which I took to be a kind of rosary.

"Tell Lady Baskerville we will come as soon as we have changed our clothing, Atiyah." Atiyah continued to stare blankly and finger her beads, so I added, "There is nothing to be afraid of."

These consoling words had precisely the opposite effect from what I had intended. Atiyah started violently and began to speak. Her voice was so low and her discourse so poorly organized that I was obliged to shake her—gently, of course—before I could make any sense of what she said. I then dismissed her, with appropriate reassurances, and hastened to find Emerson.

He had finished bathing and was in the process of putting on his boots. "Hurry up," he said. "I want my tea."

"I assure you, I want it too. Emerson, I have just had a most interesting conversation with Atiyah. She tells me that last night, about the time Hassan was murdered, she saw the figure of a woman, robed and veiled in filmy white, flitting through the palm grove. She is in a state of pitiable terror, poor thing; I was obliged to—"

Emerson had paused in the act of putting on his second boot. Now he flung it across the room. It struck a china vessel, which fell to the floor and smashed into bits. Mingled with the crash was Emerson's roar. I bowdlerize the comment, which concluded with a request that I spare him further examples of local superstition, a subject with which he was only too well acquainted.

As he spoke I began my ablutions. When he finally ran out of breath I said calmly, "I assure you, Emerson, that the woman's story was replete with a wealth of detail that gave it an air of convincing verisimilitude. She saw something, there is no doubt of that. Has it not struck you that not a thousand miles from here dwells a lady who is in the habit of wearing ancient Egyptian dress?"

Emerson's apoplectic countenance relaxed. He let out a snort of laughter. " 'Flit' is hardly the word I would use to describe Madame Berengeria's movements."

"Nor was it the word Atiyah used. I resorted to some permissible poetic license. Help me with these buttons, Emerson, we are late."

I fully expected that we would be even later, for the process of fastening buttons has the effect of arousing Emerson's amative instincts. On this occasion he simply did as he was asked before retrieving his boot and finishing his toilette. I confess—since I have determined to be completely candid about such matters— that I was a trifle put out.

When we reached the drawing room Lady Baskerville was pacing up and down, clearly annoyed at our tardiness, so—as is my invariable custom—I attempted to cast oil on the troubled waters.

"I hope we did not keep you waiting, Lady Baskerville. Had you paused to consider the matter, I am sure you would have realized we required time to freshen up after our arduous labors."

My graceful apology was received with a malignant look, but when the lady turned to Emerson, she was all charm. Mr. Milverton and Karl were also present. The latter still wore his crumpled work clothes. By contrast, Mr. Cyrus Vandergelt was the picture of sartorial elegance in a white linen suit of snowy freshness. A diamond the size of a cherry sparkled in his cravat.

"Here I am again," he remarked cheerfully, as he took my hand. "Hope you aren't tired of seeing my weather-beaten old face, Mrs. Emerson."

"Not at all," I replied.

"Glad to hear it. To tell you the truth, I've been pestering Lady Baskerville for an invitation. Do you think you could persuade her to offer a bed to a poor homeless Yankee?"

His eyes twinkled and the creases in his cheeks deepened as they always did when he was amused; but I had the impression that there was something serious beneath his seemingly humorous suggestion.

"There is something serious beneath your seemingly humorous suggestion," I said. "What are you driving at?"

"Amazing acumen!" Mr. Vandergelt exclaimed. "As always, Mrs. Emerson, you are one hundred percent correct. I'm downright unhappy about the way things are going. You folks haven't spent much time in Luxor, but take my word for it, the town is humming like a beehive. Somebody broke into Madame Berengeria's room this afternoon while she was taking her siesta, and made off with her jewelry—"

"That cannot have been a great loss," Lady Baskerville murmured.

"Maybe not, but it scared the poor woman half to death when she woke up and found the place all topsy-turvy. I happened to be at the hotel when the servants pelted in yell Poor little Miss Mary is in for a hard time when she gets home; Madame was raving about ungrateful daughters who abandon their mothers, and so on." Mr. Vandergelt took a handkerchief from his pocket and mopped his brow as he relived the painful interview. "I know as well as you do that sneak thieves aren't unusual," he went on. "But I can't remember any thief being quite as bold as this one; it's a sign of rising feelings against foreigners, especially the ones connected with this expedition. I'm proposing to move in to help protect you ladies in case of trouble. That's what it amounts to."

"Humph," said Emerson. "I assure you, Vandergelt, I am perfectly capable of protecting not only Amelia and Lady Baskerville but any indeterminate number of helpless females."

I opened my mouth, an indignant comment trembling on my lips; but I was not allowed to make it. With rising heat Emerson went on, "Curse it, Vandergelt, there are three able-bodied men here, not to mention my men from Aziyeh, who are completely reliable and who would defend Amelia and myself to the death. What are you up to?"

"The Professor has it correct," said Karl, in his Germanic way. "We can defend the ladies; never will they be in danger when here I am."

There was a faint murmur of agreement from Mr. Milverton. I found the murmur and the young man's troubled countenance far from reassuring, but Karl was the picture of manly devotion as he rose to his feet, his muscular frame (and his mustache) vibrant with emotion and his gold-rimmed spectacles gleaming. He added, "I only wish, ladies and sirs, that Miss Mary could be here. It is not right that she should be alone in Luxor with her aging and peculiar maternal parent."

"We can't ask her to come here unless we invite her mother," said Mr. Vandergelt.

There was a brief pause while everyone considered the idea. Karl was the first to break the silence. "If it must be—"

"Certainly not," Lady Baskerville exclaimed. "I will

not tolerate that woman's presence. But if you wish to join us, Cyrus, you know you are always welcome. Not that I feel there is any real danger."

"Wait until the townspeople hear about the white lady," I said ruefully.

Lady Baskerville let out an exclamation and gazed on me with burning eyes. "Have you had..." She checked herself for a moment and then went on, "...a conversation with my foolish Atiyah?"

I had the distinct impression that this was not what she had meant to say. "She mentioned seeing a figure in white robes last night, about the time Hassan was killed," I replied. "To be sure, it might have been imagination."

"What else could it have been?" Lady Baskerville demanded. "The woman is hopelessly superstitious."

"It doesn't matter." Vandergelt shook his head. "That's the kind of talk you folks don't need."

"It is perfectly ridiculous," Lady Baskerville exclaimed angrily. She walked toward the windows. The swift desert night had fallen; the evening breeze set the flimsy curtains billowing and carried the sweet, cloying scent of jasmine into the room. With one white hand holding the curtains, Lady Baskerville stood with her back to us, looking out into the night. I had to admit she made a handsome picture in her softly draped black gown, her queenly head with its crown of shining hair poised on her slender throat.

The discussion continued. Emerson could hardly refuse to receive Mr. Vandergelt when the mistress of the house had made him welcome, but he did not attempt to conceal his displeasure. Vandergelt replied with perfect good humor, but I rather thought he enjoyed Emerson's discomfiture and, in numerous sly ways, added to it.

Suddenly Lady Baskerville gave a sharp cry and stepped away from the window. The warning was too late. With the celerity of a speeding bullet (though of considerably larger dimensions), a missile hurtled through the open window and crossed the room, landing with a crash on the tea table and sending broken china flying in all directions. Before it reached its final destination, however, it achieved its aim. With a violent (and, I am sorry to report, profane) exclamation, Emerson clapped his hand to his head, staggered, and fell full length upon the floor. The impact of his body toppled several small fragile objects from the tables and shelves where they stood, so that the collapse of the colossus (if I may be permitted a literary metaphor) was accompanied by a perfect symphony of breaking glass.

As one man (speaking figuratively, in my case) we rushed to Emerson's side. The only exception was Lady Baskerville, who stood frozen to the spot like Lot's wife. Needless to say, I was the first to reach my husband; but before I could clasp him to my bosom he sat up, his hand still pressed to his temple. From beneath his fingers, already horribly stained with his gore, a crimson stream flowed down his brown cheek.

"Curse it," he said; and would have said more, no doubt, but dizziness overcame him; his eyes rolled up, his head fell back, and he would have collapsed again had I not flung my arms about him and cradled his head on my breast.

"How many times have I told you that you must not

move suddenly after receiving a blow on the head?" I demanded.

"I hope you have not had occasion to offer that advice frequently," said Mr. Vandergelt. He proffered his handkerchief.

Believe me, reader, I did not mistake his coolness for callousness. Like myself, he had observed that the missile had only grazed Emerson's cranium in passing. I admire a man of that temperament; I gave him a quick, approving smile before I accepted the handkerchief and applied it to Emerson's head. The stubborn man was beginning to struggle, attempting to rise.

"Lie still," I said sharply, "or I will have Mr. Milverton sit on your legs."

Mr. Milverton gave me a startled look. Fortunately the expedient I had proposed was not necessary. Emerson relaxed, and I was able to lower his head onto my lap. At this point, as things were calming down, Lady Baskerville created a new sensation.

"The woman in white!" she shrieked. "I saw her—there—"

Mr. Vandergelt reached her just in time to catch her as she fainted. If I were an evil-minded woman, I would have suspected she delayed her collapse long enough to give him time.

"I will go for a doctor," Mr. Milverton exclaimed.

"There is no need," I replied, pressing the handkerchief against the gash on Emerson's temple. "The cut is superficial. There is a possibility of a mild concussion, but I can deal with that."

Emerson's eyes opened. "Amelia," he croaked, "remind

me to tell you, when I am feeling a little stronger, what I think of your—"

I covered his lips with my hand. "I know, my dear," I said soothingly. "You need not thank me."

Now at ease with regard to Emerson's condition, I could turn my attention to Lady Baskerville, who was draped becomingly over Mr. Vandergelt's arm. Her eyes were closed; her long black hair had broken free of its pins and hung in a dark, shining waterfall, almost touching the floor. For the first time since we had met, Mr. Vandergelt looked mildly disconcerted, though he held the lady's limp form to his breast with considerable fervor.

"Put her on the couch," I said. "It is only a faint."

"Mrs. Emerson, just look at this," said Karl.

In his outstretched hand he held the projectile that had inflicted so much damage. At first I thought it was only a rough-hewn rock, approximately eight inches in diameter. A shudder passed through my body as I contemplated what might have occurred if it had struck its target squarely. Then Karl turned the rock over, and I found myself staring into a human face.

The eyes were deep-set, the chin unnaturally long, the lips curved in a strange, enigmatic smile. Traces of blue paint still marked the helmet-shaped headdress— the Battle Crown of an Egyptian pharaoh. I had seen that peculiar physiognomy before. It was, in fact, as familiar to me as the face of an old friend.

"Khuenaton!" I exclaimed.

In my excitement I had forgotten that this—among other archaeological terms—would have aroused Emerson from a deep coma, much less a bump on the head.

Casting off my hand, which I had kept absentmindedly pressed to his lips, he sat up and snatched the carved head from Karl's hand.

"That is wrong, Amelia," he said. "You know Walter believes the name should be read Akhenaton, not Khuenaton."

"He will always be Khuenaton to me," I replied, giving him a meaningful look as I recalled the days of our first acquaintance in the derelict city of the heretic pharaoh.

My tender reference was wasted on Emerson, who continued to study the object that had nearly crushed his skull.

"Amazing," he muttered. "It is genuine—not a copy. Where on earth—"

"This is no time for archaeologizing," I said severely. "You must get to bed at once, Emerson, and as for Lady Baskerville—"

"Bed? Nonsense." Emerson got to his feet, assisted by the assiduous Karl. Dazedly his eyes scanned the room and finally focused on the limp body of Lady Baskerville. "What is wrong with her?" he demanded.

As if on cue, Lady Baskerville opened her eyes.

"The woman in white!" she cried.

Vandergelt dropped to one knee beside the couch and took her hand. "You are perfectly safe, my dear. Don't be alarmed. What did you see?"

"A woman in white, obviously," I said, before the lady could reply. "Who was it, Lady Baskerville? Did she hurl the missile?"

"I don't know." Lady Baskerville passed her hand over her brow. "I caught a glimpse of her—a dim white figure, ghostly, with a gleam as of gold on her arms and brow. Then something came rushing at me, and involuntarily I recoiled. Oh! Oh, Radcliffe, you are covered with blood! How ghastly!"

"I am perfectly well," Emerson replied, oblivious of the crimson stains that disfigured his face. "Where the devil do you suppose the fellow found this carved head?"

This sort of thing might have gone on indefinitely—Emerson speculating about the origin of the head, and Lady Baskerville keening about blood like a banshee—if someone had not intervened. To my surprise, it was Mr. Milverton. An amazing transformation had passed over him. His step was elastic, his color good, his tone firm yet respectful.

"Forgive me, Professor, but we really must have an interlude for rest and reflection. You took quite a crack on the head, you know, and we can't risk anything going wrong with you. Lady Baskerville ought to rest too, she has had a frightful shock. If you will allow me."

With a smiling, conspiratorial glance at me, he took Emerson's arm. My husband allowed himself to be led from the room. He was still crooning over the lethal little head, which he held cupped in his hands.

Lady Baskerville followed, leaning weakly on Mr. Vandergelt's arm. After escorting Emerson to our room, Mr. Milverton drew me aside.

"I will go and tidy up the drawing room," he said. "We don't want the servants to know of this."

"I fear it is already too late," I replied. "But it is a good thought, Mr. Milverton; thank you."

The young fellow went out, whistling under his

breath. I looked at my husband, who was staring as if mesmerized into the strange carved eyes of the heretic pharaoh. But as I tended Emerson's wound and thanked the Almighty for his miraculous escape, I realized that there was an explanation for Mr. Milverton's sudden access of good spirits. He could not be suspected of hurling the deadly missile. Was he relieved because a second party—a confederate, perhaps—had cleared him of suspicion?

CHAPTER EIGHT

When I attempted to lead my wounded spouse to his bed I discovered that he was determined to go out. "I must talk to the men," he insisted. "They will have heard of this latest incident, you may be sure, and if I am not completely honest with them—"

"I see your point," I said coldly. "At least change your shirt, will you, please? That one is ruined. I told you you should have ordered another dozen before we left England; you are the most destructive man—"

At this point Emerson precipitately left the room. Of course I followed him.

The men were housed in a building that had been meant to be a storeroom. It was a little distance from the house, and we had had it fitted up with all the necessary comforts. When we reached the place I saw that Emerson had been right. The men *had* heard the news, and were talking it over.

They stared at Emerson as if he were a ghost. Then Abdullah, who had been squatting by the fire, rose to his impressive height.

"You live, then," he said, the glow of repressed

emotion in his eyes belying his calm tone. "We had heard—"

"Lies," Emerson said. "An enemy threw a stone at me. It struck a glancing blow."

He swept the thick waving locks from his brow, baring the ugly wound. The red glow of the fire illumined his stalwart frame. The bloodstains on his shirt looked black. He stood unmoving, his brown hand raised to his brow, his countenance as proudly calm as that of a sculptured pharaoh. Shadows deepened the cleft in his chin and framed his firm lips in dark outline.

After he had given them time to look their fill, he lowered his hand, allowing his black locks to fall back in place.

"The spirits of the dead do not throw stones," he said. "What man of Gurneh hates me enough to wish me dead?"

At that the men nodded and exchanged meaningful glances. It was Abdullah who replied, a humorous gleam warming his austere bearded face.

"Emerson, there are many men in Gurneh and elsewhere who hate you so much. The guilty man hates the judge, and the chidden child resents a stern father."

"You are not guilty men, or children," Emerson replied. "You are my friends. I came at once to you, to tell you what happened. *Allah yimmessikum bilkheir.*"

II

Of course if I had really felt Emerson should stay in bed I would have seen that he stayed there, by one means or another. It was apparent, however, that he was in the rudest possible health; he bounded out of bed next morning with all the panache of d'Artagnan preparing to storm La Rochelle. Disdaining my offer of assistance, he affixed a huge square of sticking plaster to his forehead, as if scorning to conceal his injury.

I was out of temper with him. The primeval drama of the confrontation with our men had aroused correspondingly primeval emotions in me; but when I expressed them to Emerson he replied that he had a headache. This was certainly a reasonable excuse, but I could not help being vexed.

Naturally I concealed my feelings with my customary dignity, and as we set out for the Valley my spirits rose. It was a typically glorious Upper Egyptian morning. The rising orb of the sun lifted majestically over the eastern mountains, and its golden rays seemed to caress us with loving arms, as the arms of the god Aten embraced the divine king who was his son.

Yet the day, which began so auspiciously, turned out to be replete with disasters. No sooner had we arrived at the tomb than we came face to face with the imam. Brandishing a long staff, he burst into an impassioned harangue, threatening us with death and damnation and pointing dramatically to Emerson's bandaged brow as evidence of the latest demonstration of the pharaoh's curse.

Emerson may deny it, but I am convinced he enjoys these encounters. His arms folded, he listened with an air of courteous boredom. Once he even yawned. Instead of interrupting, he let the man go on and on and on; and eventually the inevitable happened. The listeners also showed signs of boredom as the imam started to repeat himself, and the hoped-for battle of words degenerated into a monologue. Eventually the imam ran out of imprecations, as even the most fanatical man must. When he had stopped ranting, Emerson waited a little longer, his head tilted at an expectant angle. Then he said politely, "Is that all? Thank you, Holy One, for your interest," and, circling respectfully around the infuriated religious person, he descended into the tomb.

Scarcely an hour later there was another disturbance. Hearing angry voices from the tomb, I went to see what was the matter and found Karl and Mr. Milverton facing one another in combative attitudes. Milverton stood with his feet apart and his fists raised; Karl, restrained by Emerson, was struggling and demanding to be let loose so he could administer some unspecified punishment. A rising lump on Karl's jaw showed that the struggle had gone beyond words.

"He insulted Miss Mary," Milverton cried, without abandoning his pugilistic stance.

Karl burst into impassioned German. He had not insulted the lady; Milverton had. When he had objected, Milverton had struck him.

Milverton's normally pale countenance turned red, and the fight would have broken out again if Emerson had not clamped an iron hand over one young man's bicep and throttled the other by catching hold of his collar.

"How ridiculous!" Mary, who had been standing quietly to one side, now came forward. Her cheeks were flushed and her eyes sparkled. She looked amazingly pretty; and for a moment all the men, including my husband, stopped arguing and stared at her in open admiration.

"No one insulted me," she declared. "I appreciate your efforts to defend me; but you are being very silly, and I insist you shake hands and make up, like good boys."

This speech—accompanied by a languishing glance from under her thick black lashes, impartially divided between Milverton and Karl—did not do much to improve relations between the two, but it forced them to make a pretense at reconciliation. Coldly they touched fingertips. Mary smiled. Emerson threw up his hands. I returned to my rubbish heap.

Early in the afternoon Emerson came up to join me.

"How is it going?" he inquired genially, fanning himself with his hat.

We were talking quietly, about one thing and another, when Emerson's eyes wandered from my face and his own countenance underwent such a dreadful alteration that I turned in alarm.

A fantastic cortege was approaching. Leading it were six men whose bowed shoulders supported two long poles on which was balanced a boxlike structure completely enclosed by curtains. This object swayed dangerously as the bearers staggered along under what was clearly a considerable weight. A straggling crowd of natives in turbans and long robes accompanied the apparition.

The procession made its laborious way to where we stood staring. I then saw a man in European garb walking behind the palanquin. His hat was drawn down over his brows, but a few locks of red hair had escaped to betray an identity he seemed not eager to proclaim.

The panting, sweating bearers came to a halt and lowered the carrying poles. Unfortunately they did not move in unison; the palanquin tilted and spilled a stout form out onto the ground, where it lay emitting cries of pain and alarm. I had already surmised who the occupant of the weird structure must be. No one else in Luxor would have attempted to travel in such a way.

Madame Berengeria was wearing her linen robe, a clumsy copy of the exquisite pleated gowns noble ladies were accustomed to wear in pharaonic times. Her fall had disarranged this garment to betray a truly appalling extent of fat, pallid flesh. Her black wig, which was surrounded by a cloud of small insects, had tumbled over her eyes.

Emerson stood with his hands on his hips, staring down at the writhing form of the lady. "Well, help her up, O'Connell," he said. "And if you want to avert a nasty scene, shove her back into that ridiculous contraption and take her away."

"Mr. O'Connell has no desire to avoid a scene," I said. "He promotes them."

My acerbic comment restored the young man's composure. He smiled and pushed his hat back so that it rested at a jaunty angle.

"How unkind, Mrs. Emerson. Will one of you give me a hand? I can't manage the job alone, and that's the truth."

The bearers had collapsed onto the ground, panting and cursing. It was clear that we would get no help from them. Seeing that Emerson had no intention of touching the prostrate form—and indeed, I could not blame him—I joined Mr. O'Connell in his attempt to hoist Madame Berengeria to her feet. We succeeded, though I think I strained several muscles in my back.

Hearing the altercation, the others emerged from the tomb. I distinctly heard Mary pronounce a word I never expected a well-bred English girl to say.

"Mother, what in heaven's name are you doing here? You should not have come. The sun—the exertion—"

"I was called!" Madame Berengeria flung off the hand her daughter had placed on her shoulder. "I was told to come. The warning must be passed on. My child, come away!"

"Curse it," Emerson said. "Clap your hand over her mouth, Amelia, quickly."

Of course I did nothing of the sort. The damage was done. The watching tourists, the natives who had followed the palanquin—all were listening avidly. Striking an imposing attitude, Madame went on.

"It came to me as I meditated before the shrine of Amon and Serapis, lord of the underworld. Danger! Disaster! It was my duty to come, at whatever effort, to warn those who profane the tomb. A mother's heart gave a dying woman strength to fly to the aid of her child—"

"Mother!" Mary stamped her foot. So might the divine Cleopatra have looked as she defied Caesar—if one could picture Cleopatra in a shirtwaist and walking skirt, with tears of embarrassment flooding her eyes.

Madame Berengeria stopped speaking, but only because she had finished what she wanted to say. Her mean little mouth was set in a self-satisfied smirk.

"I am sorry, Mother," Mary said. "I didn't mean to be impertinent, but—"

"I forgive you," Madame said.

"But you must not talk like this. You must go home at once."

One of the bearers understood English. He let out a howl and addressed Mary in impassioned Arabic. Though embroidered with expletives and complaints, the gist of his speech was simple enough. His back was broken, the backs of his friends were broken; they could not carry the lady another step.

Emerson settled the difficulty with a combination of threats and bribery. When the price had gone high enough the men discovered that their backs were not broken after all. We bundled Madame Berengeria unceremoniously into her palanquin, resisting her efforts to embrace Emerson, whom she addressed affectionately as Ramses the Great, her lover and husband. Groaning piteously, the men were preparing to lift the palanquin when Madame's disheveled head once more appeared between the curtains. Thrusting out an arm, she prodded the nearest bearer.

"To the house of Lord Baskerville," she said.

"No, Mother," Mary exclaimed. "Lady Baskerville does not want... It would be rude to call on her without an invitation."

"An errand of mercy requires no invitation," was the reply. "I go to cast the mantle of my protection over that house of blood. By prayer and meditation I will avert the danger." Then, with a sudden descent from her lofty tone, she added, "I have brought your things too, Mary; there is no need for you to return to Luxor tonight."

"You mean—you mean you are planning to stay?" Mary gasped. "Mother, you cannot—"

"I certainly don't intend to spend another night in that house where I was almost murdered in my bed yesterday."

"Why don't you avert the danger by prayer and meditation?" I inquired.

Madame Berengeria glowered at me. "You are not the mistress of Baskerville House. Let her ladyship deny me, if she can." Again she prodded the bearer. "Go—now—Baskerville House."

"It may be just as well," I said to Emerson in a low voice. "We can keep her under observation if she is actually living in the house."

"What an appalling idea," said Emerson. "Really, Amelia, I don't think Lady Baskerville—"

"Then stop her. I don't see how you can do it, short of binding and gagging her. But if that is your desire—"

"Oh, bah!" Emerson folded his arms. "I wash my hands of the entire affair."

Mary, overcome by shame, had also withdrawn from the discussion. Seeing she had won, Madame Berengeria's face split into a narrow toadlike grin. The procession set out, leaving Mr. O'Connell behind like a small dapper whale stranded on a sandy beach.

Emerson's chest swelled as he turned on the young man, but before he could speak Mary anticipated him.

"How dare you, Kevin? How could you encourage her to do this?"

"Ah, my dear, but I did my best to stop her, and that's the truth. What else could I do but come along to protect her in case of trouble? You do believe me, don't you, Mary?"

He attempted to take her hand. She snatched it away

with a gesture of ineffable disdain. Tears of distress sparkled in her eyes. Quickly she turned and walked back toward the tomb.

Mr. O'Connell's freckled face fell. The faces of Karl and Milverton took on identical expressions of smug pleasure. As one man they wheeled and followed Mary.

O'Connell caught my eye. He shrugged and tried to smile. "Spare me your comments, Mrs. Emerson. I'll be back in her good graces soon, never fear."

"If one word of this incident gets into the newspapers," I began.

"But what can I do?" O'Connell's china-blue eyes widened. "Every journalist in Luxor will know of the affair by dinnertime, if they don't know of it already. I would lose my position if I let personal feelings interfere with my duty to my readers."

"You had better take yourself off," I said, seeing that Emerson was beginning to shuffle his feet and growl, like a bull preparing to charge. Mr. O'Connell grinned broadly at me. With the assistance of Mr. Vandergelt I managed to remove my husband; and after an interval of profound cogitation he remarked glumly, "Vandergelt, I believe I will have to accept your offer after all—not to protect the ladies, but to protect *me* from *them*."

"I'm tickled to death," the American said promptly.

Returning to my rubbish heap, I saw that Mr. O'Connell had taken himself off. As I proceeded with the methodical and monotonous chore of sifting the debris I considered an idea that had come to me during my conversation with the young journalist. It was clear that he would cheerfully endure personal violence in his pursuit of a story, and sooner or later Emerson, if goaded, would oblige him. Since we could not rid ourselves of his attentions, why not turn them to our own advantage and control his comments by offering him the exclusive rights to our story? In order to maintain this advantageous position he would be obliged to defer to our wishes and refrain from baiting my excitable husband.

The more I thought about this scheme, the more brilliant it seemed to me. I was tempted to propose it to Emerson at once; but since his immediate reaction to my suggestions is usually an emphatic negative, I decided to wait till later, when he had, hopefully, recovered from the ill temper induced by the latest encounter with Madame Berengeria.

An alarming development occurred later that afternoon, when a section of the exposed ceiling of the passageway collapsed, narrowly missing one of the men. The rumbling crash and cloud of dust emerging from the stairwell caused a flutter of excitement among the watchers and brought me rushing to the spot. Through the fog of dust I saw Emerson, dimly visible like a demon in a pantomime, wiping his face with his sleeve and cursing nobly.

"We will have to shore up the ceiling and walls as we proceed," he declared. "I saw that the rock was in bad condition, but hoped it would improve as we proceeded. Unhappily the reverse seems to be the case. Abdullah, send Daoud and his brother back to the house to fetch wood and a bag of nails. Curse it, this will slow the work even more."

"But it must be done," I said. "A serious accident

now would convince the men that we are indeed under a curse."

"Thank you for your tender concern," Emerson snarled. "What are you doing down here anyway? Get back to work."

Obviously the time was not ripe for me to discuss my scheme regarding Mr. O'Connell.

No one can accuse me of being an uncritically doting wife. I am fully cognizant of Emerson's many faults. In this case, however, I recognized his evil temper as a manifestation of that well-nigh supernatural force of character which drove the men to efforts exceeding their natural powers. The ill-omened words of Madame Berengeria, closely followed by the rockfall, had rendered even more uneasy temperaments not wholly unaffected by earlier uncanny events. With a lesser man than my husband at the helm, they might have walked off the job that very day.

Unfortunately Emerson's mood of majestic authority is accompanied, in the domestic sphere, by an arrogance that any woman less understanding than I would refuse to tolerate for an instant. I put up with it only because I was as anxious as he to see the work proceed apace.

Only with the imminence of night did Emerson dismiss the exhausted men. It was a weary group that started back along the rocky path. I had attempted to persuade Mary to go the long way around, on donkeyback, but she insisted on accompanying us, and of course the two young men followed her like sheep. Vandergelt had left earlier, assuring us he would meet us at the house after he had collected his luggage from the hotel.

I was still pleased with my idea of enlisting Mr.

O'Connell, but I knew better than to mention it to Emerson. Hands in his pockets, head bowed, he tramped along in grim silence. In addition to the other disasters of the day, the final hours of work had brought to light some ominous evidence. The men had cleared almost ten metres of the corridor and had finally exposed the figure of a royal personage, probably the owner of the tomb; but, alas, the head of this figure had been savagely mutilated, and the royal name in the inscription above it had been similarly defaced. This proof that the tomb had been violated depressed us all. After moving mountains of stone, would we find only an empty sarcophagus?

This fear would have been enough in itself to justify my husband's gloomy silence. The prospect of facing Madame Berengeria and Lady Baskerville, whose mood would undoubtedly be unpleasant, further depressed him.

If Mary was concerned about the social embarrassment awaiting her she showed no signs of it. She had endured the long day's labor far better than her fragile appearance had led me to expect. She and the young men were ahead of us, for Emerson was not in any hurry, and I heard her chatting merrily and even laughing. I observed that she had accepted Karl's arm and was addressing most of her comments to him. Milverton, on her other side, attempted without success to attract her attention. After a time Milverton stopped and let the others draw ahead. As Emerson and I came up to him, I saw that he was watching the girl's slim figure with a look of poignant distress.

Emerson plodded on without so much as a glance at the disconsolate young man, but I did not feel it right to neglect such obvious signs of mental perturbation. I therefore let my husband go ahead and, taking Milverton's arm, requested his assistance. I do not scruple to employ mendacity and a fictitious appearance of female incompetence when the occasion demands it.

Milverton responded like a gentleman. We walked in silence for a time and then, as I had expected, his wounded heart sought the relief of conversation.

"What can she see in him?" he burst out. "He is plain, pedantic, and poor!"

I was tempted to laugh at this damning and alliterative catalog of deficiencies. Instead I sighed and shook my head.

"I fear she is a heartless flirt, Mr. Milverton."

"I beg to differ," Mr. Milverton said warmly. "She is an angel."

"She is certainly as beautiful as an angel," I agreed amiably.

"She is; she is! She reminds me of that Egyptian queen, don't you know?—I forget the name—"

"Nefertiti?"

"Yes, that's the one. And her figure.... Look how gracefully she walks."

This was not easy to do, for dusk was far advanced, and as I realized this a new uneasiness shadowed my mind even as twilight shadowed the scene. The path was difficult enough in daylight; the rocky descent would not be easy in the dark. Also, night would serve as a cloak to enemies. I only hoped that Emerson's stubbornness had not exposed us to accident or worse. I took a firmer hold of Milverton's arm and quickened my pace. We had fallen far behind the others, and

Emerson's form, some distance ahead, was now no more than a shadowy outline against the blossoming stars.

Milverton was still alternately rhapsodizing and reproaching Mary. Conquering my apprehension, I attempted to make him see the situation in the calm light of reason.

"Perhaps she doubts your intentions, Mr. Milverton. They are, I assume, those of an honorable gentleman?"

"You wound me inexpressibly, Mrs. Emerson," the young man exclaimed. "My feelings are so profound, so respectful—"

"Then why don't you express them to their object? Have you proposed to her?"

Milverton sighed. "How can I? What have I to offer her, in my situation—"

He stopped speaking with a sharp intake of breath.

I verily believe that my own respiration halted for an instant as the import of that betraying pause dawned on me. If he had ended his sentence with that word, or allowed it to trail off into the mournful silence of indecision, I would have assumed he was referring to his subordinate position, his youth, and his lack of financial security. My detective instincts—the result of natural aptitude and of a certain not inconsiderable experience—immediately showed me the true meaning of his gasp. The comfortable cloak of darkness and the seductive influence of womanly sympathy had lowered his guard. He had been on the verge of confessing!

The detective instinct, when in full bloom, ruthlessly suppresses softer feelings. I am ashamed to admit that my next speech was dictated, not by sympathy, but by guile. I was determined to break through his guard, to trick him into an admission.

"Your situation is difficult," I said. "But I know Mary will stand by you, if she loves you. Any true woman would."

"Would she? Would you?" Before I could reply he turned and caught me by the shoulders.

I confess that a slight qualm dampened my detective ardor. The darkness was now complete, and the tall form of Milverton hovered over me like a creature of night, no longer entirely human. I felt his hot breath on my face and felt his fingers pressing painfully into my flesh. It occurred to me that possibly I might have been guilty of a slight error in judgment.

Before I was stampeded into committing some foolish act, such as calling for help or striking Mr. Milverton with my parasol, a silvery light illumined the darkness as the moon, almost at the full, rose over the cliffs. I had forgotten that this phenomenon must inevitably occur; for almost never are there cloudy skies in Luxor. So pure, so limpid is the lunar illumination in that southern clime that it is possible to read a book by its rays; but who would dream of turning his eyes to a sterile page of print when a magical landscape of shadow and silver lies before him? Moonlight in ancient Thebes! How often and how understandably has this theme formed the subject of literary masterpieces!

My feeble pen, moved by a mind more susceptible to cold reason than to poetry (though not untouched by its influence, never think that)...my feeble pen, as I say, will not attempt to rival the effusions of more gifted writers. More to the point, the light enabled me to see

Mr. Milverton's face which, in his extremity, he had pressed close to mine. I saw, with considerable relief, that his handsome features bore a look of anxiety and distress, with no trace of the mania I had feared to see.

The same light allowed him to see *my* face, which must have betrayed discomfort. Immediately he loosened his grasp.

"Forgive me. I—I am not myself, Mrs. Emerson, indeed I am not. I think I have been half mad these past weeks. I can endure it no longer. I must speak. May I confide in you? May I trust you?"

"You may!" I cried.

The young man took a deep breath and drew himself up to his full height, his broad shoulders squared. His lips parted.

At that precise moment a long-drawn-out shriek echoed across the wilderness of tumbled stone. For a moment I thought Mr. Milverton was howling like a werewolf. But he was as startled as I; and almost at once I realized that the peculiar acoustical qualities of the area had made a sound whose origin was some distance away sound mysteriously close at hand. The moon was fully up by then, and as I scanned the terrain, seeking the source of the eerie cry, I beheld an alarming sight.

Bounding across the plateau came Emerson, leaping boulders and soaring over crevasses. His speeding form was followed by a silvery cloud of dust, and his unearthly cries, combined with this ectoplasmic accompaniment, would have struck terror into a superstitious heart. He was moving in our direction, but at an angle to the path. Waving my parasol, I immediately set off on a course that would cross his.

I was able to intercept him, for I had calculated the intersecting angles accurately. Knowing him well, I did not attempt to stop him by touching him or grasping him lightly; instead I threw the whole weight of my body against his, and we both went tumbling to the ground. As I had planned, Emerson was underneath.

Once he had gotten his breath back, the moonlit scene again echoed to the fervor of his cries, now entirely profane and almost entirely directed at me. Taking a seat on a convenient boulder, I waited until he had calmed himself.

"This is too much," he remarked, raising himself to a sitting position. "Not only am I under attack by every malcontent and religious maniac in Luxor, but my own wife turns against me. I was in pursuit, Amelia—hot pursuit! I would have caught the rascal if you had not interfered."

"I assure you, you would not," I said. "There was no one else in sight. He undoubtedly crept away among the rocks while you were rushing around and howling. Who was it?"

"Habib, I suppose," Emerson replied. "I caught only a glimpse of a turban and a fluttering robe. Curse it, Amelia, I was just about—"

"And I was just about to become the repository of a confidence from Mr. Milverton," I said, in considerable bitterness of spirit. "He was on the verge of confessing to the crime. I do wish you could learn to control that juvenile joie de vivre which leads you to act before you—"

"That is certainly a case of the pot reprimanding the kettle," Emerson cried. "Joie de vivre is too kind a

word for the inveterate conceit that leads you to believe yourself—"

Before he could finish this insulting comment we were joined by the others. Agitated questions and explanations followed. We then proceeded, Emerson conceding reluctantly that there was no sense in continuing a pursuit of someone who had long since vanished. Rubbing his hip and limping ostentatiously, he headed the procession.

Once again I found myself with Mr. Milverton. As he offered me his arm I saw that he was struggling to repress a smile.

"I could not help overhearing part of your conversation," he began.

I tried to recall what I had said. I knew I had made some references to a confession. But when Milverton continued I was relieved to learn that he had not heard that part of my speech.

"I don't mean to be impertinent, Mrs. Emerson, but I am intrigued by the relationship between you and the Professor. Was it really necessary for you to knock him flat?"

"Of course it was. Nothing short of physical violence can stop Emerson when he is in a rage, and if I had not stopped him he would have gone on running until he tumbled over the cliffs or caught his foot in a hole."

"I see. He did not seem to—er—appreciate your concern for his safety."

"Oh, that is just his manner," I said. Emerson, still limping in a vulgar and unconvincing fashion, was not far ahead, but I did not trouble to lower my voice. "Like all Englishmen, he does not care to display his true emotions in public. In private, I assure you, he is the tenderest and most affectionate—"

This was too much for Emerson, who turned and shouted, "Hurry up, you two; what are you doing, dawdling along back there?"

So, with considerable vexation, I abandoned hope of regaining Milverton's confidence. As we made our way down the winding and dangerous descent, there was no opportunity for a private conversation. We had gone only a short distance toward the house, whose lights we could see gleaming through the palm fronds, when we were met by Mr. Vandergelt, who, anxious at our tardiness, had come out in search of us.

As we entered the courtyard Milverton caught my hand.

"Did you mean it?" he whispered. "You assured me—"

A flame of exultation soared from the dying embers of hope.

"Every word," I whispered back. "Trust me."

"Amelia, what are you muttering about?" Emerson demanded pettishly. "Hurry up, can't you?"

I took a firm grip on my parasol and managed not to hit him with it.

"I am coming," I replied. "Do you go on."

We were almost at the door. I heard a voice in my ear murmur, "Midnight; on the loggia."

II

As soon as we stepped into the house Emerson fled toward our room like a man pursued by demons, and, indeed, the distant echo of a resounding voice which could only be that of Madame Berengeria gave him some excuse for flight. When I entered our room he began to groan and wince. Displaying a large area of scraped, reddened skin, he accused me of being responsible for it.

I paid no attention to this childish exhibition.

"Emerson," I cried eagerly, "you will never guess what has happened. Despite your stupid interference..." Here he began to expostulate. I raised my voice and went on, "I have won Mr. Milverton's confidence. He is going to confess!"

"Well, do shout a little louder," Emerson said. "There must be a few people in the house who haven't heard you."

The reproof was justified, if rudely expressed. I dropped my voice to a whisper. "He is deeply disturbed, Emerson. I am sure the murder was unpremeditated; no doubt he was driven to it."

"Humph." Standing on a mat, Emerson pulled off his shirt and began to sponge himself off. "What precisely did he say?"

"You are very calm," I exclaimed. I took the sponge from his hand and washed the sand and dust from his back. "He was unable to give me any details. That will come later. I am to meet him at midnight, in—"

"You have lost your wits," said Emerson. His voice was calmer, however, and as I continued to move the sponge rhythmically over the hard muscles of his back, he let out an absurd purring murmur of pleasure. "Do you really suppose, my dear Peabody, that I will let you go out to meet a murderer in the middle of the night?"

"I have it all planned," I said, replacing the sponge with a towel. "You will be in hiding nearby."

"No, I won't," said Emerson. He took the towel from me and hastily finished drying himself. "I am spending the night at the tomb, and you are going to lock yourself in this room and stay in it."

"What are you talking about?"

"We are getting near the end of the passageway. Another day or two should see it cleared. A couple of determined thieves, working in haste, can dig a tunnel through in a few hours."

I did not ask how he knew the end of the corridor was near. In professional matters Emerson is the greatest archaeologist of this, and perhaps any, age. It is only in the routine aspects of life that he displays a normal degree of masculine incompetence.

"But our men are on guard, are they not?" I asked.

"Two men, who are, by this time, in such a state of nerves that a howling jackal could send them scampering for cover. And two men could not hold out against an assault in force. The Gurnawis have attacked archaeologists before."

"So you are proposing yourself as one of the victims?"

"They won't dare attack an Englishman," Emerson said sublimely.

"Ha," I said. "I see your real motive for wishing to absent yourself. You are afraid of Madame Berengeria."

"Ridiculous." Emerson let out a hollow laugh. "Let us not argue, Peabody. Why don't you get out of that dusty costume? You must be hot and uncomfortable."

I skipped agilely back as he put out his hands. "That

device will not work, Emerson. And do put on some clothes. If you think the sight of your admittedly muscular and well-developed frame will seduce me from my plain duty—"

This time it was not Emerson who interrupted me, though he was advancing in a manner indicative of intentions along those lines. A knock at the door caused him to fumble for his trousers; and a voice announced that we were summoned by Lady Baskerville.

By the time I had washed and changed, the others had assembled in the drawing room. The atmosphere was not that of a social gathering, but a council of war. I was pleased to see that Madame Berengeria had relapsed into a state of semi-stupor, and the strong smell of brandy that surrounded her did not surprise me in the least. She simpered sleepily at Emerson, but was otherwise incapable of speech or movement.

Relieved of his greatest fear by Madame's collapse, Emerson expressed his intentions and plans with his usual forcefulness. Lady Baskerville let out a cry of distress.

"No, Radcliffe, indeed you must not think of risking yourself. I would rather have the entire tomb vandalized than see one hair of your head injured."

This idiotic statement, which would have won me a blistering reproof, brought a look of fatuous pleasure to Emerson's face. He patted the white hand that clung to his sleeve.

"There is not the slightest danger, I promise you."

"You're probably right about that," said Vandergelt, who had not appreciated this display of concern by the lady. "Howsoever, I think, I'll just mosey along with you, Professor. Two six-shooters are better than one, and a fellow is safer with a pal to watch his back."

But at this Lady Baskerville cried out in greater alarm. Would they abandon her to the mercies of the ghostly form that had already killed one man and attempted a murderous assault on Emerson? Vandergelt, to whom she was now clinging, showed himself just as susceptible to amateur theatrics as my husband.

"She's right, I reckon," he said in a worried voice. "We can't leave the ladies unprotected."

At this both Milverton and Karl expressed their willingness to be of service. It was finally decided that Karl would join Emerson in guarding the tomb. So impatient was Emerson to be gone that he would not even wait to dine, so a picnic basket was prepared, and he and Karl made ready to depart. Despite Emerson's efforts to avoid me, I managed to draw him aside for a moment.

"Emerson, it is absolutely necessary that I speak with Mr. Milverton while his mood is chastened. By tomorrow he may have decided to brazen it out."

"Amelia, there is not the slightest possibility that Milverton intends to confess. Either the meeting is meant as a trap—in which case it would be infinitely stupid of you to fall into it—or, as I suspect, it is solely the product of your rampageous imagination. In either case I forbid you to leave the house tonight."

His grave, quiet tone made a deep impression on me. Nevertheless, I should have replied to his arguments had he not suddenly caught me in his arms and pressed me close, oblivious of Mary, who was passing through the courtyard toward her room.

"For once in your life, Peabody, do as I ask! If anything happens to you, I will murder you!"

With an emphatic squeeze that completely robbed me of breath, he was gone. A moment later I heard him shouting for Karl to hurry.

I leaned against the wall, holding my bruised ribs and struggling to control the emotion induced by this tender parting. A gentle hand touched my shoulder, and I beheld Mary beside me.

"Don't worry about him, Mrs. Emerson. Karl will watch over him; he is devoted to the Professor."

"I am not at all worried, thank you." Unobtrusively I applied my handkerchief to my face. "Heavens, how I am perspiring. It is very hot here."

The girl put her arm around me. "It is *very* warm," she agreed. "Come, let us go back to the drawing room."

The evening was one of the most uncomfortable I have ever passed. Lady Baskerville concentrated her undeniable charms on Mr. Vandergelt. Milverton was silent and moody, avoiding my attempts to catch his eye. Madame Berengeria had been removed to her room, but her presence seemed to hover over us like a squat, threatening shadow. Above all else, coloring every word that was spoken and spoiling the taste of every bite that went into my mouth was the thought of Emerson on guard at the tomb, vulnerable to that malice that had already displayed itself as intent on his life. If there had been no other enemy—and I felt sure there was—the malevolent Habib had a double motive to inspire an attack, greed and revenge.

The party broke up early. It was only ten o'clock when I got into bed and tucked the netting in place.

So softened was I by the thought of my husband's peril that I had almost decided to obey his last command. However, I was unable to sleep. I watched the mystic path of moonlight glide across the floor, and after a time its lure was as irresistible as the charm of a road leading into strange, unknown lands. I had to follow.

I rose. Cautiously I opened my door.

The dreaming silence of the night was broken only by the buzzing of nocturnal insects and the mournful howls of jackals far back in the hills. The household had succumbed to slumber. I continued to wait and watch; and after a while I saw the dark form of a man pass silently through the courtyard. After Hassan's death Emerson had assigned one of our own people to the watchman's post.

Not a whit discouraged, for I had never intended to go that way, I softly closed my door and put on my clothing. Another peep out the door assured me that the house was quiet and that the watchman was still in the courtyard. I then went to the window.

I had one knee on the sill and was preparing to draw the other foot up when a dark bulk loomed up, and a familiar voice murmured in Arabic, "The Sitt desires something? Her servant will bring it."

If I had not had a firm grip on the sill, I would have tumbled over backward. Recovering myself, I climbed up into the embrasure.

"The Sitt desires to climb out the window, Abdullah," I replied. "Give me a hand or get out of my way."

The tall form of the reis did not move. "Efreets and evildoers haunt the darkness," he remarked. "The Sitt will be better in her bed."

Seeing that discussion could not be avoided, I sat down, with my feet dangling. "Why did you not go with Emerson, to protect him?"

"Emerson left me here, to guard the treasure dearer to him than the gold of the pharaoh."

I doubted that Emerson had put it quite that way—though he was florid enough when he spoke Arabic. My compunctions at ignoring his request quite vanished. He had not trusted me!

"Help me down," I said, holding out my hands.

Abdullah let out a groan. "Sitt Hakim, please do not do this. Emerson will have my head on a pole if harm comes to you."

"How can harm come to me if you are guarding me? I am not going far, Abdullah. I want you to follow, making sure you are not seen, and conceal yourself behind a bush or a tree when I have reached the loggia."

I lowered myself to the ground. Abdullah shook his head despairingly, but he knew better than to try and prevent me. As I stole through the shrubbery, trying to avoid the bright patches of moonlight, I knew he was following, though I did not hear a sound. For all his size Abdullah could move like a bodiless spirit when he had to.

Turning the corner of the house I saw the loggia before me, the bright paint of its pillars strangely altered by the eerie light. Its interior was deep in shadow. I made out the shapes of the white wicker chairs and tables, but saw no sign of a human form. Pausing, I spoke softly.

"Wait here, Abdullah. Do not make a sound, or intervene unless I call for help."

I crept on. Emerson may accuse me of lack of caution, but I knew better than to approach the place openly. I meant to survey the scene from the shelter of a pillar before venturing in.

Emerson's suggestion that the midnight rendezvous was solely the product of my imagination was of course ridiculous. However, cool reflection had reminded me that I could not be absolutely sure Milverton intended to confess to Lord Baskerville's murder. He might have other, less interesting information, or—disconcerting thought—he might only wish to avail himself of my sympathy while he talked about Mary. Young men commonly suffer from the delusion that the rest of the world is absorbed in their love affairs.

I felt a thrill pass through me when I saw the round red tip of a cigar at the far end of the loggia. Abandoning my place of concealment, I glided toward it.

"Mrs. Emerson!" Milverton rose and crushed out his cigar. "You did come. God bless you."

"You must have eyes like a cat's," I said, chagrined because I had not been able to reach him unobserved.

I spoke in a low murmur, as did he. "My hearing is preternaturally sharp," he replied. "I heard you approach."

I groped for a chair and sat down. Milverton followed my example, selecting a chair next to mine. The cool breeze rustled the vines that wound green arms around the pillars.

For a few moments neither of us spoke. Realizing that the situation was delicate, fearing I would say the wrong thing, I said nothing. Milverton was wrestling with his fears and his awareness of guilt. At least I hoped that was what he was doing, rather than planning

the quickest method of dispatching me. If he grasped
me by the throat I would not be able to call Abdullah. I
wished I had brought my parasol.

Milverton's first remark did nothing to calm my
apprehension. "You are a courageous woman, Mrs.
Emerson," said he, in a sinister voice. "To come here
alone, in the middle of the night, after a mysterious
death and a series of strange accidents."

"It was rather stupid of me," I admitted. "I fear that
overconfidence is one of my failings. Emerson often
accuses me of that."

"I had no intention of suggesting anything so insulting," Milverton exclaimed. "I would rather believe that
your decision was based on a profound knowledge of
human nature and on that womanly compassion for the
unfortunate which is so conspicuous in your conduct."

"Well, since you put it that way . . ."

"And you were right," Milverton continued. "Your
appraisal of my character was correct. I am weak and
foolish, but not vicious, Mrs. Emerson. You are in no
danger from me. I am incapable of harming a woman—
or, indeed, of harming anyone; and your confidence in
me has raised you to a lofty place in my esteem. I would
die to defend you."

"Let us hope the necessity for that does not arise,"
I said. Though reassured, I felt a certain flatness. This
speech did not sound like the prelude to a confession of
murder.

"But," I went on, "I appreciate the offer, Mr. Milverton. The hour is late; may I request that you tell
me . . . whatever it was you wanted to tell me?"

From the man beside me, no more than a dim outline in the darkness, came an odd stifled sound that might have been a laugh. "You have hit on the essence of my confession, Mrs. Emerson. You have addressed me by a name that is not my own."

"Who are you, then?" I demanded in surprise.

"I am Lord Baskerville," was the astonishing reply.

CHAPTER NINE

Milverton had gone out of his mind. That was my first thought. Guilt and remorse take strange forms; wishing to deny the vile deed, his conscience had persuaded the young man that Lord Baskerville yet lived—and that he was he (Lord Baskerville, to be precise).

"I am glad to make your acquaintance," I said. "Obviously the reports of your death were greatly exaggerated."

"Please don't joke," Milverton said with a groan.

"I was not joking."

"But...Oh, I see." Again came the stifled laugh that was more like a cry of pain. "I cannot blame you for thinking me mad, Mrs. Emerson. I am not—not yet—though I am not far from it at times. Let me make myself plain."

"Please do," I said emphatically.

"I call myself Lord Baskerville because that is now my title. I am the nephew of his late lordship, and his heir."

The explanation was as unexpected as my original idea. Even *my* agile brain required several seconds to assimilate the fact and its sinister connotations.

"Then what on earth are you doing here under an assumed name?" I asked. "Did Lord Baskerville—the late Lord Baskerville—know your true identity? Good Gad, young man, don't you realize what a suspicious position you have placed yourself in?"

"Of course I do. I have been in such distress since my uncle died that I verily believe it added to the severity of the fever I caught. Indeed, but for that I would have taken to my heels long ago."

"But, Mr. Milverton…What am I to call you, then?"

"My name is Arthur. I would be honored to have you use it."

"Then, Arthur—it is just as well you could not flee. That would have been tantamount to an admission of guilt. And you claim, if I understand you, that you had nothing to do with your uncle's death."

"On my honor as a British nobleman," came the tense, thrilling whisper from the darkness.

It was hard to doubt that impressive oath, but my reservations lingered. "Tell me," I said.

"My father was his late lordship's younger brother," Arthur began. "When only a boy he incurred the displeasure of his stern parent because of some youthful peccadillo. From what I have heard, the old gentleman was a tartar, who would have been more at home in the Puritan Commonwealth than in the present century. Following the precepts of the Old Testament, he promptly cut off the right hand that had offended him and cast the prodigal son out in the cold. My poor father was dispatched to Africa with a small monthly stipend, to live or die as Fate decreed."

"Did not his brother intercede for him?"

Arthur hesitated for a moment. "I will hide nothing from you, Mrs. Emerson. The late Lord Baskerville was in complete agreement with his father's cruel behavior. He came to the title only a year after his brother had been sent into exile, and one of his first acts was to write Pater informing him that he need not waste time applying for assistance, for both personal conviction and filial respect compelled him to cast his brother off as he had been cast off by their parent."

"How unfeeling," I said.

"I was brought up to consider him a veritable fiend," Arthur said.

A shudder passed through my body when I heard this damning admission. Did not the young man realize that every word deepened the pit he was digging for himself? Did he believe I would keep silent about his identity—or did he count on other means of rendering himself safe from detection?

Arthur went on with his story. "I heard my father curse him nightly, when he was . . . Well, not to put too fine a face upon it, when he had taken too much to drink. This happened, I regret to say, with increasing frequency as time went on. Yet when he was himself, my father was the most delightful of men. His engaging character won the heart of my mother, who was the daughter of a gentleman of Nairobi and, despite her parents' objections, they were wed. My mother had a small income of her own, and on this we lived.

"She loved him devotedly, I know. Never did I hear a word of complaint or accusation from her lips. But six months ago, after he had succumbed to the inevitable consequences of his indulgence, it was my mother who persuaded me that my hatred of my uncle might be unjust. She did this, mark you, without the slightest criticism of my father—"

"Which must have been no small feat," I interrupted. I had formed a clear mental picture of Arthur's father and I felt great sympathy for his wife.

Ignoring my comment, Arthur continued. "She also pointed out that since Lord Baskerville was childless, I was his heir. He had made no attempt to communicate with me, even though she had, in duty bound, notified him of his brother's death. But as she said, omissions and unfairness on his part did not justify my behaving badly. I owed it to myself and to my family to present myself to the man whom in the course of time I must succeed.

"She convinced me; but I never admitted to her that she had, for I had formed a foolish, thoughtless scheme of my own. When I left Kenya I told her only that I meant to seek my fortune in the wide world, by means of the photography which had been my youthful hobby. I am sure she has read of the mystery surrounding my uncle's death, but she does not dream that the Charles Milverton of the newspapers is her miserable son."

"But she must be beside herself with worry about you," I exclaimed. "She has no idea where you are?"

"She believes I am on my way to America," the young man confessed in a low voice. "I told her I would send an address when I was settled."

I could only shake my head and sigh. But there was no point in urging Arthur to communicate at once with his mother; the truth would be far more painful than any uncertainty she presently felt, and though I had only the most dismal forebodings as to his future, there was always a possibility, however remote, that I might be wrong.

"My scheme was to present myself to my uncle as a stranger and win his regard and confidence before proclaiming my true identity," Arthur said. "You needn't comment, Mrs. Emerson; it was a naive idea, worthy of a sensational novel. But it was harmless. I swear to you, I had no intention of doing anything except proving myself, by hard work and devotion. Naturally I knew of my uncle's plans to winter in Egypt—most of the English-speaking population of the globe must have known. I journeyed to Cairo and applied to him as soon as he arrived. My credentials—"

"Forged?" I inquired.

"I could hardly offer him genuine recommendations, now could I? The ones I produced were impressive, I assure you. He hired me on the spot. And that is how matters stood when he died. He did not know my identity, although . . ."

He hesitated. Feeling sure I knew what he was about to say, I finished the sentence for him. "You think he suspected? Well, that does not matter now. My dear Arthur, you must make a clean breast of this to the authorities. Admittedly it places you under grave suspicion of murder—"

"But there is no evidence of murder," Arthur interrupted. "The police were satisfied that his lordship died a natural death."

He was correct; and his quickness to point out this minor flaw in my reasoning did not augur well for his innocence. However, unless I could prove *how* Lord Baskerville was murdered, there was no sense in asking *who* had murdered him.

"All the more reason for you to tell the truth," I insisted. "You must proclaim yourself in order to claim your inheritance—"

"Sssh!" Arthur clapped his hand over my mouth. The fear for my own safety, which had been forgotten in the interest of his narrative, now came back to me; but before I had time to experience more than a momentary alarm he went on in a whisper, "There is someone out there in the shrubbery. I saw movement—"

I pulled his hand from my mouth. "It is only Abdullah. I was not so foolish as to come alone. But he did not overhear—"

"No, no." Arthur rose to his feet and I thought he was about to rush out into the shrubbery. After a moment he relaxed. "It is gone now. But it was not Abdullah, Mrs. Emerson. It was slighter, and shorter— dressed in gauzy robes of snowy pallor."

I caught my breath. "The Woman in White," I gasped.

II

Before we parted I asked Arthur's permission to tell his story to Emerson. He agreed, probably because he realized I meant to do so with or without his approval. My suggestion that he go next day to Luxor to confess his true identity was rejected, and after some argument I had to admit that his reasoning had validity. The proper persons to receive this intelligence were, of course, the British authorities, and there was no one in Luxor of sufficient rank to deal with the matter, the consular agent being an Italian whose primary occupation was to supply Budge of the British Museum with stolen antiquities. Arthur promised he would accept Emerson's judgment as to what action he ought to take, and I promised I would assist him in any way I could.

They say confession is good for the soul. It had certainly improved Arthur's peace of mind. He went off with a springy step, whistling softly.

But oh, my own heart was heavy as I went to reassure my faithful Abdullah of my safety. I liked the young man—not, as Emerson claims, because he was a handsome specimen of English manhood, but because he was kind and amiable. However, I was unfavorably impressed with certain aspects of his character, which reminded me of his description of the charming ne'er-do-well who had sired him. The levity he had displayed concerning his forged credentials, the immature folly of his romantic scheme of gaining his uncle's regard, and other things he had said indicated that his good mother's influence had not overcome the shallowness he had inherited from the paternal side. I wished him well; but I was afraid his plausible story was only an attempt to win my goodwill before the truth came out, as it inevitably would when he claimed his title.

I found Abdullah concealed (more or less) behind a palm tree. When I questioned him about the apparition in white, he denied having seen anything. "But," he added, "I was watching you, or rather the dark place into which you went; never did I take my eyes away. Sitt Hakim, there is no need to tell Emerson of this."

"Don't be such a coward, Abdullah," I replied. "I will explain that you did your best to stop me."

"Then will you strike me hard on the head so I may have a bruise to show him?"

I would have thought he was joking, but although Abdullah does have quite a sense of humor, this was not the sort of joke he would be likely to make.

"Don't be ridiculous," I said.

Abdullah groaned.

III

I could hardly wait to tell Emerson I had solved the murder of Lord Baskerville. Of course there were a few small details to be worked out, but I felt sure that if I applied myself seriously to the matter I would soon discover the answers. I meant to begin working on it that very night, but unfortunately I fell asleep before I could arrive at any conclusions.

My first thought on awakening was a renewal of concern over Emerson's safety. Reason assured me that the household would have been roused if there had been a disturbance; but affection, never susceptible to logic, hastened my preparations to proceed to the Valley.

Early as I was, Cyrus Vandergelt was already in the courtyard when I emerged from my room. For the first time I saw him in his working costume, instead of one of the snowy linen suits he habitually wore. His tweed jacket was as beautifully tailored as his other clothes; it bore little resemblance to the shabby garments in which Emerson was wont to attire himself. On his head

the American wore a military-looking solar kepi with
a band of red, white, and blue ribbon. He doffed this
with a flourish when he saw me and offered his arm to
escort me to the breakfast table.

Lady Baskerville seldom joined us at this meal. I had
heard the men speculating on her need for prolonged
rest; but of course I knew she spent the time on her toilette, for the artificial perfection of her appearance was
obviously the result of hours of work.

Imagine my surprise, therefore, when we found the
lady already at her place. She had not taken the time
that morning to make up her face, and consequently
she looked her age. Shadows circled her heavy-lidded
eyes, and there were lines of strain around her mouth.
Vandergelt was so struck by her appearance that he
exclaimed with concern. She admitted that her night's
sleep had been disturbed and would have elaborated
had not Milverton—or rather, Arthur Baskerville—
rushed in full of apologies for having overslept.

Of all the persons in the room he, the guilty man,
alone appeared to have had a refreshing, dreamless
rest. The looks of smiling gratitude he kept shooting
at me assured me he had quite cast off his melancholy.
It was another demonstration of the immaturity that
had already struck me; having confessed to an older,
wiser individual, he now felt completely relieved of
responsibility.

"Where is Miss Mary?" he asked. "We ought not
linger; I am sure Mrs. Emerson is anxious to see her
husband."

"Attending on her mother, I suppose," Lady Baskerville replied, in the sharp tone she always employed

when referring to Madame Berengeria. "I cannot imagine what you were thinking of, to allow that dreadful woman to come here. Since the damage is done, I must accept it, but I absolutely refuse to be left alone in the house with her."

"Come with us," Vandergelt suggested. "We'll fix you up a nice little place in the shade."

"Thank you, my friend, but I am too tired. After what I saw last night…"

Vandergelt rose to the bait, expressing concern and demanding details. I summarize the lady's reply, for it was replete with gasps and sighs and theatrical descriptions. Stripped of these meaningless appendages, it was simple enough. Unable to sleep, she had gone to the window and seen the now notorious white-clad apparition gliding through the trees. It had disappeared in the direction of the cliffs.

I looked at Arthur and read his intentions in his ingenuous countenance. The young idiot was on the verge of exclaiming that we had also seen the White Lady—which would have brought out the whole story of our midnight meeting. It was necessary to stop him before he could speak. I kicked out under the table. In my haste I missed my object and administered a sharp blow on Mr. Vandergelt's calf. This served the purpose, however; his shout of pain and the ensuing apologies gave Arthur time to recollect himself.

Vandergelt continued to beg Lady Baskerville to join us, and, when she refused, offered to stay with her.

"My dear Cyrus," she said, with an affectionate smile, "you are burning to get to your nasty, dirty tomb. Not for the world would I deprive you of this opportunity."

A prolonged and foolish discussion ensued; it was finally decided that Arthur would stay with the ladies. So Vandergelt and I started out and at the last minute Mary joined us, breathless and apologetic. Made even more anxious by the delay, I set a pace that even the long-legged American was hard pressed to match.

"Whoa, there, Mrs. Amelia" (or perhaps it was "Gee"—some American cattle term, at any rate). "Poor little Miss Mary is going to be all tuckered out before she starts working. There's no cause for alarm, you know; we'd have heard by this time if some early bird had found the Professor weltering in his gore."

Though the thought was meant to be comforting, I did not think it particularly well expressed.

After a night spent apart I expected that Emerson would greet me with some degree of enthusiasm. Instead he stared at me blankly for a moment, as if he could not remember who I was. When recognition dawned, it was immediately followed by a scowl.

"You are late," he said accusingly. "You had better get to work at once; we are far ahead of you, and the men have already turned up a considerable number of small objects in the rubble."

"Have they?" Vandergelt drawled, stroking his goatee. "Doesn't look too salubrious, does it, Professor?"

"I said before that I suspected the tomb had been entered by robbers in antiquity," Emerson snapped. "That does not necessarily mean—"

"I get you. How about letting me have a gander at what has been done? Then I promise I'll get to work. I'll even tote baskets if you want."

"Oh, very well," Emerson said in his most disagreeable manner. "But be quick."

No one but the most fanatical enthusiast would have found the effort of inspection worthwhile, for the interior of the passage, now cleared to a length of about fifteen metres, had reached an unbelievable degree of discomfort. It sloped sharply down into abysmal and stifling darkness lighted only by the wan glow of lanterns. The air was foul with the staleness of millennia, and so hot that the men had stripped off all their garments except those required by decency. Every movement, however slight, stirred up the fine white dust left by the limestone chips with which the corridor had been filled. This crystalline powder, clinging to the men's perspiring bodies, gave them a singularly uncanny appearance; the pallid, leprous forms moving through the foggy gloom resembled nothing so much as reanimated mummies, preparing to menace the invaders of their sleep.

Partially concealed by the rough scaffolding, the procession of painted gods marched solemnly down into the darkness. Ibis-headed Thoth, patron of learning, Maat, goddess of truth, Isis and her falcon-headed son Horus. But what caught my attention and made me forget the extreme discomfort of heat and stifling air was the pile of rubble. In the beginning this had entirely closed the passageway. Now it had shrunk to a height barely shoulder high, leaving a gap between its top and the ceiling.

After a quick glance at the paintings, Vandergelt caught up a lantern and went straight to the pile of rubble. Standing on tiptoe, I peered over his arm as he moved the light forward, over the top of the pile.

The debris sloped sharply downward from that point on. In the shadows beyond the lantern rays loomed a solid mass—the end of the passageway, blocked, as the entrance had been, by a barrier of stone.

Before either of us could comment, Emerson made a commanding gesture and we followed him out into the vestibule at the foot of the stairs. Wiping dust from my streaming brow, I gazed reproachfully at my husband.

"So this is the true explanation for your decision to remain on guard last night! How could you, Emerson? Have we not always shared the thrill of discovery? I am cut to the quick by your duplicity!"

Emerson's fingers nervously stroked his chin. "Peabody, I owe you an apology; but honestly, I had no intention of stealing a march on you. What I said was true; from now on the tomb is in imminent peril of being robbed."

"And when have I shrunk from the prospect of peril?" I demanded. "When have you sunk to the contemptible practice of attempting to shield me?"

"Quite often, actually," Emerson replied. "Not that I often succeed; but really, Peabody, your inclination to rush headlong where angels fear to tread—"

"Hold on," Vandergelt interrupted. He had removed his hat and was methodically wiping the sticky dust from his face. He seemed unaware of the fact that this substance, which, when mixed with perspiration, took on the consistency of liquid cement, was running down into his goatee and dripping off the end.

"Don't get into one of your arguments," he went on.

"I don't have the patience to wait till you finish fighting. What the hades is down there, Professor?"

"The end of the passageway," Emerson answered. "And a well or shaft. I couldn't cross it. There were a few scraps of rotten wood, the remains of a bridge or covering—"

"Brought by thieves?" Vandergelt asked, his blue eyes alert.

"Possibly. They would have come prepared for such pitfalls, which were common in tombs of the period. However, if they did find a door at the far end, there is no sign of it now—only a blank wall surface painted with a figure of Anubis."

"Humph." Vandergelt stroked his goatee. This action produced a stream of mud that ran down the front of his once-neat coat. "Either the door is hidden behind the plaster and paint, or the wall is a blind alley and the burial chamber lies elsewhere—perhaps at the bottom of the shaft."

"Correct. As you see, we have quite a few more hours' work ahead of us. We must test every foot of the floor and ceiling carefully. The closer we get to the burial chamber, the greater the chance of encountering a trap."

"Then let us get to work," I cried excitedly.

"Precisely what I have been suggesting," Emerson replied.

His tone was decidedly sarcastic, but I decided to overlook it, for there was some excuse for his behavior. My brain teemed with golden visions. For the moment archaelogical fever supplanted detective fever. I was actually at work, sifting the first portion of rubble, before I remembered I had not told Emerson of Arthur's confession.

I assured myself that there was no need for haste. Emerson would undoubtedly insist on finishing the day's work before returning to the house, and Arthur had agreed to take no action until we had had a chance to confer. I decided to wait until the noon break before confiding in Emerson.

Jealous persons might claim, in the light of later events, that this was an error of judgment on my part. I cannot see it this way. Only another Cassandra, gifted or cursed with the ability to foresee the future, could have predicted what transpired; and if I *had* had a premonition, I could not possibly have convinced Emerson to act on it.

Proof positive of this assertion is given by his reaction when I did tell him about my conversation with Arthur. We had gone to eat our frugal meal and rest for a while under the canvas canopy that had been erected to shelter me from the sun's rays while I worked. Mary was below, attempting to trace the most recently uncovered paintings. The only time she could work was while the men were resting, for the clouds of dust their feet stirred up made vision, much less breathing, virtually impossible. Needless to say, Karl was in attendance upon her. Vandergelt had wolfed down his food and returned at once to the tomb, which exerted a powerful fascination over him. Emerson would have followed had I not restrained him.

"I must tell you of my conversation with Arthur last night," I said.

Emerson was grumbling and trying to free his sleeve

from my grasp. This statement had the effect of catching his attention.

"Curse it, Amelia, I ordered you not to leave our room. I ought to have known Abdullah wasn't man enough to stop you. Just wait till I get my hands on him!"

"It was not his fault."

"I am well aware of that."

"Then stop fussing and listen to me. I assure you, you will find the story interesting. Arthur confessed—"

"Arthur? How friendly you have become with a murderer! Wait a moment—I thought his name was Charles."

"I call him Arthur because if I were to use his last name and title it would be confusing. His name is not Milverton."

Emerson flung himself down on the ground with a look of bored patience, but when I reached the climax of my story he abandoned his efforts to appear disinterested.

"Good Gad," he exclaimed. "If he is telling the truth—"

"I am sure he is. There would be no reason for him to lie."

"No—not when the facts can be checked. Doesn't he realize what an extremely awkward position this places him in?"

"He certainly does. But I have persuaded him to make a clean breast of it. The question is, to whom should he tell his story?"

"Hmmm." Emerson drew his feet up and rested his forearms on his knees while he considered the question.

"He must show proof of his identity if he wants to establish his claim to the title and estate. We had better communicate directly with Cairo. They will certainly be surprised."

"To find him here, yes. Though I feel sure his existence, as the next heir, is known to whatever government persons concern themselves with such matters. I wonder I did not think of that myself. For, of course, Lord Baskerville's heir would be the most logical suspect."

Emerson's heavy brows drew together. "He would be, if Lord Baskerville's death *was* murder. I thought you had concluded that Armadale was the criminal."

"That was before I knew Milverton's—I mean Arthur's—real identity," I explained patiently. "Naturally he denies having killed his uncle—"

"Oh, he does?"

"You would hardly expect him to admit it."

"*I* would not; *you* did, if you recall. Ah, well; I will talk with the young fool tonight—or tomorrow—and we will see what steps ought to be taken. Now we have wasted enough time. Back to work."

"I feel we ought to act on this matter without delay," I said.

"I don't. The tomb is the matter that will not brook delay."

Her copy of the paintings completed, Mary returned to the house, and the rest of us resumed work. As the afternoon wore on, I found increasing numbers of objects in the rubble—potsherds and bits of blue faience, and many beads molded of the same glasslike substance. The beads were a nuisance, for they were very small, and I had to sift every cubic centimeter to make sure I had not missed any.

The sun declined westward, and its rays crept under my canvas canopy. I was still looking for beads when a shadow fell across my basket; looking up, I saw Mr. O'Connell. He doffed his hat with a flourish and squatted down beside me.

"Sure and it's a pity to see a lovely lady spoiling her hands and her complexion with such work," he said winsomely.

"Don't waste your Hibernian charm on me," I said. "I am beginning to think of you as a bird of ill omen, Mr. O'Connell. Whenever you appear, some disaster follows."

"Ah, don't be hard on a poor fellow. I'm not my usual cheery self today, Mrs. Emerson, and that's the truth."

He sighed heavily. I remembered my scheme to enlist this presumptuous young person in our cause, and moderated my sharp voice. "You have not managed to regain your place in Miss Mary's affections, then?"

"You're a canny lady, Mrs. E. Indeed she's still vexed with me, God bless her for a darling little tyrant."

"She has other admirers, you know. They leave her little time to miss an impertinent red-haired journalist."

"That's what I'm afraid of," O'Connell replied gloomily. "I have just come from the house. Mary refused even to see me. She sent a message telling me to take myself off or she would have the servants throw me out. I'm beaten, Mrs. E., and that's the truth. I want a truce. I'll accept any reasonable terms if you will help me make my peace with Mary."

I bowed my head, pretending to concentrate on my work, in order to hide my smile of satisfaction. Having been about to propose a compromise, I was now in the happy position of being able to dictate terms.

"What are you suggesting?" I asked.

O'Connell appeared to hesitate; but when he spoke the words poured forth so glibly that it was obvious he had already formulated his plan.

"It's the most charming of fellows I am," he said modestly. "But if I never see the girl, my charm is not of much use. If I were to be invited to stay at the house, now…"

"Oh, dear me, I don't see how I could possibly arrange that," I said in a shocked voice.

"There would be no difficulty with Lady Baskerville. She thinks the world of me."

"Oh, I've no doubt you can get round Lady Baskerville. Unfortunately Emerson is not so susceptible."

"I can win him over," O'Connell insisted.

"How?" I demanded bluntly.

"If, for instance, I promised to submit all my stories to him for approval before sending them to my editor."

"Would you really agree to that?"

"I hate like the very devil—excuse me, ma'am, my feelings got the better of me—I hate the idea. But I would do it to gain my ends."

"Ah, love," I said satirically. "How true it is, that the tender emotion can reform a wicked man."

"Say rather that it can soften the brain of a clever man," O'Connell replied morosely. He caught my eye; and after a moment the corners of his mouth curved in a rueful smile, devoid of the mockery that so often marred his expression. "You've got a bit of charm yourself, Mrs. E. I think you have a great deal of sentiment in your nature, though you try to hide it."

"Absurd," I said. "Take yourself off now, before Emerson discovers you. I will discuss your proposal with him this evening."

"Why not now? I am on fire to begin my wooing."

"Don't press your luck, Mr. O'Connell. If you come by the dig tomorrow at about this time, I may have good news for you."

"I knew it!" O'Connell exclaimed. "I knew a lady with a face and figure like yours could not be cruel to a lover!" Seizing me around the waist he planted a kiss on my cheek. I immediately seized my parasol and aimed a blow at him, but he skipped back out of reach. Grinning broadly and blowing me a kiss, the impertinent young man sauntered off.

He did not go far away, however; whenever I looked up from my work I saw him among the staring tourists. When his eyes met mine he would either sigh and press his hand to his heart or wink and smile and tip his hat. Though I did not show it, I could not help being amused. After an hour or so he evidently felt that his point had been made; he vanished from the scene and I saw him no more.

The molten orb of the sun was low in the west and the blue gray shadows of evening were cool on the ground when a cessation in the monotonous flow of loaded baskets made me sense that something had occurred. I looked up to see the crew file out of the tomb. Surely, I thought, Emerson cannot have dismissed them for the day; there is still an hour of daylight left. I went at once to see what had happened.

The heap of rubble had been considerably reduced. No longer did it consist solely of moderate-sized stones and pebbles. One end of a massive stone block was now visible. Emerson and Vandergelt stood by it, looking down at something on the floor.

"Come here, Peabody," said Emerson. "What do you think of this?"

His pointing finger indicated a brown, brittle object covered with limestone dust, which Vandergelt began to remove with a small brush.

Experienced in such matters, I realized immediately that the strange object was a mummified human arm—or rather the tattered remains of one, for a great deal of the skin was missing. The bared bones were brown and brittle with age. The patches of skin had been tanned to a hard leathery shell. By some strange quirk of chance the delicate fingerbones had been undisturbed; they seemed to reach out as if in a desperate appeal for air—for safety—for life.

CHAPTER
TEN

I was peculiarly moved by the gesture, though I realized it was only a fortuitous arrangement of skeletal material. However, sangfroid is necessary to an archaeologist, so I did not voice my sentiments aloud.

"Where is the rest of him?" I inquired.

"Under the slab," replied Vandergelt. "We seem to have here a case of poetic justice, Mrs. Amelia—a thief who was caught in the act in the most literal sense."

I looked up at the ceiling. The rectangular gap in the surface formed a pocket of deeper darkness. "Could it have been an accident?" I asked.

"Hardly," Emerson replied. "As we have learned to our sorrow, the rock here is dangerously brittle. However, the symmetrical shape of this block shows that it was deliberately freed from the matrix and balanced so that it would fall if a thief inadvertently disturbed the triggering mechanism. Fascinating! We have seen other such devices, Peabody, but never one so effective."

"Looks as if the slab is a couple of feet thick," Vandergelt remarked. "I opine there won't be much left of the poor rascal."

"Quite enough, however, to rattle our workmen," Emerson replied.

"But why?" I asked. "They have excavated hundreds of mummies and skeletons."

"Not under these particular circumstances. Could there possibly be a more convincing demonstration of the effectiveness of the pharaoh's curse?"

His last word echoed from the depths beyond: "Curse...curse..." and yet again the faintest murmured "curse..." before the final sibilant faded into silence.

"Hey, cut it out, Professor," Vandergelt said uneasily. "You'll have *me* gibbering about demons in a minute. What do you say we quit for the night? It's getting late, and this appears to be a sizable job."

"Quit? Stop, you mean?" Emerson stared at him in surprise. "No, no, I must see what is under the slab. Peabody, fetch Karl and Abdullah."

I found Karl sitting with his back against the fence, making a fair copy of an inscription. Urgent as Emerson's summons had been, I could not help pausing for a moment to admire the rapidity with which his hand traced the complex shapes of the hieroglyphic signs: tiny birds and animals and figures of men and women, and the more abstruse symbols derived from flowers, architectural shapes, and so on. So absorbed was the young man in his task that he did not notice my presence until I touched him on the shoulder.

With the aid of Karl and the reis we managed to lift the slab, though it was a delicate and dangerous procedure. By means of levers and wedges it was gradually raised and at last tipped back onto its side, exposing the remains of the long-dead thief. It was hard to think of those brittle scraps as having once been human. Even the skull had been crushed to fragments.

"Curse it, this is when we need our photographer," Emerson muttered. "Peabody, go back to the house and—"

"Be reasonable, Professor," Vandergelt exclaimed. "This can wait till morning. You don't want the missus wandering around the plateau at night."

"Is it night?" Emerson inquired.

"Permit that I make a sketch, Herr Professor," Karl said. "I do not draw with the grace and facility of Miss Mary, but—"

"Yes, yes, that is a good idea." Emerson squatted. Taking out a little brush, he began to clean the muffling dust from the bones.

"I don't know what you expect to find," Vandergelt grunted, wiping his perspiring brow. "This poor fellow was a peasant; there won't be any precious objects on his body."

But even as he spoke a brilliant spark sprang to life in the dust Emerson's brush had shifted. "Wax," Emerson snapped. "Hurry, Peabody. I need wax."

I moved at once to obey—not the imperious dictates of a tyrannical husband, but the imperative need of a fellow professional. Paraffin wax was among the supplies we commonly kept on hand; it was used to hold broken objects together until a more permanent adhesive could be applied. I melted a considerable quantity over my small spirit lamp and hastened back to the tomb to find that Emerson had finished clearing the object whose first glitter had told us of the presence of gold.

He snatched the pan from me, careless of the heat,

and poured the liquid in a slow stream onto the ground. I saw only flashes of color—blue and reddish orange and cobalt—before the hardening wax hid the object.

Emerson transferred the mass to a box and, with his prize in his hand, was persuaded to stop work for the night. Abdullah and Karl were to remain on guard.

As we neared the house, Emerson broke a long silence. "Not a word of this, Vandergelt, even to Lady Baskerville."

"But—"

"I will inform her in due course and with the proper precautions. Curse it, Vandergelt, most of the servants have relatives in the villages. If they hear that we have found gold—"

"I get you, Professor," the American replied. "Hey—where are you going?" For Emerson, instead of following the path to the front gate, had started toward the back of the house.

"To our room, of course," was the reply. "Tell Lady Baskerville we will be with her as soon as we have bathed and changed."

We left the American scratching his disheveled head. As we climbed in through our window, I reflected complacently on the convenience of this entrance—and, less complacently, on its vulnerability to unauthorized persons.

Emerson lighted the lamps. "Bolt the door, Peabody."

I did so, and drew the curtains across the window. Meanwhile Emerson cleared the table and placed a clean white handkerchief on its surface. Opening the box, he carefully slid the contents out onto the kerchief.

His wisdom in using wax to fasten the broken pieces

together was immediately manifest. Crushed and dispersed as they were, they yet retained traces of the original pattern. Had he plucked them out of the dust one by one, any hope of restoring the object would have been lost.

It was a pectoral, or pendant, in the shape of a winged scarab. The central element was cut from lapis, and this hard stone had survived almost intact. The delicate wings, formed of thin gold set with small pieces of turquoise and carnelian, were so badly battered that their shape could only be surmised by an expert—which, of course, I am. Enclosing the scarab was a framework of gold which had held, among other elements, a pair of cartouches containing the names of a pharaoh. The tiny hieroglyphic signs were not incised in the gold, but inlaid, each small shape being cut out of a chip of precious stone. These were now scattered at random, but my trained eye immediately fell on an "ankh" sign shaped from lapis and a tiny turquoise chick, which represented the sound "u" or "w."

"Good Gad," I said. "I am surprised it was not crushed to powder."

"It was under the thief's body," Emerson replied. "His flesh cushioned and protected the jewel. When the flesh decayed the stone settled and the gold was flattened, but not smashed to bits as it would have been had the slab fallen directly onto it."

It was not difficult for my trained imagination to reconstruct the ancient drama, and its setting: the burial chamber, lighted only by the smoky flame of a cheap clay lamp, the lid of the great stone sarcophagus flung aside, and the carved face of the dead man staring enigmatically at the furtive figures that darted hither and thither, scooping up handfuls of jewelry, stuffing golden statues and bowls into the sacks they had brought for that purpose. Hardened men, these thieves of ancient Gurneh; but they could not have been entirely immune to terror, for one of them had flung the dead king's amulet over his head so that the scarab rested on his wildly beating heart. Fleeing with his loot, he had been caught by the trap, whose thunderous fall must surely have roused the cemetery guards. The priests, coming to restore the damage, had left the fallen monolith as a warning to future thieves; and indeed, as Emerson had said, no better proof of the disfavor of the gods could have been found.

With a sigh I returned to the present, and to Emerson, who was carefully restoring the object to the box.

"If we could only read the cartouche," I said. "The ornament must belong to the owner of our tomb."

"Ah, you missed that, did you?" Emerson grinned maliciously at me.

"Do you mean—"

"Of course I do. You are letting your feminine weakness for gold cloud your wits, Peabody. Use your brain. Unless you would like me to enlighten you—"

"That will not be necessary," I replied, thinking rapidly. "From the fact that the name and figure of the tomb owner have been hacked out, we may suppose that he was one of the heretic pharaohs—possibly even Akhenaton himself, if the tomb was begun in the early days of his reign before he left Thebes and forbade the worship of the old gods. However, the fragments of the remaining hieroglyphs do not fit his name. There is only one name that does fit...." I hesitated, hastily searching my memory. "The name of Tutankhamon," I concluded triumphantly.

"Humph," said Emerson.

"We know," I went on, "that the royal personages of—"

"Enough," Emerson said rudely. "I know more about the subject than you do, so don't lecture me. Please hurry and change. I have a great deal to do, and I want to get at it."

Ordinarily Emerson is as free of professional jealousy as any man can be, but occasionally he reacts badly when my wits prove to be sharper than his. So I let him sulk, and as I dressed I tried to remember what I knew of the pharaoh Tutankhamon.

Not much was known of him. He had married one of Akhenaton's daughters, but had not followed the heretical religious view of his father-in-law after he returned to Thebes. Though it would be an unparalleled thrill to discover any royal tomb, I could not help but wish we had found someone other than this ephemeral and short-reigned king. One of the great Amenhoteps or Thutmosids would have been much more exciting.

We found the others awaiting us in the drawing room. I really believe Emerson had forgotten about Madame Berengeria in the delight of his discovery. A stricken expression crossed his face when he beheld the lady's ample form, decked in its usual bizarre costume. But the others paid us little heed; even Madame was listening openmouthed to Vandergelt's dramatic description of the thief's remains. (He did not mention the gold.)

"Poor fellow," Mary said gently. "To think of him

lying there all these thousands of years, mourned by wife and mother and children, forgotten by the world."

"He was a thief and criminal who deserved his fate," said Lady Baskerville.

"His accursed soul writhes in the fiery pits of Amenti," remarked Madame Berengeria in sepulchral tones. "Eternal punishment...doom and destruction....Er, since you insist, Mr. Vandergelt, I believe I will take another drop of sherry."

Vandergelt rose obediently. Mary's lips tightened but she said nothing; no doubt she had long since learned that any attempt to control her mother only resulted in a strident argument. So far as I was concerned, the sooner the lady drank herself into a stupor, the better.

Lady Baskerville's black eyes flashed contemptuously as she gazed at the other woman. Rising, as if she were too restless to sit still, she strolled to the window. It was her favorite position; the whitewashed walls set off the grace of her black-clad figure. "So you believe we are nearing our goal, Professor?" she asked.

"Possibly. I want to get back to the Valley at first light tomorrow. From now on, our photographer's aid will be essential. Milverton, I want...But where the devil is he?"

How well I remember the premonitory chill that froze the blood in my veins at that moment. Emerson may scoff; but I knew instantly that something dreadful had happened. I ought to have observed at once that the young man was not with the others. My only excuse is that my archaeological fever was still in the ascendency.

"He is in his room, I suppose," Lady Baskerville

said casually. "I thought this afternoon that he looked feverish and suggested that he rest."

Across the width of the room Emerson's eyes sought mine. In his grave countenance I read a concern that matched my own. Some wave of mental vibration must have touched Lady Baskerville. She paled visibly and exclaimed, "Radcliffe, why do you look so strange? What is wrong?"

"Nothing, nothing," Emerson replied. "I will just look in on the young man and remind him we are waiting. The rest of you stay here."

I knew the order did not apply to me. However, Emerson's longer legs gave him an advantage; he was the first to reach the door of Milverton's room. Without pausing to knock he flung it wide. The room was in darkness, but I knew at once, by means of that sixth sense that warns us of another human presence—or its absence—that no one was there.

"He has fled," I exclaimed. "I knew he was weak; I ought to have anticipated this."

"Wait a moment, Amelia, before you jump to conclusions," Emerson replied, striking a match and lighting the lamp. "He may have gone for a walk, or . . ." But as the lamp flared up, the sight of the room put an end to this and every other innocent explanation.

Though not equipped with the degree of luxury that marked the quarters of Lord Baskerville and his lady, the staff rooms were comfortable enough; Lord Baskerville held, quite correctly in my opinion, that people could work more effectively when they were not distracted by physical discomfort. This chamber contained an iron bedstead, a table and chair, a wardrobe and chest of drawers, and the usual portable offices, chastely concealed behind a screen. It was in a state of shocking disarray. The wardrobe doors stood open, the drawers of the dresser spilled garments out in utter confusion. In contrast, the bed was made with almost military precision, the corners of the spread tucked in and the folds falling neatly to the floor.

"I knew it," I groaned. "I had a feeling of..."

"Don't say it, Peabody!"

"...of impending doom!"

"I asked you not to say that."

"But perhaps," I went on, more cheerfully, "perhaps he has not fled. Perhaps the disorder is the result of a frantic search—"

"For what, in God's name? No, no; I am afraid your original idea is correct. Curse the young rascal, he has a ridiculously large wardrobe, doesn't he? We shall never be able to determine whether anything is missing. I wonder..."

He had been rummaging through the strewn garments as he spoke. Now he kicked the screen away and examined the washbasin. "His shaving tackle is still here. Of course he may have had an extra set, or planned to purchase replacements. I confess it begins to look bad for the new Lord Baskerville."

A sharp cry from the doorway betokened the presence of Lady Baskerville. Her eyes wide with alarm, she leaned on the arm of Mr. Vandergelt.

"Where is Mr. Milverton?" she cried shrilly. "And what did you mean, Radcliffe, by your reference to... to..."

"As you see, Milverton is not here," Emerson replied.

"But he is not...that is to say, his real name is Arthur Baskerville. He is your late husband's nephew. He promised to go to the authorities today, but it looks as if he—Here—look out, Vandergelt—"

He jumped to assist the American; for on hearing the news Lady Baskerville had promptly fainted, in the most graceful manner imaginable. I watched in aloof silence as the two men tugged at the lady's limp form; finally Vandergelt won out, and lifted her into his arms.

"By Jimminy, Professor, tact is not your strong point," he exclaimed. "Was that the truth, though, about Milverton—Baskerville—whoever he is?"

"Certainly," Emerson replied haughtily.

"Well, this has sure been a day of surprises all around. I'll just take the poor lady to her room. Then maybe we'd better have a little council of war, to decide what to do next."

"I know what we ought to do next," Emerson said. "And I mean to do it."

Scowling in magisterial fashion, he strode to the door. Vandergelt vanished with his burden. I lingered, scanning the room in hopes of seeing a hitherto unnoticed clue. Though Arthur's cowardly flight had confirmed my suspicions of his guilt, I felt no triumph, only chagrin and distress.

Yet—why should he flee? That very morning he had seemed cheerful, relieved of his anxiety. What had happened in the intervening hours to make him a fugitive?

I do not claim, nor have I ever claimed, any powers of spiritual awareness. Yet I will assert to this day that a cold wind seemed to touch my shrinking flesh. Something was amiss. I sensed it, even though none of the conventional senses confirmed my feeling of disaster. Again my eyes scanned the room. The wardrobe doors were open, the screen had been flung aside. But there was one place we had not searched. I wondered that I had not thought of it, since it was usually the first place I looked. Dropping to my knees beside the bed, I lifted the edge of the coverlet.

Emerson claims that I shrieked out his name. I have no recollection of doing so, but I must admit he was instantly at my side, panting from the speed with which he had returned.

"Peabody, my dear girl, what is it? Are you injured?" For he assumed, as he afterward told me, that I had collapsed or been struck to the floor.

"No, no, not I—it is he. He is here, under the bed...."

Again I raised the coverlet, which in my shock I had let fall.

"Good Gad!" Emerson exclaimed. He grasped the limp hand that had been my first intimation of young Arthur's presence.

"Don't," I cried. "He is still alive, but in dire straits; we dare not move him until we can ascertain the nature of his injury. Can we lift the bed, do you think?"

In a crisis Emerson and I act as one. He went to the head of the bed, I to the foot; carefully we lifted the bed and set it to one side.

Arthur Baskerville lay on his back. His lower limbs were stiffly extended, his arms pressed close to his sides; the position was unnatural, and horribly reminiscent of the pose in which the Egyptians were wont to arrange their mummified dead. I wondered if my appraisal had been too optimistic, for if he was breathing, there was no sign of it. Nor was there any sign of a wound.

Emerson slipped his hand under the young man's head. "No mystery about this," he said quietly. "He has been struck a vicious blow on the head. I fear his skull is fractured. Thank God you stopped me when I was about to drag him out from under the bed."

"I will send for a doctor," I said.

"Sit down for a moment, my love; you are as white as paper."

"Don't worry about me; send at once, Emerson, time may be of the essence."

"You will stay with him?"

"I will not leave his side."

Emerson nodded. Briefly his strong brown hand rested on my shoulder—the touch of a comrade and a friend. He had no need to say more. Again our minds were as one. The person who had struck Arthur Baskerville down had intended to commit murder. He (or she) had failed on this occasion. We must make sure he had no chance to try again.

II

It was past midnight before Emerson and I were able to retire to our room, and my first act was to collapse across the bed with a long sigh.

"What a night!"

"An eventful night indeed," Emerson agreed. "I believe it is the first time I ever heard you admit you had encountered a case that was beyond your skill."

But as he spoke he sat down beside me and began loosening my tight gown with hands as gentle as his voice had been sarcastic. Stretching luxuriously, I allowed my husband to remove my shoes and stockings. When he brought a damp cloth and began to wipe my face, I sat up and took it from his hand.

"Poor man, you deserve consideration too," I said. "After a sleepless night on a rocky bed you worked all day in that inferno; lie down and let me take care of you. I am better, indeed I am; there was no reason for you to treat me like a child."

"But you enjoyed it," Emerson said, smiling. I gave him a quick, tactile demonstration of my appreciation. "I did. But now it is your turn. Get into bed and try to snatch a few hours' sleep. I know that in spite of everything you will be up at daybreak."

Emerson kissed the hand with which I was wiping his brow (as I have had occasion to remark, he is amazingly sentimental in private), but slipped away from me and began pacing up and down the room.

"I am too keyed up to sleep, Peabody. Don't fuss over me; you know I can go for days without rest if need be."

In his rumpled white shirt, open down the front to display his muscular chest, he was again the man I had first adored in the desert wilds, and I watched him for a time in tender silence. I sometimes compare Emerson's physique to that of a bull, for his massive head and disproportionately wide shoulders do resemble that animal in form, as his fits of temper resemble it in disposition. But he has a surprisingly light and agile walk; when in motion, as on this occasion, one is rather reminded of a great cat, a stalking panther or tiger.

I was in no mood for sleep either. I arranged a pillow behind me and sat up.

"You have done all you could for Arthur," I reminded him. "The doctor has agreed to spend the night, and I fancy Mary will not leave him either. Her concern was very touching. It would be quite a romantic situation if it were not so sad. I am more sanguine than Dr. Dubois, though. The young fellow has a strong constitution. I believe he has a chance of recovery."

"But he will not be able to speak for days, if ever," Emerson replied, in a tone that told me romance and tragedy alike were wasted on him. "This is getting out of hand, Peabody. How can I concentrate on my tomb with all this nonsense going on? I see I must settle the matter or I will have no peace."

"Ah." I sat up alertly. "So you agree with the suggestion I made some time ago—that we must find Armadale and force him to confess."

"We must certainly do something," Emerson said gloomily. "And I admit that with Milverton-Baskerville out of the picture, Mr. Armadale is the leading suspect. Curse the fellow! I was prepared to let him escape justice if he would leave me alone, but if he persists in interfering with my work, he will force me to take action."

"What do you propose?" I asked. Of course I knew quite well what ought to be done, but I had decided it would be more tactful to let Emerson work it out for himself, assisted by occasional questions and comments from me.

"We will have to look for the rascal, I suppose. It will be necessary to enlist some of the Gurneh men for that job. Our people are not familiar with the terrain. I know some of these sly devils quite well; in fact, there are a few old debts owing me which I now intend to call in. I had been saving them for an emergency. Now, I believe, the emergency has come."

"Splendid," I said sincerely. Emerson is always surprising me. I had no idea he was so unscrupulous, or that his acquaintance with the criminal element of Luxor was so extensive—for his reference to old debts, I felt sure, must refer to the trade in forgeries and stolen antiquities which is always going on in this region. What he was proposing, in short, was a form of blackmail. I approved heartily

"It will take me all morning to arrange it," Emerson went on, continuing to pace. "These people are so cursed leisurely. You will have to take charge of the dig, Amelia."

"Of course."

"Don't sound so blasé. You will have to proceed with extreme caution, for fear of rockfalls and traps; and if you do find the burial chamber and enter it without me, I will divorce you."

"Naturally."

Emerson caught my eye. His frown turned to a sheepish smile, and then to a hearty laugh. "We don't make such a bad team, do we, Peabody? By the way, that costume you are wearing is singularly becoming; I am surprised that ladies haven't adopted it for daytime wear."

"A pair of drawers and a camisole, lace-trimmed though they are, would hardly constitute fitting daytime wear," I retorted. "Now don't try to change the subject, Emerson; we still have a great deal to talk about."

"True." Emerson sat down on the foot of the bed. Taking my bare feet in his hands, he pressed his lips to them in turn. My attempts to free myself were in vain; and, to be honest, I did not try very hard.

CHAPTER
ELEVEN

The following morning Arthur's condition was unchanged. He lay in a deep coma, barely breathing. But the mere fact that he had lived through the night was a hopeful sign. I finally forced the physician to admit this. He was a fussy little Frenchman with ridiculous waxed mustaches and a large stomach, but he had quite a reputation among the European colony of Luxor, and after I had questioned him I was forced to admit that he seemed to know the rudiments of his trade. We agreed, he and I, that a surgical operation was not called for at that time; the bone of the skull, though cracked, did not appear to be pressing on the brain. I was, of course, relieved at this, but it would have been most interesting to assist at such an operation, which was successfully performed by several ancient cultures, including the Egyptian.

In short, there was nothing we could do for Arthur but wait until nature performed her task, and since there was no good hospital closer than Cairo, it would have been folly to move him.

Lady Baskerville offered to do the nursing. She would

have been the logical person to assume the responsibility, but Mary was equally determined to tend the young man, and the argument became rather heated. Lady Baskerville's eyes began to flash and her voice took on the rasping quality indicative of rising temper. When summoned to settle the dispute, Emerson aggravated both ladies by announcing that he had already asked for professional assistance. The professional, a nun from a nursing order in Luxor, duly arrived; and although I have no sympathy with the idolatrous practices of Popery, the sight of the calm, smiling figure in its severe black robes had an amazingly comforting effect.

Emerson and I then set out for the Valley; for he could not bear to carry out his business with the Gurnawis without at least looking in on his beloved tomb. I had a hard time keeping up with him; he went loping along the path as if a few seconds' delay could be disastrous. I finally persuaded him to slow down because there were several questions I wanted to ask him. But before I could speak, he burst out, "We are so cursedly shorthanded! Mary won't be worth much today, she will be mooning over that worthless young man."

This seemed an auspicious time to introduce the proposal I had formed concerning Mr. O'Connell. Emerson responded more calmly than I had hoped.

"If that young——comes within six feet of me, I will kick him in the rear," he remarked.

"You will have to abandon that attitude. We need him."

"No, we don't."

"Yes, we do. In the first place, giving him the exclusive rights to report on our activities means that we can exercise control over what he writes. Moreover, we are increasingly short of able-bodied men. I include myself in that category, of course—"

"Of course," Emerson agreed.

"Even so, we are shorthanded. Someone ought to be at the house, with the women. The rest of us are needed at the dig. O'Connell knows nothing about excavation, but he is a sharp young fellow, and it would relieve my mind to know that a capable person was watching over the household. Mary is not incapable, I don't mean to imply that, but between her work at the tomb and her duties to her mother, she will have more than enough to do."

"True," Emerson admitted.

"I am glad you agree. After all, Armadale may strike again. You may think me fanciful, Emerson—"

"I do, Amelia, I do."

"—but I am worried about Mary. Armadale once proposed to her; he may yet cherish an illicit passion. Suppose he decides to carry her off?"

"Across the desert on his fleet white camel?" Emerson inquired with a grin.

"Your levity is disgusting."

"Amelia, you must overcome your ridiculous weakness for young lovers," Emerson exclaimed. "If Armadale is skulking in the mountains, he has a great deal more on his mind than making love to some chit of a girl. But I agree with your earlier remark. Why do you suppose I called in a professional nurse? The blow aimed at Milverton-Baskerville (curse these people who travel under assumed names) was meant to silence him forever. The attacker may try again."

"So that occurred to you, did it?"

"Naturally. I am not senile yet."

"It is not kind of you to expose the poor nun to the attentions of a murderer."

"I don't believe there is any danger until Milverton shows signs of returning consciousness—if he ever does. All the same, your proposal about O'Connell has some merit, and I am willing to consider it. However, I refuse to speak to that fiend of a journalist myself. You will have to make the arrangements."

"I will gladly do so. But I think you are a little hard on him."

"Bah," said Emerson. "The Egyptians knew what they were about when they made Set, the ancient equivalent of Old Nick, a redheaded man."

Our workmen had already arrived at the tomb. All of them, as well as Abdullah and Karl, were gathered around Feisal, the second in command, who was telling them about the attack on Arthur. Feisal was the best raconteur in the group, and he was going at it in great style, with furious gestures and grimaces. Our two guards, who of course had known nothing of the event until now, had forgotten their dignity and were listening as avidly as the men. Arabs greatly enjoy a well-told story and will listen over and over to a tale they know by heart, especially if it is narrated by a skilled storyteller. I suspected that Feisal had added a few embellishments of his own.

Emerson erupted onto the scene and the group hastily dispersed, except for Abdullah and Karl. The former turned to Emerson, stroking his beard in obvious agitation. "Is this true, Emerson? That liar"—with a contemptuous gesture at Feisal, who was pretending not to listen—"will say anything to get attention."

Emerson responded with an accurate description of what had happened. The widening of Abdullah's eyes and his increasingly rapid manipulation of his beard indicated that the bare facts were distressing enough.

"But this is terrible," Karl said. "I must to the house go. Miss Mary is alone—"

I tried to reassure him. The mention of Mr. O'Connell as the prospective protector of the ladies did not soothe the young German at all, and he would have continued to expostulate if Emerson had not cut the discussion short.

"Mrs. Emerson will be in charge today," he announced. "I will return as soon as I can; in the meantime you will, of course, obey her as you would me." And, with a forlorn glance into the depths of the tomb—the sort of a look a lover might have cast on his beloved as he took leave of her before a battle—he strode away, followed, I was distressed to observe, by a little tail of curiosity seekers and journalists, all shouting questions. My beleaguered husband finally snatched the bridle of a donkey from a surprised Egyptian, leaped onto the beast, and urged it into a trot. The cavalcade disappeared in a cloud of dust, with the infuriated owner of the beast leading the pursuit.

I looked in vain for the fiery-red head of Mr. O'Connell. I was surprised at his absence, for I felt sure that with his sources of information he had already heard of the latest catastrophe and would be eager to rush to Mary's side. The mystery was explained shortly thereafter when a ragged child handed me a note. I gave the messenger some baksheesh and opened the note.

"I hope you have been able to convince the Professor," it began abruptly. "If you haven't, he will have to evict me personally and by force. I have gone to the house to be with Mary."

Much as I deplored the young man's impetuosity, I could not but respect the depth of his devotion to the girl he loved. And it was certainly a relief to know that the able-bodied man we needed was on duty. With my mind at ease on this point—if on few others—I could turn my attention to the tomb.

The first order of business was to photograph the area we had uncovered the previous evening. I had caused Arthur's camera to be fetched to the tomb, since I felt perfectly confident that with a little study I could operate it. With the help of Karl I set up the apparatus. Mr. Vandergelt, who arrived at about that time, was also useful. We took several exposures. Then the men were set to removing the remains, which included a number of beads and bits of stone that had been overlooked. It was then necessary to remove the massive stone from the passageway. Its appearance outside caused a great buzzing and shoving among the sightseers. Two of them actually fell over the edge of the excavation into the stairwell and had to be removed, bruised and threatening legal action.

Now the way was clear for the removal of the remaining fill, but when I was about to direct the men to carry out this task, Abdullah pointed out that it was time for the noon rest. I was not averse to stopping; for I was becoming increasingly anxious about Emerson.

Do not suppose, reader, that because I have not expressed my fears they did not exist. To say that my husband was unpopular with the thieves' guild of Gurneh is to express a laughable understatement. Certain other archaeologists tacitly cooperate with these

gentry in order to have first chance at the illicit antiquities they dig up, but to Emerson an object ripped
from its location lost much of its historical value, and
it was often damaged by ignorant handling. Emerson
insisted that if people would not buy illicit antiquities,
the thieves would have no reason to dig. He was therefore anathema to the entrepreneurs of the trade on economic grounds, and personally—I think I have made it
clear that tact is not his strong point. I was fully cognizant of the risk he ran in approaching the Gurnawis.
They might decide not to pay blackmail but to remove
the blackmailer.

It was therefore with profound relief that I beheld the
familiar form striding vigorously toward me, brushing
away tourists as one might swat at gnats. The journalists followed at a respectful distance. I observed that the
man from the *Times* was limping, and hoped devoutly
that Emerson had not been responsible for his injury.

"Where is the donkey?" I inquired.

"How is the work going?" Emerson asked simultaneously.

I had to answer his question first or he would never
have answered mine, so I gave him a summary of the
morning's activities while he seated himself beside me
and accepted a cup of tea. When his speech was tempo-
rarily impeded by the medium of a sandwich, I repeated
my question.

Emerson stared blankly around him. "What donkey?
Oh—that donkey. I suppose the owner retrieved it."

"What happened at Gurneh? Did you succeed in
your mission?"

"We ought to be able to remove the rest of the fill

today," Emerson said musingly. "Curse it, I knew I had forgotten something—all that hullaballoo last night distracted me. Planks. We need more—"

"Emerson!"

"There is no need to shout, Amelia. I am sitting next to you, in case you failed to observe that."

"What happened?"

"What happened where? Oh," Emerson said, as I reached for my parasol. "You mean at Gurneh. Why, just what I had planned, of course. Ali Hassan Abd er Rasul—he is a cousin of Mohammed—was quite cooperative. He and his friends have already begun searching for Armadale."

"As simple as that? Come now, Emerson, don't assume that air of lofty competence, you know how it enrages me. I have been sick with worry."

"Then you weren't thinking clearly," Emerson retorted, holding out his cup to be refilled. "Ali Hassan and the rest have every incentive to do what I asked, quite aside from the—er—private matters we discussed to our mutual satisfaction. I offered a sizable reward for Armadale. Also, this search gives them a legitimate reason to do what they habitually do on the sly—prowl around the mountains looking for hidden tombs."

"Naturally I had thought of that."

"Naturally." Emerson smiled at me. He finished his tea, dropped the cup (he is almost as hard on crockery as he is on shirts) and rose to his feet. "Back to work. Where is everyone?"

"Karl is sleeping. Now, Emerson," I added, as his brows drew together in a scowl, "you can hardly expect the young man to watch all night and work all day.

Vandergelt returned to the house for luncheon. He wanted to make sure everyone was all right and get the latest news about Arthur."

"He wanted to lunch in comfort and bask in Lady Baskerville's smiles," Emerson snapped. "The man is a dilettante. I suspect him of desiring to steal my tomb."

"You suspect everyone of that," I replied, picking up the pieces of the broken cup and packing away the remainder of the food.

"Come along, Amelia, you have wasted enough time," Emerson said and, shouting for Abdullah, he bounded away.

I was about to resume my labors when I saw Vandergelt approaching. He had taken advantage of the opportunity to change his clothes and was wearing another immaculately tailored set of tweeds, of which he seemed to have an endless number. Leaning on my parasol, I watched him stride toward me, and wondered what his real age might be. In spite of his graying hair and lined, leathery face he walked like a young man, and the strength of his hands and arms was remarkable.

Seeing me, he raised his hat with his usual courtesy. "I am glad to report that all is well," he said.

"You mean that Lady Baskerville has not yet murdered Madame Berengeria?"

The American looked at me quizzically and then smiled. "That British sense of humor! To tell you the truth, Mrs. Amelia, when I got there the two ladies were squaring off like prizefighters. I had to play peacemaker, and I flatter myself I did it neatly. I suggested that Madame intercede with the gods of Egypt and beg them to spare young Arthur's life. She jumped on that like a duck on a June bug. When I left she was squatting in the middle of the parlor crooning to herself and making mystical gestures. It was sure a horrible sight."

"There is no change in Arthur's condition?" I asked.

"No. But he is holding his own. Say, Mrs. Amelia, I have to ask you—did you really tell that young rapscallion O'Connell he could move in? He was buttering up to Lady Baskerville for all he was worth, and when I asked him why he was there, he told me you had given him permission."

"That will not please Lady Baskerville. I assure you, Mr. Vandergelt, I had no intention of impinging on her prerogatives. Emerson and I felt that under the circumstances—"

"I get you. And I've got to admit I felt easier leaving the ladies there with him. He's a scoundrel, but I think he would be a good man in a fight."

"Let us hope it does not come to that," I said.

"Sure . . . . All right, ma'am, let's get to work before the Professor comes out and accuses me of making eyes at you. I have to confess that I'm torn between my duty to Lady Baskerville and my interest in the tomb. I'd sure hate to miss the opening of the burial chamber."

In this latter hope he was doomed to disappointment, for that day at least. By late afternoon the men had carried out the last of the limestone fill and the corridor lay clear before us. They then withdrew, to enable the dust to settle, and the four of us gathered at the edge of the well.

Emerson held a lantern whose dust-fogged light cast eerie shadows across the faces of the men—Vandergelt, considerably more disheveled but no less excited than he had been four hours earlier; Karl, showing the signs of sleeplessness in his sunken eyes and weary face; Emerson, alert and energetic as ever. I was conscious of not looking my best.

"It's not so wide," Vandergelt remarked, appraising the width of the shaft. "I reckon I could jump it."

"I reckon you won't," said Emerson, with a scornful look at the speaker. "You might clear the gap, but where would you land? The space is less than a foot wide and it is backed by a sheer wall."

Advancing to the rim of the pit he lay flat, with his head and shoulders protruding over emptiness, and lowered the lantern as far as his arm would reach. The dim flame burned bluer. The air in those deep recesses was still bad, for there was no circulation, and in the depths of the shaft it was even worse. Though I had immediately followed Emerson's example, I could make out very few details. Far below, at the utmost extremity of the light, was a pale amorphous glimmer—more of the omnipresent limestone chips, so many tons of which he had already removed from the tomb.

"Yes," Emerson said, when I had voiced this observation. "The shaft is partially filled. The upper part was left open in the hope that a thief would tumble into it and break his bones." Rising, he directed the light toward the far wall. There, in ominous dignity, the jackal-headed guide of the dead raised his hands in greeting.

"You see, Amelia, and gentlemen, the options open to us," Emerson said. "The continuance of the passageway is concealed. Either it lies behind that figure of Anubis, on the far wall, or it is on a lower level, opening out from the depths of the shaft. Obviously we must investigate both possibilities. We can do neither tonight. I must have a clear copy of the figure of Anubis before we bring in planks to bridge the gap and begin chopping away at the wall. To investigate the shaft we will need ropes, and it would be advisable for us to wait for the air to clear a little more. You saw how blue the lamp burned."

"Shucks," Vandergelt exclaimed. "Listen here, Professor, I'll take my chances down there; you've got some ropes here, just you lower me down and I'll—"

"*Aber nein*, it is the younger and stronger who will descend," Karl exclaimed. "Herr Professor, let me—"

"The first person to descend will be myself," Emerson said, in a tone that silenced further comment. "And that will be tomorrow morning." He looked hard at me. I smiled, but did not speak. It was obvious that the lightest person in the group should be the one to make the descent, but there would be time to discuss that later.

After a moment Emerson cleared his throat. "Very well, we are agreed. I propose that we stop for the day and make an early start tomorrow. I am anxious to learn how matters are going at the house."

"And who will be on guard tonight?" Vandergelt asked.

"Peabody and I."

"Peabody? Who is—oh, I see. Now look here, Professor, you wouldn't cheat on me, would you? No fair you and Mrs. Amelia going ahead with the work tonight."

"May I remind you that I am the director of this expedition?" Emerson said.

When he speaks in that tone it is seldom necessary for him to speak twice. Vandergelt, a man of strong personality, recognized a stronger, and fell silent.

However, he dogged our footsteps all the way back, and it was impossible for me to speak privately to my husband, as I had hoped to do. My heart had leaped with exultation at hearing him name me the partner of his watch, and the decision had confirmed my hunch that he meant to do more than watch. Whom else could he trust as he trusted me, his life and professional partner? His decision to stop work early made excellent sense; so long as there was light, of sun or moon, the tomb was safe. The ghouls of Gurneh, like other evil creatures of the night, worked only in darkness. When the moon set behind the hills the danger began; and by then, perhaps, we would have penetrated the secret of the pharaoh.

Although this thought roused me to the highest pitch of archaeological excitement, never believe I neglected my duties. I went first to the chamber where Arthur lay. The silent, black-garbed figure of the nun might not have moved since morning. Only the faint clack of the beads that slipped through her fingers showed she was a living woman and not a statue. She did not speak when I asked about the patient, only shook her head to indicate there had been no change.

Madame Berengeria was next on my agenda. I decided it would be more convenient for everyone if she were safely tucked away for the night before I left. I assumed she was still in the parlor communing with the gods, and as I walked in that direction I pondered how my aim might best be achieved. A wholly contemptible and unworthy idea occurred to me. Dare I confess it? I have vowed to be completely honest, so, at the risk of incurring the censure of my readers, let me admit that I contemplated making use of Madame's weakness for drink to render her inebriated and unconscious. If those who would condemn me had faced the situation that confronted me, and had seen the dreadful woman in action, they would, I daresay, be more tolerant of this admittedly reprehensible plan.

I was spared the necessity of acting, however. When I reached the room in question, I found that Berengeria had anticipated me. The sound of her rasping snores was audible at some distance; even before I saw her sprawled in an ungainly and indecent heap on the carpet, I knew what had happened. An empty brandy bottle lay by her right hand.

Lady Baskerville was standing over her, and I trust I may not be accused of malice if I remark that one of the lady's dainty slippers was lifted as if in preparation for a kick. Seeing me, she hastily lowered her foot.

"Abominable!" she exclaimed, her eyes flashing. "Mrs. Emerson, I insist that you remove this dreadful woman from my house. It was an act of extreme cruelty to bring her here when I am in such a state of nerves, worn by grief—"

"Let me point out, Lady Baskerville, that the decision was not mine," I broke in. "I fully sympathize with your viewpoint; but we can hardly send her back to Luxor in this condition. How did she get at the brandy? I thought you kept the liquor cabinet locked."

"I do. I suppose she managed to get at the keys; drunkards are amazingly cunning when it comes to feeding their weakness. But good heavens, what does it matter?" She raised her white hands to her breast and wrung them vigorously. "I am going mad, I tell you!"

Her theatrics assured me that she had a new audience, for she knew I was impervious to that approach; I was therefore not surprised to see Vandergelt enter.

"Holy Jehoshaphat," he said, with a horrified look at the snoring mound on the floor. "How long has she been like that? My poor girl." Here he clasped the hand Lady Baskerville had extended, and pressed it tenderly in his.

"We must take her to her room and lock her in," I said. "Do you take her head, Mr. Vandergelt; Lady Baskerville and I will take—"

The lady let out a plaintive scream. "You jest, Mrs. Emerson; surely you jest!"

"Mrs. Emerson never jokes about such things," said Vandergelt, with a smile. "If you and I refuse to help, she will do it alone—dragging the woman by her feet. Mrs. Emerson, I suggest we call one—or two, or three—of the servants. There is no hope of concealing the poor creature's condition, or preserving her reputation."

This procedure was duly carried out; and I went next to the kitchen to tell Ahmed that Emerson and I would be dining out. As I strode along, deep in thought, out of the corner of my eyes I caught a glimpse of something moving among the trees. A corner of pale fabric, like the blue zaaboots worn by Egyptian men, fluttered and disappeared.

It might have been one of our own people. But there had been something hasty and surreptitious about the darting movement. I therefore took a firm grip of my parasol and went in pursuit.

Since the night on the loggia with poor Arthur I had determined never to go abroad without this useful instrument. To be sure, I had not needed it then; but one never knew when an emergency might arise. I had therefore attached the parasol to my belt, by means of one of the hooks with which this article of clothing was supplied. This was occasionally inconvenient, for the shaft had a tendency to slip between my legs and trip me up; but better to bruise one's knees than be left defenseless in case of attack.

I moved quietly over the soft grass, taking cover when I could. Peeping out from behind a thorny bush, I beheld the form of a man in native garb behind another bush. After glancing around in a furtive manner that assured me he was up to no good, he glided serpentlike across the turf and passed through the doorway of a small building, one of the mud-brick auxiliary structures used for storage of tools. I caught a glimpse of his face as he glanced slyly over his shoulder, and a villainous countenance it was. A livid scar twisted his cheek and ran down into his heavy grizzled beard.

Normally the door of the storage shed was padlocked. Theft, or worse, was obviously the man's aim. I was about to raise the alarm when I realized that an outcry would warn the felon and enable him to escape. I decided I would capture him myself.

Dropping flat, in Red Indian style, I slid forward. I did not rise to my feet until I had reached the shelter of the wall, where I pressed myself flat. I heard voices within, and marveled at the effrontery of the thieves.

There were at least two of them—unless the original miscreant was talking to himself. They were speaking Arabic, but I could only make out an occasional word.

I took a deep breath and rushed into the hut, striking out with my parasol. I heard a grunt of pain as the iron shaft thudded against a soft surface. Hands seized me. Struggling, I struck again. The parasol was wrenched from my grasp. Undaunted, I kicked my attacker heavily on the shin, and was about to call out when a voice bade me cease. I knew that voice.

"What are you doing here?" I demanded somewhat breathlessly.

"I might echo that question," replied Emerson, in the same style. "But why ask? I know you are ubiquitous. I don't mind that, it is your impetuosity that distresses me. I believe you have broken my leg."

"Nonsense," I said, retrieving my parasol. "If you would condescend to inform me of your plans, these tiring encounters might be avoided, to our mutual benefit. Who is with you?"

"Allow me to present Ali Hassan Abd er Rasul," said Emerson. He finished the introduction in Arabic, referring to me as his learned and high-born chief wife—which would have been very flattering if his tone had not been so sarcastic. Ali Hassan, whom I now saw huddled in the corner, rolled his eyes till the whites showed, and made an extremely insulting remark.

"Son of a one-eyed camel and offspring of a deceased goat," I said (or words to that effect; the original Arabic is far too emphatic for decent English), "keep your infected tongue from comments about your betters."

Emerson amplified this statement at some length,

and Ali Hassan cowered. "I had forgotten that the honored Sitt has our language," he remarked. "Give me my reward and I will go."

"Reward!" I exclaimed. "Emerson, do you mean—"

"Yes, my honored chief wife, I do," Emerson replied. "Ali Hassan sent a message by one of the servants to meet him here. Why he won't come to the house I do not know and frankly I do not care; but he claims he has found Armadale. Of course I have no intention of paying him until I am sure."

"Where is Armadale?"

"In a cave in the hills."

I waited for him to go on, but he said no more; and as the silence lengthened, a shiver of comprehension ran through me.

"He is dead."

"Yes. And," Emerson said gravely, "according to Ali Hassan, he has been dead for quite some time."

CHAPTER
TWELVE

The declining sun thrust a long red-gold arm through the open doorway, lighting the shadowy corner where Ali Hassan crouched. I saw that Emerson was watching me quizzically.

"Throws your theories off a bit, doesn't it?" he inquired.

"I can hardly say at present," I replied. "'Quite a long time' is a rather indefinite term. But if it should prove that after all Armadale was already dead when the latest attack took place...No, that would really not surprise me; the alternative theory I had formulated—"

"Curse it, Amelia, have you the infernal gall to pretend..." Emerson cut the comment short. After a few moments of heavy breathing he bared his teeth at me. The expression was evidently meant to be a smile, for when he continued his voice was sickeningly sweet. "I will say no more; I don't want Ali Hassan to think we are at odds with one another."

"These Arabs do not understand Western means of expressing affection," I agreed, somewhat absently.

"Emerson, we must act at once. We face a dilemma of considerable proportions."

"True. Armadale's body must be brought back here. And someone must go to the tomb. It has never been more vulnerable than at this moment."

"Obviously we must divide forces. Shall I go after Armadale or guard the tomb?"

"Armadale," was the prompt reply. "Though I don't like to ask you, Peabody."

"You are giving me the less dangerous task," I said, much moved by the expression on Emerson's face as he looked at me. But there was no time for sentiment. With every passing moment the sun sank lower in the west.

Ali Hassan grunted and got to his feet. "I go now. You give me—"

"Not until you have taken us to the body of Armadale," Emerson answered. "The Sitt will go with you."

An avaricious gleam brightened Ali Hassan's eyes. He began to whine about his advanced age and state of exhaustion. After some bargaining he accepted Emerson's offer of an additional fifty piasters to lead me to the cave. "And," Emerson added, in a soft, menacing growl, "you answer for the Sitt's safety with your life, Ali Hassan. Should she suffer so much as a scratch, should a single hair be missing from her head, I will tear out your liver. You know I speak truly."

Ali Hassan sighed. "I know," he said mournfully.

"You had better go at once, Peabody," Emerson said. "Take Abdullah and one or two other men; and perhaps Karl—"

"Won't I do instead?" a voice inquired.

The sun set O'Connell's hair ablaze. Only his head was visible around the doorjamb, and that gave the impression of being ready to disappear at the slightest sign of hostility. His smile was as broad and cocky as ever, though.

"Humph," said Emerson. "I looked for you earlier, Mr. O'Connell."

"I thought I had better keep out of your way at first," the journalist replied. Emerson's mild tone had reassured him; he stepped out from behind the shelter of the wall, his hands tucked in his pockets. "I couldn't help overhearing," he went on.

"Grrr," said Emerson. (I assure you, there is really no other way of reproducing this sound.)

"Honestly." O'Connell's blue eyes widened. "And it's as well I did, now isn't it, Professor? You don't want Mrs. E. wandering off into the hills without a man to protect her."

"I don't need a man to protect me," I said indignantly. "And if I did, Abdullah would be more than adequate."

"To be sure, to be sure. You'd be a match for Cormac himself, ma'am, and that's the truth. Just let me come along now, for my own sake, like the sweet lady you are; and I swear by the gods of old Ireland that after I've written my story I'll bring it straight to you."

Emerson and I exchanged glances.

"What about Mary?" I inquired. "Will you leave her here, with Karl? He admires her very much, you know."

"She's still not speaking to me," O'Connell admitted. "But, don't you see, this is the story of the year! 'New Victim of the Pharaoh's Curse! Our correspondent on the scene! The Courage of Mrs. Emerson, parasol in hand!'" Emerson growled again at this. I confess I found it rather amusing.

After a moment Emerson said grumpily, "Very well. O'Connell, fetch Abdullah. Ask him to bring the necessary equipment—ropes, lanterns—and meet us here in ten minutes, with two of his best men."

Grinning from ear to ear like an Irish Brownie, O'Connell rushed off. Heedless of the staring Ali Hassan, Emerson caught me in a fond embrace.

"I hope I shan't regret this," he muttered. "Peabody, take care."

"And you." I returned his embrace. "Go now, Emerson, before darkness falls to endanger us even more."

II

It was, of course, impossible to organize an expedition of that nature in ten minutes; but scarcely half an hour had passed before Abdullah arrived with the required supplies. His grave face was its usual copper mask, but I knew him well enough to sense a deep perturbation, and the behavior of the two men he had selected to accompany us was even more revealing. They looked like prisoners being led to execution.

"Do they know what we seek?" I whispered to Abdullah.

"I could not keep the redheaded man silent," Abdullah replied, with a hostile glance at O'Connell. "Sitt Hakim, I fear—"

"So do I. Let us go, quickly, before they have time to think and become more afraid."

We set out, with Ali Hassan slouching along ahead. O'Connell also seemed subdued; his eyes constantly darted from side to side, as if he were taking note of the surroundings for the story he would later write.

Ali Hassan led us directly to the cliffs behind Deir el Bahri. Instead of taking the path that led to the Valley of the Kings, he went south and soon began to climb, scrambling over the jagged rocks with the agility of a goat. I rejected O'Connell's attempts to assist me. Thanks to my parasol and my training I was in far better shape than he, and he was soon forced to use both hands in the climb. Abdullah came close behind me. I could hear him muttering, and although I could not make out the words I fancied I knew what was bothering him. Ali Hassan seemed to choose, deliberately, the most difficult path. At least twice I saw easier ways of ascent than the ones he selected.

At last, however, we reached the top of the plateau, and the going became easier. If we had had leisure to enjoy it, the view was spectacular. The broad reach of the river was stained crimson by the setting sun. The eastern cliffs were washed in soft shades of pink and lavender. Above them the sky had darkened to cobalt, with a few diamond points of starlight showing. But this view lay behind us. Ali Hassan headed toward the west, where the sun hung suspended, a swollen orb of fiery copper. Before long it would set and darkness would rush in like a black-winged bat; for there is little twilight in these climes. I tried to remember when the moon was due to rise. This part of the plateau was unfamiliar to me: an uninhabited wilderness of barren rock cut by innumerable cracks and fissures. It would make for dangerous walking after dark, even with the aid of the lanterns we had brought.

O'Connell was in some distress, having cut his hand rather badly during the climb. Since time was of the essence, I had not paused to attend him, except to wrap a handkerchief around the injured member. Abdullah was now close behind me, his quickened breathing betraying his agitation. He had ample cause for concern—the natural dangers of the terrain, the possibility of ambush, and the uneasiness of our own men, fearful of night demons and efreets.

Trotting along several feet ahead of me, Ali Hassan was singing, or keening, to himself. He showed no signs of fearing the supernatural terrors of the night; and indeed a man who practiced the sinister trade of robbing the dead might not be expected to be susceptible to superstition. His good spirits had precisely the opposite effect on me. Whatever pleased Ali Hassan was likely to prove unpleasant for me. I suspected he was deliberately leading us astray, but without proof I could hardly accuse him.

My eyes were fixed on the tattered robe of Ali Hassan, alert for the first sign of treachery; I did not see the creature until it brushed against my ankle. One's first thought, in that region, is of snakes; automatically I took a quick sideward step, catching Mr. O'Connell off balance, so that he went sprawling. Reaching for my parasol, I turned to confront the new danger.

The cat Bastet perched atop a nearby boulder. It had leaped out of my way, as I had leaped away from it, and its outraged expression showed how little it approved of my rude greeting.

"I beg your pardon," I said. "But it is your own fault; you ought to give notice of your approach. I trust I have not hurt you."

The cat only stared; but Ali Hassan, who had come back to see why we had stopped, invoked the name of Allah in a voice fraught with emotion.

"She speaks to the cat," he exclaimed. "It is a demon, a spirit; and she is its mistress." He turned so quickly that his robe ballooned out; but before he could flee I hooked him around the neck with the crook of my parasol.

"We have played this game long enough, Ali Hassan," I said. "You have been leading us in circles. The cat, who is indeed the spirit of the goddess Sekhmet, came to tell me of your treachery."

"I thought as much," Abdullah growled. He tried to seize hold of Ali Hassan. I waved him away.

"Ali Hassan knows what Emerson will do to him if I report this. Now, Ali, take us directly to the place—or I will send the cat goddess to tear you in your sleep."

I released the miscreant and Abdullah moved forward ready to seize him if he tried to run. But there was no need. Ali Hassan stared wild-eyed at the cat, who had leaped down from the rock and was standing by my side, its tail lashing ominously.

"She was there, when I found the dead man," he muttered. "I should have known then. I should not have tried to strike her with a stone. O Sekhmet, lady of terror, forgive this evildoer."

"She will if I ask her," I said pointedly. "Lead on, Ali Hassan."

"Why not?" Ali shrugged fatalistically. "She knows the way; if I do not lead, she will show you."

When we went on Abdullah accompanied Ali Hassan, his big hand firmly clamped over the Gurneh man's arm. Ali Hassan sang no more.

"How did you know?" O'Connell asked respectfully. "I had no suspicion at all."

"I simply acted on my suspicions, knowing the man's character; and he was stupid enough to confess."

"You are a wonder, ma'am, and that's the truth," O'Connell exclaimed.

I smiled in acknowledgment of the compliment, well deserved though it was. "Hurry, Ali Hassan," I called. "If darkness falls before we reach the cave…"

The cat had disappeared, almost as if, having completed her mission, she had no need to stay. Ali Hassan's pace increased. I was not at all surprised to see that our path now led eastward, in the direction from which we had come. The lower rim of the sun dipped below the horizon. Ali Hassan broke into an undignified trot, his blue robe flapping. Our shadows rushed along before us, elongated gray-blue shapes like the protective *kas* of the ancient Egyptians.

Though the lengthening shadows made it easier to see obstructions in the path, it was necessary to keep a sharp lookout to avoid falling. I was aware that our general direction was eastward, but because I had to watch my footing I did not realize where we were heading until Ali Hassan came to a stop.

"We are here, oh, Sitt Hakim," he said, between pants. "We have come to the place and the sun is not down; I have done what you asked. Tell this man to take his hands from me and assure the divine Sekhmet that I have obeyed her command."

He had spoken the literal truth. A last thin crescent of fiery red marked the place where the sun had sunk. Dusk was gathering fast. Not until I raised my eyes from the immediate surroundings did I realize that we were near the edge of the cliff, only a few hundred yards north of where we had ascended.

"Son of a rabid dog," snarled Abdullah, shaking Ali Hassan till his teeth rattled, "you have led us in a circle. There is no cave here. What trick are you playing?"

"It is here," Ali Hassan insisted. "I lost my way at first; anyone might lose his way; but we have come to the place. Give me my money and let me go."

Naturally we paid no attention to this ridiculous demand. I ordered the men to light the lanterns. By the time they had done so only a faint lingering afterglow relieved the black of the star-sprinkled heavens. In the lamplight Ali Hassan's malevolent countenance might have belonged to one of the night demons whose baleful influence he flouted so contemptuously. His open mouth was a cavern of darkness, ringed by rotting fangs of teeth.

Abdullah took a lantern and led the way, pushing our reluctant robber ahead of him. The path led down the cliff. It proved less hazardous than I had feared; but the descent was breathtaking enough, in almost total darkness and with an inexperienced companion. Poor Mr. O'Connell had lost his Gaelic joie de vivre; groaning and swearing under his breath he followed me down, and when the light shone on the bloodstained bandage that covered his hand I had to admire his courage, for I knew the injury must pain him considerably. We were close to the bottom of the cliff when Ali Hassan turned to one side and pointed.

"There. There. Now let me go."

Trained as I am, I would never have seen the opening without the aid of his pointing finger. The cliffs are so seamed by cracks and fissures, each one of which casts its own shadow, that only prolonged investigation can tell which leads to an opening. While Abdullah held the lantern—and Ali Hassan—I investigated the indicated crevice.

It was low and very narrow. My height is not much over five feet and I had to stoop in order to enter. Once under the rock lintel the space opened up; I could tell by the feel of the air that a cave lay before me, but it was as black as ink and I am not ashamed to admit that I had no intention of proceeding without light. I called to Abdullah to hand me the lantern. Advancing, I held it high.

Imagine a hollow sphere, some twenty feet in diameter. Bisect the sphere and close off the open section, leaving only a narrow slit for entrance. Such was the extent and the shape of the space I now beheld, though the interior was as jagged and rocky as a hollowed sphere would be smooth. These observations were made at a later moment; just then I had no eyes for anything but the object that lay crumpled on the floor at my feet.

It lay on its side, with its knees drawn up and its head back. The tendons in the bared throat looked like dried rope. One hand was so close to my shoe that I was almost treading on it. My hand was not as steady as it might have been; the tremor of the lantern I held made the shadows shift, so that the bent fingers seemed to clutch at my ankle.

I had seen photographs of Armadale, but if I had not known the body must be his I would not have recognized this ghastly face. In life the young man had been boyishly attractive rather than handsome, with a long, narrow face and delicate features that explained the Arabs' nickname for him. He had attempted to conceal the almost feminine structure of his face with a cavalry-style mustache. This facial adornment was now missing. A heavy lock of brown hair concealed the eyes, and I cannot say I was sorry for that.

As I stood attempting to control the uncharacteristic tremors that passed through my frame, an eerie event occurred. From the shadows at the back of the cave, pacing with slow dignity, came the cat Bastet. She walked to the head of the corpse and sat down, ears pricked, whiskers bristling.

Abdullah's increasingly agitated cries finally roused me from the paralysis that had taken hold of me. I called back a reassuring reply; and my voice, I think, was steady. But before summoning my faithful reis or the inquisitive young reporter, I knelt by the pitiful remains and made a brief examination.

The skull was intact and the visible parts of the corpse were without a wound. There was no blood. Finally I forced myself to brush the dry, lifeless hair from the forehead. No wound marred its tanned surface. But traced in flaking red paint was the rough sketch of a snake—the royal uraeus serpent of the pharaoh.

III

I cast a veil over the hour that followed, not, I assure
you, because the memory is intolerable—I have had
worse hours, many of them—but because so much happened in such a short time that a detailed description
would be interminably long.

Removing Armadale's body was not difficult, since
we were only fifteen minutes' walk from the house
and our efficient reis had brought along materials with
which to construct a makeshift litter. The difficulty
arose from the reluctance of the men to touch the body.
I knew both these persons well; in fact, I considered
them friends of mine. Never before had I seen them
daunted. Yet on this occasion it required all my elo-
quence to persuade them to do what was necessary; and
as soon as the remains had been deposited in an empty
storeroom the litter bearers fled as if pursued by fiends.

Ali Hassan watched them go with a cynical smile.
"They will work no more in the accursed tomb," he
said, as if to himself. "Fools they may be, but they are
wise enough to fear the dead."

"A pity you don't feel the same," I said. "Here is your
money, Ali Hassan; you do not deserve it, after playing us
such a trick, but I always keep my word. Remember this:
if you attempt to enter the tomb, or interfere with our
work, I will call down the wrath of Sekhmet upon you."

Ali Hassan burst into loud protestations, which did
not end until Abdullah started toward him with his fist
clenched. After the Gurneh man had left, Abdullah
said gravely, "I go to talk to my men, Sitt. The robber is

right; it will be hard to make them return to the tomb once this news gets out."

"A moment, Abdullah," I said. "I understand your reasoning, and agree with it; but I need you. I am going to the Valley. Emerson must know of this at once. It may be that Ali Hassan was delaying us in order to give his friends a chance to attack the tomb."

"I'll go with you," O'Connell said.

"Is it the journalist speaking, or the gentleman?" I inquired.

A flush spread over the young man's face. "I deserved that," he said, with unusual humility. "And I confess that my reporter's instincts yearn to observe the Professor's reaction when you tell him the latest news. But that is not my reason for wishing to be of service to you. Abdullah is needed here."

Under the cold moonlight the rocky cliffs might have been part of a lunar landscape, desolate of life for millions of years. We spoke little at first. Finally O'Connell let out a deep sigh.

"Is your hand paining you?" I inquired. "I apologize for not tending to your wound; concern for my husband must be my excuse."

"No, the wound, as you call it, is a mere scratch and does not trouble me. I am concerned about other things. Mrs. Emerson, this situation was only a journalistic sensation to me before—the greatest story of my life, perhaps. Now that I find myself acquainted with all of you, and increasingly attached to some of you, my viewpoint has changed."

"May I assume, then, that we have your whole-hearted cooperation?"

"You may indeed! I only wish I could do more to relieve you. How did that poor chap meet his end? So far as I could tell there was not a mark on him—just like Lord Baskerville."

"He may have died a natural death from hunger and thirst," I said cautiously. I was inclined to believe O'Connell's protestations, but he had tricked me too often to deserve my full confidence. "Remember," I went on, "you have promised to show me your stories. No more speculations about curses, if you please."

"I feel like Dr. Frankenstein," O'Connell admitted with a rueful laugh. "I have created a monster which has come to life. The curse was my own invention, and a wholly cynical one; I have never believed in such things. But how are we to explain—"

He did not finish the sentence. Breaking into his speech came the sharp crack of a gunshot.

In the silence the sound carried and echoed, but I knew whence it had come. Logic would have told me as much even if domestic affection had not sharpened my senses. I broke into a run. Another round of firing followed. Loosening my revolver from its holster and removing my parasol from its hook in order to prevent it from tripping me, I plunged down the slope into the Valley at a speed that would have been unsafe even in daylight. Perhaps it was my very velocity that prevented me from falling. My parasol in my left hand, my revolver in my right, I rushed on, firing the latter as I went. I shot most often into the air, I believe, though I would not care to take my oath on it; my aim was to assure the attackers that assistance was rapidly approaching.

I heard no more shots. What did the deadly silence presage? Victory for us, the robbers wounded or in flight? Or…But I refused to consider an alternative theory. Running ever faster I saw before me, pallid in the moonlight, the pile of limestone chips we had removed from the tomb. The opening itself was just ahead. There was no sign of life.

Then a dark form loomed up before me. Leveling my revolver, I pulled the trigger.

A click sounded as the hammer struck the empty chamber. The voice of Emerson remarked, "You had better reload, Peabody; you fired the last bullet some time ago."

"All the same," I said breathlessly, "it was very fool-hardy of you to step out in front of me."

"I assure you I would not have done so had I not counted the shots. I know your reckless temperament too well."

I was unable to reply. A belated realization of what I had done robbed me of my remaining breath. Although I knew Emerson had spoken the truth when he said he would not have faced me without the knowledge that my revolver was empty, I was sick with remorse and distress. Sensing my emotion, Emerson put his arm around me.

"Are you all right, Peabody?"

"I am sick with remorse and distress. Indeed, in the future I must endeavor to act more calmly. I believe the situation is affecting my nerves. Ordinarily I would never behave so foolishly."

"Humph," said Emerson.

"Truly, my dear Emerson—"

"Never mind, my dear Peabody. The panache with which you plunge headlong into danger is what first drew me to you. But devil take it, you didn't come alone, did you?"

"No, Mr. O'Connell is with me or he was. Mr. O'Connell?"

"Is it safe to come out now?" inquired the young man's voice.

"You heard me say her revolver is empty," Emerson replied.

"Hers, yes," said O'Connell, still invisible. "What about yours, Professor?"

"Don't be a coward, man! The danger is over; I fired a few warning shots to keep the rascals off. Though," Emerson added, smiling at me, "I might not have gotten off so easily had not Mrs. Emerson arrived, masquerading as an entire squad of policemen. She made enough noise for a dozen men."

"That was what I planned," I said.

"Ha," said Emerson. "Well, well; sit down, both of you, and tell me what you found."

So we took seats on the blanket he had spread out before the entrance to the tomb and I narrated the events of the evening.

A lesser man than Emerson might have exclaimed in horror at the dreadful experiences I had undergone— but then a lesser man would never have allowed me to face them. When I had finished my story he simply nodded.

"Well done, Peabody. I have no doubt that it was Ali

Hassan's band of burglars who attacked just now; if you had not caught on to his trick and forced him to move more quickly, you might not have arrived here in time to rescue me." I thought I detected a trace of amusement in the last words and looked at him suspiciously; but his face was quite serious, and so was his voice when he continued. "Never mind that; we have scared them off, for this evening at least. What interests me more is the news about Armadale. There was no indication of how he died?"

"None," I said.

"But there was the scarlet cobra on his brow," O'Connell said.

I gave the young man a hard stare. I had been careful to brush Armadale's hair back over his forehead before I allowed the others to enter the cave, and I had hoped this omen had escaped the reporter.

"Then," said Emerson, "we must face the probability that he was murdered, even though no signs of violence were visible. Furthermore, I cannot believe that the body would have reached the state you describe in less than three or four days. Who, then, was responsible for the attack on young Arthur?"

"Madame Berengeria," I said.

"What?" It was Emerson's turn to give me a hard stare. "Amelia, the question was rhetorical. You cannot possibly—"

"I assure you, I have been thinking of nothing else since I found Armadale. Who had an interest in his death? Who but the madwoman who clings like a leech to her daughter's youthful strength, and who would be loath to relinquish her to a husband? Mr. Armadale had proposed marriage to Mary—"

"The spalpeen!" Mr. O'Connell exclaimed. "Did he have the infernal gall to do that?"

"He was not the only one to find Miss Mary an object worthy of devotion," I retorted. "Is not jealousy one motive for murder, Mr. O'Connell? Would you commit the sin of Cain to win the woman you love?"

Mr. O'Connell's eyes popped. The moonlight drained all color from the scene; his face had the pallor of death— or guilt.

"Amelia," said my husband, grinding his teeth. "I beg you to control yourself."

"I have barely begun," I cried indignantly. "Karl von Bork is also a suspect. He also loves Mary. Don't forget that the other person who was murderously attacked is also an admirer of the young lady. But I consider Madame Berengeria the most likely person. She is mentally deranged, and only a mad person would commit murder for such a trivial reason."

Emerson clutched his hair with both hands and appeared to be trying to pull it out by the roots. "Amelia, you are arguing in circles!"

"Wait, now, Professor," O'Connell said thoughtfully. "I think Mrs. E. may be on to something. The only reason I've been allowed to be friends with Mary was because I pretended to admire her mother. The old—er—witch has frightened off a good many men, I can tell you."

"But murder!" Emerson exclaimed. "Curse it, Amelia, there are too many holes in your theory. The old—er—witch hasn't the figure or the stamina to go running around the Theban hills striking down strong young men."

"She may have hired assassins," I said. "I admit I have not worked out the idea in detail, but I hope to do so soon. There is no sense in discussing it further tonight; we all need rest."

"You always say that when I am winning an argument," grumbled Emerson.

I saw no reason to dignify this childish comment with a reply.

CHAPTER THIRTEEN

As soon as the first streaks of light blossomed in the eastern sky we were up and stirring. I had slept well, though of course I insisted on taking my turn to stand watch. Emerson was fairly twitching, he was so anxious to attack the tomb; but the presence of the journalist restrained him, and he reluctantly agreed that we had better return to the house and deal with the latest crisis before starting work. We left O'Connell on guard, promising to send a relief, and the last thing I saw as we climbed the path was his red head glowing with the rays of the rising sun. Emerson had locked the iron grille so that he would not be tempted to sneak into the tomb while we were gone.

Despite the grim tasks that awaited us I felt an upsurge of pleasure as we strode along hand in hand through the crisp morning air and watched the sky brighten to greet the rising majesty of the sun. The great god Amon Ra had survived another nightly journey through the perils of darkness, as he had done millions of times before and would continue to do long after we who watched this day's sunrise were dust and ashes. A humbling thought.

Such were my poetic and philosophical musings when Emerson, as is his habit, spoiled my mood with a rude remark.

"You know, Amelia, what you were saying last night was bloody nonsense."

"Don't swear."

"You drive me to it. Furthermore, it was irresponsible of you to discuss your suspicions in front of one of the major suspects."

"I only said that to shake him up a bit. I don't suspect Mr. O'Connell."

"Who is it this morning? Lady Baskerville?"

Ignoring the raillery in his voice, I replied seriously, "I cannot eliminate her from suspicion, Emerson. You seem to have forgotten that Lord Baskerville was the first to die."

"I seem to have forgotten? I?" Emerson sputtered for a few moments. "You were the one who insisted last night that jealousy on Miss Mary's account was the motive."

"I presented it as one possibility. What we have here, Emerson, is a series of murders, designed to cover up the real motive. We must first determine the principal murderee, if you will permit me to use that expression."

"I do not see how I can prevent you from doing so. Offensive as the expression is, it offends me less than the theory you propose. Are you seriously suggesting that two of the murderous attacks—three, if you include Hassan—were no more than camouflage, and that a killer is slaughtering people at random in order to cover his tracks?"

"What is so ridiculous about that? Murders are solved by determining the motive. The principal suspects are those who have most to gain by the victim's death. Here we have four victims—for I certainly do include Hassan—and, consequently, a confusing plethora of motives."

"Humph," said Emerson in a milder tone. He stroked his chin thoughtfully. "But Lord Baskerville was the first."

"And if he had died under ordinary circumstances, without all this nonsense about a curse, who would have been the major suspects? His heirs, of course—young Arthur (when he arrived to claim his inheritance) and Lady Baskerville. However, if my ideas are right, Lord Baskerville's was not the primary murder. That would be too obvious. It is more likely that the killer committed the first murder to confuse us, and that the principal murderee was Armadale or Arthur."

"Heaven help the world if you ever take to crime," Emerson said feelingly. "Amelia, the idea is so mad that it has a sort of insane seductiveness. It charms me, but it fails to convince me. No"—as I started to speak—"while I agree that in most cases motive is of great importance in solving a crime, I do not believe it will help us here. There are too many motives. The ones you have suggested pertaining to Lord Baskerville are only two of many possibilities. The fact that these events began after the discovery of a new royal tomb is surely significant. The local thieves, led by Ali Hassan, may have hoped Baskerville's death would halt work long enough to allow them to rob the tomb. The imam may have been moved by religious fervor to destroy the desecrator of the dead. Vandergelt seems to have designs on Lord Baskerville's wife as well as his excavation firman. An examination of the personal life of his lordship might turn up half a dozen other motives."

"True enough. But how do you explain Armadale's death and the attack on Arthur?"

"Armadale may have witnessed the murder and attempted to blackmail the killer."

"Weak," I said, shaking my head. "Very weak, Emerson. Why would Armadale run away and remain in hiding so long?"

"Perhaps he has not been in hiding. Perhaps he has been dead all this time."

"I don't think he has been dead for over a month."

"Well, we won't know until the doctor has examined him. Let us abjure speculation until we have more facts."

"Once we have the facts, we will not need to speculate," I replied smartly. "We will know the truth."

"I wonder," Emerson said morosely.

II

I had hoped to have time to bathe and change before facing the uproar that would result when Armadale's death became known to the others. Though I am accustomed to "roughing it," I had not changed my attire for almost twenty-four hours, and it showed the effects of the strenuous activities I had engaged in since. However, as soon as we entered the courtyard I knew that indulgence must be postponed again. The first thing to strike me was the unnatural silence. The servants ought to have been up and about their labors long since. Then I saw Mary running toward us. Her hair was disheveled and her eyes stained with tears. "Thank God you are here," she exclaimed.

"Steady, my dear," I said gently. "Is it Arthur? Has he—"

"No, I thank heaven; if anything, he seems a little better. But, oh, Amelia, everything else is so terrible...."

She seemed on the verge of breaking down, so I said firmly, "Well, my dear, we are here and you have nothing more to worry about. Come into the drawing room and have a cup of tea, while you tell us what has happened."

Mary's quivering lips shaped themselves into a valiant attempt at a smile. "That is part of the trouble. There is no tea—and no breakfast. The servants have gone on strike. One of them discovered poor Alan's body a few hours ago. The news spread rapidly, and when I went to the kitchen to order breakfast for the Sister, I found Ahmed packing his belongings. I felt I had to arouse Lady Baskerville, since she is his employer, and..."

"And Lady Baskerville promptly went into hysterics," I finished.

"She was not herself," Mary replied tactfully. "Mr. Vandergelt is talking with Ahmed, trying to persuade him to stay on. Karl has gone to the village to ascertain whether he can hire replacements—"

"Idiotic!" Emerson exclaimed. "He has no business going off like that without consulting me. Besides, it will prove a futile errand. Amelia, do you go and—er—persuade Ahmed to unpack. His decision will be an example to the others. I had planned to send Karl to relieve O'Connell; now I must send Feisal or Daoud. I will see them directly. First things first."

He started to stride away. Mary put out a timid hand. "Professor..." she began.

"Don't delay me, child, I have much to do."

"But, sir—your men are also on strike."

The words caught Emerson in midstride. His boot remained poised six inches off the ground. Then he lowered it, very slowly, as if he were treading on glass. His big hands clenched into fists and his teeth were bared. Mary gasped and shrank closer to me.

"Now calm yourself, Emerson, or one of these days you will have a stroke," I said. "We might have anticipated this; it would have happened days ago, if your charismatic personality had not influenced the men."

Emerson's mouth snapped shut. "Calm myself," he repeated. "Calm myself? I cannot imagine what leads you to suppose I am not calm. I hope you ladies will excuse me for a moment. I am going to speak calmly to my men and calmly point out to them that if they do not immediately turn out and prepare to go to work I will calmly knock them unconscious, one by one."

Whereupon he departed, walking with slow, stately strides. When I saw him open the door of our room I started to expostulate; then I realized he was taking the most direct route, through our room and out the window. I only hoped he would not step on the cat or smash my toilette articles as he proceeded on his single-minded path.

"It really astonishes me that the male sex is so completely devoid of a sense of logic," I said. "There is little danger of an attack on the tomb by daylight; Emerson might have waited until we had settled other, more pressing, matters. But, as usual, everything is left to me. Go back to Arthur's room, my dear. I will send someone to you with breakfast shortly."

"But," Mary began, her eyes widening. "But how—"

"Leave that to me," I said.

I found Mr. Vandergelt with Ahmed. The cook was squatting on the floor completely surrounded by the bundles that held his worldly possessions, including his prized cooking pots. His wrinkled face serene, he was staring pensively at the ceiling while Vandergelt waved fistfuls of American greenbacks at him.

When I left the kitchen, Ahmed was at work. I cannot claim all the credit; Ahmed's exaggerated disinterest had betrayed the fact that the sight of the money was beginning to affect him, and the salary he eventually agreed to accept was truly princely. But I flatter myself that my passionate appeals to honor, loyalty, and friendship had their effect.

Gracefully I disclaimed the compliments Mr. Vandergelt lavished on me, and asked him to carry the good news to Lady Baskerville. Then at last I was free to strip off my work-stained garments. I was relieved to find that the water jars in the bathroom were full. Much as I would have liked to prolong my immersion in the cool water, I made as much haste as I could, for although the immediate crisis had been resolved I felt sure other problems awaited me. I was half dressed when Emerson climbed in through the window and, without so much as a glance in my direction, walked into the bathroom and slammed the door.

I knew from his face that his mission had been unsuccessful. Though I yearned to comfort him I could not linger—nor, indeed, was he in any mood to accept condolences just then.

I went first to the dining room, where a waiter was arranging a tray of steaming dishes on the sideboard, and ordered him to prepare a tray and follow me to Arthur's room. When I entered, Mary rose from her chair with a cry of surprise.

"Have you convinced the servants to remain, then?"

"The strike is settled," I replied wittily. "Good morning, Sister."

The nun nodded benignly at me. Her round rosy face was as fresh as if she had had eight hours' sleep, and I observed there was not a drop of perspiration on her brow, despite her muffling garments. While she applied herself to her well-deserved breakfast, I examined my patient.

I saw at once that Mary's optimism was justified. The young man's face was still sunken, his eyes tightly closed; but his pulse was distinctly stronger. "He cannot continue without nourishment, however," I mused. "Perhaps some broth. I will have Ahmed boil a chicken. There is nothing as strengthening as chicken broth."

"The doctor suggested brandy," Mary said.

"The worst possible thing. Mary, go to your room and rest. If you go on this way you will fall ill yourself, and then what will I do?"

This argument halted the girl's objections. When she had gone, with a last lingering look at the still face of her lover, I sat down beside the bed. "Sister, I must speak frankly."

Again the nun nodded and beamed at me, but did not speak.

"Are you dumb?" I inquired sharply. "Answer, if you please."

The good woman's placid brow grew troubled. *"Quoi?"* she inquired.

"Oh, dear," I sighed. "I suppose you speak only French. A fine help you will be if Arthur awakens and tries to tell us what happened. Ah, well, we must do the best we can."

So, in the plainest possible terms, I explained the situation. From the startled look on the nun's face I saw that she had believed her patient to be the victim of an accident. No one had mentioned attempted murder, and alarm replaced her surprise as I pointed out that the murderer might return to try again.

"Alors," I concluded, *"vous comprenez bien, ma soeur,* that the young man must not be left alone for a single instant. Guard yourself as well. I do not think you are in danger, but it is possible that the villain may try to drug you so he can reach his victim. Touch no food that I have not brought you with my own hands."

"Ah, mon Dieu," the Sister exclaimed, reaching for her rosary. *"Mais quel contretemps!"*

"I could not have put it better myself. But you will not abandon us in our need?"

After a moment of struggle, the nun bowed her head. "We are all in the hands of God," she remarked. "I will pray."

"An excellent idea, so far as it goes," I replied. "But I suggest you also keep your eyes open. Do not be alarmed,

Sister, I am about to arrange for a guard. You can trust him completely."

On this errand I went, via my window, to the building where our men were housed. Several of them were lounging on the grass in carefree attitudes. At the sight of me they precipitately vanished inside the house. Abdullah alone remained, his back against a palm tree, a cigarette between his fingers.

"I am unworthy of your confidence, Sitt," he murmured, as I sat down beside him. "I have failed you."

"It is not your fault, Abdullah; the circumstances are extraordinary. I promise you, before many hours have passed Emerson and I will settle this case as we settled the other you know of, and will convince the men that these tragedies were also caused by human evil. I come now to ask a favor. Will the men help with the work at the house? I want someone to watch under the window of the sick man and protect him and the holy woman in black."

Abdullah assured me that the men would be glad to relieve their guilty consciences by assisting me in any way that did not directly involve the accursed tomb, and I found myself able to choose between a dozen volunteers. I selected Daoud, one of Abdullah's many nephews, and introduced him to the sister. With my mind at ease on that point, I could at last go to my breakfast.

Emerson was already at the table, attacking his bacon and eggs furiously. Karl had returned; sitting as far as possible from Emerson, he ate in timid little bites, his mustache drooping. I deduced that he had felt the sharp edge of Emerson's tongue, and felt sorry for him.

Vandergelt, always the gentleman, rose to hold a chair for me.

"Things are sure in a mess," he said. "I don't know how much longer we can go on this way. How is the patient today, Mrs. Amelia?"

"No change," I replied, helping myself to tea and toast. "I doubt that he will ever speak again, poor fellow. Where is Lady Baskerville?"

Scarcely had I spoken when the lady swept into the room. She was in dishabille—gray chiffon ruffles, sweeping flounces, her hair flowing around her shoulders. Seeing my astonished gaze, she had the grace to blush.

"Forgive my attire; my stupid maid has run away and I am too nervous to be alone. What are we to do? The situation is dreadful."

"Not at all," I replied, eating my toast. "Sit down, Lady Baskerville, and have some breakfast. You will feel better when you have eaten."

"Impossible!" Lady Baskerville paced up and down wringing her hands. She required only an armful of weedy flowers to make a somewhat mature Ophelia. Karl and Vandergelt followed her, trying to calm her. Finally she allowed herself to be helped to a chair.

"I cannot eat a mouthful," she declared. "How is poor Mr. Milverton—Lord Baskerville, I suppose I should say; I cannot take it all in. I tried to see him earlier, but was denied, most officiously. Mary had the effrontery to tell me, Radcliffe, that it was by your orders."

"I feared it would distress you," he replied coolly. "Rest assured that everything possible is being done.

It is little enough, I am sorry to say. Don't you agree, Amelia?"

"He is dying," I said bluntly. "I doubt that he will ever regain consciousness."

"Another tragedy!" Lady Baskerville wrung her long white hands, a gesture that displayed their slender beauty. "I can endure no more. Radcliffe, much as I regret the decision, I must bow to fate. The expedition is canceled. I want the tomb closed, today."

I dropped my spoon. "You can't do that! Within a week it will be stripped by robbers."

"What do I care for robbers or tombs?" Lady Baskerville cried. "What are ancient relics compared with human life? Two men have died, one lies near death—"

"Three men," Emerson said quietly. "Or do you not consider Hassan the watchman a human being? He was not much of a man, to be sure, but if he were the only victim I would still feel obliged to bring his murderer to justice. I intend to do that, Lady Baskerville, and I also intend to finish excavating the tomb."

Lady Baskerville's jaw dropped. "You can't do that, Radcliffe. I hired you and I can—"

"I think not," Emerson replied. "You begged me to take on the job and told me, if I recall correctly, that his lordship left funds with which to carry on the work. Furthermore, I have Grebaut's order appointing me archaeologist in charge. Oh, it may involve a long, complex legal battle, when all is said and done, but"—and his eyes sparkled wickedly—"but I enjoy battles, legal or otherwise."

Lady Baskerville took a deep breath. Her bosom swelled to alarming proportions. Vandergelt leaped to his feet. "Goldurn you, Emerson, don't you talk to the lady like that."

"Keep out of this, Vandergelt," Emerson said. "It is none of your affair."

"You just bet it is." Vandergelt moved to Lady Baskerville's side. "I have asked the lady to be my wife, and she has done me the honor to accept."

"A bit sudden, is it not?" I inquired, spreading marmalade on another piece of toast (my busy day and night had given me quite an appetite). "With your husband dead less than a month—"

"Naturally we will not announce our engagement until the proper time," Vandergelt said in shocked tones. "I wouldn't have told you folks if the situation had not been so perilous. This poor lady needs a protector, and Cyrus Vandergelt, U.S.A., is privileged to take that part. My dear, I think you ought to leave this cursed place and move to the hotel."

"I will obey your slightest wish, Cyrus," the lady murmured submissively. "But you must come with me. I cannot flee, leaving you in danger."

"That's right, Vandergelt, desert the sinking ship," Emerson said.

A look of embarrassment spread over the American's rugged features. "Now you know I'm not about to do that. No, sir; Cyrus Vandergelt is no four-flusher."

"But Cyrus Vandergelt is a dedicated archaeology buff," said Emerson mockingly. "Admit it, Vandergelt; you cannot tear yourself away until you know what lies beyond that wall at the end of the passageway. What is it to be, wedded bliss or Egyptology?"

I smiled quietly to myself, seeing the agonized

indecision that twisted the American's features. The hesitation did not flatter his promised bride (though I confess that, faced with a similar dilemma, Emerson might have hesitated too).

Lady Baskerville saw the signs of struggle on her fiancé's face and was too wise in the ways of the male sex to force him into a reluctant sacrifice. "If that is how you feel, Cyrus, of course you must stay on," she said. "Forgive me. I was distraught. I am better now."

She applied a dainty kerchief to her eyes. Vandergelt patted her shoulder distractedly. Then his face brightened.

"I have it! There is no need to make such a choice. At a time like this, convention must yield to necessity. What do you say, my dear girl—will you defy the world and be mine at once? We can be married in Luxor, and I will then have the right to be at your side day and—er—that is, at all times and in all places."

"Oh, Cyrus," Lady Baskerville exclaimed. "This is so sudden. I should not...and yet..."

"Congratulations," I said, seeing that she was about to yield. "I trust you will excuse us if we do not attend the ceremony. I expect to be occupied with a mummy at about that time."

With a sudden rush Lady Baskerville left her chair and flung herself at my feet. "Do not be harsh with me, Mrs. Emerson! Conventional minds may condemn me; but I had hoped that *you* would be the first to understand. I am so alone! Will you, a sister woman, abandon me because of an old-fashioned, senseless rule?"

Snatching my hands, toast and all, in hers, she bowed her head.

Either the woman was a consummate actress or she was genuinely distressed. Only a heart as hard as granite could be unmoved.

"Now, Lady Baskerville, you must not act this way," I said. "You are getting marmalade all over your sleeve."

"I will not rise until you say you understand and condone my decision," was the murmured response from my lap, where the lady's head had sunk.

"I do, I do. Please rise. I will be your matron of honor, or your flower girl, or I will give you away, whatever you wish; only stand up."

Vandergelt added his appeals, and Lady Baskerville consented to restore my hands and my crumbling toast. As she rose I caught the eye of Karl von Bork, who was watching in openmouthed astonishment. Shaking his head, he murmured low, *"Die Engländer! Niemals werde ich sie verstehen!"*

"Thank you," Lady Baskerville sighed. "You are a true woman, Mrs. Emerson."

"That's right," Vandergelt added. "You're a brick, Mrs. Amelia. I'd never have proposed this if matters weren't so doggoned desperate."

The door burst open and Madame Berengeria billowed in. Today she was enveloped in a tattered cotton wrapper and her wig was not in evidence. Her wispy hair, which I saw for the first time, was almost pure white. Swaying, she scanned the room with bloodshot eyes.

"A person could starve to death," she muttered. "Insolent servants—wretched household—where is the food? I require....Ah, there you are!" Her eyes focused on my husband, who pushed his chair back from the table and sat poised, ready for retreat. "There you are, Tut—Thutmosis, my lover!"

She rushed at him. Emerson slid neatly out of his chair. Berengeria tripped and fell face- or rather, stomach-down across the seat. Even I, hardened as I am, felt constrained to avert my eyes from the appalling spectacle thus presented.

"Good Gad," said Emerson.

Berengeria slid to the floor, rolled over, and sat up. "Where is he?" she demanded, squinting at the table leg. "Where has he gone? Thutmosis, my lover and my husband—"

"I suppose her attendant has run away with the other servants," I said resignedly. "We had better get her back to her room. Where on earth did she get brandy at this hour of the morning?"

It was a rhetorical question, and no one tried to answer it. With some difficulty Karl and Vandergelt, assisted by me, lifted the lady to an upright position and steered her out of the room. I sent Karl to seek out Madame's missing attendant, or any reasonable fac- simile thereof, and returned to the dining room. Lady Baskerville had left, and Emerson was coolly drinking tea and making notes on a pad of paper.

"Sit down, Peabody," he said. "It is time we had a council of war."

"Did you, then, succeed in convincing the men to return to work? You seem much more cheerful than you were earlier, and I am sure the admiration of Madame Berengeria is not the cause of your good humor."

Emerson ignored this quip. "I did not succeed," he replied, "but I have worked out a plan that may have the desired effect. I am going across to Luxor. I wish I could ask you to go with me, but I dare not leave the house unguarded by at least one of us. I can trust no one else. Too many matters hang on a sword's edge. Amelia, you must not leave young Baskerville unattended."

I told him what I had done, and he looked pleased. "Excellent. Daoud is dependable; but I hope you will keep a watchful eye out as well. Your description of the young man's worsening condition was designed to mislead, I hope?"

"Precisely. In actual fact he seems stronger."

"Excellent," Emerson repeated. "You must be on the qui vive, Peabody. Trust no one. I think I know the identity of the murderer, but—"

"What?" I cried. "You know—"

Emerson clapped a large hard hand over my mouth. "I will make the announcement myself, at the proper time," he growled.

I peeled his fingers from my lips. "That was unnecessary," I said. "I was only surprised at your statement, after you have consistently disclaimed any interest in the matter. In fact, I too have discovered the identity of the person in question."

"Oh, you have, have you?"

"Yes, I have."

We studied one another warily.

"Would you care to enlighten me?" Emerson inquired.

"No. I think I know; but if I am wrong you will never let me hear the end of it. Perhaps *you* will enlighten *me*."

"No."

"Ha! You are not sure either."

"I said as much."

Again we exchanged measuring glances.

"You have no proof," I said.

"That is the difficulty. And you—"

"Not yet. I hope to obtain it."

"Humph," said Emerson. "Peabody, please refrain from any reckless actions while I am away. I wish you could bring yourself to confide in me."

"Truly, Emerson, I would if I had anything useful to suggest. At the present time my suspicions are based on intuition, and I know how scornful you are of that; you have mocked me often enough. I promise that the moment I obtain concrete evidence I will tell you."

"Very well."

"You might return the compliment," I said pointedly.

"I will tell you what I will do. Let us both write down the name of the person we suspect and put it in a sealed envelope. When this is over, the survivor, if there is one, can see who was right."

I found this attempt at humor not at all amusing, and said so. We proceeded to do as Emerson had suggested, placing the sealed envelopes in a table drawer in our room.

Emerson then departed. I had hoped to have a few moments to myself, in order to jot down a few notes about the case and consider methods of obtaining the evidence I had spoken of. I was not given time for reflection, for one duty succeeded the next. After sending Karl to the Valley to relieve Mr. O'Connell I interviewed Dr. Dubois, who had come to visit Arthur.

When I suggested broth to strengthen the patient, his response was positively rude.

I then led the medical man to the building where Armadale's body had been placed. I was pleased to see that an attempt had been made to lend some dignity to the poor fellow's resting place. The body had been decently swathed in a clean white sheet and upon the breast of the still form lay a bouquet of flowers. I fancied that Mary must have supplied these, and regretted I had not been there to support the girl as she carried out this sad task.

Dubois was of no help whatever. His examination was cursory in the extreme; his conclusion was that Armadale had died of exposure—a perfectly ridiculous idea, as I pointed out. He was even more vague about the time of death. The atmospheric conditions that produced so many excellent mummies prevailed in the cave where Armadale had been found, so that desiccation rather than decay had affected the body. Dubois declared he had been dead no less than two days and no more than two weeks.

I then turned to the needs of the living, first ordering the chicken broth from Ahmed and then hastening to my room to carry out a task which had been too long delayed. Only the succession of unnerving incidents that had required all my attention had made me neglect this pressing duty. At least by waiting I had more hopeful news to send Arthur Baskerville's long-suffering mother. As I sat trying to compose a message that would be both peremptory and soothing, it occurred to me that I did not know Mrs. Baskerville's full name or address. After some thought I decided to send the message to the authorities in Nairobi; surely, with all the publicity attendant on Lord Baskerville's death, they would be able to locate his brother's widow.

Scarcely had I finished this task when I was summoned to the drawing room to assist Lady Baskerville in explaining to the police how Armadale's body had been discovered. After much fuss and bureaucratic delay the requisite documents were completed. Armadale had no living relatives, except for distant cousins in Australia. It was decided that he should be buried in the small European cemetery in Luxor, delay in this matter being both insanitary and unnecessary; and when Lady Baskerville showed signs of relapsing into sobs and sighs, I assured her I would make the necessary arrangements.

It was midafternoon before Emerson returned, and by then even my iron constitution was beginning to feel some strain, for in the meantime, in addition to the tasks I have described, I had visited the sick man and forced some broth down his throat, had interviewed Mr. O'Connell on his return from the Valley, dressed his injured hand and put him to bed, and had enjoyed an acrimonious argument with Madame Berengeria over the luncheon table. Like many drunkards, she had astonishing powers of recuperation; a few hours' rest completely restored her, and when she forced her way into the dining room she was again dressed in her appalling costume. The strong perfume she had poured over her frame did not entirely cover the unmistakable olfactory evidences of her lack of interest in the most rudimentary personal cleanliness. She had learned of Armadale's death, and her dire predictions of further disasters to come were interrupted only by intervals of munching and mumbling as she crammed food into her mouth. I did not blame Lady Baskerville for her precipitate departure from the table. Vandergelt followed, but I felt obliged to remain until Madame had eaten herself into a semistupor. My request that she return to her room revived her and was the cause of the argument, during the course of which she made a number of unwarranted personal remarks and asserted her intention of reclaiming her reincarnated lover, Thutmosis-Ramses-Amenhotep the Magnificent-Setnakhte.

When Emerson entered our room, by way of the window, he found me recumbent on the bed with the cat at my feet. He hastened to my side, dropping the armful of papers he was carrying.

"Peabody, my dear girl!"

"Everything is under control," I assured him. "I am a little tired, that is all."

Emerson sat down beside me and wiped the perspiration from his brow. "You cannot blame me for being alarmed, my love; I don't recall ever seeing you in bed during the daytime—to rest, that is. And," he added, with an amused glance at the sleeping cat, "you looked for all the world like a small Crusader on a tombstone with your faithful hound at your feet. What is the cause of this unusual weariness? Have the police been here?"

I gave him a succinct, well-organized summary of the events of the day.

"What a frightful time you have had," he exclaimed. "My poor girl, I only wish I could have been with you."

"Bah," I said. "You don't wish that at all. You are relieved to have missed all the fuss, particularly Madame."

Emerson smiled sheepishly. "I confess that the lady comes as close to throwing me off balance as any living creature—with the exception of yourself, my love."

"She is more appalling every day, Emerson. The ways of Providence are inscrutable, to be sure, and I would never dream of questioning its decree; but I cannot help but wonder why Madame Berengeria is allowed to flourish when good young men like Alan Armadale are cruelly cut off. It would be an act of positive benevolence to remove her from this world."

"Now, Amelia, be calm. I have something for you that will restore your equanimity; the first mail from home."

Shuffling through the envelopes I came upon a familiar hand and a sentiment long repressed, through stern necessity, would not be denied. "A letter from Ramses," I exclaimed. "Why did you not open it? It is addressed to both of us."

"I thought we could read it together," Emerson replied. He stretched out across the bed, his hands supporting his head, and I opened the envelope.

Ramses had learned to write at the age of three, disdaining the clumsy art of printing. His hand, though unformed, proclaimed the essentials of his character, being large and sprawling, with emphatic punctuation marks. He favored very black ink and broad-nibbed pens.

"'Dearest mama and papa,'" I read. "'I miss you very much.'"

Emerson let out a choked sound and turned his head away.

"Do not yield to emotion yet," I said, scanning the

next lines. "Wait till you hear his reasons for missing us. 'Nurse is very cruel and will not give me any sweets. Aunt Evelyn would, but she is afraid of Nurse. So I have not been to a sweetshop since you left and I think you were cruel and vishus [I reproduce Ramses' spelling literally] to leave me. Uncle Walter spanked me yesterday—'"

"What?" Emerson sat up. The cat, disturbed by his violent movement, let out a grumble of protest. "The wretch! How dare he lay hands on Ramses! I never thought he had it in him."

"Neither did I," I said, pleased. "Pray let me continue, Emerson. 'Uncle Walter spanked me yesterday only because I tore some pages out of his dikshunary. I needed to use them. He spanks very hard. I will not tear any more pages out of his dikshunary. Afterwards he taught me how to write "I love you, mama and papa," in hieroglyphs. Here it is. Your son, Ramses.'"

Together Emerson and I contemplated the untidy little row of picture signs. The signs blurred a trifle as I looked at them; but, as always when Ramses was concerned, amusement and irritation tempered sentimentality.

"How typical of Ramses," I said, smiling. "He misspells dictionary and vicious, but misses not a letter of hieroglyphs."

"I fear we have bred a monster," Emerson agreed, with a laugh. He began to tickle the cat under the chin. The animal, annoyed at being awakened, promptly seized his hand and began to bite it.

"What Ramses needs is discipline," I said.

"Or an adversary worthy of his steel," Emerson

suggested. He pried the cat's teeth and claws from his hand and studied the animal thoughtfully. "I have just had an inspiration, Amelia."

I did not ask what it was. I preferred not to know. Instead I turned to the rest of the mail, which included a long, loving letter from Evelyn reassuring me as to Ramses' health and happiness. Like the good aunt she was, she did not even mention the dictionary incident. Emerson opened his own mail. After a while he handed two items to me for perusal. One was a telegram from Grebaut, canceling Emerson's permission to excavate and demanding that he re-hire the guards he had dismissed. After I had read it Emerson crumpled it up and tossed it out the window.

The second item was a clipping from a newspaper, sent us by Mr. Wilbour. The story, under the byline of Kevin O'Connell, described in vivid detail not only the kicking of the reporter down the stairs of Shepheard's Hotel, but also the knife in the wardrobe. Mr. O'Connell's informant had played him false with the latter incident, however; the knife, "a bejeweled weapon worthy of being worn by a pharaoh," was said to have been found driven into the center of the bedside table.

"Wait till I get my hands on that young man," I muttered.

"At least he did not break his word," Emerson said with surprising tolerance. "This story was written some days ago, before we made our agreement. Do you want to change the name in that envelope, Amelia?"

It took me a moment to understand what he meant.

When I did, I replied, "Certainly not. Though this does raise a point I cannot yet explain. What about you?"

"My opinion is unchanged."

A low growl from the cat warned us that someone was approaching. A moment later there was a knock at the door. I opened it and admitted Daoud.

"The holy woman calls you to come," he said. "The sick man is awake and speaking."

"Curse it," Emerson exclaimed, shaking his fist in the astonished man's face. "Keep your voice down, Daoud. No one must know of this. Now get back to your post and hold your tongue."

Daoud obeyed and we proceeded, posthaste, to Arthur's room.

The Sister was bending over the sick man, as was Mary. Worn by illness as he was, it required both women's strength to keep him from sitting up.

"He must not move his head!" I exclaimed in alarm.

Emerson went to the bed. His big brown hands, so strong and yet so gentle, took hold of the injured member, immobilizing it. Arthur immediately left off struggling. So intense is the degree of animal magnetism Emerson projects that it seemed to flow through his fingers into the injured brain. Arthur opened his eyes.

"He is awake," Mary cried. "Do you know me, Mr. . . . . I mean, Lord Baskerville?"

But there was no awareness in the dazed blue orbs. If they focused at all, it was on some object high in midair, invisible to the rest of us.

I have always held that the various states of semiconsciousness, even deep coma, do not necessarily involve the complete cessation of sensation. The means of communication may be interrupted, but who is to say that the brain does not function or the ears do not hear? I therefore seated myself by the bed and approached my mouth close to the ear of the injured man.

"Arthur," I said. "It is Amelia Emerson who speaks to you. You have been struck down by an assailant as yet unknown. Have no fear; I am watching over you. But if you could possibly answer a question or two—"

"How the devil do you expect him to do that?" Emerson demanded, in the muted roar that passes, with him, for a whisper. "The poor chap has all he can do to continue breathing. Ignore her, Milverton—er—Baskerville."

Arthur paid no attention to either speech. He continued to stare raptly into space.

"He seems calmer now," I said to the nun, in French. "But I fear a repetition of this; should we tie him to the bed, do you think?"

The Sister replied that Dr. Dubois had predicted the possibility of such a violent awakening and had given her medicine to administer should it occur. "I was taken by surprise," she added apologetically. "It happened so suddenly; but do not fear, madame, I can deal with him."

Mary had collapsed into a chair, pale as...I was about to say "snow" or "paper" or one of the common comparatives; however, in strict accuracy I must say that a complexion as brown as hers could never turn ashy white. Her pallor was in reality a delicate shade of coffee well laced with milk; three quarters milk to one quarter coffee, let us say.

Suddenly we were all electrified at hearing a strange

voice. It was young Arthur's; but I identified it only because I knew it could belong to no one else. The soft, droning tone was totally unlike his normal speaking voice.

"The beautiful one has come....Sweet of hands, beautiful of face; at hearing her voice one rejoices...."

"Good Gad," Emerson exclaimed.

"Ssssh!" I said.

"Lady of joy, his beloved....Bearing the two sistrums in her two beautiful hands...."

We waited, after that, until my chest ached with holding my breath, but Arthur Baskerville spoke no more that day. His darkly stained lids closed over his staring eyes.

"He will sleep now," the nun said. "I give you felicitations, madame; the young man will live, I believe."

Her calm struck me as inhuman until I realized that she was the only one who had not understood a word. To her the patient had simply been babbling nonsense syllables, in his delirium.

Mary's reaction was inclined more toward confusion than the awestruck disbelief that had effected Emerson and me.

"What was he talking about?" she asked.

"Don't ask," Emerson said, with a groan.

"He was delirious," I said. "Mary, once again I am going to ask that you go to your room. It is ridiculous for you to sit here hour after hour. Touching, but ridiculous. Go and take a nap, or a walk, or talk to the cat."

"I second the motion," Emerson added. "Get some rest, Miss Mary; I may want you later this evening."

We escorted the girl to her room and then confronted one another with identical expressions of disbelief.

"You heard, Peabody," Emerson said. "At least I hope you did; if not, I was experiencing auditory hallucinations."

"I heard. They were the titles of Queen Nefertiti, were they not?"

"They were."

"Such tender phrases...I am convinced, Emerson, that they were the compliments of Khuenaten—excuse me, Akhenaton—to his adored wife."

"Amelia, you have an absolutely unparalleled talent for straying from the point. How the devil did that ignorant young man know those words? He told us himself that he was untrained in Egyptology."

"There must be a logical explanation."

"Of course there must. All the same—he sounded rather like Madame Berengeria in one of her fits, didn't he? Though his ravings were a great deal more accurate than hers."

"Curse it," I exclaimed, "he must have heard the titles from Lord Baskerville or Armadale at some time. They say the sleeping brain retains everything, though the waking mind cannot recall it."

"Who says?"

"I forget. I read it somewhere—one of those new-fangled medical theories. However farfetched it may be, it makes more sense than..."

"Precisely," Emerson agreed. "All that aside, Peabody, has it struck you that the young man's ravings may have a bearing on who murdered Lord Baskerville?"

"Naturally that aspect of the matter had not escaped me."

Emerson let out a roar of laughter and flung his arms

around me. "You are indestructible, Peabody. Thank God for your strength; I don't know what I would do without it, for I feel like an antique chariot driver trying to control half a dozen spirited steeds at once. Now I must be off again."

"Where?"

"Oh—here and there. I am arranging a little theatrical performance, my dear—a regular Egyptian *fantasia*. It will take place this evening."

"Indeed! And where is the performance to take place?"

"At the tomb."

"What do you want me to do? I don't promise," I added, "that I will do it; I simply ask."

Emerson chuckled and rubbed his hands together. "I rely on you, Peabody. Announce my intentions to Lady Baskerville and Vandergelt. If they wish to spend the night at the hotel, they may do so, but not until my performance is ended. I want everyone there."

"Including Madame Berengeria?"

"Humph," said Emerson. "As a matter of fact, yes; she might add a certain *je ne sais quoi*."

Alarm seized me. Emerson never speaks French unless he is up to something.

"You are up to something," I said.

"Certainly."

"And you expect me to submit tamely—"

"You have never submitted to anything tamely in your life! You will work with me, as I would with you, because we are as one. We know one another's minds. You suspect, I am sure, what I intend."

"I do."

"And you will assist me?"

"I will."

"I need not tell you what to do."

"I ... No."

"Then *à bientôt,* my darling Peabody."

He embraced me so fervently that I had to sit down on a bench for a few moments to catch my breath.

In fact, I had not the slightest idea what he meant to do.

When he rises to heights of emotional intensity Emerson can carry all before him. Mesmerized by his burning eyes and fervent voice, I would have agreed to anything he proposed, up to and including self-immolation. (Naturally, I never let him know he has this effect on me; it would be bad for his character.) Once he had departed I was able to think more calmly, and then, indeed, a glimmer of an idea occurred to me.

Most men are reasonably useful in a crisis. The difficulty lies in convincing them that the situation has reached a critical point. Being superior to others of his sex, Emerson was more efficient than most—and harder to convince. He had finally admitted that there was a murderer at large; he had agreed that the responsibility of identifying the miscreant was ours.

But what, in fact, was Emerson's chief concern? Why, the tomb, of course. Let me be candid. Emerson would cheerfully consign the entire globe and its inhabitants (with a few exceptions) to the nethermost pits to save one dingy fragment of history from extinction. Therefore, I reasoned, his activities of that evening must be designed to attain his dearest wish, the resumption of work on the tomb.

I am sure, dear reader, that you can follow my reasoning to its logical conclusion. Remember Emerson's fondness for playacting; bear in mind the regrettable susceptibility of all segments of the human race to crass superstition; stretch your imagination—and I have no doubts you will forward as eagerly as I did to Emerson's *fantasia*.

CHAPTER FOURTEEN

The moon was up when we set out on our journey to the Valley. It was on the wane, no longer a perfect silver globe; but it emitted enough light to flood the plain with silver and cast deep shadows across the road.

I would have preferred to lead our caravan over the lofty path behind Deir el Bahri, but such a walk would have been beyond Lady Baskerville's powers, and Madame Berengeria was also incapable of self-locomotion. Therefore I resigned myself to a prolonged and bumpy ride. I was the only one of the ladies who was sensibly dressed. Being unable to anticipate what might eventuate from Emerson's performance, I thought it best to be prepared for anything; so my working costume was complete, down to the knife, the revolver, and the parasol. Madame Berengeria was decked out in her decaying Egyptian costume; Lady Baskerville was a vision in black lace and jetty jewels; and Mary wore one of her shabby evening frocks. The poor child did not own a gown that was less than two years old. I wondered if she would be offended if I made her a present of the best Luxor had to offer. It would have to be done tactfully, of course.

Though I did not really believe Arthur was in any danger that evening, since all the suspects would be under my watchful eyes, I had taken the precaution of requesting Daoud to remain on guard at the window, with his cousin Mohammed at the door. They were not pleased at missing the *fantasia*, but I promised to make it up to them. I also told them the truth about Arthur's identity. I felt sure they already knew, since such news has a way of spreading, but they appreciated being taken into my confidence. As Daoud remarked, nodding sagely, "Yes; if he is rich, it is not surprising that someone should wish to kill him."

It was easier to arrange matters with my loyal men than to persuade the others to agree with my plans. Lady Baskerville at first refused to join the party; it had required all my persuasion, and that of Mr. Vandergelt, to convince her. The American was mightily intrigued and kept pestering me (as he put it) to give him a hint of what was going to transpire. I did not yield to his importunities, in order to maintain an air of mystery and suspense (and also because I was not sure myself).

Knowing that Emerson would appreciate any little dramatic touches I could add, I had mounted several of our men on donkeys and set them at the head of the procession with lighted torches in their hands. Any superstitious fears they may have had were overcome by anticipation, for Emerson had already spoken to them, promising them wonders and revelations. I suspected that Abdullah had some idea of what my husband meant to do, but when I asked him he only grinned and refused to answer.

As the carriages proceeded along the deserted road, the scene cast its spell on all our hearts; and when we turned into the narrow cleft in the cliffs I felt myself an intruder, pushing rudely into byways that rightfully belonged to the thronging ghosts of the past.

A great fire blazed before the entrance to the tomb. Emerson was there; and when he advanced to meet us I did not know whether to laugh or exclaim in astonishment. He wore a long flowing crimson gown and a most peculiar cap with a tassel on top. The cap and the shoulders of the robe were trimmed with fur; and although I had never seen this particular dress before, my familiarity with the academic world enabled me to deduce that it was the robe of a doctor of philosophy, probably from some obscure European university. It had obviously been designed for a much taller person, for as Emerson reached out to help me from the carriage, the full sleeves fell down and enveloped his hand. I assumed he had bought this amazing creation in one of the antiquities shops of Luxor, where a remarkable variety of objects is to be found; and although its effect on me, at least, was rather more productive of hilarity than awe, Emerson's complacent expression indicated that he was enormously pleased with the ensemble. Shaking back his sleeve, he took my hand and led me to one of the chairs that had been arranged in a semicircle facing the fire. Surrounding us on all sides was a sea of brown faces and turbans. Among the Gurnawis I saw two faces I recognized. One was that of the imam; the other was Ali Hassan, who had had the audacity to take up a position in the front row of the spectators.

The others took their chairs. No one spoke, though Vandergelt's lips were twitching suspiciously as he watched Emerson bustling about in his trailing finery. I had feared Madame Berengeria would be unable to resist the opportunity to make a spectacle of herself, but she sat down in silence and folded her arms across her breast like a pharaoh holding the twin scepters. The flames were beginning to die down, and in the growing gloom her bizarre costume was much more effective than it had been in the brightly lighted hotel. As I studied her somber and unattractive countenance I found a new source of uneasiness. Had I, after all, underestimated this woman?

With a loud "hem!" Emerson called us to attention. My heart swelled with affectionate pride as I looked on him, his hands tucked in his flowing sleeves like a Chinese mandarin, the silly cap perched on top of his thick black hair. Emerson's impressive presence invested even that absurd garb with dignity, and when he began to speak no one had the slightest inclination to laugh.

He spoke in English and in Arabic, translating phrase by phrase. Instead of making the audience impatient, this deliberate pace was all the more effective theatrically. He mocked the cowardice of the men of Gurneh and praised the courage and intelligence of his own men, tactfully omitting their recent lapse.

Then his voice rose to a shout that made his audience jump.

"I will tolerate this no longer! I am the Father of

Curses, the man who goes where others fear to tread, the fighter of demons. You know me, you know my name! Do I speak the truth?"

He paused. A low murmur responded to this peculiar jumble of ancient formulas and modern Arabic boasting. Emerson went on.

"I know your hearts! I know the evildoers among you! Did you think you could escape the vengeance of the Father of Curses? No! My eye can see in the blackness of night, my ear can hear the words you think but do not utter!"

He strode quickly back and forth, moving his arms in mystic gestures. Whenever his steps took him toward the staring crowd, those in the front ranks drew back. Suddenly he came to a complete standstill. One arm lifted, the forefinger rigid and quivering. An almost visible current of force emanated from this extended digit; the awestruck watchers fell back before it. Emerson bounded forward and plunged into the crowd. The blue and white robes undulated like waves. When Emerson emerged from the human sea he was dragging a man with him—a man whose single eye glared wildly in the firelight.

"Here he is," Emerson bellowed. "My all-seeing eye has found him where he cowered among his betters."

The surrounding cliffs flung his words back in rumbling echoes. Then he turned to the man he held by the throat.

"Habib ibn Mohammed," he said. "Three times you have tried to kill me. Jackal, murderer of children, eater of dead man's bones—what madness seized you, that you dared to threaten me?"

I doubt that Habib could have produced a reply worthy of that eloquent demand even if he had been capable of speaking. Turning again to the circle of rapt faces, Emerson cried, "Brothers! What punishment does the Koran, the word of the Prophet, decree for a murderer?"

"Death!" came the answer, thundering among the echoing cliffs.

"Take him away," Emerson said and flung Habib into the waiting arms of Feisal.

A sigh of pure delight went up from a hundred throats. No one appreciates a good theatrical performance more than an Arab. An audience of Luxor men had sat enthralled through *Romeo and Juliet*—in English—a few years earlier. This was much more entertaining. Before they could turn to their friends and begin an animated critique of the show, Emerson spoke again.

"Habib was not the only evildoer among us," he called out.

Agitated eddies appeared here and there, as certain members of the audience hastily headed for the obscurity of darkness. Emerson made a contemptuous gesture.

"They are even smaller jackals than Habib; let them go. They did not cause the deaths of the English lord and his friend. They did not kill the watchman Hassan."

Vandergelt stirred uneasily. "What is he up to now?" he whispered. "That was a first-rate performance; he ought to let the curtain down."

I was myself a trifle apprehensive. Emerson has a tendency to overdo things. I hoped he knew what he was doing. His next sentence made me doubt that he did.

"Were they slain by the curse of the pharaoh? If so..." Emerson paused; and not one pair of eyes in that assemblage blinked or moved from his face. "If so, I take that curse on myself! Here and now I challenge the gods to strike me down or give me their blessing. O Anubis, the High, the Mighty, the Chief over the mysteries of those in the underworld, O Horus, son of Osiris, born of Isis, O Apet, mother of fire..."

He turned to face the fire, which had died to a bed of red coals, against which his form was darkly silhouetted. Arms raised, he invoked the gods of Egypt in a sonorous but rather oddly pronounced form of their own language. All at once the dying fire soared heavenward in a rainbow flame, blue and sea-green and ghastly lavender. A gasp went up from the crowd; for in the uncanny light they saw on the topmost step of the tomb entrance an object that had certainly not been there before.

It had the form of a giant black cat with glowing yellow eyes. The play of firelight along the lean flanks gave the illusion of tensed muscles, as if the weird beast were preparing to spring on its prey.

The cat shape was a hollow shell, covered with bituminous pitch, and had once contained, if it did not still, the mummified figure of a real cat. Emerson had presumably acquired this object in Luxor, from one of the dealers, and had undoubtedly paid a pretty penny for it. No doubt many of the watchers were as cognizant as I of the true nature of the feline mummy case; but its seemingly miraculous appearance had as dramatic effect as any showman could wish.

Emerson broke into a weird, stiff-kneed dance, waving his arms. Vandergelt chuckled. "Reminds me of an old Apache chief I used to know," he whispered. "Suffered terribly from rheumatism, but wouldn't give up the rain dance."

Fortunately the rest of the audience was less critical. Watching Emerson's hand, I saw the same movement that had preceded the burst of multicolored flame. This time the substance he tossed onto the fire produced a huge puff of lemon-colored smoke. It must have contained sulfur, or some similar chemical, for it was singularly odorous and the spectators who were on its fringes began to cough and flap their hands.

For a few seconds the tomb entrance was completely veiled in coiling smoke. As it began to disperse we saw that the cat coffin had split down the middle. The two sections had fallen, one to each side, and between them, in the exact pose of the coffin, sat a living cat. It wore a jeweled collar; the gleaming stones winked emerald and ruby-red in the firelight.

The cat Bastet was extremely annoyed. I sympathized with her feelings. Caged, boxed, or bagged, as the case might be, she had been kidnapped and then thrust into a cloud of evil-smelling smoke. She sneezed and rubbed her nose with her forepaw. Then her glowing golden eyes lit on Emerson

I feared the worst. But then came the crowning wonder of that night of wonders, which would be the subject of folktales in the nearby villages for years to come. The cat walked slowly toward Emerson—who was invoking it as Sekhmet, goddess of war, death, and destruction. Rising on its hind feet, it clung to his trouser leg with its claws and rubbed its head against his hand.

Emerson flung his arms high. "Allah is merciful! Allah is great!" Another mighty puff of smoke burst from the fire, and the majestic invocation ended in a fit of violent coughing.

The performance was ended. Murmuring appreciatively, the audience drifted away. Emerson emerged from the fog and walked toward me.

"Not bad, eh?" he inquired, grinning demonically.

"Let me shake your hand, Professor," Vandergelt said. "You are as smooth a crook as I ever met, and that's saying something."

Emerson beamed. "Thank you. Lady Baskerville, I took the liberty of ordering a feast for our men once they get back to the house. Abdullah and Feisal particularly deserve an entire sheep apiece."

"Certainly." Lady Baskerville nodded. "Really, though, Radcliffe, I hardly know what to say about this—this peculiar business. Was it, by chance, my emerald-and-ruby bracelet around that beast's neck?"

"Ah—hem," said Emerson. He fingered the dent in his chin. "I must apologize for the liberty. Never fear, I will restore it."

"How? The cat has run away."

Emerson was still trying to think what to say when Karl joined us.

"Herr Professor, you were splendid. One little point, if you permit—the imperative form of the verb *iri* is not *iru,* as you said, but—"

"Never mind," I said quickly. Emerson had directed

an outraged scowl at the earnest young German, rather like Amon Ra glowering at a priest who ventured to criticize his pronunciation. "Had we not better return to the house? I am sure everyone is tired out."

"There will be no sleep for the guilty tonight," said a sepulchral voice.

Madame Berengeria had risen from her chair. Her daughter and Mr. O'Connell, who flanked her on either side, made ineffectual attempts to keep her quiet and move her on. She waved them away.

"A fine show, Professor," she went on. "You remember more of your past lives than you admit. But not enough; you fool, you have mocked the gods, and now you must suffer. I would have saved you if you had let me."

"Oh, the devil," Emerson exclaimed. "Really, I can't tolerate much more of this. Amelia, do something."

The woman's bloodshot eyes moved to me. "You share his guilt and will share his fate. Remember the words of the sage: 'Be not proud and arrogant of speech, for the gods love those who are silent.'"

"Mother, please," Mary said, taking the woman by the arm.

"Ungrateful girl!" With a twist of her shoulder, Madame sent Mary staggering back. "You and your lovers...You think I don't see, but I know! Filth, uncleanliness...Fornication is a sin, and so is failure to revere your mother. 'It is an abdomination to the gods, going into a strange woman to know her...'"

The last comment was apparently aimed at Karl and O'Connell, whom she indicated by a wild gesture. The journalist was ashen with rage. Karl's reaction seemed to be chiefly one of surprise. I half-expected to hear him repeat, "The English! Never will I understand them."

Yet neither spoke to deny the vile allegations. Even I was momentarily nonplussed. I realized that Berengeria's earlier exhibitions had contained a certain element of deliberate calculation. She was not acting now; beads of froth oozed from the corners of her mouth. She turned her burning gaze on Vandergelt, who had thrown a protective arm around his bride-to-be.

"Adultery and fornication!" shouted Madame. "Remember the two brothers, my fine American gentleman; by the wiles of a woman Anubis was driven to murder his younger brother. He put his heart in the cedar tree and the king's men chopped it down. The lock of hair perfumed the garments of pharaoh; the talking beasts warned him to beware..."

The narrow cord of sanity had finally snapped. This was madness and delirium. I suspected that not even a brisk slap, my usual remedy for hysteria, would avail in this case. Before I could decide what to do, Berengeria pressed her hand to her heart and slowly subsided onto the ground.

"My heart...I must have a stimulant...I have overtaxed my strength..."

Mr. Vandergelt produced an elegant silver flask of brandy, which I administered to the fallen woman. She lapped it greedily, and by holding it in front of her, like a carrot in front of a balky mule, I was able to get her into the carriage. Mary was weeping with embarrassment, but when I suggested she ride with us she shook her head.

"She is my mother. I cannot abandon her."

O'Connell and Karl offered to go with her, and so

it was arranged. The first carriage set out on the return journey and the rest of us were about to follow when I remembered that Lady Baskerville had planned to spend the night at the hotel. I assured her that if she wanted to carry out her plan, Emerson and I could walk back.

"How can you suppose me capable of abandoning you?" was the heated reply. "If that wretched woman has suffered a heart attack you will have two sick persons on your hands, in addition to all your other responsibilities."

"That's my noble girl," said Mr. Vandergelt approvingly.

"Thank you," I said.

When we reached the house I rolled up my sleeves and went first to Arthur's room. He was deep in slumber, so I proceeded to see how Madame was getting on. The Egyptian woman who had been assigned to attend the lady was leaving her room as I approached. When I asked her where the devil she thought she was going she informed me that the Sitt Baskerville had sent her for fresh water. I therefore allowed her to proceed on her errand.

Lady Baskerville was bending over the gross shape that sprawled across the bed. In her elegant gown and delicate lace shawl she was an incongruous figure to be found in a sickroom, but her movements were quick and efficient as she straightened the sheets.

"Will you have a look at her, Mrs. Emerson? I don't believe her condition is serious, but if you feel we ought to call Dr. Dubois, I will send someone at once."

After taking Berengeria's pulse and heartbeat I nodded agreement. "It can wait till morning, I think.

There is nothing wrong with her now, except that she is dead drunk."

Lady Baskerville's full red lips curved in a wry smile. "Blame me, if you wish, Mrs. Emerson. As soon as she had been placed on the bed she reached under the mattress and brought out a bottle. She did not even open her eyes! At first I was too surprised to interfere. Then...well, I told myself that to attempt to wrest the bottle from her would only lead to a struggle which I must lose; but to be honest I wanted to see her insensible. I am sure you must despise me."

In fact, I rather admired her. For once, she was being honest with me, and I could not blame her for carrying out a scheme which I had myself once contemplated.

After directing the servant, who had returned with the water, to keep a close watch and wake me if there was any change in Madame's condition, I went with Lady Baskerville to the drawing room, where the others were assembled. Emerson had commanded their presence, and as we entered we heard Kevin O'Connell berating my husband for his lack of consideration.

"Miss Mary is on the verge of collapse," he cried. "She ought to be in bed. Just look at her!"

The young lady's appearance did not support this diagnosis. Her cheeks were tear-stained and her costume somewhat the worse for wear, but she sat upright in her chair, and when she spoke her voice was calm.

"No, my friend, I do not require pity. I need to be reminded of my duty. My mother is a tormented, unhappy person. Whether she is ill or mad or simply evil-minded I do not know, but it does not matter. She is my cross and I will bear it. Lady Baskerville, we will leave you tomorrow. I am ashamed that I have allowed this to go on as long as it has."

"Very well, very well," Emerson burst out, before anyone else could speak. "I am sure we all sympathize with you, Miss Mary, but at the moment I have more pressing matters to discuss. I must have a copy of the painting of Anubis before I demolish the wall. You had better be at work early, before—"

"What the—" O'Connell sprang to his feet, red as a turkey cock. "You cannot be serious, Professor."

"Be still, Kevin," Mary said. "I made a promise and I will keep it. Work is the best medicine for a wounded heart."

"Humph," said Emerson, kneading his chin. "I agree with the sentiment, at least. You might think about it too, Mr. O'Connell; how long has it been since you sent off a story to your newspaper?"

O'Connell sank limply into a chair and shook his disheveled red head. "I will probably lose my position," he said gloomily. "When one is living the news, it is hard to find time to write about it."

"Cheer up," Emerson said. "In forty-eight hours— perhaps less—you will be able to steal a march on your colleagues with a story that will restore you to the good graces of your editor. You may even be able to demand a rise in pay."

"What do you mean?" Fatigue forgotten, O'Connell sat up alertly and reached for his notebook and pencil. "You hope to enter the tomb by then?"

"Of course. But that is not what I meant. You will be one to announce to the world the identity of the murderer of Lord Baskerville."

CHAPTER
FIFTEEN

The listeners were galvanized by this announcement. Vandergelt let out a loud "by Jimminy!" Mary's eyes opened wide. Even the phlegmatic young German stared at Emerson in surprise.

"Murderer?" O'Connell repeated.

"He was murdered, of course," Emerson said impatiently. "Come now, Mr. O'Connell, you have always suspected as much, though you did not have the effrontery to suggest it in your newspaper stories. The succession of violent tragedies that has occurred here makes it impossible that Lord Baskerville could have died a natural death. I have been working on the case and I will soon be in a position to announce results. I await one last piece of evidence. It will be here late tomorrow or the following morning. By the way, Amelia," he added, looking at me, "don't try to intercept my messenger; the news he carries has meaning only to me; you won't understand it."

"Indeed?" I said.

"Well, well," said O'Connell. He crossed his legs, put his notebook on his knees, and gazed at Emerson with the impish grin that betokened his professional mood. "You wouldn't care to drop a hint, would you, Professor?"

"Certainly not."

"There is nothing to prevent me from speculating a bit, is there?"

"At your own risk," Emerson replied.

"Never fear, I am no more anxious to commit myself prematurely than you are. Hmmm. Yes, this will require some rather delicate phrasing. Excuse me, please; I had better get to work."

"Don't forget your promise," I said.

"You may see the story before I send it off," O'Connell said. He departed with a springy step, whistling.

"The rest of us had better retire too," Emerson said. "Vandergelt, can I count on your assistance tomorrow morning when I reopen the tomb?"

"I wouldn't miss it for . . . That is, if you don't mind, my dear?"

"No," Lady Baskerville replied wearily. "Do as you like, Cyrus. This latest news has quite overwhelmed me."

When she had taken her departure, leaning on Vandergelt's arm, Emerson turned to me. Before he could speak I made a warning gesture.

"I believe Karl wishes to ask you something, Emerson. Either that, or he has fallen asleep there in the shadows."

Emerson looked startled. Karl had been so still, and the corner where he sat was so far distant from the nearest lamp, that he might have fallen into a doze; but I suspected another, more sinister explanation. Now he roused himself and came forward.

"Not to ask do I wish, Herr Professor, but to warn. An act very foolish it was, to say what you said. A gauntlet of defiance you have thrown down to a killer."

"Dear me," Emerson said. "That was careless of me."

Von Bork shook his head. He had lost considerable weight during the past week, and the lamplight emphasized the new hollows under his cheekbones and in his eye sockets.

"A stupid man you are not, Professor. I myself ask why you have so acted. But," he added, with a faint smile, "I do not an answer expect. *Gute Nacht,* Herr Professor, Frau Professor—*Schlafen Sie wohl.*"

Frowning, Emerson watched the young man go. "He is the most intelligent of the lot," he muttered. "I may have made a mistake there, Peabody. I ought to have handled him differently."

"You are tired," I said magnanimously. "No wonder, after all that shouting and jumping around. Come to bed."

Arm in arm, we sauntered across the courtyard, and as we went Emerson remarked, "I believe I detected a slight note of criticism in your comment, Amelia. To describe my masterful performance as 'shouting and jumping around' is hardly—"

"The dancing was an error."

"I was not dancing. I was performing a grave ritual march. The fact that the space was limited—"

"I understand. It was the only flaw in an otherwise superb performance. The men have agreed to return to work, I take it?"

"Yes. Abdullah will be on guard tonight, though I don't expect any trouble."

I opened our door. Emerson struck a match and lighted the lamp. The wick flared up and a hundred fiery sparks reflected the light from the neck of the cat Bastet, who sat on the table by the window. As soon as she caught sight of Emerson she let out an eager, throaty mew and trotted toward him.

"What did you use to attract the animal?" I inquired, watching Bastet claw at Emerson's coattails.

"Chicken," Emerson replied. He withdrew a greasy packet from his trouser pocket. I was pained to observe that it had left a nasty spot. Grease is so difficult to get out.

"I spent an hour training her earlier this afternoon," Emerson said, feeding the remainder of the chicken to the cat.

"You had better get Lady Baskerville's bracelet off her neck," I said. "She has probably knocked half the stones out already."

And indeed it proved that she had. Seeing Emerson's face fall, as he tried to calculate the weight and value of the rubies and emeralds he would be obliged to replace, I quite forgave him for being so puffed up about his performance.

II

When I went to see Arthur next morning the Sister gave me a smiling *"bon jour"* and informed me that the patient had spent a quiet night. His color was much better—which I attributed to the strengthening effect of the chicken broth—and when I placed my hand on his brow he smiled in his sleep and murmured something.

"He is calling for his mother," I said, brushing a tear from my eye with my sleeve.

"Vraiment?" the sister asked doubtfully. "He has spoken once or twice before, but so softly I could not make out the word."

"I am sure he said *'Mother.'* And perhaps by the time he wakes he will see that good lady's face bending over him." I allowed myself the pleasure of picturing that exquisite scene. Mary would be there, of course (I really must do something about the child's clothes; a pretty white gown would be just the thing); and Arthur would hold her hand in his thin, wasted fingers as he told his mother to greet her new daughter.

To be sure, Mary had announced her intention of devoting the rest of her life to her mother, but that was just a young girl's romantic fancy. A fondness for martyrdom, especially of the verbal variety, is common to the young. I had dealt with this phenomenon before and did not doubt my ability to bring this love affair also to a happy conclusion.

However, time was passing, and if I expected to see Mary become the new Lady Baskerville, it was up to me to make sure her bridegroom survived to take that step. I repeated my caution to the nun, to give the sick man nothing except what was brought to her by myself or by Daoud.

I then went to my next patient. A peep into the room assured me that Madame was in no need of my attention. She slept the calm, deep-breathing sleep of the wicked. It is a misconception that the innocent sleep

315 THE CURSE OF THE PHARAOHS

well. The worse a man is, the more profound his slumber; for if he had a conscience, he would not be a villain.

When I reached the dining room Emerson growled at me for being late. He and Mary had already finished breakfast.

"Where are the others?" I inquired, buttering a piece of toast and ignoring Emerson's demands that I bring it with me and eat as we walked.

"Karl has gone ahead," Mary said. "Kevin has crossed to Luxor, to the telegraph office—"

"Emerson!" I exclaimed.

"It is all right, he showed the story to me," Emerson replied. "You will enjoy reading it, Amelia; the young man has an imagination almost as uncontrolled as yours."

"Thank you. Mary, your mother seems better this morning."

"Yes, she has had these attacks before and made a remarkable recovery. As soon as I have finished the copy of the painting I will make arrangements to move her back to Luxor."

"There is no hurry," I said sympathetically. "Tomorrow morning will be soon enough; you will be worn out this evening after working in the heat."

"Well, if you really think so," Mary said doubtfully. Her morose expression lightened a little. One may be determined to embrace martyrdom gracefully, but a day of reprieve is not to be sneezed at. I am sure even the early Christian saints raised no objection if Caesar postponed feeding them to the lions until the next circus.

Tiring of Emerson's nagging, I finished my breakfast

and we prepared to leave. "Where is Mr. Vandergelt?" I asked. "He wanted to be with us, I thought."

"He has taken Lady Baskerville over to Luxor," Emerson replied. "There were matters to arrange for their approaching nuptials; and I persuaded the lady to stay there and do a little shopping. That always cheers ladies, does it not?"

"Why, Professor," Mary said with a laugh. "I had no idea you were so well acquainted with the weaknesses of our sex."

I looked suspiciously at Emerson. He had turned his back and was attempting to whistle. "Well, well," he said, "Let us be off, shall we? Vandergelt will join us later; it will be some time before we can actually breach the wall."

III

It was, in fact, midmorning before our preparations were complete. The air in the depths of the tomb was still bad, and the heat was so unbelievable that I refused to let Mary work for more than ten minutes at a time. Impatient as Emerson was, he had to agree that this was reasonable. In the meantime he occupied himself with supervising the construction of a stout wooden cover for the well. Karl had taken over the operation of the camera. And I?

You know little of my character, dear reader, if you are unable to imagine the nature of the thoughts that occupied my mind. I sat under the shade of my awning, supposedly making scale drawings of pottery fragments, but the sound of Emerson's cheerful shouts and curses as he supervised the carpenter work roused the gravest suspicions. He seemed very sure of himself. Was it possible, after all, that he was right in his identification of Lord Baskerville's murderer, and that I was wrong? I could not believe it. However, I decided it might be advisable to go over my reasoning once more, in the light of the most recent developments. I could always think of a way of changing the name in my envelope if I had to.

Turning over a page of my sketching pad, I abandoned pots for plans. I would make a neat little chart, setting forth the various motives and means and so on.

So I began.

THE DEATH OF LORD BASKERVILLE

Suspect: Lady Baskerville.

Motive in the murder of:

Lord Baskerville. Inheritance. (How much Lady Baskerville would inherit I, of course, did not know yet; but I felt sure it was enough to account for her willingness to do away with her husband. By all accounts he had been a singularly boring man.)

Armadale. He witnessed the crime. The room he had occupied was next to Lady Baskerville's. (To be sure, this did not explain why Armadale had disappeared. Had he lost his mind from horror after seeing Lady B. massacre her husband? And how the devil—as Emerson might have said—did she massacre him? If some obscure and unidentifiable poison had been used, all Armadale could have seen was Lord Baskerville sipping a cup of tea or a glass of sherry.)

Hassan. Hassan had seen Armadale and observed something—perhaps the particular window to which the "ghost" had gone—that betrayed the identity of the murderer. Attempted blackmail; destruction of blackmailer.

I read over this last paragraph with satisfaction. It made sense. Indeed, the motive for Hassan's murder would apply to all the suspects.

The next section of my little chart was not so neat. Lady Baskerville's motives for bashing Arthur on the head were obscure, unless there was some clause in his lordship's will that allowed certain properties to revert to his wife in the event of the death of his heir. That seemed not only unlikely, but positively illegal.

I went doggedly on to the question of opportunity.

Lord Baskerville. His wife's opportunity of getting at him was excellent. But how the devil had she done it?

Armadale. No opportunity. How had Lady Baskerville known the location of the cave? If she had killed Armadale at or near the house, she would have had to transport his body to the cave—obviously impossible for a woman.

Weak, very weak! I could almost hear Emerson's jeer. The truth of the matter was I wanted Lady Baskerville to be the murderer. I never liked the woman.

I gazed disconsolately at my chart, which was not working as I had hoped. With a sigh I turned to a fresh page and tried another arrangement.

THE DEATH OF LORD BASKERVILLE

Suspect: Arthur Baskerville, alias Charles Milverton.

That had a fine, professional look to it. Emboldened, I went on:

Motive: inheritance and revenge. (So far, so good.)

In fact, Arthur's motive was particularly strong. It accounted for his imbecilic behavior in presenting himself to his uncle incognito. This was the act of a romantic young idiot. Arthur *was* a romantic young idiot; but if he had planned in advance to kill his uncle, he had a very good reason for taking a false name. Once Baskerville was dead (how? curse it, how?) Arthur could return to Kenya, and it was most unlikely that anyone would have connected Arthur, Lord Baskerville, with the former Charles Milverton. He would probably claim the title and estates without ever going to England, and if he did have to go, he could make excuses to avoid Lady Baskerville.

With a start I realized that my chart had taken to wandering all over the page. I took a firm grip on my wits and my pencil, and returned to the proper form.

THE DEATH OF LORD BASKERVILLE

Suspect: Cyrus Vandergelt. His motives were only too clear. Contrary to the stern warning of Scripture, he had coveted his neighbor's wife.

It was at that point I realized I had not discussed Arthur's means or opportunity, or explained who had struck him down if he was the original killer.

Gritting my teeth, I turned the page over and tried again.

THE MURDER OF ALAN ARMADALE

This approach was based on the assumption that Lord Baskerville's death was a red herring—or, to put it more elegantly, that his lordship had died a natural death; that the so-called mark on his brow was a meaningless stain, misinterpreted by sensation-seekers; and that the murderer had taken advantage of the furor following his lordship's death to commit a murder whose true motive would be obscured.

The obvious suspect here was Mr. O'Connell. He had not only taken advantage of the story of the curse, he had invented it. I did not suppose that he had murdered Armadale in cold blood; no, the killing had obviously resulted from a sudden rush of jealous passion. Once the deed was done, a clever man—which O'Connell undoubtedly was—might have seen how he could avert suspicion by making Armadale's death seem related to that of Lord Baskerville.

The same motive—love of Mary—could apply in the case of Karl von Bork. In my opinion he was not capable of the sort of grand passion that might drive a man to violence. But still waters run deep. And once or twice Karl had displayed hidden depths of feeling and of cunning.

By this time my chart had abandoned all pretense of form, and my random jottings, embodying the thoughts I have expressed in more developed form above, were sprawling all over the page. I studied it in some exasperation. My thought processes are always orderly. The case was simply not susceptible to this means of organization. It is all very well for writers of crime fiction; they invent the crime and the solution, so they can arrange things the way they like.

I decided to abandon the outline and let my thoughts stray where they would.

Solely on the basis of opportunity one would have to eliminate all the women from suspicion. Madame Berengeria's motive was excellent; she might not be mad in the medical sense, but she was mad enough to destroy anyone who might wish to interfere with her selfish hold on her daughter. However, she and Mary resided on the east bank. The bodies had all been discovered on the west bank. I could not visualize either Mary or her mother scampering through the dark streets of Luxor, hiring a boat and bribing the boatmen to silence, then running through the fields of the western shore. The idea that Madame could have done this not once but several times was ludicrous—unless she had hired accomplices to do the actual killing. And although Lady Baskerville had been on the scene, such activity on the part of a lady of elegant and languid habits seemed equally unlikely. The murder of Armadale presented particular difficulties, as I had indicated in my initial attempt at a chart.

At this point in my cogitations Mr. Vandergelt and Mr. O'Connell arrived, having met at the quay. I was glad to abandon my futile outlines; for I had decided I had been right all along.

Mr. Vandergelt's first question concerned the state of our operations on the tomb.

"You haven't broken through that wall yet, have you?" he demanded. "I'll never forgive you, Mrs. Amelia, if you didn't wait for me."

"I think you are just in time," I retorted, hastily hiding my notebook under a pile of chips. "I was about to go down myself to see how matters are progressing."

We met Mary on her way out. She was in an indescribable state of dampness and dirt, but her eyes shone triumphantly as she displayed a splendid drawing, the result of her uncomfortable labors. It was not, I thought, quite equal to Evelyn's efforts; but perhaps I am prejudiced. Certainly it was a fine piece of work, and I knew Emerson would be pleased with it.

Crooning in an exaggerated Irish brogue, Mr. O'Connell carried Mary off to rest, and Vandergelt and I descended the steps.

Already the newly constructed wooden structure

was in place over the shaft, and the men were preparing to make a hole in the wall.

"Ah, there you are," Emerson remarked unnecessarily. "I was just about to go and fetch you."

"Like fun you were," said Vandergelt. "Never mind, Professor; if I were in your shoes I wouldn't want to wait either. What's the plan?"

I will spare the reader further technical details; they can be found in Emerson's superb report, which is to appear this fall in the *Zeitschrift für Aegyptische Sprache*. Suffice it to say that the hole was drilled and Emerson looked through it. Waiting with bated breath, Vandergelt and I heard him groan.

"What is it?" I cried. "A dead end? An empty sarcophagus? Tell us the worst, Emerson."

Silently Emerson made way for us. Vandergelt and I each put one eye to the opening.

Another corridor stretched down into darkness. It was half filled with debris—not the deliberate limestone fill of the first corridor, but fragments of a collapsed ceiling and wall, mingled with scraps of gilded wood and brown linen—the remains of mummy wrappings.

Withdrawing the candle from the hole, I held it up, and in its light we three contemplated one another's disappointed faces.

"That is surely not the burial chamber," Vandergelt exclaimed.

Emerson shook his untidy head, now gray with dust. "No. It appears that the tomb was used for later burials, and that the ceiling has collapsed. It is going to be a long, tedious job clearing that mess out and sifting the debris."

"Well, then, let's get to it," Vandergelt exclaimed, mopping his streaming brow.

Emerson's lips curved in a reluctant smile as he studied the American. Fifteen minutes in the heat of the corridor had changed Vandergelt from a dapper, handsome man of the world to a specimen that would have been denied entrance to the cheapest London hotel. His goatee dripped, his face was white with dust, and his suit sagged. But his face shone with enthusiasm.

"Quite right," Emerson said. "Let us get at it."

Vandergelt took off his coat and rolled up his shirt sleeves.

IV

The sun had passed the zenith and begun its westward journey before Emerson halted the work. I remained up above, having a comfortable woman-to-woman chat with Mary. She proved to be remarkably resistant to my efforts to ascertain which of her suitors she preferred. She kept insisting that since she did not intend to marry, her preference did not matter; but I think I was on the verge of winning her confidence when we were interrupted by the approach of two dusty, disheveled ragamuffins.

Vandergelt collapsed under the awning. "I sure hope you ladies will excuse me. I'm not in a fit state for the company of the gentler sex just now."

"You look like an archaeologist," I said approvingly. "Have a cup of tea and a little rest before we start back. What results, gentlemen?"

Again I refer the reader to the technical publications about to appear. We had an animated and extremely enjoyable discussion on professional matters. Mary seemed to enjoy it too; her timid questions were very sensible. It was with visible reluctance that she finally rose and declared she must get back.

"May I escort Miss Mary?" Karl asked. "It is not right that she should go alone—"

"I need you here," Emerson replied absently.

"I'll be escorting the lady," O'Connell announced, smirking triumphantly at his rival. "Unless, Professor, that matter of which we spoke last night is imminent?"

"What on earth is he talking about?" Emerson asked me.

"You remember," O'Connell insisted. "The message—the evidence that would—er—"

"Message? Oh, yes. Why can't you speak out, young man, instead of being so confoundedly mysterious? It must be the effect of your profession; always sneaking and spying. As I think I told you, the messenger will probably not arrive until tomorrow morning. Run along, now."

Emerson then drew me aside. "Amelia, I want you to go back to the house also."

"Why?"

"Matters are rapidly approaching the final crisis. Milverton—curse it, I mean young Baskerville—may not be out of danger. Watch him. And make sure everyone knows that I expect the fatal message tomorrow."

I folded my arms and looked at him steadily. "Are you going to confide your plans to me, Emerson?"

"Why, surely you know them already, Amelia."

"It is impossible for any rational mind to follow the

peculiar mental convolutions that pass for logic among the male sex," I replied. "However, the course of action you have suggested happens to suit my own plans. I will therefore do as you ask."

"Thank you," said Emerson.

"You are quite welcome," I replied.

Mary and Mr. O'Connell had gone off in Vandergelt's carriage. I took the path over the hills, so was the first to arrive at the house. Though climbing in and out my bedroom window had now become a natural and convenient procedure, I decided on this occasion to make a formal entrance, by way of the gate. I wanted my presence to be noted.

As I entered the courtyard Lady Baskerville came out of her room. She greeted me with unusual warmth. "Ah, Mrs. Emerson. Another hard day's work accomplished? Is there any news?"

"Only of an archaeological variety," I replied. "That would not interest you, I suppose."

"Once it did. My husband's enthusiasms were my own. He spoke of them constantly. But can you blame me for now regarding the entire subject as darkly stained by unfortunate memories?"

"I suppose not. Let us hope, however, those memories will fade. It is unlikely that Mr. Vandergelt will ever abandon his absorption in Egyptology, and he will want his wife to share it."

"Naturally," said Lady Baskerville.

"Was your trip to Luxor a success?" I asked.

The lady's somber countenance brightened. "Yes, the arrangements are being made. And I found a few things that were not too bad, considering. Do come to my room and let me show you my purchases. Half the pleasure in new clothes is in showing them to another woman."

I was about to refuse, but Lady Baskerville's sudden fondness for my company struck me as highly suspicious. I decided to go along with her in order to ascertain her true motives.

I thought I understood one such motive when I saw the disorder of her room, every surface being strewn with garments that she had taken from their boxes. Automatically I began to shake them out and fold them neatly away.

"Where is Atiyah?" I asked. "She ought to be performing this service for you."

"Didn't you know? The wretched woman has run away," was the careless reply. "What do you think of this shirtwaist? It is not very pretty, but—"

The rest of her speech went unheard by me. I was seized by a grim foreboding. Had Atiyah become another victim?

"Some effort ought to be made to locate the woman," I said, interrupting Lady Baskerville's criticism of an embroidered combing mantle. "She may be in danger."

"What woman? Oh, Atiyah." Lady Baskerville laughed. "Mrs. Emerson, the poor creature was a drug addict; did you not realize that? She has probably spent her wages on opium and is in a stupor in some den in Luxor. I can manage without a maid for a few more days; thank heaven I will soon be back in civilization, where decent servants are to be found."

"Let us hope you will," I agreed politely.

"But I count on Radcliffe to free me. Did he not

promise all our doubts and questions would be settled today? Cyrus—and I, of course—would be reluctant to leave you all unless we were sure you were no longer in danger."

"Apparently that longed-for moment will not occur until tomorrow," I said drily. "Emerson tells me his messenger has been delayed."

"Today, tomorrow, what matter? So long as it is soon." Lady Baskerville shrugged. "Now this, Mrs. Emerson, is to be my wedding hat. How do you like it?"

She placed the hat, a broad-brimmed straw trimmed with lavender ribbons and pink silk flowers, on her head and skewered it in place with a pair of jeweled pins. When I did not reply at once, she flushed and a spark of anger shone in her black eyes.

"You think me wrong to wear something so frivolous when I am supposed to be in mourning? Should I replace the ribbons with black and dye the flowers sable?"

I took the question as it was meant, a display of sarcasm rather than a request for information, and did not reply. I had other things on my mind. Lady Baskerville was visibly annoyed at my lack of interest, and when I rose to leave she did not press me to remain.

The carriage was just passing through the gate when I emerged from Lady Baskerville's room. The young people had had no reason to hurry. After greeting me, Mary asked if I had seen her mother.

"No, I have been with Lady Baskerville. If you can wait a few minutes, until I have visited Arthur, I will accompany you."

Mary was glad to agree to this.

The nun greeted us with shining eyes and a look of genuine happiness in the news she had to give. "He has shown signs of regaining consciousness. It is a miracle, madame. How great is prayer!"

How great is chicken soup, I thought to myself. But I did not say so; let the good creature enjoy her delusions.

Arthur was painfully thin—there are limits even to the powers of chicken broth—but his improvement in the past twenty-four hours had indeed been astonishing. As I leaned over the bed he stirred and murmured. I motioned to Mary.

"Speak to him, my dear. Let us see if we can rouse him. You may hold his hand, if you like."

Scarcely had Mary taken the wasted hand in her own and called the young man's name in a voice tremulous with emotion than his long golden lashes fluttered and his head turned toward her.

"Mary," he murmured. "Is it you, or a heavenly spirit?"

"It is I," the girl replied, tears of joy trickling down her cheeks. "How happy I am to see you better!"

I added a few appropriate words. Arthur's eyes moved to me. "Mrs. Emerson?"

"Yes. Now you know you have not died and gone to heaven." (I always feel that a little touch of humor relieves situations of this nature.) "I know you are still weak, Arthur," I went on, "but for your own safety I hope you can answer one question. Who struck you?"

"Struck me?" The sick man's pallid brow wrinkled. "Did someone . . . I cannot remember."

"What is the last thing you remember?"

"Lady . . . Lady Baskerville." Mary gasped and looked at me. I shook my head. Now, of all times, we could not leap to conclusions on the basis of a wounded man's confused recollections.

"What about Lady Baskerville?" I asked.

"Told me . . . rest." Arthur's voice grew even weaker. "Went to my room . . . lay down . . ."

"You remember nothing more?"

"Nothing."

"Very well, my dear Arthur, don't tire yourself any further. Rest. There is nothing to worry about; I am on the job."

A smile curved the young man's bearded lips. His weary lids drooped shut.

As we went toward Madame's room, Mary said with a sigh, "I can leave with a lighter heart. Our fears for his safety are now relieved."

"True," I said, half to myself. "If he was struck during his sleep, as seems to be the case, he never saw the villain's face, so there is no reason why he should be attacked again. However, I do not regret the precautions we took. We had to make sure."

Mary nodded, though I do not think she really heard what I was saying. The closer we came to that room which must seem to her like a goblin's foul lair, the more slowly she moved. A shudder passed through her frame as she reached for the knob.

The room was in shadow, the shades having been drawn to keep out the afternoon sun. The attendant lay huddled on a pallet at the foot of the bed. She looked like a corpse in her worn brown robes, but she was only asleep; I could hear her breathing.

Mary touched her mother gently on the arm. "Mother, wake up. I am back. Mother?"

Suddenly she reeled back, her hands clasped on her breast. I leaped to support her. "What is it?" I cried. She only shook her head dumbly.

After helping her into a chair I went to the bed. It required no great stretch of imagination to anticipate what I would find.

When we entered, Madame Berengeria had been lying on her side with her back to the door. Mary's touch, gentle as it was, had disturbed the balance of the body and caused it to roll onto its back. One glance at the staring eyes and lax mouth told the story. It was not even necessary for me to seek a nonexistent pulse, though I did so, as a matter of routine.

"My dear child, this could have happened at any time," I said, taking Mary by the shoulders and giving her a sympathetic shake. "Your mother was a sick woman, and you should regard this as a blessed release."

"You mean," Mary whispered. "You mean it was—her heart?"

"Yes," I said truthfully. "Her heart stopped. Now, child, go and lie down. I will do what needs to be done here."

Mary was visibly heartened by the false assumption I had allowed her to form. Time enough for her to learn the truth later. The Arab woman had awakened by this time; she cringed when I turned to her, as if expecting a blow. I did not see how she could be blamed, so I spoke gently to her, instructing her to take care of Mary.

When they had gone, I went back to the bed. Madame's fixed stare and sagging jowls were not a pleasant sight, but I have seen worse things and done worse; my hands were quite steady as I went about my ghoulish but necessary tasks. The flesh was still warm. That proved little, since the temperature of the room was hot, but the eyes gave away the truth. They were so widely dilated as to appear black. Berengeria's heart had certainly stopped, but it had stopped as the result of a large dose of some narcotic poison.

CHAPTER
SIXTEEN

I sent a message at once to Emerson, although I never supposed for a moment that he would allow the small matter of another murder to distract him from his work. In fact, it was not until teatime that he returned. I was waiting for him; and as he stripped off his work-stained garments I brought him up to date on the events of the day. He seemed more struck by what Arthur had told me.

"Very interesting," he said, stroking his chin. "Ve-ry interesting! That should relieve us of one concern; if he did not see the killer we may assume, may we not, that he is not liable to a second attack. I say, Amelia, did you think of summoning Dr. Dubois to look at Madame, or did you do the postmortem yourself?"

"I did call him, not because he could add anything to what I already knew, but because he had to sign the death certificate. He agreed with me that death was due to an overdose of laudanum or some similar poison; even he could not overlook the signs of that. He claims, however, that the drug was self-administered, by accident. Apparently all Luxor knew Madame's habits."

"Humph," said Emerson, rubbing his chin so hard it turned pink. "Ve-ry interest—"

"Do stop that," I said crossly. "You know as well as I do that it was murder."

"Are you sure you didn't do it? You said the other day that the world would be a better place if the lady were removed from it."

"I am still of that opinion. Apparently I was not the only one who thought so."

"I would say the viewpoint was virtually unanimous," Emerson agreed. "Well, well, I must change. Do you go to the parlor, Amelia; I will be with you shortly."

"Don't you want to discuss the motives for Madame's murder? I have a theory."

"I felt sure you would."

"It has to do with her wild ravings last night."

"I prefer to defer discussion of that."

"You do, eh?" Absently I stroked my own chin, and we eyed one another suspiciously. "Very well, Emerson. You will find me ready for you."

I was the first one in the drawing room. By the time Emerson made his appearance the others had assembled. Mary, in a black dress borrowed from Lady Baskerville, was tenderly supported by Mr. O'Connell.

"I persuaded her to come," the young man explained in a proprietary manner.

"Quite right," I agreed. "After all, there is nothing like a nice hot cup of tea to comfort one."

"It will take more than a cup of tea to comfort me," Lady Baskerville announced. "Say what you will, Radcliffe, there is a curse on this place. Even though Madame's death was an unfortunate accident—"

"Ah, but are we sure of that?" Emerson inquired.

Vandergelt, who had taken his agitated fiancée in the shelter of his white linen arm, looked sharply at my husband.

"What do you mean, Professor? Why look for trouble? It's no secret that the poor woman was—er—"

He broke off, with an apologetic look at Mary. She was staring at Emerson in wide-eyed surprise. I quickly passed her a cup of tea.

"We may never know the truth," Emerson replied. "But it would have been easy to slip a dose of poison into the lady's favorite beverage. As for the motive . . ." He glanced at me, and I took up the narrative.

"Last night Madame made a number of wild accusations. Pure malice and hysteria, most of them; but now I wonder if there might not have been a grain of wheat in all that chaff. Do any of you know the ancient tale to which she referred?"

"Why, sure," Vandergelt replied. "Anyone who knows the least little thing about Egyptology must be familiar with it. 'The Tale of the Two Brothers,' isn't that right?"

His reply was prompt. Too prompt, perhaps? A stupid man might have pretended ignorance of that potentially dangerous story. A clever man might know his ignorance would be suspect, and admit the truth at once.

"What are you talking about?" Mary asked pathetically. "I don't understand. These hints—"

"Let me explain," Karl said.

"As a student of the language you probably know the story best," Emerson said smoothly. "Go on, Karl."

The young man cleared his throat self-consciously. I noted, however, that when he spoke his verb forms were in perfect English alignment. That meant something.

"The tale concerns two brothers. Anubis the elder and Bata the younger. Their parents were dead, and Bata lived with his older brother and his wife. One day when they were working in the fields, Anubis sent Bata back to the house to fetch some grain. The wife of Anubis saw the young man's strength and desired—er—that is, she asked him—er—"

"She made advances to him," Emerson said impatiently.

"*Ja, Herr Professor!* The young man indignantly refused the woman. But, fearing that he would betray her to her husband, she told Anubis Bata had—er—made advances to *her.* So Anubis hid in the barn, meaning to kill his younger brother when he came in from the field.

"But," Karl continued, warming to the tale, "the cattle of Bata were enchanted; they could speak. As each entered the barn it warned Bata that his brother was hiding behind the door, intending to murder him. So Bata ran away, pursued by Anubis. The gods, who knew Bata was innocent, caused a river full of crocodiles to flow between them. And then Bata, across the river, called out to his brother, explaining what had really happened. As a sign of his innocence he cut off—er—that is—"

Karl turned fiery-red and stopped speaking. Vandergelt grinned broadly at the young man's discomfiture, and Emerson said thoughtfully, "There really is no acceptable euphemism for that action; omit it, Karl.

In view of what happens later in the story, it does not make much sense anyway."

"*Ja, Herr Professor.* Bata told his brother he was going away to a place called the Valley of the Cedar, where he would put his heart in the top of a great cedar tree. Anubis would know his brother was in good health so long as his cup of beer was clear; but when the beer turned cloudy he would know Bata was in danger, and then he must search for Bata's heart and restore it to him."

Lady Baskerville could restrain herself no longer. "What is this nonsense?" she exclaimed. "Of all the stupid stories—"

"It is a fairy tale," I said. "Fairy tales are not sensible, Lady Baskerville. Go on, Karl. Anubis returned to the house and destroyed his faithless wife—"

For once—the first and last time—Karl interrupted me instead of the other way around.

"*Ja, Frau Professor.* Anubis regretted his injustice to his poor young brother. And the immortal gods, they also felt sorry for Bata. They determined to make a wife for him—the most beautiful woman in the world—to keep him company in his lonely exile. And Bata loved the woman and made her his wife."

"Pandora," Mr. O'Connell exclaimed. "I never heard this story, and that's the truth; but it's just like the tale of Pandora, that the gods made for . . . begorrah, but I can never remember the fellow's name."

No one enlightened him. I would never have taken the young man for a student of comparative literature; it seemed much more likely that he was trying to emphasize his ignorance of the story.

"The woman was like Pandora," Karl admitted. "She was a bringer of evil. One day when she was bathing, the River stole a lock of her hair and carried it to the court of pharaoh. The scent of the hair was so wonderfully sweet that pharaoh sent soldiers to find the woman from whose head it had come. With the soldiers went women who carried jewels and beautiful garments and all the things women love; and when the woman saw the fine things she betrayed her husband. She told the soldiers about the heart in the cedar tree; and the soldiers cut down the tree. Bata fell dead, and the faithless woman went to the court of pharaoh."

"Bedad, but it's the Cinderella story," said Mr. O'Connell. "The lock of hair, the glass slipper—"

"You have made your point, Mr. O'Connell," I said.

Unabashed, O'Connell grinned broadly. "It never hurts to make sure," he remarked.

"Go on, Karl," I said.

"One day the older brother Anubis saw that his cup of beer was clouded, and he knew what it meant. He searched, and he found his brother, and he found the heart of his brother in the fallen tree. He put the heart in a cup of beer and Bata drank it and came back to life. But the woman—"

"Well, well," Emerson said, "that was splendidly told, Karl. Let me synopsize the rest, it is just as long and even more illogical than the first part. Bata eventually avenged himself on his treacherous wife and became pharaoh."

There was a pause.

"I have never heard anything so nonsensical in my life," said Lady Baskerville.

"Fairy tales are meant to be nonsensical," I said. "That is part of their charm."

II

The general reaction to "The Tale of the Two Brothers" was approximately the same as Lady Baskerville's. All agreed that Madame's references to it had been meaningless, the product of a deranged mind. Emerson seemed content to let the subject drop, and it was not until we were almost finished with dinner that he again electrified the company by introducing a controversial topic.

"I intend to spend the night at the tomb," he announced. "After tomorrow's revelations I will be able to procure all the workmen and guards I need; until then, there is still some slight risk of robbery."

Vandergelt dropped his fork. "What the devil do you mean?"

"Language, language," Emerson said reproachfully. "There are ladies present. Why, you have not forgotten my messenger, have you? He will be here tomorrow. Then I will know the truth. A simple 'yes' or 'no'; the message will be no more than that; and if it is 'yes' . . . Who would suppose that one person's fate could hang on such a little word?"

"You are overdoing it," I said, out of the corner of my mouth. Emerson scowled at me, but took the hint.

"Are we all finished?" he inquired. "Good. Let us retire. I am sorry to rush you, but I want to get back to the Valley."

"Then perhaps you wish to be excused now," said Lady Baskerville, her raised eyebrows showing what she thought of this piece of rudeness.

"No, no. I want my coffee. It will help keep me awake."

As we left the room, Mary came up to me. "I don't understand, Mrs. Emerson. The story Karl told was so strange. How can it have any bearing on my mother's death?"

"It may have no bearing at all," I said soothingly. "We are still walking in a thick fog, Mary; we cannot even see what objects are hidden by the mist, much less know if they are landmarks to guide us on our quest."

"How literary we all are tonight," remarked the ubiquitous Mr. O'Connell, smiling. It was his professional, leprechaun's smile; but it seemed to me his eyes held a glint of something more serious and more sinister.

With a defiant glance at me Lady Baskerville took her place behind the coffee tray. I smiled tolerantly. If the lady chose to make this trivial activity a show of strength between us, let her. In a few more days I would be in charge officially, as I already was in actuality.

We were all extremely polite that evening. As I listened to the genteel murmurs of "black or white?" and "two lumps, if you please," I felt as if I were watching the commonplace, civilized scene through distorting glasses, like those in a fairy tale I had once read. Everyone in the room was acting a part. Everyone had something to conceal—emotions, actions, thoughts.

Lady Baskerville would have done better to let me serve the coffee. She was unusually clumsy; and after she had managed to spill half a cup onto the tray, she let out a little scream of exasperation and clapped her hands to her head.

"I am so nervous tonight I don't know what I am doing! Radcliffe, I wish you would reconsider. Stay here tonight. Don't risk yourself, I could not stand another..." Smiling, Emerson shook his head, and Lady Baskerville, summoning up a faint answering smile, said more calmly, "I ought to know better. At least you will take someone with you? You will not go alone?"

Stubborn creature that he is, Emerson was about to deny this reasonable request, but the others all joined in urging him to accept a companion. Vandergelt was the first to offer his services.

"No, no, you must stay and guard the ladies," Emerson said.

"As ever, Herr Professor, I would be honored to be of service to the most distinguished—"

"Thank you, no."

I said nothing. There was no need for me to speak; Emerson and I habitually communicate without words. It is a form of electrical vibration, I believe. He felt my unspoken message, for he avoided looking at me as he scanned the room in a maddeningly deliberate fashion.

"The chosen victim must be Mr. O'Connell, I believe," he said at last. "I hope we will have a restful night; he can work on his next dispatch."

"That suits me, Professor," said the young Irishman, taking his cup from Lady Baskerville.

Suddenly Emerson rose to his feet with a cry. "Look there!"

Every eye went to the window, where he was pointing.

O'Connell rushed across the room and pulled back the curtains.

"What did you see, Professor?"

"A flutter of white," Emerson said. "I thought some-one passed rapidly by the window."

"There is nothing there now," O'Connell said. He went back to his chair.

No one spoke for a time. I sat gripping the arms of my chair, trying to think; for a new and terrible idea had suddenly occurred to me. I had no idea what Emerson was up to, with his ridiculous suggestions of flutters of white and his dramatic cries; the matter that concerned me was of quite another nature. I might be wrong. But if I was not wrong, something had to be done, and without delay.

"Wait," I cried, rising in my turn.

"What is it?" Emerson demanded.

"Mary," I exclaimed. "Quickly—she is about to swoon—"

The gentlemen all converged on the astonished girl. I had hoped, but had not really expected, that she would have the wits to follow my lead. Evelyn would have done it instantly. But Evelyn is used to my methods. It did not matter; the distraction gave me the opportunity I needed. Emerson's coffee cup and mine were on a low table next to my chair. Quickly I exchanged them.

"Honestly, there is nothing wrong with me," Mary insisted. "I am a little tired, but I don't feel at all faint."

"You are very pale," I said sympathetically. "And you have had such a dreadful day, Mary; I think you ought to retire."

"So should you," Emerson said, looking at me suspiciously. "Drink your coffee, Amelia, and excuse yourself."

"Certainly," I said, and did so without hesitation.

The group dispersed soon thereafter. Emerson offered to escort me to our room; but I informed him I had other matters to take care of before I retired. The first and most imperative I will not describe in detail. It had to be done, and I did it; but the process was unpleasant to experience and distasteful to recount. If I had been able to anticipate Emerson's plans I would not have eaten quite so much at dinner.

I then felt obliged to look in on Mary. She was still in the state of false composure that often follows a shock, whether the shock be one of joy or sorrow—but sooner or later she must give way to the bewildering mixture of emotions that filled her heart. I treated her as I would a hurt or frightened child, tucking her into bed, and leaving a candle burning for comfort; and she seemed pathetically grateful for the attentions, which, I have no doubt, were new to her. I took the opportunity of speaking to her about Christian fortitude and British spunk in the face of adversity, adding that, with all due respect to her mother, the future could only appear bright. I might have said more; but at this point in the conversation she fell asleep. So I tucked the netting around her and tiptoed out.

Emerson was waiting outside the door. He was leaning against the wall with his arms folded and his look of "I would stamp and shout if I were not such an unusually patient man" on his face.

"What took you so cursed long?" he demanded. "I am in a hurry."

"I did not ask you to wait for me."

"I want to talk to you."

"We have nothing to talk about."

"Ah!" Emerson exclaimed, in the surprised tone of someone who has just made a discovery. "You are angry because I didn't ask you share the watch with me tonight."

"Ridiculous. If you wish to sit there like Patience on a monument waiting for a murderer to attack you, I will not interfere."

"Is that what you are thinking?" Emerson laughed loudly. "No, no, my dear Peabody. I was bluffling about the message, of course—"

"I know."

"Humph," said Emerson. "Do you suppose the others know?"

"Probably."

"Then what are you worried about?"

He had me there. The message was such a transparent subterfuge that only a fool would fail to see it for the trick it was.

"Humph," I said.

"I had hoped," Emerson admitted, "that the device would stimulate our suspect, not to murder me—I am no hero, my dear, as you may have observed—but to flee. Like you, I believe now that the trick has failed. However, just in case the killer is more nervous or more stupid than we believe, I want you here to observe whether anyone leaves the house."

We had been pacing slowly around the courtyard as we spoke. Now we reached the door of our room;

Emerson opened it, shoved me in, and enveloped me in a bruising embrace.

"Sleep well, my darling Peabody. Dream of me."

I flung my arms around his neck. "My dearest husband, guard your precious life. I would not attempt to keep you from your duty, but remember that if you fall—"

Emerson pushed me away. "Curse it, Peabody, how dare you make fun of me? I hope you fall over a chair and sprain your ankle."

And with this tender farewell he left me, cursing under his breath.

I addressed the cat Bastet, whose sleek form I had seen outlined against the open window.

"He deserved that," I said. "I am inclined to agree with you, Bastet; cats are much more sensible than people."

III

Bastet and I kept watch together while the hands of my little pocket watch crept on toward midnight. I was flattered that the cat stayed with me; always before she had seemed to prefer Emerson. No doubt her keen intelligence told her that the truest friend is not always the one who offers chicken.

I had not been deceived for a moment by Emerson's glib excuses. He did hope the murderer would believe his lies about messages and decisive clues; he expected to be attacked that very night. The more I thought about it, the more uneasy I became. A sensible murderer (if there is such a thing) would not have been fooled for a moment by Emerson's playacting. But if my theory was correct the murderer was stupid enough, and desperate enough, to react as Emerson had planned.

After I put on my working costume I blackened my face and hands with soot from the lamp and removed every touch of white from my attire. Opening my door a crack, I ascertained that the watchman was on duty in the courtyard. I could not see anyone outside the window. When midnight finally came I left the cat sleeping quietly on my bed and slipped out the window.

The moon was gibbous, but it gave too strong a light for my purposes. I would rather have walked unseen under heavy clouds. Despite the cool of the night air I was perspiring by the time I reached the cliff that overlooked the Valley.

Below me the abode of the dead lay at peace under the light of Egypt's eternal moon. The fence around the tomb obstructed my view until I was quite near. I had not expected to hear sounds of revelry, so the dead silence that enveloped the place was not in itself alarming, nor was the fact that I saw no glow from the lantern Emerson usually kept burning. He might have left it unlit in the hope of luring the killer close. Yet the now only too familiar grue of apprehension chilled my limbs as I glided on.

I approached the barrier cautiously. I did not want to be mistaken for the criminal and knocked down by my own husband. My approach was certainly not noiseless, for the stony ground was littered with pebbles and gravel that crunched underfoot. Reaching the fence, I peered through the gap between two stakes.

"Emerson," I whispered. "Don't shoot; it is I."

No voice replied. Not the slightest sound broke the uncanny stillness. The enclosed space was like a badly focused photograph, crisscrossed by the shadows of the fence stakes and blurred by the shapes of boulders and miscellaneous objects. Instinct told me the truth even before my straining eyes made out a huddled, darker shape beside the stairwell. Abandoning caution, I ran forward and flung myself down beside it. My groping hands found creased fabric, thick tumbled hair, and features whose shape would have been familiar to me in the darknest night.

"Emerson," I gasped. "Speak to me! Oh, heavens, I am too late. Why did I wait so long? Why did—"

The motionless body was suddenly galvanized into life. I was seized—throttled—muffled—pulled down to the ground with a force that left me breathless—enclosed in an embrace that held the ferocity of a deadly enemy instead of the affection of a spouse.

"Curse you, Amelia," Emerson hissed. "If you have frightened my quarry away I will never speak to you again. What the devil are you doing here?"

Being unable to articulate, I gurgled as meaning-fully as I could. Emerson freed my mouth. "Softly," he whispered.

"How dare you frighten me so?" I demanded.

"How did you . . . Never mind; get back out of sight, with O'Connell, while I resume my position. I was pre-tending to be asleep."

"You *were* asleep."

"I may have dozed off for a moment....No more talk. Retire to the hut where O'Connell—"

"Emerson—where is Mr. O'Connell? This encounter has not been exactly silent; should he not have rushed to your assistance by this time?"

"Hmmm," said Emerson.

We found the journalist behind a boulder on the hillside. He was breathing deeply and regularly. He did not stir, even when Emerson shook him.

"Drugged," I said softly. "This is a most alarming development, Emerson."

"Alarming but hopeful," was the reply, in tones as soft as Emerson could make them. "It confirms my theory. Stay here out of sight, Peabody, and for heaven's sake don't give the alarm too soon. Wait till I actually have my hands on the wretch."

"But, Emerson—"

"No more. I only hope our animated discussion has gone unheard."

"Wait, Emerson—"

He was gone. I sat down beside the boulder. To pursue him and insist on being heard was to risk the failure of our scheme; and besides, the information I had meant to give him was no longer pertinent. Or was it? Chewing on my lip, I tried to sort out my thoughts. O'Connell had been drugged. No doubt Emerson's coffee, which I had drunk, had also been doctored. Fearing such an eventuality, I had drunk Emerson's coffee, and rid myself of it. Yet when I came upon him just now he had been sound asleep. I could not have mistaken pretense for reality. I had felt the limpness of his body, and if he had only been feigning sleep he would have heard my whispers. He had drunk *my* coffee. Or had someone else exchanged cups with him? I felt as if my head were spinning like a top.

A soft glow of artificial light roused me from my disquieting thoughts. Emerson had lit the lantern. I approved this decision; if my reasoning was correct, the murderer would expect to find him drugged and helpless, and the lamplight would enable this prostrate condition to be observed more readily. I only wished I could be certain he was free of the influence of some drug. I took a deep breath and clenched my hands. It did not matter. I was on the job. I had my knife, my gun, my parasol; I had the resolve of duty and affection to strengthen every sinew. I told myself that Emerson could not have been in better hands than mine.

I told myself that; but as time wore on I began to doubt my own assurances—not because I had lost faith in my abilities, but because I stood to lose so much if, by some unexpected mischance, I should fail to act in time. Emerson had seated himself on the ground by the stairs, his back against a rock, his pipe in his mouth. After smoking for a while he knocked out the pipe and sat motionless. Gradually his head drooped forward. The pipe fell from his lax hand. Shoulders bowed, chin on his breast, he slept—or was he pretending to sleep? A breeze ruffled his dark hair. I beheld his unmoving form with mounting apprehension. I was at least ten yards away. Could I reach him in time, if action proved necessary? Beside me, Mr. O'Connell rolled over and began to snore. I was tempted to kick him, even though I knew his comatose condition was not his fault.

The night was far advanced before the first betraying sound reached my ears. It was only the soft click of a pebble striking stone, and it might have been made by a wandering animal; but it brought me upright, with every sense alert. Yet I almost missed the first sign of movement. It came from behind the fence, outside the circle of light.

I had known what to expect; but as the shadowy shape emerged cautiously into view, I caught my breath. Muffled from head to foot in clinging muslin that covered even its face, it reminded me of the first appearance of Ayesha, the immortal woman or goddess, in Mr. Haggard's thrilling romance *She*. Ayesha veiled her face and form because her dazzling beauty drove men mad; this apparition's disguise had a darker purpose, but it conveyed the same sense of awe and terror. No wonder the persons who had seen it had taken it for a demon of the night or the spirit of an ancient queen.

It stood poised, as if prepared for instant flight. The night wind lifted its draperies like the wings of a great white moth. So strong was my desire to rush at it that I sank my teeth in my lower lip and tasted the saltiness of blood. I had to wait. There were too many hiding places in the nearby cliffs. If it escaped us now, we might never bring it to justice.

Almost I waited too long; for when the figure finally moved it did so with such speed that I was caught unawares. Rushing forward, it bent over Emerson, one hand raised.

It was apparent by this time that Emerson really had dozed off and was not mimicking sleep. Naturally

I would have cried out if the danger had been imminent; but seeing the ghostly figure, I knew all. My theories had been right, from start to finish. Knowing the
method of attack, I knew it required a certain delicacy
and deliberation of execution. I had plenty of time. Triumph soared within me as I rose slowly to my feet.

As soon as I put my weight on it, my left ankle gave
way, tingling with the pain of returning circulation.
The crash of my fall, I am sorry to say, was quite loud.

By the time I had recovered myself, the white form
was in rapid retreat. Emerson had tumbled over onto
his side and was stirring feebly, like an overturned bee-
tle. I heard his bewildered curses as I staggered past
him, leaning on my parasol for support.

A woman in less excellent physical condition might
have continued to stagger till all was lost; but my blood
vessels and muscles are as well trained as the rest of me.
Strength returned to my limbs as I progressed. The
white apparition was still visible, some distance ahead,
when I broke into my famous racing form, arms swing-
ing, head high. Nor did I scruple to make the echoes
ring with my demands for assistance from anyone who
might be listening.

"Help! *Au secours! Zu Hilfe!* Stop thief," accompanied my progress, and I daresay these cries had an effect
on the person I pursued. There was no escape for it, but
it continued to run until I brought my parasol down
on its head with all the strength I could muster. Even
then, as it lay supine, it reached out with clawed hands
for the object it had dropped in its fall. I put my foot
firmly on the weapon—a long, sharp hatpin. With my

parasol at the ready, I looked down on the haggard, no longer beautiful face that glared up at me with Gorgonlike ferocity.

"It is no use, Lady Baskerville," I said. "You are fairly caught. You should have known when we first met that you were no match for me."

CHAPTER
SEVENTEEN

Emerson was unreasonably annoyed with me for what he called my unwarranted interference. I pointed out to him that if I had not interfered he would have moved on to a better, but probably less interesting, world. Unable to deny this, but reluctant to admit it, he changed the subject.

We made a little ceremony of opening the envelopes to which we had earlier committed our deductions as to the identity of the murderer. I suggested we do this publicly. Emerson agreed so readily that I knew he had either guessed correctly or been able to substitute a new envelope for the original.

We held our conference in Arthur's room. Though still very weak, he was out of danger, and I felt his recovery would be hastened if he knew he was no longer under suspicion of murder.

Everyone was there except Mr. Vandergelt, who had felt duty-bound to accompany Lady Baskerville to Luxor, where, I had no doubt, she was proving a considerable embarrassment to the authorities. They seldom had a criminal of such exalted social status, and a woman to boot. I only hoped they would not let her escape out of sheer embarrassment.

After Emerson and I had opened our envelopes and displayed the two slips of paper, each bearing the name of Lady Baskerville, Mary exclaimed, "You amaze me, Amelia—and you too, of course, Professor. Though I cannot say I admired her ladyship, it would never have occurred to me that she could be guilty."

"It was obvious to an analytical mind," I replied. "Lady Baskerville was shrewd and vicious but not really intelligent. She committed one error after another."

"Such as asking the Professor to take command of the expedition," Karl said. "She ought to have known a man so brilliant, so distinguished—"

"No, that was one of her more intelligent actions," Emerson said. "The work would have been carried on, with or without her approval. His late lordship's will specifically directed that it be done. She had a role as a devoted widow to play; and at the time she approached us she took it for granted that the matter was ended. Armadale, she hoped, would either die in the desert or flee the country. She underestimated his stamina and the depth of his passion; but, though she was not very intelligent, she knew how to act promptly and decisively when action was necessary."

"And," I added, "the idea of disguising herself as a lady in white was one of her brighter notions. The veils were so voluminous that there was no way of identifying the figure; it might even have been that of a man. Also, its ghostly appearance made some of those who saw it reluctant to approach it. Lady Baskerville made good use of the white lady by pretending to see it herself the night Emerson was so nearly hit by the stone head. It was, of course, Habib who threw the stone. Other indications, such as Lady Baskerville's preference for an inefficient and timid Egyptian servant, were highly suspicious. I have no doubt that Atiyah observed a number of things that a sharper attendant would have understood, and perhaps reported to me."

I would have gone on had not O'Connell interrupted me.

"Just a minute, ma'am. All this is very interesting but, if you will pardon me, it is the sort of thing anyone might see, after the fact. I need more details, not only for my editor, but to satisfy my own curiosity."

"You already know the details of one incident in the case, though you may not care to describe them to your readers," I said meaningfully.

Mr. O'Connell blushed fiery red, so that his face almost matched his hair. He had confessed to me in private that he had been responsible for the knife in the wardrobe. He had bribed a hotel servant to place an elaborate, ornamented knife—of the sort that is made for the tourist trade—in a prominent place in our room. His inefficient and underpaid ally had replaced the expensive trinket with a cheaper weapon and put it in the wrong place.

Seeing the journalist's blushes, I said no more. In the last few days he had earned my goodwill, and besides, he was due for a comeuppance if my suspicions about Mary and Arthur were correct.

"Yes, well, let us proceed," said O'Connell, gazing intently at his notebook. "How did you—and Professor Emerson, of course—arrive at the truth?"

I had decided I had better hear what Emerson had to say before I committed myself. I therefore remained silent and allowed him to begin.

"It was evident from the first that Lady Baskerville had the best opportunity to dispose of her husband. It is a truism in police science—"

"I can only allow you ten minutes, Emerson," I interjected. "We must not tire Arthur."

"Humph," said Emerson. "You tell it, then, since you consider my narrative style too verbose."

"I'll just ask questions, if you permit," said Mr. O'Connell, looking amused. "That will save time. I am trained, you know, to a terse journalistic style."

"Terse" was not the word I would have used; but I saw no reason to interfere with the procedure he suggested.

"You have mentioned opportunity," he said. "What about motive? Professor?"

"It is a truism in police science," said Emerson stubbornly, "that a victim's heirs are the primary suspects. Though I was unaware of the stipulations of the late Lord Baskerville's will, I assumed his wife stood to inherit something. But I suspected an even stronger motive. The archaeological world is small. Like all small communities, it is prone to gossip. Lady Baskerville's reputation for—er—let me think how to put it..."

"Extramarital carrying on," I said. "I could have told you that."

"How?" Emerson demanded.

"I knew it the moment I set eyes on her. She was that sort of woman."

"So," Mr. O'Connell intervened, as Emerson's face

reddened, "you inquired about the lady's reputation, Professor?"

"Precisely. I had been out of touch for several years. I spoke with acquaintances in Luxor and sent off a few telegrams to Cairo, to ascertain whether she had continued her old habits. The replies confirmed my suspicions. I concluded that Lord Baskerville had learned of her affairs—the husband is always the last to know—and had threatened her with divorce, disgrace, and destitution."

In reality, he had discovered these facts only that morning, when Lady Baskerville broke down and confessed all. I wondered how many other facets of that most interesting confession would turn up, in the form of deductions, as he went along.

"So she killed her husband in order to preserve her good name?" Mary asked incredulously.

"To preserve her luxurious style of living," I said, before Emerson could reply. "She had designs on Mr. Vandergelt. He would never have married a divorced woman—you know how puritanical these Americans are—but as an unhappy widow she did not doubt she could capture him."

"Good," said Mr. O'Connell, scribbling rapidly. "Now, Mrs. E., it is your turn. What clue gave away the murderer's identity to you?"

"Arthur's bed," I replied.

Mr. O'Connell chuckled. "Wonderful! It is almost as deliciously enigmatic as one of Mr. Sherlock Holmes's clues. Elucidate, please, ma'am."

"The evening we found our friend here so near his end," I said, with a nod at Arthur, "his room was in disorder. Lady Baskerville had tossed his belongings around in order to suggest a hasty flight. She had, however—"

"Forgotten to take his shaving tackle," Emerson interrupted. "I knew then that the murderer must be a woman. No man would overlook such an obvious—"

"And," I said, raising my voice, "no man could have made Arthur's bed so neatly. Remember, he was resting on it when he was attacked. The killer had to remake the bed so that the counterpane hung all the way down to the floor and concealed his unconscious form. The longer the delay, the more difficult it would have been for innocent persons to establish an alibi. Those neat hospital corners were a dead giveaway."

"Good, good," crooned Mr. O'Connell, scribbling. "But how did she commit the crime, Mrs. E.? That is the most baffling thing of all."

"With a hat pin," I replied.

Exclamations of astonishment followed. "Yes," I went on. "I confess that I puzzled over that for a long time. Not until yesterday afternoon, when Lady Baskerville was trying on her trousseau, did I realize how deadly a hat pin can be. Lady Baskerville had been a nurse, and she had known—er—been acquainted with—medical students and doctors. A sharpened steel needle inserted into the base of the brain will penetrate the spinal column and kill the victim instantly. A small puncture, hidden by the victim's hair, would not be observed; or, if it was, it would be taken for an insect bite. She killed Mr. Armadale the same way."

"But why Armadale?" O'Connell asked keenly, his pencil poised. "Did he suspect her?"

"Quite the contrary," I replied. (My breath control is much better than Emerson's; I could start speaking while he was still inhaling.) "Mr. Armadale thought *he* had killed Lord Baskerville."

A gratifying burst of surprised exclamations interrupted me.

"It is only conjecture, of course," I said modestly, "but it is the only explanation that fits all the facts. Lady Baskerville had cold-bloodedly seduced Mr. Armadale. Mary noticed that he was distracted and depressed for several weeks preceding Lord Baskerville's death. More significantly, he did not renew his offer of marriage. He had found another love, and the torment of knowing he had betrayed his patron was tearing him apart. Lady Baskerville pretended to feel the same. She informed Armadale that she intended to tell her husband the truth and, professing fear of his reaction, asked the young man to wait in her room while the confrontation took place. Not unnaturally her husband began to shout at her. She screamed; Armadale rushed in and struck the enraged husband, thinking he was protecting his mistress. As soon as Lord Baskerville fell, his wife bent over him and cried, 'You have killed him!'"

"And Armadale believed her?" O'Connell asked skeptically. "My readers are going to love this, Mrs. E., but it's a little hard to swallow."

"He loved her," Arthur said weakly. "You don't understand true love, Mr. O'Connell."

I reached for Arthur's wrist. "You are flushed," I said. "You are becoming overexcited. We had better adjourn."

"No, no." The sick man took hold of my hand. His golden beard had been neatly trimmed and his hair arranged. His pallor and emaciation made him handsomer than ever, like a young Keats (except, of course, that the poet was dark).

"You can't leave the story unfinished," Arthur went on. "Why did she attack me?"

"Yes, why?" Emerson said, catching me off guard this time. "I'll warrant even my omniscient wife does not know that."

"Do you?" I inquired.

"No. It makes no sense. Arthur never saw her; she entered his room while he was asleep, and why she did not use the handy hat pin on him—"

"She had to render him unconscious first," I explained. "The insertion of the needle into the pertinent spot requires some dexterity; it cannot be done while the victim is awake and capable of resistance. Once she had struck him, she believed him to be dead. Perhaps, also, she was afraid of being interrupted. In Arthur's case she had to act during the daylight hours. Something may have startled her, and she had only time to hide him under the bed. The question is, why did she feel it necessary to silence you, Arthur? If someone had become suspicious of how Lord Baskerville died, you were the obvious suspect. Your naive folly in telling no one of your identity—"

"But I did tell someone," Arthur said innocently. "I told Lady Baskerville, barely a week after I came here."

I exchanged glances with Emerson. He nodded. "So that was it," he said. "You did not mention that to my wife, when you bared your soul to her."

The young man flushed. "It hardly seemed cricket. Mrs. Emerson had told me in no uncertain terms what she thought of my stupidity. To admit that Lady Baskerville had encouraged me to retain my anonymity would be to accuse her..." He broke off, looking startled. Handsome Arthur Baskerville might be; wealthy and endowed with all the good things of this world. Oustandingly intelligent he was not.

"Hold on now." O'Connell's pencil had been racing across the page. He now looked up. "This is all good stuff, but you are not following the right order. Let's go back to the murder of Armadale. I presume that she persuaded the poor booby to flee after Baskerville collapsed and then did his lordship in with her hat pin. Hey—wait a minute. No one mentioned a bruise on Baskerville's face—"

"Dr. Dubois would not notice if the man's throat had been cut," I said. "But, to do him justice, he was looking for the cause of death, not a slight swelling on the jaw or chin. Lord Baskerville seems to have been astonishingly prone to self-mutilation. He probably had many bruises, cuts, and scrapes."

"Good." O'Connell wrote this down. "So Armadale ran away—disguised himself as a native, I suppose, and hid in the hills. I am surprised he didn't flee the country."

"And leave his mistress behind?" I countered. "I doubt that the young man's mental state was quite normal. The horror of what he thought he had done was enough to turn his brain and render him incapable of decisive action of any kind. If he *had* wanted to confess, he would have been deterred by the knowledge that by doing so he must incriminate the woman he loved, as an accessory after the fact. But when Lady Baskerville returned he could bear it no longer. He came to her window at night and was seen by Hassan. That foolish man tried to blackmail Lady Baskerville—for of course he had seen which window Armadale approached. She disposed of both of them the next night, Armadale at the cave, where he had told her to meet him, and Hassan on the way back, when he intercepted her. I am not surprised that she appeared so exhausted next day."

"But what about—"

"No more at the present time," I said, rising. "Arthur has had all the excitement he ought to have. Mary, will you stay with him and make sure he rests? As soon as the good Sister finishes her well-deserved nap, I will send her to relieve you."

As we left the room, I saw Arthur reach for Mary's hand. Mary blushed and lowered her lashes. I had arranged that matter as well as I could, they must do the rest. Avoiding Mr. O'Connell's reproachful glance, I led the way to the sitting room.

"There are a few more loose ends to tie up," I said, taking a chair. "I did not want Mary to hear us discuss her mother's death."

"Quite correct," said Karl approvingly. "I thank you, Frau Professor, for—"

"That is all right, Karl," I said, wondering why he was thanking me, but not really caring very much.

Before I could continue, the door opened to admit Mr. Vandergelt. He gave the impression of having shrunk several inches since the day before. No one knew what to say, until Emerson, rising to the sublime heights of which he is sometimes capable, uttered the mot juste.

"Vandergelt, have a drink!"

"You're a real pal, Professor," the American said with a long sigh. "I think maybe I will."

"Did she send you away, Mr. Vandergelt?" I inquired sympathetically.

"With language that would make a mule-skinner blush," was the reply. "She sure enough took me in. I guess you think I'm a blamed silly old fool."

"You were not the only one to be deceived," I assured him.

"*Aber nein,*" Karl exclaimed. "I had for her always the most respectful, most—"

"That is why I refused your offer to stand guard with me last night," said Emerson, from the table where he was pouring whiskey for the afflicted Vandergelt. "Your respect for the lady might have prevented you from acting, if only for a split second; and even that brief time could have meant the difference between life and death."

"And naturally you turned *me* down," said Vandergelt gloomily. "I tell you, Professor, I'd have been too flabbergasted to move if I had seen her."

Emerson handed him the glass and he nodded his thanks before continuing. "You know that confounded woman expected me to marry her after all? She started cursing at me when I said I had to respectfully decline. I felt like a rat, but, gee whiz, folks, marrying a woman who has already murdered one husband just isn't sensible. A fellow would always be wondering if his morning coffee tasted peculiar."

"It would also be impractical to wait twenty or thirty years before enjoying the pleasures of connubial bliss," I said. "Cheer up, Mr. Vandergelt; time will heal your wound, and I know happiness awaits you in the future."

My well-chosen words lifted a little of the gloom from the American's countenance. He raised his glass in a graceful salute to me.

"I was just about to discuss the death of Madame Berengeria," I went on. "Will it pain you too much to hear..."

"One more whiskey and it wouldn't pain me to hear that Amalgamated Railroads had fallen twenty points," Mr. Vandergelt replied. He handed his empty glass to Emerson. "Join me in the next round, won't you, Professor?"

"I believe I will," Emerson replied, with an evil look at me. "We will drink, Vandergelt, to the perfidy of the female sex."

"I will join you both," I said gaily. "Emerson, your jests are sometimes a bit ill-timed. Mr. O'Connell is sitting on the edge of his chair, his pencil poised; explain in your own inimitable fashion the meaning of the little fairy tale we discussed last evening, and why that seemingly harmless story caused a murder."

"Ahem," said Emerson. "Well, if you insist, Peabody."

"I do. In fact, I will be barmaid and wait on you both." I took Vandergelt's empty glass from his hand. Emerson gave me a sheepish smile. He is pathetically easy to manage, poor man. The slightest kind gesture quite softens him.

"May I impose on your good nature too, ma'am?" O'Connell asked.

"Certainly," I replied graciously. "But none of your brash Irish gestures at the barmaid, Mr. O'Connell."

This little sally completed the atmosphere of good humor I was endeavoring to create. As I served the gentlemen—including Karl, who thanked me with a smile—Emerson took the floor.

"Lady Berengeria's death was in its way a masterpiece of tragic irony, for the poor stupid woman did not have the slightest intention of accusing Lady Baskerville of murder. Like all the good ladies of Luxor, who, in their infinite Christian charity spend most of their time dissecting their fellow women, she knew Lady Baskerville's reputation. 'The Tale of the Two Brothers' was a slam at an adulteress, not a murderess. And it could not have been more apt. The heart in the cedar tree is the heart of a lover—vulnerable, exposed, trusting in the love of the beloved. If the object of adoration proves false the lover has no defense. Lord Baskerville trusted his wife. Even when he had ceased to love her he did not think of defending himself against her. It is a tribute to some long-buried streak of intelligence and sensitivity in Madame Berengeria that she sensed the meaning of the metaphor. Who knows what she might have been, if the vicissitudes of life had not proved too great for her will?"

I gazed at my husband with tears of affection dimming my sight. How often is Emerson misjudged by those who do not know him! How tender, how delicate are the feelings he conceals beneath a mask of ferocity!

Unaware of my sentiments, Emerson took a stiff drink of whiskey and resumed, in a more practical vein. "The first part of the story of the Two Brothers concerns a faithless wife who turns one man against another by her lies. Think of that story, gentlemen and Peabody, in terms of our tragic triangle. Again, the metaphor was apt; and Lady Baskerville's guilty conscience led her to choose the wrong reference. She thought herself in danger of exposure—and it was so easy to slip a fatal dose of opium into Madame Berengeria's bottle of brandy. What was one more murder? She had already committed three. And what was the death of one dreadful old woman? A blessing in disguise, really."

Silence followed the conclusion of his remarks. Then he addressed Mr. O'Connell, whose pencil had been racing across the page. "Any questions?" he said.

"Wait, just let me get the last part. 'What was the death of one dreadful…'"

"Old woman," Emerson supplied.

"Silly old fool," Mr. Vandergelt muttered, staring into his empty glass.

The door opened and Mary entered.

"He is asleep," she said, smiling at me. "I am so happy for him. He will so enjoy being Lord Baskerville."

"And I am happy for you," I replied, with a meaningful look.

"But how did you know?" Mary exclaimed, blushing prettily. "We have not told anyone yet."

"I always know these things," I began.

Fortunately I said no more; for even as I spoke Karl von Bork crossed to Mary's side. He put his arm around her and she leaned against him, her flush deepening into a rosy glow.

"We have you to thank, Frau Professor," he said, his mustaches positively curling in the ardor of his happiness. "It is not proper to speak of this so soon after the unhappy, the unfortunate occurrence we have been discussing; but my dear Mary is quite alone in the world now, and she needs me. I have confidence that you will be to her a true friend until comes the blissful time when I can take her to the place which is—"

"What?" Emerson exclaimed, staring.

"Begorrah!" cried Mr. O'Connell, flinging his pencil across the room.

"Silly old fool," said Mr. Vandergelt to his empty glass.

"My very best wishes to both of you," I said. "Of course I knew it all along."

II

"Has it occurred to you," Emerson inquired, "that you have quite a number of acquaintances in prisons around the world?"

I considered the question. "Why, really, I can only think of two—no, three, since Evelyn's cousin was apprehended last year in Budapest. That is not a great number."

Emerson chuckled. He was in an excellent mood, and with good reason. The surroundings, the state of his career, the prospects before us—all were conducive to the most unexampled good spirits.

Two and a half months had passed since the events I have narrated, and we were on our way home. We were sitting on the deck of the steamer *Rembrandt;* the sun shone down and the white-capped waves curled away from the prow as the boat plunged rapidly toward Marseilles. The rest of the passengers were huddled at the farthest end of the boat (I can never remember whether it is the poop or the stern). Whatever it was, they were there, leaving us strictly alone. I had no objection to the privacy thus obtained, though I failed to understand their objections to our mummies. The poor things were dead, after all.

They were also very damp. That is why Emerson carried them out on deck every day to let them dry out. They lay in their brightly painted coffins staring serenely up at the sun, and I have no doubt they felt quite comfortable; for was not the sun-god the supreme deity they once worshiped? Ra Harakhte was performing his last service for his devotees, enabling them to survive for a few more centuries in the solemn halls of a modern temple of learning—a museum.

Our tomb had proved a disappointment after all. It had once been a royal sepulcher, there was no doubt of that; the design and the decorations were too grand for a commoner. But the original inhabitant had been anathema to someone; his name and portrait had been viciously hacked to bits wherever they appeared, and his mummy and funerary equipment had long since vanished. Some enterprising priest of a later dynasty had used the tomb for his own familial burial ground. Still later, the ceiling had collapsed and water had gotten into the burial chamber. We had found the remains of no less than ten mummies, all more or less battered, all more or less equipped with jewelry and amulets.

M. Grebaut had been generous in his division of the spoils, giving Emerson the nastiest and most water-logged of the mummies. So the Chantress of Amon, Sat-Hathor, and the First Prophet of Min, Ahmose, enjoyed a few last days in the sun.

Karl and Mary had spoken their vows the day before we left Luxor. I had been matron of honor, and Emerson had given the bride away, with Mr. Vandergelt acting as best man. Mr. O'Connell had not been present. I had no fear for his broken heart, however; he was too dedicated a newsman to make a good husband. His account of the wedding had appeared in the Cairo newspaper and had been more notable for sensationalism—the last chapter of the Curse of the Pharaoh—than for spite.

As I remarked to Emerson at the time, there is nothing like a hobby to take a person's mind off personal troubles. Mr. Vandergelt was a good example of this, although I did not think his attraction to Lady Baskerville had ever been more than superficial. He had applied to the Department of Antiquities for Lord Baskerville's concession and was eagerly planning a new season of digging.

"Are you going to accept Mr. Vandergelt's offer of a position as chief archaeologist next season?" I asked.

Emerson, lying back in his chair with his hat over his eyes, simply grunted. I tried a new approach. "Arthur—Lord Baskerville—has invited us to stay with him this summer. He will soon find a substitute for his lost love; a young man with his personal and financial attractions can take his pick of young ladies. But Mary was quite right not to accept him. Luxor is home to her, and she is deeply interested in Egyptology. She is far more intelligent than Arthur; such a match would never work out. I liked Arthur's mother, though. I was quite moved when she kissed my hand and wept and thanked me for saving her boy."

"Shows what a fool the woman is," Emerson said from under his hat. "Your carelessness almost killed the young man. If you had only thought to ask him——"

"What about you? I never asked you this before, Emerson, but confess, now that we are alone; you did not know the guilty party was Lady Baskerville until the last night. All that nonsense about clues and deductions was drawn from her confession. If you had known, you would not have been so careless as to allow her to drop laudanum into your cup of coffee."

Emerson sat up and pushed his hat back. "I admit that was an error in judgment. But how the devil was I to know that her maidservant was an opium addict and that her ladyship had obtained supplies of the drug from Atiyah? You say you knew; you might have warned me, you know."

"No one could possibly have anticipated that," I said, back-tracking with my usual skill. "It is ironic, is it not? If Atiyah had not been an addict, she would probably have made an addition to the long list of Lady Baskerville's victims. Though she saw the lady several times on her nocturnal journeys, she was too befuddled by the drug to realize what she was seeing. Nor would she have been a convincing witness."

"When it comes to that," said Emerson, now thoroughly aroused, and on the defensive, "how did you come to suspect Lady Baskerville? And don't tell me it was intuition."

"I told you before. It was Arthur's bed. Besides," I added, "it was not difficult for me to understand why a woman might be driven to murder her husband."

"Vice versa, Peabody, vice versa." Emerson slid down into a semirecumbent position and pushed his hat over his eyes.

"There is one other point I never raised with you," I said.

"And what is that?"

"You," I said, "were overcome with sleepiness that last night. Don't deny it; you were stumbling and muttering for hours afterward. If I had not tied Lady Baskerville up with her own veils, she would have escaped. What did you put in my coffee, Emerson?"

"I never heard such nonsense," Emerson mumbled.

"You drank my coffee," I continued remorselessly. "Unlike you, I suspected Lady Baskerville might take steps to ensure that you would be asleep and helpless that night. I therefore drank the poison myself, like... well, like a number of heroines I have read about. So, my dear Emerson—what was in *my* coffee, and who put it there?"

Emerson was silent. I waited, having discovered that cold forbearance is more effective than accusations in loosening a witness's tongue.

"It was your own fault," Emerson said at last.

"Oh?"

"If you would stay peacefully at home, like a sensible woman, when you are told to—"

"So you put opium in my coffee. Lady Baskerville put it in yours, and in Mr. O'Connell's, after you had chosen him to accompany you. Really," I said, in some vexation, "the affair is positively farcical. Emerson, your carelessness astonishes me. What if Lady Baskerville had wished to render *me* hors de combat too? Your little contribution, which I presume you obtained from my medical chest, added to hers, would have put an end to my nocturnal activities permanently."

Emerson leaped to his feet. His hat, lifted from his head by the vigor of his movement, floated around for a few seconds and then dropped onto the head of Sat Hathor, the Chantress of Amon. It was a rather amusing sight, but I had no impulse to laugh. Poor Emerson's face had gone white under his deep tan. Careless of the watchers on the lower deck he lifted me up out of my chair and crushed me to him.

"Peabody," he exclaimed, in a voice hoarse with emotion, "I am the stupidest idiot in creation. My blood runs cold when I think... Can you forgive me?"

I forgave him, with gestures instead of words. After a long embrace he released me.

"In fact," he said, "we should call it a draw. You tried to shoot me, I tried to poison you. As I said before, Peabody, we are well matched."

It was impossible to resist him. I began to laugh, and after a moment Emerson's deep-throated chuckle blended with mine.

"What do you say we go down to the cabin?" he inquired. "The mummies will do very well alone for a while."

"Not just yet. Bastet was just waking when we came up; you know she will prowl and howl for some time before she resigns herself."

"I should never have brought that cat," Emerson

growled. Then he brightened up. "But just think, Peabody, what a pair she and Ramses will make. Never a dull moment, eh?"

"It will toughen him up for next season," I agreed.

"Do you really think—"

"I really do. Good heavens, Emerson, Luxor is becoming known as a health resort. The boy will be better off there than in that nasty damp winter climate of England."

"No doubt you are right, Peabody."

"I always am. Where do you think we should excavate next winter?"

Emerson retrieved his hat from the Chantress of Amon and clapped it onto the back of his head. His face had the look I loved to see—baked as brown as a Nubian's by the Egyptian sun, his eyes narrowed speculatively, a half-smile on his lips.

"I fear the Valley is exhausted," he replied, stroking his chin. "There will be no more royal tombs found. But the Western Valley has possibilities. I will tell Vandergelt we ought to work there next season. And yet, Peabody..."

"Yes, my dear Emerson?"

Emerson took a turn around the deck, his hands clasped behind his back. "Do you remember the pectoral we found on the crushed body of the thief?"

"How could I forget it?"

"We read the cartouche as that of Tutankhamon."

"And decided that our tomb must have belonged to him. It is the only possible conclusion, Emerson."

"No doubt, no doubt. But, Peabody, consider the dimensions of the tomb. Would such a short-lived and ephemeral king have time enough and wealth enough to construct such a sepulchre?"

"You discussed that in your *Zeitschrift* article," I reminded him.

"I know. But I cannot help wondering...You don't suppose a gang of thieves would rob two tombs in the same night?"

"Not unless the said tombs were practically side by side," I said, laughing.

"Ha, ha." Emerson echoed my mirth. "Impossible, of course. That part of the Valley cannot contain any other tombs. All the same, Peabody, I have a strange feeling that I have missed something."

"Impossible, my dear Emerson."

"Quite, my dear Peabody."

ELIZABETH PETERS was named a 1998 Grand Master by the Mystery Writers of America. A prolific author, she has written dozens of acclaimed mysteries, including *The Hippopotamus Pool*, *The Mummy Case*, and *Crocodile on the Sandbank*. She can also be credited with numerous other suspense novels written under the *New York Times* bestselling pseudonym Barbara Michaels.

Ms. Peters earned a Ph.D. in Egyptology at the University of Chicago, and she has established a scholarship for minority women mystery writers. In 1990 she was awarded an honorary doctorate of Humane Letters by Hood College. She lives in Frederick, Maryland.